BLACK
DOG

A CRIME NOVEL

Stephen Booth

SCRIBNER

New York   London   Toronto   Sydney   Singapore

SCRIBNER
1230 Avenue of the Americas
New York, NY 10020

First Scribner Edition 2000
Published by arrangement with the author

SCRIBNER and design are trademarks of Macmillan Library Reference USA, Inc.,
used under license by Simon & Schuster, the publisher of this work.

DESIGNED BY ERICH HOBBING

Text set in Adobe Garamond

Manufactured in the United States of America

10 9 8 7 6 5 4 3 2 1

Library of Congress Cataloging-in-Publication Data
Booth, Stephen, 1952–
Black dog: a crime novel/Stephen Booth.—1st Scribner ed.
p. cm.
1. Peak District (England)—Fiction. 2. Country life—Fiction. I. Title.

PR6052.064 B58 2000
823'.92—dc21
00–037154

ISBN 0-684-87301-X

For Lesley

BLACK DOG

black dog: 1. melancholy, depression of spirits; ill humor. In some country places, when a child is sulking, it is said "the black dog is on his back."

—*Oxford English Dictionary*

-1-

The sudden glare of colors beat painfully on the young woman's eyes as she burst from the back door of the cottage and hurled herself into the brightness. She ran with her bare feet slapping on the stone flags and her hair streaming in red knots from her naked shoulders.

A harsh voice was cut off suddenly when the door slammed behind her, isolating her from the house. As she sprinted the length of the garden, she stirred the dust from a flagged path whose moisture had been sucked out and swallowed by the sun. A scarlet shrub rose trailed halfway across the path and a thorn slit the flesh of her arm as she brushed against it, but she hardly felt the pain.

"Wait!" she called.

But the old wooden garden gate had banged shut on its spring before she could reach it. She threw herself onto the top of the drystone wall, flinging out an arm to clutch at the sleeve of the old man on the other side. He was wearing a woolen jacket despite the heat, and his arm felt stiff and sinewy under the cloth. The young woman scrabbled for a firmer grip, feeling his muscles slide against the bones under her fingers as if she had plunged her hand deep into his body.

Harry Dickinson paused, held back only by the hand that touched his arm, turning his face away from the appeal in his granddaughter's eyes. The only change in his expression was a slight tightening in the creases at the sides of his mouth as his gaze slipped past Helen to the row of stone cottages. The stone walls and the white-mullioned back windows were at last starting to cool in the early evening shade, but the sun still glared low over the slate roofs, bad-tempered and unrelenting. The pupils of Harry's eyes narrowed to expressionless black points until he tilted his head sideways to turn the peak of his cap into the sun.

Helen could smell the impregnated odors of earth and sweat and animals in the wool, overlaid by the familiar scent of old tobacco smoke. "It's no good walking away, you know. You'll have to face it in the end. You can't run away from things forever."

A loud juddering sound made Harry flinch as it passed across the valley behind him. For an hour now the noise had been moving backward and forward over the dense woodland that covered the slope all the way down to the valley bottom. The sound echoed against the opposite hillside like the beating wings of an angry bird, battering the gorse and heather and alarming the sheep scattered on the upper slopes.

"We'll understand," said Helen. "We're your family. If only you'd tell us . . ."

The old man's right arm was held out at an unnatural angle, creasing the sleeve of his jacket into an ugly concertina of fabric. She knew that Harry felt himself being physically tugged toward the woods along the valley side; his body was tense with the effort of resisting the pull. But emotionally he was being drawn in two directions. The conflicting pressures seemed only to strengthen and toughen him, setting his shoulders rigid and hardening the line of his jaw. His face held no possibility of turning away from whatever he had decided to do.

"Granddad? Please."

The sharp edges of the stone wall were digging into her thighs through her shorts, and the skin of the palm on her left hand stung where she had scraped it on the jagged topping stones. There had been a sudden, desperate rush, a moment of overwhelming emotion, and now she didn't know what to say. She felt the impotence of the conventions that surrounded the communication between one adult and another, even when they were members of the same family. She shared with her grandfather an inborn shortage of the words she needed to be able to express her feelings to those closest to her.

"Grandma is very upset," said Helen, "but she'll calm down in a minute. She's worried about you."

Helen had never needed many words before, not with Harry. He had always known exactly what she wanted, had always responded to the message in her eyes, to the shy, adoring smile, to the gleam of sun on a wave of flame-colored hair, and to a small, trusting hand slipped into his own. She was no longer that child, and hadn't been for years. A teacher learned a different way of communicating, a calculated performance that was all surface gloss and scored no marks for feeling. Harry still understood, though. He knew what she wanted him to do now. But it was too hard for him, a thing completely against a lifetime's habit.

Gradually the juddering noise was fading to the edge of audibility, muffled to a dull rattle by the trees and the folds of the land. Its temporary absence released the subtler sounds of the evening—a current of air stirring the beech trees, a cow moaning for the bull across the valley, a skylark spilling its song over the purple heather. Harry cocked an ear, as if listening for a voice that no one else could hear. It was a voice that deepened the sadness in his eyes but stiffened his back and tautened the clench of his fists and his grip on the loop of worn black leather held in one hand.

"Come back and talk to us. Please?" she said.

Helen had never heard that voice. She had often tried, staring intently up at her grandfather's face, watching his expression change, not daring to ask what it was he heard but straining her own ears, desperate to catch an elusive echo. Like most men who had worked underground, Harry spent as much of his time as he could outside in the open air. As she stood at his side, Helen had learned to hear the sounds of the woods and the sky, the tiny movements in the grass, the shifting of the direction of the wind, the splash of a fish in a stream. But she had never heard what her grandfather heard. She had grown up to believe it was something uniquely to do with being a man.

"If you don't want to talk to Grandma, won't you tell me about it, Granddad?"

And then the noise began to grow steadily louder again, clattering toward them as it followed the invisible line of the road that meandered along the valley bottom. It drew nearer and nearer across the rocky slopes of Raven's Side, skirting a sudden eruption of black basalt cliff and veering north once more toward the village until it was almost overhead. The din was enough to drown out normal speech. But it was then that Harry chose to speak, raising his voice defiantly against the clattering and roaring that beat down on him from the sky.

"Noisy bastards," he said.

The helicopter banked, its blue sides flickering in the fragmented shadows of its blades. A figure could be seen, leaning forward in the cabin to stare at the ground. The lettering on his door read POLICE.

"They're looking for that girl that's gone missing," said Helen, her voice scattered and blown away by the roar. "The Mount girl."

"Aye, well. Do they have to make so much row about it?"

Harry cleared his throat noisily, sucking the phlegm onto the top of his tongue. Then he pursed his thin lips and spat into a clump of yellow ragwort growing by the gate.

As if taking offense, the helicopter moved suddenly away from the edge of the village, sliding toward a row of tall conifers that grew in the grounds of a large white house. The pitch of the noise changed and altered shape as it passed the house, tracing the outline of the roofs and chimneys like an echo locator sounding the depths of an ocean trench.

"At least it'll wake that lot up as well."

"Granddad—"

"There's nowt more to be said. Not just now."

Helen sighed, her brain crowding with thoughts she couldn't express and feelings she couldn't communicate. The old man only grimaced as his arm was stretched at an even sharper angle.

"Have to go, love," he said. "Jess'll pull me arm off, else."

Helen shook her head but dropped her hand and let him go. A thin trickle of blood ran down her arm from the scratch made by the thorn. It glittered thickly on her pink skin, clotting and drying fast in the warm sun. She watched as her grandfather set off down the hillside toward the woods at the foot of the cliffs. Jess, his black Labrador, led the way along the familiar path, tugging eagerly at the end of her lead, impatient to be allowed to run free when they reached the stream.

No, you couldn't run away from things forever, thought Helen. But you could always bugger off and walk the dog for a bit.

Down on the lower slopes of the hill, Ben Cooper was sweating. The perspiration ran in streams through the fine hairs on his chest and formed a sticky sheen on the muscles of his stomach. The sides and back of his T-shirt were already soaked, and his scalp prickled uncomfortably.

No breeze had yet found its way through the trees to cool the lingering heat of the afternoon sun. Each clearing was a little sun trap, funneling the heat and raising the temperature on the ground into the eighties. Even a few feet into the woods the humidity was enough to make his whole body itch, and tiny black flies swarmed from under the trees in irritating clouds, attracted by the smell of his sweat.

Every man in the line was equipped with a wooden pole to sift through the long grass and push aside the dense swathes of bracken and brambles. The bruised foliage released a damp, green smell, and Cooper's brown fell boots were stained dark to an inch above the soles. His pole came out of the undergrowth thick with burrs and with small caterpillars and insects clinging to its length. Every few minutes he had to stop to knock them off against the ground or on the bole of a tree. All along the line were the sounds of men doing the same, the thumps and taps punctuating their muttered complaints and sporadic bursts of conversation.

Cooper found that walking with his head down made his neck ache after a while. So when the line stopped for a minute to allow someone in the center the time to search a patch of dense bramble, he took the chance to raise his head and look up, above the line of the trees. He found himself gazing at the side of Win Low across the valley. Up there, on the bare, rocky outcrops they called the Witches, it would be so much cooler. There would be a fresh wind easing its way from the west, a wind that always seemed to come all the way from the Welsh mountains and across the Cheshire plain.

For the last two hours he had been wishing that he had used his common sense and brought a hat to keep the sun off his head. For once, he was jealous of his uniformed colleagues down the line, with their dark peaked caps pulled over their eyes and their starburst badges glittering in the sunlight. Being in CID had its disadvantages sometimes.

"Bloody hell, what a waste of effort."

The PC next to Ben Cooper was from Matlock section, a middle-aged rural beat manager who had once had aspirations to join the Operational Support Task Force in Chesterfield. But the Task Force was deployed farther along the hillside, below the Mount itself, while PC Garnett found himself alongside an Edendale detective in a makeshift search group which included a couple of National Park Rangers. Garnett wore his blue overalls with more comfort than style, and he had been swinging his pole with such ferocity as he walked that his colleagues had gradually moved farther away to protect their shins.

"You reckon so?"

"Aye, certain," said Garnett. "They say the lass has run off with some boyfriend."

"I don't know," said Cooper. "I've not heard that. It wasn't in the briefing. Just that she was missing."

"Huh. Missing my arse. Mark my words, she'll be off shagging some spotty youth somewhere. Fifteen years old, what do you expect these days?"

"Maybe you're right. We have to go through the motions all the same."

"Mind you, if one of my two did it, I'd murder 'em all right."

Garnett thrashed at a small elder sapling so hard that the stem snapped in two, the tender young branches collapsing to the ground and leaking a tiny trickle of sticky sap. Then he trod on the broken stem and crushed it into the grass with his police issue boot. Cooper hoped that, if there were any fragile evidence to be found in the woods, he would see it before Garnett reached it.

Then he looked at the PC and smiled suddenly, recognizing that the man had no harm in him. He might be a middle-aged dad whose ambitions were withering as his waistline expanded, but he had no harm in him at all. Cooper could almost sense the ordinary little niggles that teemed in Garnett's mind, from his disappearing hairline to the recurring ache at the base of his spine and the size of his telephone bill.

"Just be thankful for the overtime," he said. "We could all do with a bit of that."

"Ah yes, you're right there, lad. Too right. It takes something like this to get the fingers of those tightfisted bastards off the purse strings these days, doesn't it?"

"It's the budget cuts."

"Budgets!" Garnett said the word like a curse, and they both paused for a moment to listen to its sound, shaking their heads as if it symbolized the end of everything they had known.

"Accountants, you can keep 'em," said Garnett. "We're not coppers to them anymore, just a load of figures on a sheet of paper. It's all flashy operations and clear-up rates. There's no room for old-style coppers these days."

He threw a bitter glance along the hillside toward where the Task Force squad was beating its way through the scrubland beyond a row of Lombardy poplars like a set of dark spikes dropped into the landscape.

"Of course, you'll know all about that, lad. You're different. A chip off the old block, they reckon. Good for you. Wish you luck, though."

"Yeah, thanks."

Cooper had only just returned from a fortnight's summer leave. On his first day back on duty he had been thrown straight into the search for Laura Vernon, fifteen years old and missing from home since Saturday night. They were looking for a girl with short dark hair dyed red, wearing a silver nose stud, five foot six inches tall, mature for her age. Failing that, they were looking for her clothes—black denims, a red short-sleeved cotton T-shirt, a white sports bra, blue bikini pants, blue ankle socks, a pair of Reeboks, size five, slim fit. Nobody thought it necessary to point out that if they found her clothes, they were also looking for a body.

"This lass, though. She's miles away, if you ask me," said Garnett. "Run off with the boyfriend. Some yob on a motorbike from Manchester, maybe. That's what teenage girls get up to these days. The schools teach them about contraceptives before they're twelve, so what can you expect? Course, the parents never have a clue. Not parents like this lot, anyway. They don't know the kids exist half the time."

Cooper's legs were still aching from the rock climbing he had done on the sheer, terrifying faces of the Cuillin Hills of Skye. His friends Oscar and Rakesh were members of the Edendale Mountain Rescue Team and could never get enough of the mountains. Just now, though, he could really have done with a quiet day behind his desk at Division, making a few phone calls maybe, catching up on what had been happening during the last fortnight, getting up to date with the gossip. Anything but clambering up and down another hillside.

But he knew this area well—he was himself from a village a few miles down the valley. Most of the men recruited for the search parties were from the section stations or even from out of the division. A few of them were city boys. On the hills around here they would be falling down old mine shafts in their dozens without someone to tell them which way was up and which was down.

And, of course, PC Garnett could well be right. It had happened so often—youngsters bored with life in the villages of the Peak District, attracted by the glamour and excitement of the big cities. And very likely there was a boyfriend, too—no doubt someone the parents found unsuitable. According to the initial reports, the Vernons claimed there had been no trouble at home, no family rows, no reason at all for Laura to walk out. But didn't parents always say that? So much could remain misunderstood among families or never even suspected. Especially if they were a family who didn't have the time or the inclination to talk to each other much.

But there were other factors in this case. Laura had taken no clothes with her, very little money, no possessions of any kind. And initial inquiries had brought a sighting of her talking to a young man on Saturday night, at the edge of the expanse of hillside scrub and woodland known as the Baulk.

Once he got out on the hill below the village of Moorhay, Cooper had remembered that he had even been to Laura Vernon's home once. It was the big white house they called the Mount, which stood somewhere above the search party, hidden behind the trees on its own spur of land. It was a former mine owner's house, big and pretentious, with formally laid out grounds full of rhododendrons and azaleas, and with a stunning view over the valley from the terrace. Cooper had been invited to the Mount for the eighteenth birthday party of a classmate, a lad everyone at the old Edendale High School knew had well-off parents even before they were given the tour of the big house. That hadn't been the Vernons but the people before them—they had been local people, the family of a man who had inherited a string of small petrol stations scattered throughout the Peak. The business had expanded from Edendale and its surrounding villages, beyond the borders of Derbyshire, in fact, into South Yorkshire and the fringes of the cities.

Eventually, of course, he had sold out to one of the larger companies, cashed in, and moved away to somewhere better. Abroad, they said. The South of France and Italy were popular guesses.

The Mount had stood empty then for some time, waiting out the recession. Photographs of its elegant facade featured regularly in the adverts of upmarket estate agents in glossy county magazines. The village people would sit in the doctor's waiting room, pointing out to each other the multiplicity of bathrooms, wondering what a utility was, and shaking their heads in astonishment at the number of noughts in the asking price. Then the Vernons had moved into the Mount. No one knew where they had come from or what Mr. Vernon did, except that he was "in business." He drove off every day in his Jaguar XJS in the direction of Sheffield, sometimes staying away from home for days on end. Was he another one just pausing for a while in the Peak while he booked his ticket to Tuscany?

"You'll be glad of the extra cash, too, though, won't you? Just been on holiday?" said Garnett.

"Scotland," said Cooper.

"Bloody hell. Scotland? It's just the Peak District, but with a bit more water, isn't it? Can't see the point of that, myself. Me, I want a bit of sun and sand when I go on leave. Not to mention the cheap booze, eh? I like Ibiza. There's loads of English pubs and casinos and stuff. A few bottles of sangria, a paella, and a go on the fruit machines. You can't beat it, that's what I say. Besides, the wife'd divorce me if I suggested anything else. She's on about the Maldives next year. I don't even know where it is."

"Somewhere east of Ibiza, I think," said Cooper. "But you'd like it."

The line was moving forward again, and Cooper waved away a cloud of flies from his face. Sun and sand and cheap booze were far from his mind. Even during his fortnight on Skye, his thoughts had kept slipping away from the rock face, back to the promotion interviews that were coming up, now just a few days away. There would soon be a detective sergeant's job available at E Division. DS Osborne had been on sick leave for weeks now, and it was said that he would go the usual way—early retirement on health grounds, another pension to be paid for from the creaking police authority budget. Ben Cooper thought he was the natural successor to Osborne. Ten years in the force, and five in CID, and he had more local knowledge than most of the rest of his shift put together. The sergeant's job was what he wanted and needed. More—it was what his family wanted. Cooper thought of his mother and the desperately hopeful look in her eye when he came home from work, the question as often unspoken as asked out loud. He thought about her many times a day, every time he saw someone ill or old. He thought of her seemingly endless pain and grief, and the one thing she thought might ease it. He ached to give her what she longed for, just this once.

The line of men were deep into the trees again now, the canopy over them muffling the noise of the police helicopter that was still moving along the valley, sweeping the woods with its thermal imaging camera. The sudden transition from glaring sun to deep shade made it difficult to make out the details of the undergrowth below the trees. In places there could have been an entire SAS platoon lying concealed in the chest-high bracken and willow herb, waiting for some bobby in blue overalls to stumble into them armed with nothing but a slug-encrusted pole.

A pheasant clattered in alarm and took off somewhere nearby. From farther away, there was another sound. The trees were too thick to tell which direction it came from or exactly how far away it was. But it was the sound of a dog, and it barked just once.

-2-

Charlotte Vernon had been in the same position for a quarter of an hour. Whether it was the effects of the tablets or the alcohol, or simply the frantic activity of her imagination, throughout the day she had been alternating between phases of restlessness and immobility. It was as though she managed to blank out her thoughts entirely for short periods before being overwhelmed afresh by surges of terror. The waiting had become an end in itself.

Now Charlotte stood on the terrace, leaning against the stone balustrade, watching the helicopter passing overhead. She followed the movement of the rotor blades as if she hoped to read a message in their flickering blur. On a table near her hand stood a half-drunk glass of Bacardi and an ashtray filled with damp and crushed butts, their filters stained with smears of vermilion.

She had been on the terrace all afternoon, hardly seeming to notice as the heat of the sun gradually moved away from her shoulders and dipped behind the house until she stood in shade and the stone flags around her began to whisper and contract. She had stirred only when the phone rang behind her in the house, her muscles tensing, her fingers gripping tighter on the balustrade for a few seconds each time, as Graham answered it. She would strain to catch his muttered words, then cover her ears as if she didn't want to hear them at all.

But all the calls were inquiries from friends. Some were even business calls, which Graham dealt with in a lowered voice, glancing toward his wife's back as he turned guiltily away. He seemed relieved to have an excuse not to look at her as she posed against the view of the Witches, her head raised to the sky like a heroine in an Arthurian romance, waiting for news of a distant battle.

After the latest call, Graham replaced the phone and turned back toward the windows.

"That was Edward Randle from AET," he said. "He sends his thoughts. And he wanted to know whether he and Martina should still come tomorrow night."

Graham waited for Charlotte to speak. But he could hear only the faint buzzing of the fans and the distant bark of a dog somewhere down in the village.

"I told him of course they should come. We can't put people off, can we? Life goes on."

Graham wondered whether she had heard what he said. She was in some world of her own where Allied Electronics and other such trivialities didn't exist. Graham moved closer to her, wondering whether he should offer to touch her, whether it would be what she wanted just now, or whether it would only make things worse. He couldn't tell.

When he stepped onto the terrace, he could smell the suntan oil on her body. Her bleached hair hung straight on her neck, falling slightly on to the collar of her wrap. The backs of her slim, well-tanned legs were visible to the edge of her bikini, her muscles tense and stretched. Graham felt a surge of physical desire but tried to suppress it. Maybe tonight his wife would be restored to her usual receptive mood. Maybe tomorrow.

"Did you hear me, Charlie?"

"I wish we could take the phone off the hook."

"But then we wouldn't hear . . . if there was news."

"When they find her, you mean."

Charlotte's voice was tired now, the strain of the past forty-eight hours taking its toll, though she would be reluctant to admit it.

"They will find her, won't they, Graham?"

"Of course they will."

Graham repeated the same reassurance he had been giving for two days. He put as much sincerity as he could into his voice, though he doubted his wife really believed him. He certainly didn't believe it himself.

The helicopter started to turn, its rotors dipping and fading from sight against the hillside behind it. Charlotte looked dejected at its disappearance, as if she had failed to decipher the message because she had not tried hard enough. From the terrace, none of the houses in the village were visible. The only human habitation in view consisted of a couple of farms high on the opposite slope, their weathered stone walls blending into the hillside as if they had grown there. No wonder Charlotte hadn't wanted the helicopter to go away. It was the only sign of life she could see from the Mount.

"You hear of girls running off and disappearing forever," she said. "To London. Would she go to London, Graham? How would she get there?"

"She's only fifteen," he said. "They would bring her back."

"How would she get there?" she repeated. "Where would she get the money? She could have hitched, I suppose. Would she know how to do that? Why didn't she take any clothes?"

For two days she had asked too many questions that Graham couldn't answer. He would have liked to tell her that he was sure Laura could have got no farther than Bakewell and that the police would pick her up before the night was over. He had tried to tell her, but the words dried up in his throat.

"Don't you want to come in now? It's time to eat."

"Not just yet," she said.

"It's starting to go dark. You'll want to change at least."

"I want to be out here," she said.

"Charlie—"

"As long as they're still looking," she said, "I want to be out here."

A book had been turned facedown on the table. Very little of it had been read, but it didn't need to be. Graham could see from the cover that it was the latest in a best-selling series about an American pathologist who was forever dissecting dead bodies and catching serial killers. The illustration showed a barely identifiable part of a naked body, set against a dark background.

"I can't think of anywhere else that she might have gone," said Charlotte. "I've been trying and trying, racking my brains. But we've tried everywhere, haven't we, Graham? Can you think of anywhere else?"

"We've tried them all," said Graham.

"There's that girl in Marple."

"We've tried there," said Graham. "Her parents said she was in France for the summer."

"Oh yes, I forgot."

"If she's met up with the wrong sort of people . . ."

"How could she?" said Charlotte quickly. "We've been so careful. How could she meet the wrong people?"

"We have to face it, it does happen. Some of her friends . . . Even if they're from the best families, they can go astray."

"I suppose so."

"I've heard there are these rave things. Some of them go on all week-end, they say."

Charlotte shuddered. "That means drugs, doesn't it?"

"We'll have to talk to her about it seriously, when she's back."

After the helicopter had moved away to hover somewhere along the valley, the faint sound of voices could be heard, carried toward the house on the evening breeze. Graham and Charlotte could see no one because of the heavy tree cover, but both of them knew, without discussing it, that there were many men out there on the hillside, calling to each other, searching for their daughter.

"Of course, there were probably friends she didn't tell us about," said Graham. "We have to face up to that. Places she went that she didn't want us to know about."

Charlotte shook her head. "Laura didn't keep secrets from me," she said. "From you, of course. But not from me."

"If you say so, Charlie."

A small frown flickered across Charlotte's face at his calm acceptance. "Is there something you know, Graham? Something that you're not telling me?"

"Of course not."

He was thinking of his last conversation with Laura. It had been late on Thursday night, when she had slipped into his study and persuaded him to let her have a glass of his whiskey. Her face had been flushed with some other excitement, even before the whiskey had begun to take effect. She had perched on the edge of his desk and stroked his arm, smiling at him with that mature, seductive smile she had learned had such an effect on their male visitors. She had dyed her hair again, a deeper red than ever, almost violet, and her fingernails were painted a color so dark it was practically black. Then she had talked to him, with that knowing look in her eyes and that sly wink, and told him what she wanted. The following morning, he had sacked Lee Sherratt. The second gardener they had lost that year.

"No, of course not, Charlie."

She accepted his word. "And the boy Lee?"

Graham said nothing. He closed the abandoned novel, slipping a soft leather bookmark between the pages. He collected the book and the half-full glass of Bacardi from the table. The sun had almost gone from their part of the valley now. But the jagged shapes of the Witches were bathed in a dull red light that was streaked with black runnels where the rocky gulleys were in shadow.

"What about *him,* Graham? What about the boy?"

He knew Charlotte still thought of Laura as pure and innocent. It was the way she would think of her daughter forever. But Graham had begun to see her with different eyes. And the boy? The boy had already been punished. Punished for not dancing to the tune that Laura had played. Lee Sherratt had been too stubborn to play the game—but of course, he had been busy playing other games by then. And so Graham had sacked him. It was what Laura had wanted.

"The police have spoken to him. He told them he hasn't seen Laura for days."

"Do you believe that?"

He shrugged. "Who knows what to believe just now?"

"I want to speak to him. I want to ask him myself. Make him tell the truth."

"I don't think that would be a good idea, Charlie. Leave it to the police."

"They know about him, don't they?"

"Of course. They've got him on their records anyway. Over that stolen car."

"What?"

"You remember. The car that was taken from the car park at the top of the cliff. It belonged to some German people. Laura told us about it."

"Did she?" said Charlotte vaguely.

At last she allowed him to lead her back into the room, where she began to touch familiar objects—a cushion, the back of a chair cover, the piano stool, a series of gilt-framed photographs in a cabinet. She opened her handbag, touched up her lipstick, and lit another cigarette.

"Who else is supposed to be coming tomorrow night?" she said.

"The Wingates. Paddy and Frances. And they're bringing some friends of theirs from Totley. Apparently, they're building up a big computer business, installing systems in Doncaster and Rotherham. Paddy says they've got a really good future. They'd make an ideal account, but I need to get in quickly and make the contact."

"I'd better see to the food then."

"Good girl."

As she turned toward Graham now, her eyes showed no sign of any tears. Graham was glad—she was not a woman given to tears, and he would not have known how to deal with it. Instead, she fiddled with the front of her wrap, letting him glimpse her brown thighs and the gentle slope of her belly above the edge of her bikini briefs.

"You like Frances, don't you?" she said.

Graham grinned, recognizing the opening. "Not as much as I like you, Charlie."

He took a step toward her, but she turned suddenly and picked up one of the photograph frames from the cabinet and began to stroke its edges.

"Won't you go and see the Sherratt boy, Graham? To help get Laura back."

"Leave it for now, Charlie."

"Why?"

"Because the police will find her."

"Will they, Graham?"

The photograph frame she was holding was empty. The picture had been given to the police to enable them to identify Laura when they found her. Graham took the frame from her and replaced it in the cabinet.

"Of course they will," he said.

The old woman's burst of anger was over, but her thin hands still jerked and spasmed on the floral-patterned arms of her chair. Helen watched her until she was calm and pulled her cardigan closer around her shoulders from where it had slipped.

"I'll put the kettle on, Grandma."

"If you like."

"Do you want your Special Blend?"

"The bags'll do. But make sure you put an extra one in the pot. You know how I like it."

Helen stood at the narrow window of the kitchen of Dial Cottage while she waited for the kettle to boil. The electrical appliances that her father had bought for his parents-in-law left hardly any room in the kitchen to turn around. There was certainly not enough space for two people between the cooker and the oversized pine table crammed in lengthwise to the sink.

The table was scattered with cooking equipment, place mats with scenes of a North Wales seaside resort, sprigs of mint and thyme tied with bits of string, a jar of marmalade, a jar filled with wooden ladles and spatulas, a potato peeler with a wooden handle, a chopping board, and half an onion soaking in a bowl of water. By the back door a pair of Wellington boots and a walking stick stood on the blue lino, and a dark green waxed coat with a corduroy collar hung from the hook where Harry's cap would normally have been. The coat had been Helen's present to him on his seventy-fifth birthday.

"He was never like this before," said her grandmother from her chair, not needing to raise her voice over the short distance to the kitchen. "Never this bad. Now he can't speak without biting my head off."

"Have you asked him what's wrong?"

"Asked him? *Him?* I might as well talk to the wall."

"Perhaps he's ill, Grandma."

"He had a cold the other week, I suppose."

Helen could see that her grandmother thought that Harry was just being a bad-tempered old man, that she had done something to annoy him. But Helen's thoughts were running on some serious illness troubling him, something he was keeping to himself, an awful secret he wouldn't want to inflict on his wife and family.

There were so many possibilities when you were in your late seventies, when you smoked, when you had spent most of your working life in a lead mine, when you had fought your way through a vicious war. Her grandmother Gwen would not think of these things. She would believe that Harry had a bad cold right up to the moment they put him in the ground at St. Edwin's.

"But if he's ill it doesn't stop him going off down there with Jess. It doesn't stop him going off with those friends of his, either."

"No, Grandma."

Helen put hot water into the teapot and emptied it out again, dropped three tea bags in, and poured on the boiling water from the electric kettle.

While she waited for the tea to brew, she looked out of the window, across the back garden toward the valley. The garden itself was bright with beds of petunias and violets, rows of potato plants with white and yellow flowers, and canes wrapped around with runner beans. But beyond the garden, the woods that ran down the valley looked dark and brooding. Helen could see the police helicopter hovering over the tops of the trees half a mile away. They were still looking. Still hoping.

"They've changed him. He thinks more of his cronies than he does of me. More than he does of his family."

"Granddad thinks the world of his family."

"They've changed him. That Wilford Cutts and the other one, Sam Beeley."

"Them? They're just Granddad's friends. His old workmates. They're nothing to do with it."

"It's them that's done it."

"I'm sure they haven't done anything, Grandma. They're just his friends from Glory Stone Mine. He's known them for years."

"Not like now. It was different before, when they were working. But now they've led him away, filled his head with thoughts."

"I don't know what you mean," said Helen.

But she had wondered herself, sometimes, about what the three old men got up to when they were together out on the hill or up on Wilford's untidy smallholding with the flock of hens and the odd little collection of aging animals. Sometimes Harry brought home a capful of speckled brown eggs from the Cuckoo Marans or a bag of potatoes from the disused paddock that he and Wilford had converted into a huge vegetable patch. At other times, the three of them just went to the pub, where Sam Beeley came into his own and bought the drinks.

"Since he's had no work, he's been different," said Gwen. "All of them have. It doesn't do for men to be at a loose end. Not men like them. The devil makes evil work."

"You're talking nonsense now, Grandma."

Helen found a carton of long-life milk in the fridge and dropped a tiny amount into a cup. Then she poured the tea, making sure it was good and strong.

Her grandmother had kept her old lino on the floor in the kitchen. She had protested so much when they had laid the new fitted carpet in the sitting room that her son-in-law, Andrew, had been forced to give in on this one point. She had said it was easy to keep clean. For Helen, looking at the blue lino now, it also seemed to be inseparable from the dark oak paneling and the bumpy walls and the whitewashed stone lintels.

"He thinks more of them than me, anyway. That's what I say. He's proved it now."

"Let's forget about it for a bit, Grandma. Enjoy your tea."

"You're a good girl. You were always his favorite, Helen. Why don't you talk to him?"

"I will try," promised Helen.

She stood by the old woman's armchair, looking down on her white hair, so thin she could clearly see the pink scalp. She wanted to put her arm around her grandmother's shoulders and hug her, to tell her it would be all right. But she knew that Gwen would be embarrassed, and in any case Helen wasn't at all sure that it *would* be all right. A sudden surge of affection and frustration made her turn away.

Then she saw her grandfather, a small figure way down at the bottom of the hillside path, just emerging from the trees at the foot of Raven's Side. Whether it was something about the way he moved or the set of his shoulders, she couldn't say. But she knew immediately that there was something badly wrong.

Gwen cocked her head and peered at Helen, sensing the tension in her silence.

"What is it, dear?"

"Nothing, Grandma."

Helen unlatched the back door and stood on the whitewashed step. Suddenly she felt an irrational flood of memories streaming out of the old cottage behind her like coils of smoke escaping from a burning house. They were childhood memories, mostly of her grandfather—memories of him taking her by the hand as they walked on this same path to look at the fish jumping in the stream or to pick daisies for a daisy chain; of her grandfather proudly sitting her on his knee as he showed her how he filled his pipe with tobacco and lit it with the long colored-paper tapers. Fleeting smells flickered by her senses, passing in a second, yet each one with enough emotional power to fill her eyes with instant tears. They were the remembered smells of pipe smoke and Brylcreem and boot polish.

Harry had always seemed to be polishing his shoes. He still did. It was one of those signs that she knew her grandfather by even as he had changed over the years. Without those signs, she thought, old age might have made him unrecognizable to the child who had known the strong, indestructible man in his fifties.

It was in just the same way that, at this moment, she knew her grandfather only by his walk. It was a slow, purposeful walk, upright and solemn, the pace of a soldier at a funeral, bearing the coffin of a dead comrade.

She heard the helicopter turn again and come straight toward her. Two faces stared down at her, expressionless behind their dark glasses. She felt as though the watching policemen could see straight into her heart. Their presence was somehow personal and intimate, and yet forever too far away.

-3-

"OK, take a break."

The word came down the line from the uniformed sergeant at the opposite end from Ben Cooper. The men in blue overalls and Wellingtons backed away from the line of search and sat on the tussocks of rough grass in a half circle. Someone produced a flask of tea, someone else a bottle of orange juice.

PC Garnett settled down comfortably, tossing his pole aside, taking off his cap to reveal receding hair cropped short at the sides. They said it was the helmets that made so many policemen start to lose their hair early. Cooper himself was conscious that one day he would start to see a thinning on either side of his forehead. Everybody told him that his fine brown hair was just like his father's, who had never been anything but halfway bald, as far as he could remember. So far, though, he was still able to let a lock of hair fall across his forehead as he had always done. Fashions had tended to pass him by.

Garnett smiled as he mopped his brow with his sleeve and eased himself into gossip mode. "So what about this new recruit in your department, Cooper? The new DC?"

"I've not met him yet. I've only just come back from leave."

"It's a 'her,' mate, a 'her.' Diane Fry, they call her."

"Right."

"She's from Birmingham."

"I've not heard anything about her. I expect she'll be all right."

"According to Dave Rennie, she's a bit of a hard-faced cow. Could be a looker, he says, but she doesn't bother. Blonde but has her hair cut short. Too tall, too skinny, no makeup, always wears trousers. A bit of a stroppy bitch."

"You haven't even met her," protested Cooper.

"Well, you know the type. Probably another lesbian."

Cooper blew out an exasperated breath. "That's ridiculous. You can't go around saying things like that. You don't know anything about her."

Garnett had the sense to hear the irritation in Cooper's voice and didn't argue. He idly pulled a clump of dandelions and shredded the leaves between his fingers. But Cooper couldn't let the subject rest.

"You know what it's like for the women as well as I do, Garnett—some of them just try too hard. She'll fit in fine after a week or two, you'll see. They usually do."

"I dunno about that. I've a feeling you'll not have time to be her best mate though, lad. She'll be up and away in no time."

"Why? Does she go ballooning?"

"Ha, ha." Garnett ignored the sarcasm, in fact was probably impervious to it when he had a good subject of gossip. "She comes with a bit of a 'rep' actually. A potential highflier, they reckon. Ambitious."

"Oh yeah? She'll have to prove herself first."

"Maybe."

The clouds of tiny flies were getting thicker as they gathered around the men's heads, attracted by their sweat and the sweet smell of the orange juice. The PC looked smug.

"Come on, what do you mean?" said Cooper. "You don't just get promotion without showing you're worth it."

"Get real, mate. She's female. You know—two tits and a fanny, always puts the toilet seat down."

"Yeah, I've noticed that. So what?"

"So what? *So what?* So the force is short of female officers in supervisory ranks, especially in CID. Don't you read the reports? You just watch, old son—provided she keeps her nose clean and always smiles nicely at the top brass, Detective Constable Fry will shoot up that promotion ladder like she's got a rocket up her arse."

Cooper was about to protest when the shout went up from the contact man. "DC Cooper! Is DC Cooper here? Your boss wants you. Urgent."

The instructions from DI Hitchens were terse, and the address he gave Cooper was in Moorhay, the village visible on the brow of the hill above the woods. Communities in this area tended to gather around the thousand-foot contour, the valley bottoms being too narrow.

"Check it out, Cooper, and fast. We either get to the girl in the next two hours or we lose the whole night. You know what that could mean."

"I'm on my way, sir."

"Take somebody with you. Who've you got?"

Cooper looked back at the group of men lounging on the grass. His gaze passed across PC Garnett and a couple of other middle-aged bobbies, the overweight sergeant, two female PCs from Matlock, and the three Rangers.

"No CID officers, sir. I'll have to borrow a uniformed PC."

There was a suggestion of a sigh at the other end of the line.

"Do it then. But get a move on."

Cooper explained as quickly as he could to the sergeant and was given a tall, muscular young bobby of about twenty called Wragg, who perked up at the prospect of some action.

"Follow me as best you can."

"Don't worry, I'm right with you," said Wragg, flexing the muscles in his shoulders.

The path up to Moorhay wound back through the trees to where a kissing gate gave access through the drystone walls into a field where black-and-white dairy cattle had recently been turned back in after milking. The field had been cut for hay a few weeks before, and the grass was short and springy underfoot as Ben Cooper ran along the side of the wall, the heat and sweat prickling on his brow and his legs spasming with pain as he forced them on. Wragg kept pace with him easily, but soon dropped his tendency to ask questions when Cooper didn't respond. He needed all his breath for running.

As they passed, the cows turned their heads to watch in astonishment, their jaws working slowly, their eyes growing huge between twitching ears. Earlier in the afternoon, the search party had had to wait for the farmer to move the cows to the milking shed before the line could work its way across the field. The air had been filled with crude jokes about cow pats.

Cooper passed a stretch of collapsed wall, where a length of electric fence had been erected to keep the cattle away until someone skilled in drystone walling could be found to repair it. Before the cows' curiosity could lead them to follow him, Cooper had already reached the next gate. He skirted another field and ran up a farm track paved with stones and broken rubble.

The steepness of the slope was increasing steadily now on the last few hundred yards, until Cooper began to feel as though he was back on the Cuillins again. Wragg was dropping farther and farther behind, slowing to a walk, using his arms against his knees to boost himself up the steeper sections.

He was carrying too much upper body weight, thought Cooper, and hadn't developed the right muscles in his thighs and calves for hill climbing. Some of the old people who had lived in these hill villages all their lives would have passed the young PC with ease.

Finally Cooper reached the high, dark wall at the corner of the graveyard at St. Edwin's Church. The church seemed to have been built on a mound, standing well above the village street at the front and presenting an elevation from the bottom of the valley like the rampart of a castle wall. The square Norman tower stood stark against the sky, tall and strangely out of proportion to the shortened nave, giving the church the appearance of a fallen letter L.

The surface of the churchyard was so high that Cooper thought the bodies buried there must be almost on his eye level, if only he could see through the stones of the wall and the thick, dark soil to where the oak caskets lay rotting.

The church was surrounded by mature trees, horse chestnuts and oaks, and two ancient yews. The damp smell of cut grass was in the air, and as Cooper passed the churchyard, climbing now toward the back of a row of stone cottages, a man in a red check shirt with his sleeves rolled up looked over the wall at him from the side gate. He was leaning on a big petrol lawn mower, pausing between a swathe of smoothly mown grass and a tussocky area he hadn't yet reached. He gazed at the running man with a grimace of distaste, as if the evening had been disturbed by something particularly unpleasant.

At the first of the cottages, a woman was in her garden with a watering can, tending the flower beds on the side where they were in the shade of the cottage wall. She held the watering can upright in a gloved hand as she watched Cooper trying to catch his breath to ask directions. He found he was gasping in the heady smells of honeysuckle and scented roses freshly dampened with water. Behind him, the lawn mower started up again in the churchyard, and a small flock of jackdaws rose protesting from the chestnuts.

"Dial Cottage?"

The woman stared at him, then shook her head almost imperceptibly, unwilling to spare him even that effort. She turned her back ostentatiously, her attention on a miniature rose with the palest of yellow flowers. On the wall in front of Cooper was a sign that said: NO PARKING. NO TURNING. NO HIKERS.

Two cottages up, he found an old woman sitting in a garden chair with a Persian cat on her knee, and he repeated his question. She pointed up the hill.

"Up to the road, turn left, and go past the pub. It's in the row of cottages on your left. Dial Cottage is one of those with the green doors."

"Thank you." With a glance at the PC still struggling up the track, Cooper ran on, glad to have tarmac under his feet at last as he approached the road.

Moorhay was off the main tourist routes and had little traffic most of the time, with no more than an occasional car coasting through toward Ladybower Reservoir or the show caverns in Castleton. A small pub called the Drover stood across the road, with two or three cars drawn up on the cobbles in front. According to the signs, it sold Robinson's beer, one of Ben Cooper's favorites. Right now, he would have died for a pint, but he couldn't stop.

He passed a turning called Howe Lane, near a farm entrance with a wooden-roofed barn and a tractor shed. A sign at the bottom of the track said that the farmhouse itself provided bed and breakfast. Trees overhung the road as it wandered away from the village. In the distance, he glimpsed a shoulder of moor with a single tree on its summit.

Two hundred yards from the church was a long row of two-storey cottages built of the local millstone grit, with slate roofs and small mullioned windows. They had no front gardens, but some had stone troughs filled with marigolds and petunias against their front walls. One or two of the cottages had plain oak plank doors with no windows. The doors were painted a dark green, with lintels of whitewashed stone tilted at uneven angles.

By the time Cooper found which of them was Dial Cottage the perspiration was running freely from his forehead and the back of his neck and soaking into his shirt. His face was red and he was breathing heavily when he knocked on the door. He could barely bring himself to speak when it was answered.

"Detective Constable Cooper, Edendale Police."

The woman who opened the door nodded, not even looking at the warrant card held in his sticky palm.

"Come in."

The old oak door thumped shut, shutting out the street, and Cooper blinked his eyes to readjust them to the gloom. The woman was about his own age, maybe twenty-seven or twenty-eight. She was wearing a halter-necked sun top and shorts, and her pink limbs immediately struck him as totally out of place in the dark interior, like a chorus girl who had wandered into a funeral parlor. Her hair shone as if she had brought a bit of the sun into the cottage with her.

They stood in a narrow hallway, made even narrower by a heavy mahogany sideboard loaded with cut glass vases and a fruit bowl, all standing on lace mats. In the middle was a color photograph of a large family group, taken at the seaside somewhere. Recently applied magnolia woodchip wallpaper could not disguise the unevenness of the walls underneath. An estate agent would have called it a charming period look.

Cooper stood still for a moment, fighting to get back his breath, his chest heaving. He wiped the back of his hand across his brow to stop the trickles of sweat running into his eyes.

"We had a report at the station," he gasped. "A phone call."

"It's *Ben* Cooper, isn't it?"

"That's right." He looked at the young woman again, recognition dawning only slowly, as he found it did when you saw someone out of their familiar surroundings.

"Helen? Helen Milner?"

"That's it. I guess I've changed a bit since the sixth form at Edendale High."

"It was a few years ago."

"Nine years, I suppose," she said. "You've not changed much, Ben. Anyway, I saw your picture in the paper a while ago. You'd won a trophy of some sort."

"The Shooting Trophy, yes. Look, can we—?"

"I'll take you through."

"Do you live here then?"

"No, it's my grandparents' house."

They stepped through into a back room, hardly less gloomy than the hallway despite a window looking out on to the back garden. There was a 1950s tiled fireplace in the middle of one wall, scattered with more photographs and incongruous holiday mementos—a straw donkey, a figure of a Spanish flamenco dancer, a postcard of Morocco with sneering camels and an impossibly blue sea. Above the fireplace, a large mirror in a gilt frame reflected a murky hunting print on the opposite wall, with red-coated figures on horseback galloping into a shadowy copse in pursuit of an unseen quarry. Cooper smelled furniture polish and the musty odor of old clothes or drawers lined with ancient newspapers.

There were two elderly people in the room—a woman wearing a floral-patterned dress and a blue cardigan sitting in one armchair and an old man in a pair of corduroy trousers and a Harris wool sweater facing her in the other chair. They both sat upright, stiff and alert, their feet drawn under them as if to put as much distance between themselves as they could.

In front of the empty fireplace stood a two-bar electric fire. Despite the warmth of the day outside, it gave the impression of having been recently used. Cooper, though, was glad of the slight chill in the room, which had begun to dry the sweat on his face as the two old people turned toward him.

"It's Ben Cooper, Granddad," said Helen.

"Aye, I can see that. Sergeant Cooper's lad."

Cooper was well used to this greeting, especially from the older residents around Edendale. For some of them, he was merely the shadow of his father, whose fame and popularity seemed eternal.

"Hello, sir. I believe somebody phoned the station."

Harry didn't answer, and Cooper was starting to form the idea that the old boy might be deaf when his granddaughter stepped in.

"It was me actually," said Helen. "Granddad asked me to."

Harry shrugged, as if to say he couldn't really be bothered whether she had phoned or not.

"I thought it'd be something you lot would want to know about, like as not."

"And your name, sir?"

"Dickinson."

Cooper waited patiently for the explanation. But it came from the granddaughter, not from the old man.

"It's in the kitchen," she said, leading the way through another door. An almost brand-new washing machine and a fridge-freezer stood among white-painted wooden cupboards, with an aluminium sink unit awkwardly fitted into place among them. Neither of the old people followed them, but watched from their chairs. The rooms were so small that they were well within earshot.

"Granddad found this."

The trainer lay on a pine kitchen table, lumpy and grotesque among the bundles of dried mint and the brown-glazed cooking pots. Someone had put a sheet from the *Buxton Advertiser* underneath it to stop the soil that clung to its rubber sole from getting onto the surface of the table. The trainer lay in the middle of an advertising feature for a new Cantonese restaurant, its laces trailing across a photograph of a smiling Chinese woman serving barbecued spareribs and bean sprouts. On the opposite page were columns of birth and death notices, wedding announcements, and twenty-first birthday greetings.

Cooper wiped his sweaty palms on his trousers and took out a pen. He gently prised open the tongue of the trainer to look inside, careful not to disturb the soil that was starting to dry and crumble away from the crevices in the sole.

"Where did you find this, Mr. Dickinson?"

"Under Raven's Side."

Cooper knew Raven's Side. It was a wilderness of rocks and holes and tangled vegetation. The search parties had been slowly making progress toward the cliff all afternoon, as if reluctant to have to face the task of searching it, with the expectation of twisted ankles and lacerated fingers.

"Can you be more specific?"

The old man looked offended, as if he had been accused of lying. Cooper began to wonder why he had thought it was cooler inside the cottage. Despite the open windows, there was no breath of air in the kitchen. The atmosphere felt stifling, claustrophobic. The only bit of light seemed to go out of the room when Helen went to answer a knock at the door.

"There's a big patch of brambles and bracken down there, above the stream," said the old man. "It's where I walk Jess, see."

Cooper was surprised by a faint scrabbling of claws near his feet. A black Labrador gazed up at him from under the table, responding hopefully to the sound of its name. The dog's paws were grubby, and it was lying on the *Eden Valley Times*. The sports section, by the look of it. Edendale FC had lost the opening match of the season.

"Was there just the trainer? Nothing else?"

"Not that I saw. It was Jess that found it really. She goes after rabbits and such when she gets down by there."

"OK," said Cooper. "We'll take a look in a minute. You can show me the exact spot."

Helen returned, accompanied by an exhausted PC Wragg.

"Is it . . . any use?" she asked.

"We'll see." Cooper took a polythene bag from his back pocket and carefully slid the trainer into it. "Would you wait here for a while, please? A senior officer will probably want to speak to you."

Helen nodded and looked at her grandfather, but his expression didn't alter. His face was stony, like a man resigned to a period of necessary suffering.

Cooper went back into the road and pulled out his personal radio to contact Edendale Divisional HQ, where he knew DI Hitchens would be waiting for a report. He held the polythene bag up to the light, staring at its contents while he waited for the message to be relayed.

The trainer was a Reebok, size five, slim fit. And the brown stains on the toe looked very much like blood.

-4-

The E Division Police Headquarters in Edendale had been new once, in the 1950s, and had even earned their architect a civic award. But in the CID room, fifty years of moldering paperwork and half-smoked cigarettes and bad food had left their mark on the walls and their smell in the carpets. The Derbyshire Constabulary budget had recently stretched sufficiently to decorate the walls, replace the window frames, and install air-conditioning in some of the offices. They had also replaced the old wooden desks with modern equivalents more in keeping with the computer equipment they carried.

DC Diane Fry was reading the bulletins. She had started off by catching up with the fresh ones for the day, then had continued casting back over recent weeks. Her intention was to make herself familiar with all the current inquiries in the division. Although she had been in Edendale nearly two weeks, she still felt as new as the white glosswork that for some reason was refusing to dry properly on the outside wall near the window. All the windows on this side of the building looked down on Gate C and the back of the East Stand at Edendale Football Club, a team struggling in the lower reaches of one of the pyramid leagues.

The priority problem of the moment was car crime at local tourist spots. From the weary tone of some of the memos Fry came across, it sounded as though it always was the priority problem in E Division at this time of year. Many thousands of visitors were drawn into the Peak District National Park during the summer, bringing with them what appeared to be their own crime wave, like the wake trailing behind a huge cruise liner. These visitors left their cars at remote spots, in makeshift car parks on rough ground, in abandoned quarries, and on roadside verges. The cars were invariably full of cameras and binoculars and purses stuffed with cash and credit cards and God knows what else. At the same time, traveling criminals from the big conurbations around Sheffield in the east and Manchester in the west were touring the Peak District looking for just such victims. A few minutes with an unattended vehicle and they were away back to their cities, leaving a trail of distraught visitors and ruined holidays.

It presented an apparently insoluble problem. It was impossible to get the message across to the car owners, since they were a constantly changing flood—here one day, then moving on the next, to be replaced by another group of visitors. It was impossible for the police to keep surveillance on vulnerable sites with the resources available; it was feasible only to identify possible perpetrators and ask neighboring forces to keep them under observation. It was called living in hopes.

Diane Fry looked across the room at DS Rennie. He was on the phone, and had been for some time. She couldn't hear what he was saying, but she was fairly sure he hadn't yet taken a single note with the ballpoint pen he was chewing. He was thick shouldered and thick necked, a veteran prop forward in the divisional rugby team, as she had learned from his conversation with one of the other DCs. She also knew that Rennie's first name was David, and that he was married with two children in their early teens.

She had soon become aware of his sly sideways appraisal, a slithering of the eyes toward her when he thought she wasn't looking. She had observed this in the past to be a common tentative first maneuver toward a junior female colleague, designed to culminate in an office affair. Many men, of course, never got past this first sign—it was more an indication of hope than intention. But there were others who were more of a nuisance, and Fry couldn't tell just yet which Rennie was. It was helpful, though, to have the early warning, so that she could decide on her own terms when the time was right to put him down. Affairs with colleagues were not on her agenda. Not at all.

She could see Rennie was not making the effort to appear busy, even though there was a DCI somewhere in the building and liable to appear in the CID room at any moment.

"Sarge?" said Fry, when at last he put the phone down.

Rennie looked around, as if surprised that she was still there. Then he smiled, contorting his face until it was almost a wink. His tie was something dark green, with a small gold crest, and his suit was a good cut for his heavy shoulders but not recently cleaned. He pulled out a stick of his habitual chewing gum, which Fry had guessed might mean he was a reformed smoker.

"What can I do for you, Diane?"

"This project group looking at the auto crime figures."

"Yeah?"

"I wondered if a check had been done on the computer. Matching up locations and timings. An analysis of MOs. We could set up a computer model."

"Ben Cooper usually does that," said Rennie. "You'd better not mess with the computer until you've asked him about it."

"A computer model could come up with a set of predictions, suggest target locations. It's worth a try, Sarge."

"I told you, speak to Ben. They've got him out at Moorhay, but he should be back in the office later, thank God."

Fry had already heard Ben Cooper's name several times during her first week in Edendale. Apparently he was some paragon of all the virtues who knew everything. DC Cooper knew the area like the back of his hand, they said. He knew all the local villains and even their families, they said. He knew how all the systems in the CID office worked, too. He knew exactly how to fill in the vast quantities of paperwork that baffled other detectives. Now, apparently, he was the only one who knew how to use the computers. But Diane Fry had an information technology qualification to her name, and she had done a course on intelligence data analysis at the National Crime Faculty in Bramshill. At the first opportunity, she would show them who knew how to use the computers around here.

For now, though, she decided to try another tack.

"Someone from the NCIS did a paper on this problem a few months ago. It was mentioned when I was at Bramshill."

"Really?"

Rennie sounded uninterested.

"The National Crime Intelligence Service."

"I know what the NCIS is, thanks."

"I wondered if someone had researched it. I can't see any mention in the paperwork. Maybe the project group have followed it through?"

"I doubt it."

"I'll look it up, if you like, Sarge."

Rennie looked sour, pulled at his tie, scrabbled about on his desk for a bit of paper, and picked up the phone to dial another number.

"Shall I, Sarge?"

"Oh, if you like."

Fry made a note for herself in her notebook and asterisked it. Then she put the car crime reports aside and picked up that morning's bulletin on the missing girl, Laura Vernon. She had already read it once and had memorized its admittedly sketchy details.

Her memory was excellent for jobs like this. She knew exactly what the girl had been wearing when last seen, down to the blue pants and the size five slim-fit Reeboks. If she was the first officer to come across any of these items, she knew she would recognize them straightaway. But she would have to be allocated to the search first, of course.

All available hands had already been called to the task of finding Laura Vernon. All hands, that was, except Detective Constable Diane Fry and Detective Sergeant David Rennie. Fry was new to the division, of course, but what had Rennie done wrong? He was currently in charge of day-to-day crime in E Division, and Fry constituted his staff. It wasn't a combination that looked likely to crush any crime waves. At this moment, they weren't even trying.

Fry got up from her desk and walked over to check the action file on the Laura Vernon inquiry. Although the inquiry was less than forty-eight hours old, the file was already getting thick. The apparatus of a major inquiry was beginning to swing into operation, even though it hadn't yet been designated a murder inquiry—not until a body was found. Teenage girls ran away from home all the time, of course, and generally turned up a few days later, hungry and shamefaced. Laura had a little money—her parents estimated there could have been ten pounds in her purse. But she had taken no clothes and no possessions with her. That was a significant factor.

And reactions had been quicker in this instance for two other reasons. One was the fact that a witness report had placed Laura Vernon talking to an unidentified young man behind her house shortly before her disappearance. It had been the last sighting of her for nearly two days now.

The other pressing reason, understated in the action file but discernible as a thread running through the reports, was the so-far unsolved murder of sixteen-year-old Susan Edson in neighboring B Division a few weeks earlier.

Everyone knew that the first two or three days of an inquiry were vital, if it did turn out to be a case of murder or other serious crime. Within the first seventy-two hours the memories of witnesses were fresh and the perpetrator had little time to dispose of evidence or construct an alibi. At the same time, speedy action also meant they had a better chance of finding Laura Vernon alive.

Fry was interested to see that a name had been offered up to police as a "possible" right from the start. A youth called Lee Sherratt had been named by the parents and had been interviewed by officers in the initial sweep. He had denied being the young man seen talking to Laura, but his alibi was unsupported. Sherratt's record had been pulled from the Police National Computer—a few petty crimes, some as a juvenile. It wasn't much, but it was enough to leave his name at the top of the file until he could be eliminated.

According to the reports, a uniformed inspector from Operational Support was now in charge of the search on the ground. DI Paul Hitchens was CID investigating officer, reporting to Detective Chief Inspector Stewart Tailby. Officers had already called at every house in the village of Moorhay, since there weren't all that many. Inquiries had been made with all known friends and relatives in the area. No sign of Laura Vernon, no leads to her possible whereabouts.

By now the painstaking inch-by-inch search of the surrounding countryside was well under way—off-duty officers had been called in, the search dog teams were out, and the helicopter was in the air. Peak Park Rangers and Countryside Rangers were helping the search, and the Mountain Rescue Team was somewhere up on the tops of the moors above the village. And, of course, Detective Constable "Mr. Perfect" was also out at Moorhay in person. Case solved, then.

Fry had met DI Hitchens on her first day. He was her CID boss—after DS Rennie, anyway, and she had already decided Rennie didn't really count. Hitchens was younger than the sergeant and better educated. So an early promotion; maybe he was a fast-track graduate, like herself. He would certainly be destined for higher things, and his voice would be listened to by more senior officers. Fry ached to be out there, on a major inquiry, at the right hand of DI Hitchens, getting the chance to impress. She wasn't intending to hang around looking at car crime statistics for long. A murder inquiry was just the thing. But it had come too soon, while she was still too new. Hence her presence in the office with Rennie.

In an hour or two they would have to call off the search for Laura Vernon anyway. Even in August dusk fell eventually over the hills, and the lines of men and women would disperse and wander dispiritedly home. Tomorrow there would be appeals in the papers and on TV, and civilian volunteers would be queueing up to swell the numbers of the search parties.

Fry knew she had two choices. She either coasted along and filled in time until Rennie thought fit to allocate her some tasks or she could speak up, take the initiative, start to show what she was made of. But she held her tongue. Now was not the time—she needed to be in a stronger position. Meanwhile, DS Rennie was not worth the effort of trying to impress.

Then the door opened and DI Hitchens put his head around. "Who's here? Oh yes."

He looked disappointed, like a captain left with the choice of the players no one wants when the teams are being chosen. Hitchens was in his shirtsleeves with his cuffs rolled up a few inches over strong wrists covered in dark, wiry hair. He was in his thirties, and seemed to be permanently about to break into a smile. Fry caught his eye, looked from him to Rennie, who had barely moved except to shift his foot from his desk.

Hitchens nodded. "All right to hold the fort for a while, Dave?"

"Sir."

Fry jumped up eagerly. "Where are we going, sir? Is it the missing girl, Laura Vernon?"

"What else? Yes, we've had a find called in. We've got a good man out in the field now checking it out, but it sounds positive. Can you be ready in two minutes?"

"I'll be ready."

When the DI had left, Diane Fry went back to her desk to clear away the car crime reports. She was careful to turn her back to Dave Rennie, so that he wouldn't see her smiling.

Edendale sat astride a wide valley in the gap between the two distinct halves of the Peak District. On one side the gentle limestone hills and wooded dales of the White Peak rolled away past Bakewell and Wyedale into B Division and the borders of Staffordshire. On the other side were the grim, bare gritstone moors of the sparsely populated Dark Peak, where the high slopes of Mam Tor and Kinder Scout guarded the remote, silent reservoirs below Snake Pass.

It was one of only two towns that sat within the boundaries of the Peak District National Park—the other being Bakewell, a few miles to the south, where one of the E Division section stations was based. Other towns, like Buxton, headquarters of B Division, had been deliberately excluded from the National Park when the boundaries were drawn.

At Buxton, as at Matlock and Ashbourne, the boundary took wide sweeps around the towns and back again. But Edendale was too deep within the hills to be excluded. It meant that the restrictive Peak Park planning regulations applied to the town as much as they did to the face of Mam Tor or to the Blue John caves of Castleton.

Diane Fry was still learning the geography of the town and the dale. So far she was familiar only with the immediate area around the Victorian house on the outskirts of Edendale, where she had rented a first floor flat, and the streets near the station—including the view of the Edendale FC stand. But she was aware that, no matter which route you chose out of Edendale, the only way was up—over the hills, to the moorland hamlets or the villages in the next valley.

Fry was a good driver, trained in the West Midlands force driving school to handle pursuit cars. But DI Hitchens chose to drive himself as they headed out of the town toward the great hump of moorland separating Edendale from the next valley.

"It's just the one shoe," said Hitchens.

"A trainer?" said Fry. "Reebok, size five?"

The DI looked at her, surprised, raising his eyebrow.

"You've been reading up on the Vernon inquiry."

"Yes, sir."

"It was always a possibility from the start that something had happened to her, though you can't tell the parents that. She had cash with her, but had taken nothing else. We'd already traced all her friends and contacts. Negative all around. It's inevitable, I'm afraid, that her body will turn up somewhere."

"What sort of girl is she?"

"Oh, comes from a well-off family, comfortable background. Never wanted for anything, I'd say. She attends a private school called High Carrs, due to take her GCSEs next year. She gets piano lessons, has a horse that her parents bought that's kept at some stables just outside Moorhay. She takes part in riding events sometimes."

"Show jumping?"

"I suppose so."

"And is she good at any of those things?"

Hitchens looked at her and nodded approvingly. "If you believe the parents, she's perfect at everything. Bound to get a place at Oxford or Cambridge and do her degree, but might decide to pursue a career as a concert musician later on. Unless she wins an Olympic gold medal in the meantime, of course. Her friends say different."

"Boys?"

"Of course. What else? Mum and Dad deny it, though. They say she's too busy with her studies and her horse riding, all that. But we're tracing the boyfriends, gradually."

"Rows at home? Anything like that?"

"Nothing. At least . . ."

"Not according to the parents, right."

"Got it."

Hitchens was smiling again. Fry liked her senior officers to smile at her, within reason. She watched his hands on the steering wheel. They were strong hands, with clean and carefully trimmed fingernails. His nose was a little too large in profile. It was what they called a Roman nose. But a man could get away with that—it gave him character. She looked again at his left hand. There was no wedding ring on his finger. But now she noticed a white scar that crawled all the way across the middle knuckles of three of his fingers.

"The parents say that Laura had been shopping with her mother that afternoon," said Hitchens. "They'd been to the De Bradelei Center at Belper."

"What's there?"

"Oh—clothes," he said vaguely.

"Not Dad?"

"I don't suppose it was his sort of thing. Anyway, the females were buying him a birthday present, so he wouldn't have been wanted, would he? He stayed at home to catch up on some work. Graham Vernon runs a financial consultancy business and says it's going well. They do seem to be pretty well-off."

"And after they got home?"

"It was about half past five by then. It was still hot, so Laura changed and went out into the garden for a while. She didn't come back for her evening meal at half past seven. That's when the Vernons began to panic."

Fry admired the way he had all the details in his mind and could produce them without effort. Hitchens obviously had the sort of brain that was much valued in the police service these days. Many coppers could not have repeated the information without reading it from their notes.

"Parents alibi each other?"

"Yes."

"But she was seen talking to a young man before she disappeared, wasn't she?"

"Very good, Diane. Yes, we found a lady who was out collecting wildflowers on the edge of the scrubland at the top of the Baulk. She's a WI member and is helping to create the decoration for a well dressing at Great Hucklow. She was embarrassed about admitting it, can you believe it? She thought we might arrest her for stealing wildflowers. Her children had told her it's a crime against the environment. But the well dressing was obviously important enough to turn her to evil ways. Anyway, she came forward and identified Laura Vernon from her photograph as the girl she saw. She couldn't describe the boy, though. Too far away."

"And now a trainer."

"Yes, that's all we've got so far, but it looks hopeful. We've got Ben Cooper on the spot there—he was with one of the search parties. Ben's got good judgment."

"I'm sure he has."

"Oh, you've met Cooper, have you? He's only back from leave today."

"No, but I've heard the others talk about him."

"Right." Hitchens said nothing for a few minutes, negotiating a crossroads where heavy lorries thundered by at regular intervals, dusting the roadside verges with a coating of lime. Fry tried to read his thoughts, wondering if she had said something wrong. But she was sure of her ability to keep any emotion out of her voice. She had practiced long and hard, and now, she felt, she only ever sounded positive.

"How's it going then, Diane? Settling into the CID room OK?"

"Fine, sir. Some things are done a bit differently from what I've been used to, but nothing I haven't been able to pick up on pretty quickly."

"That's good. Dave Rennie treating you all right?"

"No problem," said Fry. She noted that she had become "Diane" since getting into the car alone with the DI. She liked to keep a track of these things, in case they had any deeper meaning. Maybe she could manage without the "sir" in return, and see if it struck the right note—a closeness of colleagues rather than a senior officer with a junior. But no further.

"Not finding Derbyshire too quiet for you after the West Midlands?"

"It's a nice change," said Fry. "But I'm sure E Division has its own challenges."

Hitchens laughed. "The other divisions call it 'E for Easy Street.'"

Fry had already been informed by her new colleagues that Edendale had been chosen over Bakewell or Matlock as E Division Headquarters for purely alphabetical reasons. It was one of the oddities of the Derbyshire Constabulary structure that the territorial divisions were all based in towns that began with the right letter—A Division in Alfreton, B Division in Buxton, C Division in Chesterfield, and D Division in Derby.

So it was inconceivable that E Division should have been based in Bakewell or Matlock. It would have been an outrage against corporate neatness. In fact, if there hadn't already been a town called Edendale, some PR person in an office at County HQ would have had to invent one.

"But I was thinking of the social life," said Hitchens. "Edendale isn't exactly the night spot capital of Europe. A bit tame after Birmingham, I expect."

"It depends what you're looking for, I suppose."

He turned to look toward her, his hands resting casually on the wheel. "And what is Diane Fry looking for exactly?"

What indeed? There was only one thing that Fry wanted to acknowledge to herself. Maybe it wasn't what Hitchens was expecting to hear. But it was something he ought to know, now rather than later.

"I want to advance my career," she said.

"Ah." He raised his eyebrows, a smile lighting up his face. He was quite good-looking, and he wore no wedding ring.

"I'm good at my job," she said. "I'll be looking for promotion. That's what's important to me. At the moment."

"Fair enough. I like your honesty."

The main road toward Buxton climbed and climbed until it reached a plateau where the limestone quarries competed with the moors as background scenery. There was a well-placed pub here called the Light House, with tremendous views over two neighboring valleys and the hills beyond. Hitchens turned off the road before they reached the quarries, and they began a gentle roller-coaster ride over smaller valleys and hills, dipping gradually toward Wyedale. Farm gates flickered past occasionally, with black-and-white signs advertising the names of dairy herds and stacks of huge round bales of straw or black plastic–wrapped silage lying in the fields behind stone walls.

"I've seen your record, of course," said Hitchens. "It's not bad."

Fry nodded. She knew it wasn't bad. It was damn good. Her exam results had been in the top few percent all along the line. Her clear-up rate since her transfer to CID had been outstanding. She had had a good career lined up in the West Midlands, and they had been grooming her for big things; anybody could see that.

"It was a pity you had to leave your old force," said Hitchens.

She said nothing, waiting for the comment that she knew would have to come.

"But it was understandable. In the circumstances."

"Yes, sir."

In the circumstances. That was exactly how Fry herself tried to think of it now. "The circumstances." It was a wonderfully cool and objective phrase. Circumstances were what other people had, not something that turned your life upside down, destroyed your self-esteem, and threatened to ruin everything you had ever held as worthwhile. You couldn't get upset about circumstances. You could just get on with life and concentrate on more important things. In the circumstances.

They were driving along a ridge now, with a steep drop on one side down rock-strewn slopes to a little river. Gradually the view became more and more obscured by trees. Here and there was a house set back from the road, not all of them working farms.

"No ill effects though?" said Hitchens.

Fry couldn't really blame him for fishing. She had expected it sooner or later. The subject had been raised at her interview, of course, and she had answered all the carefully worded questions with the proper responses, very reasonable and unemotional. But it was bound to be in the minds of those, like DI Hitchens, that she had to rely on for her prospects of advancement. It was just another hurdle she had to get over.

"None at all," she said. "It's all behind me now. I don't think about it. I just want to get on with the business in hand."

"One of the hazards of the job, eh? Goes with the territory?"

"I suppose you might say that, sir."

He nodded, satisfied. For a brief moment, Fry wondered how he would react if she did what a tight little angry knot deep inside her really wanted to do—screamed, shouted, lashed out with her fists to wipe the smug smile off his face. She was proud that she no longer did that; she had learned to keep the knot of anger tied up tight and secure.

The houses suddenly grew thicker on either side of the road, though there had been no sign to indicate they were reaching a village. There was a small school off to the right, some farm buildings converted into craft workshops, and a tiny village post office and store in an end terrace cottage. The square tower of a church appeared over the rooftops, surrounded by tall, mature chestnut trees and sycamores.

They found a cluster of cars and vans parked in a gravel lay-by. As soon as Hitchens pulled up, a sweating PC Wragg appeared at the window of the car. He was clutching a polythene bag containing a Reebok trainer.

"Wragg? Where's DC Cooper?"

"The old bloke's showing him where he found it, sir."

"What's he playing at? He should have waited," said Hitchens.

"The old bloke wouldn't wait. He said it was dominoes night, and it was now or never."

"*Dominoes* night?"

Wragg looked embarrassed. "He really seemed to mean it," he said.

The section of footpath looked much the same as any other. It had a dry bed of dusty soil, embedded with twisted tree roots that broke through the surface to form steps in the steeper places. There were oaks and birches clinging to the slopes on either side with swathes of dense bracken clustering around their trunks. A tumble of huge rocks lay half hidden among the bracken, like the overgrown ruins of a Stone Age temple. Birds skittered away among the undergrowth, chattering their alarm calls, and there was the constant background hiss of a fast-running stream.

"Aye, about here," said Harry.

"You're sure?"

"I reckon."

Ben Cooper didn't quite know what to make of Harry Dickinson. Usually he could read some emotion in people he came into contact with in this sort of job. They were often upset, frightened, angry, or even completely knocked for six by shock and distress. These were the ones for whom violent crime was something new and horrific that had never touched their lives before. Sometimes there were those who were nervous or became unreasonably aggressive. Those were interesting reactions, too, often the first signs of guilt. He had learned to pick up those signs in the people he dealt with. He thought of it as a good detective's instinct.

Harry Dickinson, though, had showed no emotion of any kind, not when he had been in the cottage with his wife and granddaughter, and not now when he stood with Cooper at the spot where he and his dog had found the bloodstained trainer.

During the walk down the path to the foot of Raven's Side, Harry had marched ahead, silent and stiff, his back straight, his arms swinging in a steady rhythm. He had not spoken a word since they had left the cottage, communicating only with a slight tilt of the head when they reached a turning in the path. It was as if the old man was shut up tight in a body that had turned to wood. Cooper would have liked to have got in front of him, to try to read something in the old man's eyes.

"You do realize that Laura Vernon might be lying nearby, badly injured, Mr. Dickinson?"

"Yes."

"Or even dead?"

Harry met Cooper's eyes. What was the expression that passed across them so fleetingly? Amusement? No, mockery. An impatience with such a waste of words.

"I'm not daft. I know what's what."

"It's vital that we know the exact spot you found the trainer, Mr. Dickinson."

Harry spat into the grass, narrowed his eyes against the low sun like an Indian picking up a trail. He pointed the peak of his cap to the right.

"Down there? Near the stream?"

"Jess runs down there, by the water," said Harry.

"What's past those rocks?"

"A wild bit, all overgrown. There's rabbits and such in there."

"Is that where the trainer came from?"

Harry shrugged. "Take a look for yourself, lad."

Cooper walked over to the outcrop of rocks. Only their tops protruded from the grass, and their jagged shapes looked slippery and treacherous. It was not a place he would choose to walk over, given the choice of easier walking that lay in other directions. He could see that sheep must graze here, by the shortness of the coarse grass. Between the rocks, narrow tracks had been worn, and there were ancient black pellets drying on the ground.

Trying to stick to the rocks to avoid confusing any traces of footprints, Cooper clambered over into the thick undergrowth. The stream rushed over the rocks a few feet to his right, running low just here below a stretch of smooth, grassy bank. It looked like an ideal spot for two people to spend an afternoon, secluded and undisturbed.

He looked back over his shoulder. Harry Dickinson had not followed him. He stood on a flat section of rock, poised as if guarding the path, apparently oblivious of what was going on around him. His fist clenched occasionally, as if he felt that he ought to have his dog lead in his hand. He looked completely calm.

Cooper moved farther into the undergrowth, his clothes brushing against the bracken and catching on the straggling tendrils of brambles. Two or three wasps, disturbed by his passage, hovered around his head, making irritating darts at his face and evading his futile slaps at the air. The trees began to close over him again, creating a dark cave filled with summer flies.

Ahead and about thirty feet below, just across the stream, he could make out a wide footpath marked with small stones and with wooden ledges built into the ground as steps. It was almost a motorway of a footpath, cleared of vegetation, well used and worn by many feet. Cooper realized that he had almost reached the Eden Valley Trail, the path that connected to the long-distance Pennine Way a little to the north. It was a favorite with ramblers, who passed this way in their thousands in the summer.

But the spot where he stood was as remote and isolated from life on the path down there as if it had been on top of Mam Tor itself. A passing walker would not have been able to see Cooper up there among the bracken, even if he had bothered to look up.

He turned around, wafting his hand across his face against the flies. He was looking back through the trees and thick brambles as if toward the end of a dark tunnel, where the figure of Harry Dickinson stood framed in a network of grasping branches. Cooper had to squint against the contrast of a patch of dazzling light that soaked the hillside in strong colors. The old man stood in the glare of the low sun, with the hot rocks shimmering around him like a furnace. The haze of heat rising from the ground made his dark outline blur and writhe, as if he were dancing a slow shimmy. His vast shadow, flung across the rocks, seemed to wriggle and jerk as its jagged shape fragmented among the bracken and brambles.

The expression in Harry's eyes was unreadable, his face lying partly in the shade from the peak of his cap. Cooper couldn't even tell which way he was looking, whether he had turned away or was staring directly toward him into the trees.

He wanted to grab the old man by the shoulders and shake him. He wanted to tell him that somebody *had* disturbed the spot, and recently. The evidence was right there for anyone to see and to smell. There had been two people, and at least one of them had been looking for more than just rabbits. The smell that lingered under the trees was of stale blood, overripe meat, and urine. And the flies had found something even more attractive than Cooper's sweat to feed on.

-5-

"OK. Secured?"

"Officers at all points," said Hitchens promptly.

"Scenes?"

"On their way."

Diane Fry stood behind DI Hitchens and Detective Chief Inspector Tailby, twenty feet from where the body of the girl lay. The scene had already been well organized. Hitchens had made a big performance of it, posting officers along the track, calling for information so that he could pass it on to the DCI. But it had seemed to Fry that everything necessary had already been done even before Hitchens had arrived.

"Scientific support?"

"Ditto."

"Incident room?"

"DI Baxter is i/c."

Tailby was head and shoulders taller than the inspector, slim and slightly stooped around the shoulders, as very tall men often were. His hair was graying at the front but still dark at the back, and it was left to grow thicker than the cropped heads favored by most of his junior colleagues. He was wearing green Wellingtons, which were not ideal footwear for stumbling over half a mile of rough ground scattered with rabbit holes and hidden stones. He was lucky to have reached the scene without a broken ankle. Fry congratulated herself on her habit of wearing strong, flat-soled shoes and trousers.

"Photographer?" said Tailby.

"Here, ready."

"Let him get on with it."

Fry waited for the DCI to ask about the doctor, but she looked up and realized that he could already see Dr. Inglefield making his way down the path.

"Finder?" said Tailby.

"Back at the cottage, sir. With DC Cooper."

"Let's see what the doc says then."

The doctor was giving his name to a PC standing halfway up the path. Tailby waited impatiently while they compared watches to agree the time, and the PC wrote it down in his notebook. Most of the other officers who had inevitably begun to gather around the scene had been sent away to continue their search, grumbling all the more at the futility of it.

Blue and white tape hung in strands for several yards around the body, wound around the trunks of trees and a jutting stump of black rock. From where the detectives stood, all that could be seen of Laura Vernon was a lower leg. The black fabric of her jeans contrasted with the glare of a white, naked foot, its toenails painted bloodred. The rest of the body was hidden in a dense clump of bracken, and around it there were numerous signs of trampling. Fry knew that the broken stems and crushed grass raised the odds in favor of the crime scene examiners producing the sort of evidence that would lead to a quick arrest. She longed to get nearer, to get a close look at the body, to see the girl's face. How had she died? Had she been strangled or battered or what? Nobody was saying. At this stage, nobody wanted to commit themselves. They simply stood and watched the doctor do his official business as he nodded at the policemen without a word and made his way gingerly along a marked-out strip of ground to the crushed bracken.

They were, of course, assuming the body was that of Laura Vernon. There seemed little doubt, but it was not considered a fact until one of her parents had been dragged through the process of identification.

"No hope of getting the caravan down here," said Tailby.

"Nowhere near, sir," agreed Hitchens.

"Is there a farm track nearby? What's over that side of the trees?"

"Don't know, sir."

Hitchens and Tailby both turned to look at Fry. Hitchens frowned when he saw who she was, as if he had been expecting someone else.

"See if you can find out, Fry," he said. "Closest access we can get for the caravan."

"Yes, sir."

Fry wondered how she was expected to do this, when there was no habitation in sight. The village itself was invisible beyond the huge outcrop of rock. There was a cliff face at her back and dense woodland stretching in front of her down to the road.

She was aware of the tall DCI studying her. He had a thin, bony face and keen gray eyes with a vigilant air. She had not encountered him face-to-face until now—he had simply been a figure passing in the distance once, pointed out to her and noted as one of the people who mattered. The last thing she wanted to do was to look useless now, on their first meeting. First impressions lasted a long time.

"Perhaps you could find somebody who has a bit of local knowledge," suggested Tailby.

Hitchens said, "Maybe we'd better ask—"

Then Diane Fry registered the noise that she had been aware of in the background all the time they had been on the hillside. It was a juddering and clattering noise, stationary now somewhere over the trees to the east. The helicopter was holding position until its crew were given instructions to return to base.

Fry pulled out her radio and smiled. "I think I've got a better idea, sir."

The DCI understood straightaway. "Excellent. Get them to let Scenes and Scientific Support have a location as well for their vans."

Dr. Inglefield had taken only a few minutes before he was walking back up the path toward Tailby.

"Well, dead all right," he said. "Skull bashed in, I'd say, not to put too fine a point on it. You'll get the technical details from the PM, of course, but that's about it. Rigor is almost completely resolved and decomposition has started. Also, we have quite a few maggots hatching in the usual places. Eyes, mouth, nostrils. You know . . . the pathologist should be able to give you a pretty good idea of the time of death. Normally I'd say at least twenty-four hours, but in this weather . . ." He shrugged expressively.

"Sexually assaulted?" asked Tailby.

"Mmm. Some disturbance of the clothing, certainly. More than that I couldn't say."

"I'll take a quick look while we wait for the pathologist," said Tailby to Hitchens.

He pulled on plastic gloves and approached to within a few feet of the body. He would not touch it or anything around it, would not risk disturbing any of the possible forensic evidence waiting for the SOCOs. Inglefield looked at Fry curiously as she pocketed her radio. She had been listening keenly to their conversation even while she made the call.

"New, are you?" asked Inglefield. "Sorry about the maggots."

"New to the area," said Fry. "I've seen maggots on a dead body before. People don't realize how quickly flies will get into the bodily orifices and lay their eggs, do they, Doctor?"

"In weather like this the little beggars will be there within minutes of death. The eggs can hatch in another eight hours or so. How long has the girl been missing?"

"Nearly two days," said Fry.

"There you are then. Plenty of time. But don't take my word . . ."

"It's a question for the pathologist, yes."

"Mrs. Van Doon will no doubt give your chaps the chapter and verse. A forensic entomologist will be able to tell you what larval stage they're going through and all that. That can fix the time of death pretty well."

There was the sound of engines beyond the trees; and the helicopter appeared again, flying low, guiding a small convoy along the forest track that had been found.

"I'd better go and direct them," said Fry.

"Somebody was luckier than me," said the doctor. "My car's back up the hill there somewhere. Ah well, no doubt the exercise will do me good. It's what I tell my patients anyway."

Fry shepherded the Home Office pathologist and the Scenes of Crime team down the hillside. The SOCOs, a man and a woman, were sweating in their white suits and overshoes as they lugged their cases with them to the taped-off area and pulled their hoods over their heads until they looked like aliens. Tailby was backing away, leaving the way clear for the photographer to set up his lights against the lengthening shadows that were now falling across the scene. The exact position of the body had to be recorded with stills camera and video before the pathologist could get close enough to examine her maggots. Fry turned away. She knew that the next stage would involve the pathologist taking the girl's rectal temperature.

She was in time to catch DI Hitchens taking a call on his cell phone.

"Hitchens here. Yes?"

He listened for a minute, his face slipping from a frown into anger and frustration.

"Get everyone on to it that you can. Yes, yes, I know. But this is a priority. We're going to look complete idiots. Pull people in from wherever you need to."

Hitchens looked around to see where Tailby was, and saw him walking back up the slope toward them.

"Bastard!" said Hitchens as he pushed the phone into his pocket.

"Something wrong?" asked Fry.

"A team went to pick up Lee Sherratt, and he's done a runner."

Fry winced. It was bad luck to lose your prime suspect just when you were hoping that everything would click together easily—that the initial witness statements would tie your man to the scene and the results of forensic tests would sew the case up tight. It was bad luck she didn't want to be drawn into, she thought, as they watched the DCI approach, peeling off his plastic gloves.

"We need to get that time of death ascertained as close as we can," said Tailby. "Then we need the inquiry teams allocated to doing the house to house again, Paul."

"Yes, sir."

"We need to locate a weapon. Organize the search teams to get started as soon as Scenes are happy."

"Yes, sir."

"What was the call? Have they picked up the youth yet? Sherratt?"

Hitchens hesitated for the first time.

"No, sir."

"And why not?"

"They can't find him. He hasn't been at home since yesterday afternoon."

"I do hope you're joking."

Hitchens shook his head. "No, sir."

Tailby scowled, his bushy eyebrows jutting down over cold gray eyes. "I don't believe this. We interview the lad on Sunday morning when it's a missing person inquiry, and as soon as a body turns up we've lost him."

"We had no reason—"

"Well, we've got reason enough now. Reason enough down there, don't you think?" said Tailby angrily, gesturing at the spot where Laura Vernon lay.

"We've got patrols trying all possible locations now. But so many men were taken up by the search down here—"

"They'd damn well better turn the lad up soon. I want to wrap this one up quickly, Paul. Otherwise, people will be connecting it to the Edson case and we'll have all the hysteria about a serial killer on the loose. We don't want that—do we, Paul?"

Hitchens turned and looked appealingly at Fry. She kept her face impassive. If people chose to have bad luck, she wasn't about to offer to share it with them.

"Right," said Tailby. "What's next? Let's see—what's his name? The finder?"

"Dickinson," said Hitchens. "Harry Dickinson."

Harry was in the kitchen. He had finally taken off his jacket, and the sleeves of his shirt were rolled up to show white, sinewy arms. At his wrists there was a clear line like a tidemark between the pale skin untouched by sun and his brown, weathered hands, sprinkled with liver spots and something dark and more ingrained. Harry was at the sink using a small blue plastic-handled mop to scrub out the teacups and polish the spoons. His face was as serious as if he were performing brain surgery.

"He always does the washing-up," said Gwen when the detectives came to the door. "He says I don't do it properly."

"We'd just like a few words, Mrs. Dickinson," said Tailby. "Further to our inquiries."

Harry seemed to become aware of them slowly. He put down the mop and dried his hands carefully on a towel, rolled his sleeves down over his arms, and reached behind the door to put his jacket back on. Then he walked unhurriedly past them, without a word, into the dim front room of the cottage, where there was a glimpse of the road through a gap in white net curtains.

Hitchens and Tailby followed him and found him sitting upright on a hard-backed chair. He was facing them like a judge examining the suspects entering the dock. The detectives found two more chairs pushed close to a mahogany dining table and set them opposite the old man. Diane Fry slipped quietly into the room and leaned against the wall near the door with her notebook, while Hitchens and Tailby introduced themselves, showing their warrant cards.

"Harry Dickinson?" said Hitchens. The old man nodded. "This is Detective Chief Inspector Tailby, Harry. I'm Detective Inspector Hitchens. From Edendale."

"Where's the lad?" asked Harry.

"Who?"

"The one who was here before. Sergeant Cooper's lad."

Tailby looked at Hitchens, raising an eyebrow.

"Ben Cooper is only a detective constable, Harry. This is a murder inquiry now. You understand that? Detective Chief Inspector Tailby here is the senior investigating officer who will be in charge of the inquiry."

"Oh aye," said Harry. "The man in charge."

"You are aware that we have found a body, Mr. Dickinson?" said Tailby. He spoke loudly and clearly, as if he had decided that they were dealing with an idiot.

Harry's eyes traveled slowly from Hitchens to Tailby. At first he had looked unimpressed, now he looked stubborn.

"The Mount girl, is it?"

"The Vernon family live at the Mount," explained Hitchens for Tailby's sake. "That's the name of the house."

"The remains haven't yet been formally identified, Mr. Dickinson," said Tailby. "Until they have, we can't commit ourselves to a positive statement in that regard. However, it is generally known that we have been conducting an extensive search for a fifteen-year-old female by that name for some hours. In the circumstances there would seem to be a strong degree of possibility that the remains discovered in the vicinity may be those of Laura Vernon."

An old carriage clock in an oak case ticked quietly to itself on the mantelpiece, providing the only sound in the room as it counted off the seconds. Fry thought that time seemed to be passing particularly slowly within the room, as if it were sealed off from the rest of the world in a zone of its own, where normal rules didn't apply.

"You talk like a proper pillock, don't you?" said Harry.

Tailby's jaw muscles tightened, but he restrained himself.

"We'd like to hear from you how you came to find the trainer, Mr. Dickinson."

"I've told it—"

"Yes, I know you've told it before. Just tell us again, please."

"I've got other things to do, you know."

"Yes, I know," said Tailby coolly. "It's dominoes night."

Harry took his pipe from the pocket of his jacket and poked at the contents of the ceramic bowl. His movements were slow and relaxed, and his expression was studiously placid. Hitchens began to stir, but Tailby quelled him with a movement of his hand.

"You'll no doubt understand one day," said Harry, "that at my age you can't go rushing up- and downhill twice in one afternoon and be in any fit state to go out of the house later on, without having a bit of a kip in between. I don't have the energy for it anymore. There's no fighting it." He ran a hand across his neatly groomed hair, smoothing down the gray, Brylcreemed strands. "No matter how many dead bodies you've found."

"The sooner we get it over with, the sooner we'll be able to leave you in peace."

"I can't do anything more than that, not even for some top brass copper and all his big words. All this coming and going and folk clattering about the house—it wears me out."

Tailby sighed. "We'd really like to hear your story in your own words, Mr. Dickinson. Just tell us the story, will you?"

Harry stared at him defiantly. "The story. Aye, well. Do you want it with hand gestures or without, this story?"

To Diane Fry there seemed to be something wrong with the scene, a sort of subtle reversal. It was as though the two detectives were waiting to be interviewed by the old man, not the other way around. Hitchens and Tailby were unsettled, shifting uncomfortably on their hard chairs, not sure what to say to break the moment. Harry, though, was totally at ease, calm and still, his feet planted in front of him on a worn patch of carpet. He had placed himself with his back to the window, so that he was outlined against the view of the street, a faint aura forming around his head and shoulders. Hitchens and Tailby were looking into the light, waiting for the old man to speak again.

"Without, then, is it?"

"Without, if you like, Mr. Dickinson."

"I was out with Jess."

"Jess?"

"My dog."

"Of course. You were walking your dog."

Harry lit a taper, puffed on his pipe. He seemed to be waiting, to see if Tailby were going to take up the story himself.

"I were walking my dog, like you say. We always go down that way. I told the lad. Sergeant Cooper's—"

"Sergeant Cooper's lad, yes."

"Interrupt a lot, don't you?" said Harry. "Is that a, what you call it, interview technique?"

Fry thought she detected the ghost of a smile on Tailby's face. Hitchens, though, so genial at the office, did not look like smiling.

"Do go on, Mr. Dickinson," said Tailby.

"We always go down to the foot of Raven's Side. Jess likes to run by the stream. After the rabbits. Not that she ever catches any. It's a game, do you follow?"

Harry puffed smoke into the room. It drifted in a small cloud toward the ceiling, gathering around the glass bowl that hung on tiny chains below a sixty-watt lightbulb. A wide patch of ceiling paper in the center of the room was stained yellow with smoke.

Fry watched the moving cloud and realized that the old man must sit every day in this same chair, in this room, to smoke his pipe. What was his wife doing meanwhile? Watching *Coronation Street* or *Casualty* on the color television in the next room? And what did Harry do while he was smoking? There were a few books on a shelf set into the alcove formed by the chimney breast. The titles she could make out were *The Miners in Crisis and War* and *Trade Unions in Britain, Choose Freedom,* and *The Ripper and the Royals.* There seemed to be only one novel—Robert Harris's *Fatherland.* It was lined up with the other books, all regimented into a neat row between two carved oak bookends. Three or four issues of *The Guardian* were pushed into a magazine rack by the hearth. But there was no television here, no radio, no stereo. Once the newspaper had been read, it would leave nothing for the old man to do. Nothing but to listen to the ticking of the clock and to think.

Fry became aware of Harry's eyes on her. She felt suddenly as though he could read her thoughts. But she could not read his in return. His expression was impassive. He had the air of an aristocrat, forced to suffer an indignity but enduring it with composure.

"A game, Harry . . ." prompted Hitchens. He had less patience than the DCI. And every time he called the old man "Harry" it seemed to stiffen his shoulders a little bit more. Tailby was politer, more tolerant. Fry liked to observe these things in her senior officers. If she made enough observations, perhaps she would be able to analyze them, put them through the computer, produce the ideal set of character traits for a budding DCI to aim for.

"Sometimes she fetches things," said Harry. "I sit on a rock, smoke my pipe, watch the stream and the birds. Sometimes there's otters after the fish. If you sit still, they don't notice you."

Tailby was nodding. Maybe he was a keen naturalist. Fry didn't have much knowledge of wildlife. There hadn't been a lot of it in Birmingham apart from the pigeons and the stray dogs.

"And while I sit, Jess brings me things. Sticks, like. Or a stone, in her mouth. Sometimes she finds something dead."

Harry paused. It was the first time Fry had seen him hesitate unintentionally. He was thinking back over his last words, as if surprised by what he had said. Then he shrugged.

"I mean a stoat or a blackbird. A squirrel once. If they're fresh dead and not been marked too bad, there's a bloke over at Hathersage will have 'em for his freezer."

"What?"

"He stuffs 'em," said Harry. "All legal. He's got a license and everything."

"A taxidermist," said Hitchens.

Fry could see Tailby frown. Harry puffed on his pipe with extra vigor, as if he had just won a minor victory.

"But today, Mr. Dickinson?" said Tailby.

"Ah, today. Today, Jess brought me something else. She went off, rooting about in the bracken and that. I wasn't paying much attention, just sitting. Then she came up to me with something in her mouth. I couldn't make out what it was at first. But it was that shoe."

"Did you see where the dog got it from?"

"No, I told you. She was out of sight. I took the shoe off her. I remembered this lass you lot were looking for, the Mount girl. It looked the sort of object she would wear, that lass. So I brought it back. And my granddaughter phoned."

"You knew Laura Vernon?"

"I reckon I know everybody in the village," said Harry. "It isn't exactly Buxton here, you know. I've seen her all right."

"When did you last see her, Mr. Dickinson?" asked Tailby.

"Ah. Couldn't say that."

"It might be very important."

"Mmm?"

"If she was in the habit of going onto the Baulk, where you walk your dog regularly, Mr. Dickinson, you may have seen her earlier."

"You may also have seen her killer," said Hitchens.

"Doubt it," said Harry. "I don't see anyone."

"Surely—"

"I don't see anyone."

Harry glared at Hitchens, suddenly aggressive. The DI saw it and bridled immediately.

"This is a murder inquiry, Harry. Don't forget that. We expect full cooperation."

The old man pursed his lips. The skin around his mouth puckered and wrinkled, but his eyes remained hard and cool. "I reckon I've done my bit. I'm getting a bit fed up of you lot now."

"Tough. We're not messing about here, Harry. We're not playing games, like you throwing sticks for your dog to fetch. This is a serious business, and we need all the answers you can give us."

"Have you seen anybody else on the Baulk, Mr. Dickinson?" said Tailby gently.

"If I had," said Harry, "I'd remember, wouldn't I?"

Hitchens snorted and stirred angrily in his chair. "Crap."

"Hold on, Paul," said Tailby automatically.

"Right. I'll not have that in my house," said Harry. "It's high time you were off somewhere else, the lot of you, doing some good." He pointed the stem of his pipe toward Fry and her notebook. "And make sure you take the secretary lass with you. She's making a mucky mark on my wall."

"Detective Constable Fry will have to stay to take your statement."

"She'll have to wake me up first."

Tailby and Hitchens stood up, straightening their backs from the hard chairs. The DCI looked too tall for the room. The house had been built at a time when very few people stood more than six foot. He must have had to stoop to get through the door, though Fry hadn't noticed it.

"We may want to speak to you again, Mr. Dickinson," said Tailby.

"You'd be better off sending that lad next time."

"I'm afraid you'll have to put up with DI Hitchens and myself. Sorry and all that, but we expect you to cooperate fully with our inquiries, however long they may take. Are you sure there isn't anything else you'd like to say to me just now, Mr. Dickinson?"

"Oh yes," said Harry.

"What's that?"

"Bugger off."

-6-

No sooner had the police left than the little cottage was again full of people. Helen watched from the kitchen as her mother and father fussed into the back room, flapping around her grandparents as if they were naughty children who needed scolding and reassuring at the same time.

"My goodness, you two, what's been going on? All these police up here? What *have* you been doing, Harry?"

Andrew Milner was in a short-sleeved cotton shirt with a frivolous blue and green pattern, but he still had on the trousers of the dark-gray suit he wore for the office. He smelled faintly of soap and a suggestion of whiskey fumes. Helen didn't need to be told that her father had showered after arriving home from work and had already drunk his first Glenmorangie of the evening by the time she had phoned. He wore clip-on sun shades over his glasses, which he had to flip up as soon as he stepped over the threshold of the cottage. Now they stood out horizontally from his forehead like extravagant eyebrows.

Harry looked up at Andrew from his chair, no gesture of welcome breaking the rigidity of his expression.

"I dare say young Helen's told you what you need to know."

Margaret Milner was fanning herself with a straw hat. She was a large woman and felt the heat badly. Her floral dress swirled and rustled around her knees and wafted powerful gusts of body spray throughout the room.

"A dead body. How awful. You poor things."

"It was a shoe your dad found," said Gwen, who had not yet tired of the excitement. "One of those trainer things. They said there was a dead girl with it, but your dad didn't see her. Did you, Harry?"

"It was Jess," said Harry. "Jess that found it."

"But there was . . . Was there blood?"

"So they reckon."

"The young policeman took it away," said Gwen. "The first one, the young one."

"The Cooper lad," said Harry.

"Who?"

"Sergeant Cooper's son. The old copper. You remember all the fuss, surely?"

"Oh, I know." Margaret turned to her daughter. "Didn't you used to know him very well at school, Helen? Is that the one? I remember now. You liked him, didn't you?"

Helen fidgeted, ready to escape back to the kitchen to make more tea. She loved her parents and her grandparents, but she was uncomfortable when they were all together. She could communicate with them one at a time, but when they were gathered in a family group there was a kind of blanket of incomprehension that descended between them.

"Yes, Mum, Ben Cooper."

"You always seemed to get on well. But he never asked you out, did he? I always thought it was a shame."

"Mum—"

"I know, I know—it's nothing to do with me."

"Forget it, Mum. This isn't the time."

"We've had a body," said Gwen plaintively, appealing to the room, as if someone, somewhere could give her consolation, even tell her it hadn't happened.

"And it *was* the Vernons' girl?" said Andrew impatiently. Helen noticed her father's faint Scottish accent creeping through in the *r*'s, as it did when he was under stress. "Did they say it was definitely Laura Vernon?"

"She had to be *identified,* they said." Gwen looked challengingly toward Harry, letting it be known that she had been listening at the door when the police had been interviewing him. Harry took no notice. He was feeling at his pocket, as if all he wanted to do was pull out his pipe and retire to the front room, to escape to his sanctuary.

"They reckon it was her all right," said Harry.

"Poor little thing," said Margaret. "She was only a kiddie. Who would do a thing like that, Helen?"

"She was fifteen. Would you like some tea?"

"Fifteen. Just a child. They gave her everything, her mother and father did. A private school, her own horse. All that money, just think of it. And look what it comes to."

"I wonder what Graham Vernon will think," said Andrew.

"What do you mean, Dad?"

"Well, it's awkward. You know—just imagine what state he's in over the girl. And then it has to be my own father-in-law who finds her."

"What does that matter to him, for heaven's sake? Their daughter's dead—it won't make any difference to them who found her."

"Well, it's just awkward, that's all."

"Andrew thinks his role is to be Graham Vernon's loyal lackey," said Margaret. "Being involved in the murder of his daughter rather ruins the image, doesn't it?"

"*Involved?* Well, hardly," protested Andrew.

"However distantly, of course," said Margaret, with a smile of satisfaction. "I suppose it's bound to make you feel tainted by association."

"Stop it, Margaret."

"Perhaps it would have been better if Dad had just walked on and ignored it, and said nothing. Better for you, anyway. I'm surprised he didn't think of your reputation at the time. It was very remiss of you, Dad."

Harry took his empty pipe out and sucked on its stem, looking from one to the other. Helen thought he was the only one of them who was enjoying the conversation.

"Anyway, *they* haven't much of a reputation up there to be worried about, have they?" said Margaret.

"That's not fair. The Vernons are very well respected."

Margaret snorted contemptuously. "Respected. Not in this house. What do you say, Dad?"

"Rich buggers. Ignorant rubbish."

Helen smiled. "That needed saying, too. They've done enough to this family. Why should we let something like this affect us? I'm sorry for their trouble, but it's their trouble, not ours. It's nothing to do with Granddad. Blow the Vernons. We have to see that Grandma and Granddad are all right."

"Of course we do. Andrew?"

"Well, all right."

"We're lucky we're a proper family and can stand together," said Margaret. "Not like them up there. That's been their problem, of course. That's been the cause of all the trouble in the past. They don't know what a family should be. And that's the cause of this bit of trouble, too, you'll see."

"We should talk about it," said Helen. "We should have talked about it before."

"*He* won't," said Gwen. "He won't talk about it to anybody."

"There's no need for it," said Harry. "Let it rest."

Helen stood by his chair and put her hand on his arm. "Granddad?"

He patted her hand and smiled up at her. "Believe me, lass, there's no need."

She sighed. "No, we've never talked about anything important, have we? Not ever, in this family. Except when we were angry or upset. And that's not the time to talk. It's not the time to do anything."

"Well, I don't know what you mean by that, I'm sure," said Margaret. "I'm as capable as anyone of talking things over without getting upset about it."

Margaret's voice was becoming high-pitched. She tossed her head and fiddled with an earring, glaring at her husband as if challenging him not to support her. But Andrew turned away with sagging shoulders and found himself staring into the mournful eyes of Jess, who had crept into the corner of the room to listen. The dog's ears twitched from side to side as she assessed the sound of their voices, trying to judge the mood and looking dejected at what she heard.

"There was no need for you to come here, you know," said Harry. "No need at all. We were managing perfectly well, us and Helen."

"We could hardly stay away at a time like this," said Margaret. "We're your family, after all."

Harry stood and walked slowly to the stairs. "I'll be going out for a while," he said.

And before anybody could ask him where to, he had disappeared. They could hear water running and the sound of a wardrobe door creaking above them through the ancient floorboards.

"Where is he going?" asked Andrew.

"Not to the pub, surely?" said Margaret. "Not at a time like this."

"Oh, yes," said Gwen. "He'll be going to meet *them*."

Half an hour later, Harry had escaped from the cottage and was settled into an entirely different atmosphere, where he didn't need to be prompted to tell his story. When he had finished, it required a moment of quiet contemplation, a few swallows of beer, a companionable silence to emphasize the seriousness of the occasion.

"Well, Harry. Police and all."

"Oh aye, them, all right, Sam. A bucketload of 'em."

"Making a nuisance of themselves, I suppose?"

"They try, some of them. But they don't bother me."

The corner of the Drover between the fire and the window smelled strongly of old men and muddy dogs. The seats of the wooden settles the men sat on were worn smooth to the shape of their buttocks, and their boots seemed to ease themselves into familiar depressions in the dark carpet tiles.

Sam Beeley had rested his stick against the table. Its ivory handle, shaped like the head of an Alsatian dog, stared at the beaten brass surface with contempt. Occasionally, Sam stroked the ivory with a bony hand, fondling the Alsatian's worn ears in his yellow fingers or tapping it with a twisted thumbnail on the corner of the brass. His knees cracked when he moved, and he shuffled his toes uncomfortably in soft suede shoes as if he were unable to find a position that did not give him pain. He was the thinnest of the three men, but his thinness was almost masked by the multiple layers of clothes that he wore, despite the warmth of the evening. The emaciation showed most in his hands and in his face, where the flesh had sunk into his cheeks and his eye sockets were dark pools where weak blue eyes flickered.

"Bloody coppers," he said, his voice rough with cigarette smoke. "What do you reckon, Wilford?"

"We can do without 'em, Sam."

"True enough."

"Oh aye."

Wilford Cutts had removed his cap to reveal a tangle of white hair around a pale scalp that contrasted sharply with the ruddy color of his face. He had an untidy white mustache and a suggestion of sideburns that might once have been bushy around his ears. His neck was thick and sinewy and ran into heavy shoulders that could no longer be called well muscled, but sagged forward into his sweater, soft and fleshy. His palms were stained with grime, and his fingernails were dark against the side of his beer glass. Dark fibers clung to his corduroy trousers, which were worn at the knees and stiff at the calves, where they were tucked into gray woollen socks. He kept his feet pushed out of sight under the bench, in case the landlord should notice the caked soil drying on the soles of his boots.

"So it's what they call a murder inquiry then, is it, Harry? They've worked out what happened to the lass?"

"They didn't say, Wilford."

"No?"

"No."

"Bloody coppers."

Harry was keeping his cap firmly in place. He was the center of attention, the man of the moment, but it didn't do to get too excited. He had put on a clean shirt to walk to the pub, and a tie with a discreet paisley pattern fastened neatly around his throat. His feet were thrust out in front of him into the room, where the wall lights were reflected in his polished toe caps.

Now and then one of the pub's customers called to him across the room, and he acknowledged their greetings with a brief nod, not uncivil but deliberately reserved. He stared, tight-lipped, at a group of youths and girls he didn't recognize, who were laughing noisily at the far end of the bar, trying to talk above one another and now and then breaking into bursts of song.

By unspoken consent, Sam sat closest to the fire, although it was summer and the grate was empty. Wilford sat furthest away, with his back to the door, hidden in the shadow of the alcove. There were two pints of Marston's Bitter and a half of stout on the table, next to a heap of well-worn dominoes which had been emptied from their box and left untouched. With the round of drinks had come a packet of smoky bacon crisps, which Wilford slid into his pocket.

"And how are the family bearing up?" said Sam. "Bit of a shock for the womenfolk, no doubt."

Harry shrugged. "That son-in-law of mine is the worst by a long chalk," he said. "He can't stand it at all. Worried about his precious job with Vernon."

"He'd crack like a nut, that one. Sorry to say it, Harry. But if he had anything to hide, if he ever found himself under suspicion. He'd cough, all right."

The slang expression brought a small smile to Harry's face. Like Sam, he had heard it used last night in the latest television police series, set in some drug-ridden area of inner London, where the detectives were more like criminals than the criminals themselves.

"Has he?" asked Wilford suddenly.

"Has who what?"

"Has Andrew Milner got anything to hide?"

"You must be joking," said Harry. "Our Margaret knows every hole in his socks. The poor bugger couldn't hide a pimple on his arse."

"The police are useless, anyway," said Sam. "They never know who to talk to, what questions to ask. If they solve anything, it's by luck around here."

Wilford laughed. "Not like on the telly, Sam."

"Well, on the telly they always sort it out. That stands to reason. They're just stories. There wouldn't be much point putting them on the telly otherwise, would there?"

"I suppose it's a sort of warning to people, like," said Wilford. "It's telling them not to commit murders and crimes, because they'll get caught, like they always do on the telly."

"But they don't really get caught," said Sam. "Not in real life they don't. Half of 'em never get found out. And those that do get caught are let off by the judges. They get probation or one of them other things."

"Community service," said Harry. He pronounced the words carefully, as if he had never actually heard them spoken but had only seen them as an unfamiliar combination of syllables printed in the court reports of the *Buxton Advertiser*.

Sam curled his lip. "Aye. Community service. When was that ever a punishment for a crime? Making 'em do a bit of honest work. It's just like letting them off. It's true, you can get away with owt these days. Murder even."

"But the people who watch the telly don't know that," said Wilford. "Mostly they have no idea. They think it *is* real life on the box. The kids today. And the women, of course. They don't know the difference. They think when there's a crime Inspector Morse comes out and works it all out in the pub with a pencil and a bit of paper and the murderer gets banged up."

"Banged up, aye. For life."

They lapsed into silence again, staring at one another's drinks, trying to imagine the reality of spending the rest of their lives in prison. A life sentence might mean ten, twenty, or thirty years—it was all the same for a man in his late seventies or eighties. He would never be likely to see the outside again.

"You'd miss the open air something terrible in prison," said Sam.

The other two nodded, their heads turning automatically to the window, where, even in the dusk, the outline of the Witches could be made out against the southern sky, jagged and black on the horizon of Win Low. A ripple of unease ran around the table. Sam shivered and clutched at his stick, rubbing the ivory as if seeking comfort from its smooth shape. Wilford ran his hands nervously through his untidy hair and reached for his glass. Even Harry seemed to become more tight-lipped, a shade more cautious.

"No. You couldn't be doing with that," he said. "Not at all."

The three old men looked sideways at one another, unspoken messages passing between them in the tentative movements of their hands and the tilting of their heads. It was a level of communication they had learned in their working lives, when they had been isolated from the rest of the world in their own enclosed space, where conversation was unnecessary and at times impossible. At such moments, they could still cut themselves off from the world around them, pushing the noise and bustle of the pub into the distance as effectively as if they had been sitting in one of those dark tunnels a mile underground, far from the surface light.

Sam fumbled a packet of ten Embassy and a box of matches from somewhere among his clothing and lit a cigarette, squinting his pale eyes against the cloud of smoke that hung in the still air, obscuring his face. Wilford ran his dirt-stained fingers through his hair, momentarily revealing an unnaturally white patch of naked scalp at the side of his head, where the skin was stretched thin and tight like paper. Harry fiddled with his unlit pipe, poking a few dominoes about the table with the stem, separating the tiles that were facedown. He stared at them fixedly, as though hoping to read their numbers through their patterned backs.

"There are some that would have a troubled conscience, though," suggested Wilford. "They say that can be as bad as anything anybody else can do to you."

"It can drive folks mad," agreed Sam.

"Like being in your own hell, I reckon. That would be punishment, all right."

"Worse than community service, any road."

"Worse than prison?" asked Harry.

They looked unsure about that. They were picturing a narrow, confined cell and bars, the knowledge of hundreds of other men crowded together like ants, allowed out into a yard for an hour each day. Shut away from the light and the air forever.

"You'd have to have a conscience to start with, of course," said Wilford.

"There aren't many that have one these days," agreed Sam.

They both looked at Harry, waiting for his response. But Harry didn't seem to want to think about it. He got up stiffly, collected their glasses, and walked across the room to the bar. He looked to neither right nor left as he moved through the crowd of youngsters, his back upright, like a man entirely apart from those around him. Drinkers parted automatically to let him through, and the landlord served him without having to be told the order.

Harry's jacket and tie looked incongruously formal and sober among the T-shirts and shorts of the other customers. He could have been an elderly undertaker who had wandered into a wedding reception. When he turned his head, the peak of his cap swung like a knife across a background of pink limbs and sunburnt faces.

"So the bloke who killed this lass," said Harry when he returned to the corner table. "Do you reckon he'll get away with it?"

"Depends," said Wilford. "Depends whether the coppers have a bit of luck. Perhaps somebody saw something and decides to tell them about it. Or some bobby asks the right question by accident. That's the only way it happens."

"They have their suspicions, no doubt."

"It doesn't matter what they suspect. They can't do anything without evidence," said Wilford confidently.

"Evidence. Aye, that's what they'll want."

"They'll be desperate for it. Desperate for a bit of evidence."

"They reckon that Sherratt lad has gone missing," said Sam.

"Daft bugger."

"It'll keep the coppers busy, I suppose, looking for him. He'll be the number one suspect."

"Unless they fancy blaming it on one of the family," said Wilford. "That's where they always look first."

"Aye," said Sam, brightening suddenly. "Or the boyfriend."

"Ah! Which boyfriend?" asked Harry.

"That's the question. With that one, that's the first question you'd have to ask."

"And only fifteen," said Sam.

They shook their heads in despair.

"Well, that's the best bit, eh, Harry?"

"Oh aye," said Harry. "That's the best bit. When they do all their inquiring, they'll turn up all sorts. They're bound to find out about those buggers at the Mount. The Vernons."

"Maybe when they do . . ."

"They won't be so bothered about finding out who put the cat among their pigeons."

"Maybe," said Harry, "they'd even give him a medal."

The youths at the other end of the pub turned in astonishment to stare at the three old men in the corner. For once, the laughter of the old men was even louder and more unnatural than their own.

Helen stood with her grandmother on the doorstep of the cottage, watching the lights of the Renault disappear past the bend by the church. The night was clear and still quite warm, and the stars glowed in a dark blue blanket of sky. Only the streetlamps here and there and the security lights outside the Coach House and the Old Vicarage created areas that seemed truly dark.

"It was nice to see Sergeant Cooper's son, wasn't it? He's made a nice-looking young man."

"Yes, Grandma."

"Ben, is it?"

"That's right."

"He's the one you used to bring 'round to the house after school sometimes, isn't he, Helen?"

"Only once or twice, Grandma. And that was years ago."

"I remember, though. I remember how you looked at him. And then you told me one day that you were going to marry him when you grew up. I remember that."

"All little girls get crushes like that. I don't even know him now."

"I suppose so. But he has nice eyes. Dark brown."

They turned back into the house. Helen noticed that Gwen was reluctant even to look into the kitchen, let alone go near the door, although the police had long since taken away the bloodstained trainer and the pages of the *Buxton Advertiser* with it.

"They'll be up at the Mount now," said Helen. "I don't envy them the job. They have to tell Mr. and Mrs. Vernon what they've found."

Her grandmother looked at the clock, fiddled with her cardigan, folded and unfolded a small piece of pink tissue from her sleeve.

"One of them will have to go and identify the body, you know. I suppose he'll be the one who does it. But it will hit her hard, Charlotte Vernon. Don't you think so, Grandma?"

Gwen shook her head, and Helen saw a small tear gather at the corner of one eye, brightening for a moment the dry skin of her cheek.

"I know I should do," said Gwen. "I know I should feel sorry for them, but I don't. I can't help it, Helen."

Helen sat on the side of her grandmother's chair and put her arm around her thin shoulders.

"It's all right, Grandma. It's understandable. There's no need to upset yourself. What if I make some hot chocolate, then there might be something you can watch on TV until Granddad comes back."

Gwen nodded and sniffed, and found another piece of tissue that was still intact to wipe her nose. Helen patted her shoulder and began to move toward the kitchen until her grandmother's voice stopped her. It sounded harsh and full of fear, and trembling on the edge of despair.

"What's going to happen to Harry?" she said. "Oh, dear God, what will they do to Harry?"

-7-

The mortuary assistant drew back the plastic sheet from the face with care. The relatives should never be allowed to see the injuries on the body, unless it was absolutely necessary. In this case, the face was bad enough, although it had been cleaned up as far as possible in the time they had been given. The maggots had been scooped away and bottled, the eyes cleaned and closed, the dried blood scraped off for testing. With the hair pushed back, the injuries to the side of the head were not readily visible.

"Yes," said Graham Vernon without hesitation.

"You are identifying the remains as those of your daughter, Laura Vernon, sir?" asked DCI Tailby.

"Yes. That's what I said, isn't it?"

"Thank you very much, sir."

"Is that it?"

"It's a necessary formality which allows the other procedures to get under way."

The assistant was already drawing the sheet back over Laura's face, returning her to the anonymity of the recently dead, until the post-mortem examination could be completed.

"Does one of your procedures involve catching my daughter's murderer, by any chance, Chief Inspector?" said Vernon, without taking his eyes from the body.

There was no need for Tailby to have been present when Graham Vernon identified his daughter's body, but he saw it as a valuable chance to observe the reactions of relatives. He watched Vernon now as the man stepped away from the sheeted mound that had been his daughter. He saw his eyes linger with that familiar horrid fascination on the loose ridges and hollows of green plastic that concealed the dead girl's face. Vernon's hands moved constantly, touching his face and his mouth, smoothing his jacket, rubbing their soft fingers together in a series of involuntary gestures that could mean nervousness or barely concealed distress. His face told its own story.

Many parents and bereaved spouses had told Tailby that at this point their minds still refused to accept the reality of death. They would imagine their loved one sitting up suddenly and laughing at the joke, the sheet falling away from features restored to life and health. Was Graham Vernon thinking this now? Did he still see and hear a living Laura? And, if so, what was she telling him that made him look so afraid?

There was a fine line to tread in these cases. The family of a victim had to be treated with care and consideration. Yet 90 percent of murders were "domestics," in which a family member or close friend was responsible. Tailby was no longer moved by the various symptoms of distress displayed by relatives. It was a necessary ability in the job he did, this hardening of the emotions. Sometimes, though, he was forced to acknowledge that it had weakened him as a person; it was a long time since he had been able to form a close relationship.

"You appreciate that we will need to talk to you and your wife again, sir," he said, when Vernon finally turned away.

"There isn't anything else I can tell you that I haven't already."

"We need to know as much about Laura's background as we can. We need to interview all her friends and associates again. We need to identify any links that we haven't yet discovered. We need to trace her movements on the day she was killed. There's a lot to be done."

"Just find Lee Sherratt!" snapped Vernon. "That's all you need to do, Chief Inspector."

"Inquiries are being made in that respect, sir."

"And what does *that* mean, for God's sake?"

The two men walked out through the double doors into the corridor, attempting to leave behind the stink of antiseptic. Their footsteps echoed on a tiled floor as Tailby lengthened his stride to keep up with Vernon, who seemed to want to get away as quickly as possible.

"We'll find the boy, of course, sir. In time. I remain hopeful."

Vernon stopped suddenly, so that Tailby couldn't avoid bumping into him. They ended up almost eye to eye, though the detective was several inches taller. Vernon stared upward with a ferocious scowl, his handsome face swollen into a grimace. His eyes were tired and shot with tiny red veins, and he had shaved unevenly on one side of his face.

"I seem to remember you saying something like that before, Chief Inspector. Nearly two days ago. But that time you were assuring me that you would find my daughter."

Tailby waited, not blinking in the face of Graham Vernon's stare. "Yes, sir."

"But somebody else found her first. Didn't they?"

Tailby recalled the painful scene earlier in the evening, when he had visited the Mount to break the news to the Vernons. He remembered the way that neither parent had shown any surprise on seeing him, only despair and resignation.

He also remembered Charlotte Vernon's slow deterioration into sobbing hysteria, the retreat to a bedroom somewhere, and Graham Vernon's phone call to their doctor. They had been both shocked and upset, of course. But they had reacted entirely separately—there had not been the smallest gesture of mutual support in the first moments after the bad news had been broken.

The two men were through the outside door and at the top of the mortuary steps when Tailby spoke again. To their right, through a screen of dark conifers, they could see the lighted windows of the medical wards of Edendale General Hospital, a series of modern two-storey brick buildings added to the rambling Victorian original. The lights looked cheerful and bright in contrast with the plain facade of the mortuary and its discreet car park.

"Apart from the fact that he seems to have temporarily disappeared, there is no firm evidence at this stage to link Lee Sherratt with the death of your daughter," said the DCI reasonably.

"That's your job, surely, Chief Inspector. It's up to you to find the evidence. I just hope you're going to get on with it now."

His voice had grown louder once they were free of the atmosphere of the mortuary. He had reverted to the brusque and impatient businessman. It had been interesting to observe the change in him in the presence of his daughter's body. But the change had been short-lived.

"All we know of Lee Sherratt, sir, is that he was employed by you as a gardener for the last four months. You gave him employment after he answered an advertisement in the window of Moorhay post office. Until then, he seems not to have known your family at all. His skills appear to have been of a laboring nature—digging and weeding, using a lawn mower, and pushing a wheelbarrow—rather than anything requiring horticultural expertise, since he has absolutely no training and no experience in that field. Am I right?"

"That's all we wanted—a laborer. My wife has all the expertise we needed."

"Indeed. And though he is twenty years old, this was the first job Sherratt had ever obtained, apart from a short spell as a warehouse assistant at the Tesco supermarket here in Edendale. He likes drinking, he admits he has had several casual girlfriends, and he is known to follow the fortunes of Sheffield Wednesday FC. It hardly seems much to reach a conclusion from, sir."

"Look, his father's in prison for receiving stolen goods," said Vernon. "And the boy himself was involved in stealing a tourist's car. What do you make of that?"

"A criminal background, eh? Then why did you employ him, Mr. Vernon?"

Vernon turned away, staring at the police car waiting in the car park. "I wanted to give him a chance. I don't believe young men like that should be hanging around idle with nothing to do but get into trouble. Is that so wrong? Also, he looked like a strong youth who could cope with the heavy work. All right, I admit I made a mistake, but how could I have known what he would turn out to be?"

"His mother says he's just an ordinary young man who likes girls and beer and football."

"Crap!" said Vernon. "Look a bit deeper, Chief Inspector. You'll find Sherratt is a violent yob who was obsessed with my daughter. I warned him off; I sacked him. The next day she's attacked and murdered. Who else are you going to suspect?"

Vernon stalked off and got into the car that was waiting to take him home to Moorhay. But Stewart Tailby stood thoughtfully for a moment on the mortuary steps, considering the last question. On reflection, he was glad that Vernon hadn't waited to be given the answer.

Diane Fry had got a lift back into Edendale with two traffic officers. She had been sent off duty for the night, while DCI Tailby himself had made the journey up to the Mount to ask the Vernons to identify the body.

As she sat behind the traffic men rustling in their yellow fluorescent jackets, she began to feel the familiar sensation of growing despondency as the tension left her and the adrenaline subsided. Very shortly she would have to walk away from the job and face up to the bleak reality of her personal life for another depressing evening.

"Thanks, fellers!" she called as the car dropped her in the station yard.

The driver waved a hand nonchalantly in her direction, but his partner turned to look at her as the Rover pulled away. He eyed her curiously and said something to the driver that Fry couldn't make out. She dismissed it from her mind as not worth bothering about. She had seen female colleagues rushing like lemmings to destroy their own careers in the force because they had let totally petty incidents get out of proportion and fester in their minds.

First she walked up to the CID room. All the lights were on, and one or two of the computer screens were flickering with screen savers that looked like all the stars of the galaxy rushing past the flight deck of the starship *Enterprise*. But the place was devoid of human life, not even a DC on night duty. Fry sat at her desk and wrote up her notes of the interview with Harry Dickinson. She knew that Tailby would be demanding them first thing, before the morning briefing, and she wanted them to be there for him before he had to ask. It would mean another small credit to her name—and it would also mean she would be available immediately for allocation to an inquiry team.

The report didn't take her long. She was a competent typist, and her note taking was accurate and legible. She hesitated for only a moment when she reached the end of the interview, but decided to include the final comment from Harry Dickinson for the sake of completeness. As she wrote that Dickinson had told DCI Tailby to "bugger off," she was surprised to find herself smiling. She quickly changed the expression to a grimace, then a frown, looking around the empty office to be sure that no one was watching her. It wasn't her style to laugh at senior officers—she had never joined in the irreverent banter and rude jokes of the canteen, either here or at West Midlands. She couldn't understand what there was about Harry Dickinson's comment that could have made her smile.

She printed out two copies of her notes and dropped one into the tray on DI Hitchens's desk. Then she walked up to the incident room, where a DS and a computer operator were huddled together over a telephone and a screen full of data. They both ignored her as she cast around for the action file to insert the second copy of her report. She knew that, in the morning, when the regular day shift came on, the room would be buzzing with activity. From what she had seen of Tailby, she was sure he would be fully up-to-date and reminded of the details of the day by the time everyone arrived for briefing.

Then, finally, there was nothing left for her to do. She shut the incident room door quietly and walked back down through the almost empty building to the car park.

After she had deactivated the alarm on her black Peugeot, she stood for a moment, looking at the back wall of the police station. There was nothing at all to see but a few lighted windows, where shadowy outlines could be made out occasionally as officers went about their business. Probably some of them were resentful about being on duty when they would rather be at home with their families or out at the pub or whatever else police officers did in their free time. Fry guessed that very few of them would resent having to leave the station and go home. She started the Peugeot and drove too quickly out of the yard.

In Edendale, as in any other small town, the evening often meant almost deserted streets for long periods, interrupted by straggling groups of young people heading for the pubs between eight and nine o'clock, and the same groups, stumbling now, returning home at half past eleven or looking for buses and taxis to take them on to nightclubs or parties.

Many of the youngsters who littered the streets at night were not only the worse for drink but were also plainly underage. Diane Fry knew enough to turn a blind eye when she passed them. Every police officer would do so, unless some other offense was being committed—an assault, a breach of the peace, abusive language, or indecent exposure. Underage drinking could only be tackled in the pubs themselves, and there were always more urgent things to do, always other priorities.

Today was Monday, and even the young people were thin on the ground as Fry drove down Greaves Road toward the town center. She circled the roundabout at the end of the pedestrianized shopping area and automatically looked to her right down Clappergate. There were lights on in the windows of Boots the Chemists and McDonald's, where three youths slouched against the black cast-iron street furniture, eating Chicken McNuggets and large fries prior to adding their cartons to the debris already littering the paving stones.

Most of the shops were shrouded in darkness, abandoning the town to the pubs and restaurants. Fry had not yet got used to the mixture of shops in Edendale. By day, there was a small baker's shop in Clappergate with wicker baskets and an ancient delivery boy's bicycle strung with onions and a painted milk churn, all standing outside on the pavement. A few doors down was a New Age shop rich with the smell of aromatherapy oils and scented candles and the glint of crystals. In between them lay SpecSavers and the dry cleaners and a branch of the Derbyshire Building Society.

Farther along, on Hulley Road, a couple in their thirties stood looking into the darkened window of one of the estate agents near the market square. They were probably weighing up the prices of properties in Catch Wind and Pysenny Banks, the more picturesque and desirable parts of old Edendale, where the stone-walled streets were barely wide enough for a car and the river ran past front gardens filled with lobelias and lichen-covered millstones. Diane Fry wondered why the couple had chosen to visit the estate agent's at night. Where were they going, where had they come from? What intimate plans were they making for themselves, the two of them together?

She had to stop at the lights at the far end of the square. On her right, running down the hill, were steep cobbled alleys with names like Nimble John's Gate and Nick i'th Tor. Narrow pubs and tearooms and craft shops filled the corners of these alleys like latecomers crowding around the edges of the main shopping area. Of course, they really were latecomers—attracted by the twentieth century influx of tourists rather than by the traditional trade of a market town.

Fry had researched her new area and knew that a fair share of the Peak District's twenty-two million visitors found their way to Edendale each year, in one form or another. By day, the market square was frequently impassable because of the volume of traffic passing through or seeking parking spaces on the cobbles near the public toilets and the recycling skips.

A huge Somerfield's lorry rolled slowly across the junction, heading for the back of the supermarket that had recently opened on Fargate, replacing a derelict cotton mill. Beyond the junction, the Castleton Road began to climb past rows of pebble-dashed semis. On either side, close-packed residential areas spiraled up the hillsides, houses lining narrow, winding roads that took sudden twists and turns to follow the humps and hollows of the underlying contours. The roads were made even narrower up there by the cars parked nose to tail at the curb, except on the worst of the bends. The bigger houses had made room for short drives and garages, but the humbler cottages had not been built for people with cars.

Farther out, the houses became newer as they got higher, though they were built of the same white stone. On the edge of town were small council estates, where the streets were called "closes" and had grass verges. Finally, there was an area where the housing petered out in a scattering of smallholdings and small-scale dairy farms. In some places, it was difficult to see where town became country, with farm buildings converted into homes and mews-style developments lying shoulder to shoulder with muddy crew yards, fields full of black-and-white cows and pervasive rural smells.

Eventually, the pressure for more housing would force up the price of the farmland, and the town would continue its spread. But for now, Edendale was constrained in its hollow by the barrier of hills.

Turning from Castleton Road into Grosvenor Avenue, Fry finally pulled up at the curb outside number twelve. The house had once been solid and prosperous, just one detached Victorian villa in a tree-lined street. Its front door nestled in mock porticos, and the tiny bed-sitters on the top floor were reached only by hidden servants' staircases.

Her own flat, on the first floor, consisted of a bedroom, sitting room, bathroom with shower cubicle, and a tiny kitchen area. The wallpaper was striped in a faded shade of brown, and the pattern on the carpet was a complicated swirl of washed-out blues and pinks and yellows, as if designed to hide any substance spilt on it. Judging by the background smell, there must have been many things spilt in the flat over the years that she would not have liked to name. Most of the other occupants of the house were students at the High Peak College campus on the west side of town.

Fry made herself cheese on toast and a cup of tea and took a Müller low-fat yogurt from a fridge that smelled suspiciously of rotting fish and onions. No amount of cleaning had removed the smell, but in any case she intended to keep only a minimum amount of food in the fridge, preferring to visit the shops as often as required, glad to take any excuse to be out of the flat. There was an Asian corner shop a quarter of a mile away where the young couple behind the counter had seemed pleasant enough. A friendly greeting over the sliced bread and gold top could be welcome at times.

After her meal, she spent ten minutes going through some gentle exercises, winding down from the day as she would after a practice session at the dojo, flexing her muscles and stretching her joints and limbs. Then she showered and put on her old black silk kimono with the Chinese dragon on the back and the yin and yang symbols on the breast.

Tomorrow, she decided, she would make a point of getting hold of the

Yellow Pages and looking up names and addresses of local martial arts centers. She would not find an instructor quite like her old *shotokan* master in Warley, and she would have to adapt to new techniques. But she could not let her skills go rusty. The ability to defend herself had become too important to her now. Besides, she relished the renewed feeling of confidence and power that karate had brought her. And it required total concentration. With *shotokan* and her job, she might never have to think about anything else.

Fry didn't spend too much time considering the Laura Vernon killing. At present, her mind was a blank, awaiting data on which to base deductions, to make connections. She was looking forward to the morning, when she expected to be able to take in a barrage of facts that would be presented at the briefing, to see lines of inquiry open up like so many doors of opportunity.

For one brief moment, a small niggle entered her mind, a passing irritation that might have to be dealt with at some stage. It concerned DC Ben Cooper. The detective everyone loved, the man most likely to stand in her way. The picture that entered her mind was of a six-foot male with broad shoulders and perfect teeth, smiling complacently. She considered him fleetingly, then pushed him off the stage with an imaginary hand in the face. There were no obstacles that couldn't be overcome. There were no problems, only challenges.

Finally, she switched on the television in the corner to watch a late night film before bedtime. It was some sort of old horror film, in black and white. From her place in the old armchair, she was able to feel under the bed with one hand, her eyes on the TV. She pulled out a two-pound box of Thornton's Continental and fed a Viennese truffle into her mouth. On the screen, a woman walking alone at night turned at the sound of following footsteps. As a dark shadow fell across her face, she began to scream and scream.

Five miles away from Grosvenor Avenue, Ben Cooper bumped his Toyota down the rough track to Bridge End Farm, twisting the wheel at the familiar points along the way to avoid the worst of the potholes. In places, the track had been repaired with compacted earth and the odd half brick. The first heavy rain of the winter would wash it all away again when the water came rushing down from the hillside and turned the narrow track into a river.

In passing, he noticed a stretch of wall where the topping stones had fallen away and the wall was beginning to bulge outward toward the field. He made a mental note to mention it as a job he could do for Matt on his next day off.

Cooper was consciously trying to readjust his mind to such mundane things. But his thoughts were lingering on the Laura Vernon case. It was going to be an inquiry that he would not find easy to forget. He was baffled by the old man Harry Dickinson. He had seen many reactions among people who became accidentally involved in incidents of major crime, but he could not recall such a puzzling mixture of indifference and secret enjoyment.

Unable to find a ready explanation for the old man's attitude, he considered the leading suspect, the missing Lee Sherratt. He did not know Lee and had never had any dealings with him. But he did recall his father, Jackie Sherratt, a local small-time villain. He was currently serving two years in Derby for receiving, but was better known in the Edendale area as an experienced poacher.

Most of all, though, Cooper's thoughts kept straying back to the moment he had found the body of the girl. The physical impressions had stamped themselves on his senses and would not go away. Even the evening air blowing through the open windows of the Toyota could not take away the smell of stale blood and urine that seemed to linger in the car. Even a Levellers tape on the stereo could not drown out the buzzing of the flies that had laid their eggs in Laura Vernon's mouth or silence the derisive cry of the ragged-winged crow that had flapped away from her face. Directly in his field of vision, as if imprinted on the inside of the windscreen, hung the images of a ravaged eye socket and the startling contrast between a strip of bleached white thigh and a thick coil of black pubic hair. Even at the moment that he had first seen the body, Cooper had registered the fact that Laura Vernon had dyed the hair on her head a rich vermilion red.

It was not his first body by any means. But they didn't get any better with experience. Certainly not when they were like this one. He knew that the sight would stay with him for weeks or months, until something worse came along. Maybe it would never go away at all.

Cooper also knew that he had sensed something wrong in the cottage at Moorhay where Harry and Gwen Dickinson lived. Something that the granddaughter, Helen Milner, was aware of, too. It was not anything he could put his finger on—not a cold fact that he could have included in an interview report, not a logical conclusion that he could have justified in any way. There wasn't even any firm impression in his mind that the atmosphere had anything to do with the finding of Laura Vernon's body. But something wrong at Dial Cottage there had certainly been. He was sure he was not mistaken.

The Toyota rattled over a cattle grid and into the yard of Bridge End Farm. Its tires splashed through trails of freshly dropped cow manure left by the herd coming down to the milking shed from their pasture and back again after afternoon milking. A group of calves destined for Bakewell Market bellowed at him from a pen in one of the buildings at the side of the yard. But he ignored them, slowing instead as he passed the tractor shed to look in at the big green John Deere and the old gray Fergie, and the row of implements lined up against the walls. There was no sign of his brother, although Matt would normally be found tinkering with a bit of machinery at this time of the evening.

When he reached the front of the house, Cooper's heart began to sink. His two nieces, Amy and Josie, were sitting on the wall between the track and the tiny front garden. They were not playing and not talking to each other, but sat kicking their heels against the stones and stirring the dust with the toes of their trainers. They looked up as he parked the Toyota, and neither smiled a greeting. He could see that Josie, who was only six, had been crying. Her eyes were red and her nose had been running, leaving grimy tracks on her brown cheeks. A comic lay discarded on the wall, and an ice cream had melted into a raspberry-colored puddle on the ground.

"Hello, girls," he said.

"Hi, Uncle Ben."

Amy looked at him sadly, with big eyes that showed hurt but no real comprehension of what was hurting. She glanced apprehensively over her shoulder at the farmhouse. The front door stood open, but there was silence from within. A black-and-white cat emerged from the garden, walked to the doorstep, and paused, sniffing the air of the hallway. Then it seemed to change its mind and trotted quickly away toward the Dutch barn.

"Mum's in the kitchen," said Amy, anticipating the question.

"And where's your dad?"

"He had to go up to Burnt Wood straight after milking. To mend some gates."

"I see."

Cooper smiled at the girls, but got no response. They were totally unlike the two children who would normally have come running to greet him. But he didn't have to ask them any more questions to guess why they were so subdued.

In the big kitchen he found his sister-in-law, Kate. She was moving about from table to stove stiffly, like a woman with arthritis or one whose limbs were badly bruised. Her short fair hair was disheveled, and the sheen of sweat on her forehead looked as though it was caused by something more than the heat of the day or the steam from a pan that was simmering on the hot plate with nothing in it. She, too, had been crying.

When she saw him, she let go of the carving knife she was carrying as if it were a relief to part with it. The kitchen normally smelled of herbs and freshly baked bread, and sometimes of garlic and olive oil. Tonight, though, it smelled of none of those. The smell was of disinfectant and several less pleasant odors that made Cooper's stomach muscles tighten with apprehension.

"What's wrong, Kate?"

His sister-in-law shook her head, sagging against the pine table, weary with the effort of trying to keep up an appearance of normality for the girls. Cooper could have told her, even from his brief glimpse of them outside, that it had not worked.

"See for yourself," she said. "I can't bear it anymore, Ben."

He put his hand on her shoulder and saw the tears begin to squeeze from her eyes once more.

"Leave it to me," he said. "You look after the girls."

He went out into the passage that ran through the center of the house and looked up the stairs. When he was a child, the passage and the stairs had been gloomy places. The walls and most of the woodwork had been covered in some sort of dark brown varnish, and the floorboards had been painted black on either side of narrow strips of carpet. The carpet itself had long since lost its color under a layer of dirt which no amount of cleaning could prevent from being tramped into the house by his father, his uncle, their children, three dogs, a number of cats of varying habits and even, at times, other animals that had been brought in from the fields for special attention. Now, though, things were different. There were deep-pile fitted carpets on the floor and the walls were painted white. The wood had been stripped to its original golden pine, and there were mirrors and pictures to catch and emphasize what light there was from the small crescent-shaped windows in the doors at either end of the passage.

Yet he found that the stairs, light and airy and comfortable as they were, held more terrors for him now than they ever had as a child. The immediate cause of his fear lay on a step halfway up. It was a pink, furry carpet slipper, smeared with excrement.

The slipper lay on its side, shocking and obscene in its ordinariness, its gaudy color clashing with the carpet. It turned his stomach as effectively as if it had been a freshly extracted internal organ left dripping on the stairs.

Slowly, he climbed the steps, pausing to pick up the slipper gingerly between finger and thumb as he would have done a vital piece of evidence. On the first landing, he paused outside a door, cocking his head for a moment to listen to the desperate, high-pitched whimper that came from inside. It was an inhuman noise, a mumbled keening like an animal in pain, forming no words.

Then Cooper opened the door, pushing it hard as it stuck on some obstruction on the floor. When he walked into the room, he entered a scene of devastation worse than any crime scene he had ever encountered.

-8-

"Found by a man walking a dog."

There was a wary silence. Diane Fry tried to look efficient and attentive, with her notebook open on her knee. At the moment, her hand was moving slowly through an elaborate series of aimless doodles that might, from a distance, have been taken for shorthand. A bluebottle buzzed fruitlessly against a window of the conference room, someone shuffled his feet, and the metal legs of a chair creaked uneasily.

"Found by a man walking a *dog,*" repeated the superintendent dangerously.

Some of the officers in the room looked at the ceiling; others tilted their plastic coffee cups to their faces, hoping to hide their expressions from the superintendent's eyes. Fry wondered why bluebottles always chose to ignore open windows in favor of the determined futility of bashing themselves incessantly against the closed ones.

"It was some old bloke called Dickinson, sir," said DS Rennie. "Apparently he has his own regular route across the Baulk every night."

Rennie had not been involved in the search operation. But, like everyone else in the room, he recognized the time for covering your back, for limiting the damage, for claiming any shreds of credit where it could be found. Those responsible for the search were keeping sensibly silent. So it followed that if you spoke up, the super would register you as blameless. Rennie watched for the brief flicker of the blue eyes toward him that said he had been heard and acknowledged.

"So. A man walking a dog. Some old bloke called Dickinson, in fact. Thank you for that, Rennie." The superintendent nodded and smiled like a sewage worker gifted with an exceptionally keen sense of smell. "And here we are, Her Majesty's finest. We had a helicopter up in the air at God knows how much a minute, and forty officers on the ground searching those woods for five hours, without turning up so much as a decent used condom. The police, like the papers used to say, are baffled. And then— and then what happens?"

Nobody answered him this time, not even Rennie. Fry found she had drawn an entire swarm of small blue flies flitting across her page, their flimsy wings beating fast but going nowhere.

"The body," said Jepson, "is found by a *man* walking a *dog.*"

"Given another day or two—" began DI Hitchens. But it was unwise— as duty inspector, Hitchens had been technically responsible for the search, though he had not been present. The superintendent cut straight across him.

"Just tell me why," he said. "Why is there *always* a man walking a dog? You might start to suspect they were put there specifically to expose the shortcomings of the police force, eh? Lost a body somewhere in the woods? Don't worry, Chief, some old bloke walking his dog will find it for us. Got no description of the getaway car used in that armed robbery last night? No problem—some insomniac dragging poor old Rover 'round the streets is bound to have made a note of the registration number. Got no positive ID of your suspect to place him at the scene of the offense? Albert and Fido are sure to have clocked him stashing the loot while they were wetting a lamppost somewhere. Yes. Men walking dogs. If only they advertised their services in the *Eden Valley Times,* we'd save a fortune."

"Chief, I don't think—" said Hitchens.

"And then," said Jepson, "we could disband the entire Derbyshire Constabulary and replace it with a few dozen blokes walking their dogs. They'd have the detection rate up in no time."

Diane Fry relegated Hitchens a few rungs in her mental hierarchy. She had to make the best impression she could among all these new faces and stay alert, try to pick up the names and ranks and figure out who was the most likely to be influential. Hitchens had started off near the top of the scale as her DI but was gradually fading on the rails.

A detective Fry didn't recognize had put his hand up, like the bright boy in class wanting to get himself noticed. He had already drawn unwelcome attention to himself by arriving very late for the briefing, which had always been considered a disciplinary offense in stations Fry had worked at. He had looked hot and flustered and disheveled when he came in, as if he had only just got out of bed, and he had suffered a prolonged glower from Jepson. Now all eyes turned to him, welcoming a

sacrificial victim, amazed that he was throwing himself into the pit vol-
untarily. He looked to be in his late twenties but carried an air of innocence lacking in those around him. He was tall and slim, and he had
messy, light brown hair that fell untidily across his forehead.

"Excuse me, sir, but I don't understand."

"Oh aye? What don't you understand, lad?"

"Well, we got the dog section out from Ripley to go over the ground,
didn't we? So why didn't the Ripley lot find what the old bloke's dog
found?"

Jepson looked at him sharply, a scathing put-down hovering on his
lips. But he saw the expression on the detective's face, noticed his cheeks
already starting to go a shade of pink. The superintendent sighed, his irritation suddenly spent.

"I think you'll find the key to that, Cooper," he said, "is not the dog.
It's the old bloke."

Finally, Jepson handed over to DCI Tailby as senior investigating officer. Amid muffled sighs of relief and a flood of comforting conference
room jargon, the discussion moved on into safer areas—the prioritiza-
tion of lines of inquiry, the division of staff into inquiry teams, the allocation of action sheets. But several days later, Diane Fry was amazed to
find that, in among the detailed anatomical drawings of common winged
insects, she had recorded the superintendent's last words exactly.

"Preliminary report from the pathologist suggests death was caused by
two or three heavy blows to the side of the head with a hard, smooth
object. Task Force will commence a search for the weapon this morning."

All eyes in the room were fixed on the photograph of the crime scene that
had been projected onto the screen behind Tailby. The full-length shot of
the body lying in the undergrowth changed to a closer view of the head. The
color of Laura Vernon's hair looked garish and unnatural in the photograph,
and the dark, matted bloodstains were not easy to make out. Her red T-shirt
made the accuracy of the color balance even more doubtful.

"First indications, based on temperature of the body and the stage of
development of fly larvae found in the eyes, mouth, and vulva, suggest
Laura Vernon was killed within a couple of hours either side of the first
report that she was missing—i.e., eight o'clock Saturday evening. As you
know, we already have one early report that Laura was seen talking to a
young man at about six-fifteen on a footpath in the scrubland just a few

yards from her own back garden. This is some distance from where she was found, which was in the wooded area called the Baulk. Therefore, we need to retrace that final journey. House-to-house teams will concentrate on recording movements of anyone in and around the Baulk at about the time. Including, of course, any sightings of Laura Vernon herself."

The picture changed to the lower half of Laura's body. Black denims were pulled down to her knees, showing the top edge of a pair of blue pants and several inches of deathly white flesh above and below the dark bush of hair.

"As you see, Laura's clothing was disturbed. However, subject to the full postmortem, which will be carried out later this morning, the pathologist's initial view is that there is no evidence that any sexual assault took place, either before or after the victim's death. There is one possible exception to that."

Tailby nodded, and the picture changed again, the camera zooming in to a small area near the top of the dead girl's right thigh. The assembled officers frowned and peered closer. A discoloration of the skin could be seen, some sort of bruising, but bearing an oddly regular shape.

"Mrs. Van Doon," said Tailby, "believes this injury probably occurred around the time of death."

The room stirred uneasily. Some of the officers were sweating, and the atmosphere was becoming humid.

"I know you're all anxious to get started," said Tailby, sensing the restlessness. "DI Hitchens will give you your action forms very shortly. Bear with me for a few more minutes."

The picture disappeared from the wall behind the DCI, and some in the room breathed a sigh of relief.

"First of all, we are urgently inquiring into the whereabouts of one Lee Sherratt, aged twenty, recently employed as a gardener at the Mount. Details are in your files. But we also want to know about any other boyfriends Laura Vernon may have had a relationship with. Particularly those her parents might not have been aware of."

"Are we assuming the family are in the clear, sir?" asked DS Rennie.

"We never assume, Rennie," said the DCI with a little smile. "It makes an 'ASS' out of 'U' and 'ME.'"

Rennie paused for a moment, puzzled. Then someone sniggered, and he realized he had been put down.

"Thank you, sir," he said.

"Both Graham and Charlotte Vernon will, of course, be interviewed again. There is also a brother, I believe, away at university. Otherwise, we are told that Laura Vernon did not mix much with people in the village of Moorhay. This is what the parents tell us, at least. If that isn't the case, it will be your job to find out. Meanwhile, the usual checks on all our known sex offenders are being carried out. We have DI Armstrong here from B Division, who will be coordinating that aspect of the inquiry."

The chief inspector indicated a female officer to one side of the room. She was rather overweight, and the gray suit she was wearing didn't fit too well around her shoulders. Her dark hair was collar length and cut very straight.

"Some of you may know that DI Armstrong has been working on the team investigating the death of Susan Edson near Buxton five weeks ago. Some of this ground has already been covered in B Division in the last few weeks, so we are avoiding duplication of effort."

Some of the officers shifted uneasily and looked sideways at one another. Tailby seemed to sense it and responded. "For public consumption, there must be no suggestion of a link between these two cases. I do not want to hear the words 'serial killer' mentioned by any member of this team or see them appearing in the press."

He looked to one side, glaring at a civilian wearing a suit, a colorful tie, and a pair of large, blue-framed spectacles. Fry pegged him as one of the force's press officers, whose job it was to deflect press attention and distribute as little information about the case as possible.

"All these lines of inquiry will take time, of course," said Tailby, "and I don't need to remind you that the first hours are important."

Diane Fry was busy studying DI Armstrong when Ben Cooper tentatively put his hand up again. Tailby regarded him with something like pity.

"Yes, Cooper?"

"Harry Dickinson, sir. The gentleman who found the trainer."

"Ah, the old bloke," said someone, breaking the tension.

"With the dog," said someone else.

"Will he be interviewed again, sir?"

Fry wondered for a moment whether Cooper had seen her transcript of the first interview with Harry Dickinson and was taking the mickey out of the DCI. But Tailby obviously decided that it wasn't Cooper's style or intention.

"Harry Dickinson is seventy-eight years old," he said.

"Yes, sir," said Cooper. "But we're not assuming that his age rules him out. Are we, sir?"

"Of course not," said Tailby. "We assume nothing."

There was a general shuffling of feet and scraping of chair legs. Fry watched a female detective turn around to ask Ben Cooper if he was all right. She looked concerned, but he only nodded, keeping his eyes on the chief inspector. Fry noticed that there was a scuff mark on Cooper's leather jacket, and his tie needed straightening. He was really untidy, and it made him look disorganized. No way was he as perfect as everyone said he was.

"One more thing I want to emphasize before you go," said Tailby, raising his voice over the noise. "Again, this is in your files, but keep it to the forefront of your minds, all of you. DC Cooper has mentioned the trainer found by Mr. Dickinson and his dog, the find which led us to the body a short distance away. But there is one fact which could be vital to the inquiry. One thing which could lead to an early conclusion, if we are thorough with our routines—and if we get a little bit of luck. I want you to remember, all of you, that Laura Vernon's second trainer is missing."

"All right. DC Fry, here, please."

Fry stepped briskly toward Hitchens, where he leaned casually against the wall, dangling a leg over the edge of a desk. He had a stack of action forms in his hand, and Fry knew she was about to be allocated to an inquiry team.

"You're the new girl around here, Diane. So we're going to team you up with Ben Cooper for a while. He knows the area like the back of his hand."

"So I've heard."

"Well, we don't want you going and getting lost on the moors, do we, Fry? We'd have to send the dogs out again."

Fry tried a smile and hoped it was convincing. "I'm sure we'll work well together."

Hitchens studied her. "You'll get on all right," he said.

"It's OK."

"Right. DC Cooper! Where's Ben Cooper gone?"

"He had to take an urgent phone call, sir," said another detective, "in the CID room."

"OK. Well, you two are in charge of house to house in Moorhay," said

Hitchens. "There will be uniformed teams out there to assist you. These are the allocated areas. Make sure you don't miss anybody."

He held out a photocopied street map divided into three sections by blue, red, and yellow highlighter pens.

"I'll go and introduce myself to DC Cooper," said Fry, "if I can find the CID room."

Ben Cooper was hunched over a desk, staring at a sea of papers that seemed to have accumulated during his holiday. He wasn't reading the papers; in fact, he didn't appear to see them at all. His face was completely blank as he listened to the voice at the other end of the phone.

"I suppose so, if that's what they think," he said. "But how long for? Yes, I know Kate needs a break, but, Matt—"

He saw the new DC coming from the far end of the CID room. She moved with a cool deliberateness, not meeting his eyes, but glancing from side to side as she walked past the desks and filing cabinets, as if searching for evidence of misdemeanors among her absent colleagues. Cooper half expected to see her stoop to check for footprints on the carpets or turn over an envelope to examine the address. She had a lean face and short fair hair, and she was very slim—slimmer than he had grown up to expect women to be. His mother would have said she was sickening for something. But she had a certain wiry look that suggested she was no weakling. No wilting violet, this one.

He had worked out who she was, of course. She was the one PC Garnett had told him about, the new DC who had come from the West Midlands with a reputation. Garnett had been almost right in his description. The only surprise was that she was actually quite attractive—though a smile, he thought, would help to relax her face and do something about the dark shadows in her eyes.

"Yes, Matt. Yes, you're right, I know. Two days then. And we can talk about it properly on Thursday, OK? It just seems a long time to wait."

The new DC had reached Cooper's desk. She stood looking at the mess of papers, idly tapping the Moorhay file against her thigh. He turned away, shielding the phone. He knew it was obvious that the call was nothing to do with work. She would recognize a personal call when she heard one. She probably thought he was discussing a girlfriend.

He watched in amazement as she calmly took a seat and booted up his computer terminal, still without looking at him.

"Hold on a minute, Matt."

He saw her start to smile as the computer came to life and she logged into the database. It allowed her into the first two screens, but then threw up a dialogue box when she tried to extract some data.

"You need a password," said Cooper.

"What's that?" said Matt in his ear.

"Nothing."

"What is it then?" she asked.

"I can't just give it out. You need authority."

"Yeah? I'll find a way past it then."

She started tapping keys to get into the terminal settings, looking for the security program and the password function. A silver stud glinted in her ear where it was exposed by a recent trim.

"You'll never get anywhere without knowing the proper password."

"Ben, if you're busy—"

"Yes, look, Matt, I'll have to go," said Cooper. "I'll speak to you tonight."

He replaced the phone and didn't look up for a moment, as if he was adjusting himself to something, preparing to face a whole new challenge.

"Damn!"

A FATAL ERROR message was frozen on the computer screen. The terminal had objected to the unauthorized tinkering and had crashed.

"I did tell you you'd get nowhere without the password," he snapped.

"You're my new partner," said Fry. "When you're available, that is."

Cooper took a deep breath. "OK. Hi, I'm Ben Cooper. You must be DC Fry."

He waited for her to say something else. He didn't know her first name yet.

"My friends call me Diane."

He nodded cautiously, noting the ambiguity of the message. "What are we up for?"

"House to house with some wooden tops."

"Don't let them hear you call them that."

Fry shrugged. "We could get going, if you're ready. I'm only the new girl, but I understand murder inquiries are usually considered quite important."

"All right, I'm ready."

In the corridor, DI Hitchens called them back.

"I'll be out for another briefing and to take your reports myself at the end of the morning," he said. "There's a pub in Moorhay, isn't there, Cooper?"

"The Drover, sir."

"Marston's, I seemed to notice when we went through the village yesterday."

"That's right."

"We'll rendezvous there then—let's say twelve-thirty. And Ben . . ."

"Yes, sir?"

"Don't be late, will you?"

"Sorry about that, sir. Family problems."

"It's not like you. Don't make a habit of it."

"No, sir."

"One more thing everybody needs to know. Mr. Tailby pointed out how important these first few hours of an inquiry are. We all know that. But don't get too carried away when your shift is finished. There's no more overtime."

"What?"

"There's no cash in the budget. The top floor think we can get a result without it."

"It's crazy," said Cooper.

Hitchens shrugged. "That's the way it is. OK, you know what your tasks are. Off you go."

Cooper and Fry had reached the car park at the back of the police station before they hesitated. Fry felt she could read his thoughts.

"My car's over there," she said. "The black Peugeot. And I'm a good driver."

"My Toyota's got four-wheel drive," said Ben. "It might be handy for some of those lanes around Moorhay. And I know the way."

Fry shrugged, allowing him a small victory. "OK."

They found little to say to each other on the drive out of Edendale. Cooper took a route that Fry didn't know, dodging down narrow back streets that wound their way across town past the parish church and Edendale Community School. When they emerged on the Buxton Road, she realized that he had managed to bypass all the traffic snarled up on Clappergate and the other approaches to the town center. Already, she thought, he was making a point of showing off his famous local knowledge.

*   *   *

Cooper could barely keep his eyes off the landscape as he drove. It was a constant pleasure to him to escape from Edendale into the surrounding hills, where the changing moods of the scenery always surprised and delighted him.

Nowhere was the contrast between the White Peak and the Dark Peak more striking than on the climb southward out of Edendale, past the last of the housing developments, past the sports field and the religious retreat run by the Sisters of Our Lady. Right at the top of the hill was the Light House, with its stunning views across both limestone and mill-stone grit.

The patchwork of farmland and tree-covered slopes to the south looked welcoming and approachable, lit by the sun, but was full of hidden depths and unseen corners. It was crisscrossed by a pattern of white drystone walls, and it erupted here and there in steep limestone cliffs or the ripples and pockmarks of abandoned mine workings. It was, above all, a human landscape, settled and shaped by people, and still a place where thousands of years of history might be expected to come to the surface, if you cared to look.

Behind the car, to the north, the moors of the Dark Peak looked remote and forbidding, an uncompromising landscape that was anything but human. The bare faces of hardened gritstone seemed to absorb the sun instead of reflecting it as the limestone did. They seemed to stand aloof and brooding, untouched by humanity and therefore offering a challenge which many took up, to conquer their peaks. Some succeeded, but many failed, defeated by the implacability of the dark slopes and the bad weather that seemed to hover around them.

But appearances could be deceptive. Even the White Peak bore its scars—the great crude gashes where the limestone quarries and opencast workings had been blasted and ripped from its hills.

"What do you think of Edendale, then?" he asked at last, as they joined a convoy of cars crawling behind a caravan around the bends that climbed toward the summit of the hill. It promised to be another hot day, and their visors were down against the sun already scorching the windscreen and glaring off the tarmac. To their right, the outskirts of the town were gradually falling away, the stone slates of the roofs settling among the trees and petering out along the faint silver ribbon of the river Eden. There was a camping site in a meadow by the river just outside town, with rows of blue and green tents like exotic plants blooming in the morning sun.

"That's what everybody asks me," said Fry. "What do I think of Edendale. Does it matter?"

"I would have thought so," said Cooper, surprised.

"It's a place to work. It has crime, like any other place, I suppose. I expect it has a few villains, a lot of sad cases, and a whole mass of boring respectable types in between. It's the same everywhere."

"It's a better place to live than Birmingham, surely?"

"Why?"

"Well—" He gestured with one hand off the steering wheel, indicating the hills and the valley and the river and the patchwork of fields and drystone walls, the tumbling roofs and spires of the town behind them, and the deep green mass of the Eden Forest marching up toward the vast reservoirs on the heights of the gritstone moors. He hardly knew how to express what he meant, if she couldn't see it for herself.

"In any case, I didn't live in Birmingham," said Fry. "I lived at Warley."

"Where's that?"

"In the Black Country. Have you heard of it?"

"I once traveled into Birmingham by train. That went through Wolverhampton. Is that close?"

"Yeah, well, you'd know all about it, then."

They had reached a level stretch of road at the top of the hill, and Cooper accelerated to follow the stream of cars overtaking the caravan.

"So if you liked the Black Country, what brought you here, then?"

Fry grimaced and turned her face away to look at the view across the plateau toward the Wye Valley, where Moorhay waited. But Cooper didn't miss the gesture.

"I suppose everybody asks you that as well."

"I suppose they do."

"Oh well," he said. "Nice to have you on board anyway, Diane."

Fry had charge of the file Hitchens had given them. She pulled out the map to avoid having to look at Cooper.

"There's only Main Street running through the village, and a few lanes off it. Some without names that only seem to lead to farms. And there's a group of houses that seem to be called Quith Holes. Do you know it?"

"Those cottages at Quith Holes back on to the Baulk," he said, "not far from where Laura Vernon was found. There's the Old Mill there, too. It does teas and bed and breakfast now."

"Who doesn't around here?" said Fry as they passed another farmhouse advertising holiday accommodation.

She had to admit that Ben Cooper was a competent driver. She felt able to concentrate on absorbing the details from the file before they arrived at Moorhay. There was a photograph of Laura Vernon as she had been in life, though her hair was a different color from that of the dead girl Fry had seen—not quite so virulent a shade of red. The photo had been blown up from one supplied by the Vernons on the day their daughter had gone missing. Fry had seen the original picture in the action file, before the case had become a murder inquiry and had been removed from the CID room. The full shot had shown young Laura in a garden, with a clump of rhododendrons in full bloom behind her, a glimpse of a stone balustrade and the top of a flight of steps to one side, and a black-and-white Border collie asleep on the grass at her feet. But the enlargement showed only her head and the top half of her body. The background had been cut out, removing Laura from her environment as effectively as someone had removed her from life.

There was a list of the names and addresses of all Laura Vernon's known contacts in Moorhay and the surrounding area. It was a pitifully short list for a fifteen-year-old girl. Top of it was Lee Sherratt, aged twenty, of 12 Wye Close, Moorhay. He had worked as a gardener at the Mount until dismissed from his job last Friday by Laura's father, Graham Vernon. Sherratt had been interviewed when Laura was first reported missing but had not been seen since Sunday. Unlike the Vernons, the Sherratts had not reported their son missing. His name was marked in red, which meant tracing him was a priority.

Further down the list were Andrew and Margaret Milner and their daughter, Helen. Andrew was also noted as an employee of Graham Vernon's. As for Helen, Fry remembered her from her visit to Dial Cottage with Tailby and Hitchens. She had stayed close to the old man when the police had arrived—closer than his own wife, it had seemed. Close relationships within families always seemed a bit suspect to Diane Fry; she felt she didn't quite understand them.

She looked up at Cooper, watching his profile as he drove. She had a sudden urge to tell him to tidy himself up before they met the public. She wanted to straighten his tie, to push his hair back from his forehead. That boyish look did absolutely nothing for her.

But she could see that he was completely absorbed in his own thoughts, his face closed to the outside world. It struck her that they were not happy thoughts, but she dismissed it as none of her business and returned to her file.

Ben Cooper was remembering the smell. There had been a stink in the room worse than anything he had ever smelt on a farm. No cesspit, no slurry tank, no innards from a freshly gutted rabbit or pheasant had ever smelt as bad as the entirely human stench that filled that room. There was excrement daubed across the wallpaper and on the bedclothes piled on the floor. A pool of urine was drying into a sticky pool on the carpet near where other similar puddles had been scrubbed clean with disinfectant, leaving paler patches like the remnants of some virulent skin disease. A chair lay on the rug with one leg missing. A curtain had been torn off its rail, and the pages of books and magazines were scattered like dead leaves on every surface. A second pink slipper sat ludicrously in a wooden fruit bowl on the chest of drawers, and a thin trickle of blood ran down across the top drawer, splitting into two forks across the wooden handle. The drawers and the wardrobe had been emptied of their contents, which were heaped at random on the bed.

It was from beneath the heap of clothes that the noise came, monotonous and inhuman, a low, desperate wailing. When he had moved toward the bed, the mound stirred and the keening turned to a fearful whimper. Cooper knew that the crisis was over, for now. But this had been the worst so far, no doubt about it. The evidence was all around him.

He leaned closer to a coat with an imitation fur collar but was careful not to touch the bed for fear of sparking off a violent reaction. The coat was drenched in a familiar scent that brought a painful lump to his throat.

"It's Ben," he said quietly.

A white hand was visible briefly as it clutched for a sleeve and the edge of a skirt to pull them closer for concealment. The fingers withdrew again into the darkness like a crab retreating into its shell. The whimpering stopped.

"It was the devil," said a small voice from deep in the pile of clothes. "The devil made me do it."

The mingled odors of stale scent, sweat, and excrement and urine made Cooper feel he was about to be sick. He swallowed and forced himself to keep his voice steady.

"The devil's gone away."

The hand slowly reappeared, and Cooper clasped it in his fingers, shocked by its icy coldness.

"You can come out now, Mum," he said. "The devil's gone away."

"Ben?" said Fry.

"Yes?" He jerked back to attention. He looked to Fry as if he had been asleep and dreaming. Or maybe going through a familiar nightmare.

"Why did you ask about Harry Dickinson during the briefing this morning?"

She was curious why he had drawn attention to himself at the wrong time, when self-interest had clearly indicated that it was a time to keep quiet and keep his head down for a while. But she couldn't ask him that outright.

"The person who finds the body is always a possible suspect," he said.

"Oh, really? But I thought Dickinson only found the trainer. It was you who actually found the body."

"Yes, but you know what I mean."

"Anyway, Dickinson is seventy-eight years old. An awkward old sod, I'll give you that. But a definite pipe and slippers man. He hardly looked strong enough to unzip his own fly, let alone commit a violent assault on a healthy fifteen-year-old girl."

"I'm not sure you're right there, Diane."

"Oh? What are you basing your suspicion on?"

"Nothing really. Just a feeling I had when I was there, in the cottage. A feeling about that family."

"A feeling? Oh yeah, right, Ben."

"I know what you're going to say."

"You do? Is that another feeling? Tell you what, do me a favor—while we're together as a team, don't involve me in any of your feelings. I prefer the facts."

They lapsed into silence again for the rest of the drive. Fry mentally dismissed Ben Cooper's talk of feelings. She didn't believe he could know the facts about relationships in families. He was what she thought of as the social worker type of police officer—the sort who thought there were no villains in the world, only victims, that people who did anything wrong must necessarily be sick and in need of help. Not only that, but he was obviously well settled, popular, uncomplicated, with dozens of friends and relatives around him, smothering him with comfort and support until his view of the real world was distorted by affection.

She didn't think he could possibly know what it was like to have evil in the family.

-9-

Wye Close was in the center of the little council estate at the northern end of Moorhay. The houses were built of the same gray-white stone as the rest of the village, with slate roofs and unfenced grassed areas that were more roadside verge than garden. At one side stood a row of old people's bungalows, separated from the family houses by a low fence that didn't deter the children from playing on the grass under the windows of the old people.

There were no more than thirty houses on the estate; and in many other places, even in Edendale, it wouldn't have been considered a street, let alone an estate. It had been built on the top field of one of Moorhay's dairy farms. When the area had been allocated for housing on the council's local plan, the increased value of the land had proved too much of a temptation for the farmer at a time when agriculture was in increasing financial difficulties. The result was that every house backed on to pastureland or had a view across rolling slopes to the farm itself. Some of the residents of the estate worked in the small factory units on the outskirts of Edendale or in the dairy ten miles away. Many didn't work at all. Rural housing might have been provided, but not rural employment.

Outside number twelve Wye Close stood an unmarked police Vauxhall. The car, or one like it, had been there since Monday evening, waiting for the return home of Lee Sherratt. The local children, at a loose end during the day because the schools were still on holiday, had invented a new game this morning. They were acting out the part of burglars, robbers, and murderers, lurking suspiciously in the street, then pretending to see the police car suddenly and running away around the corner, screaming. The detective constable on surveillance duty was getting rapidly fed up with it. The baking heat inside the car was already enough to make him tired and irritable. The cheeky kids could be the last straw.

A green Ford entered the estate and pulled up at number twelve.

When DCI Tailby got out and glowered across the road, the children seemed genuinely frightened for once, perhaps intimidated by his size and the gray suit he wore. They retreated behind the fence of the old people's homes and watched to see what he would do. First, he crossed to speak to the detective in the Vauxhall, who sat up straight and shook his head. Then he strode to the door of number twelve and banged the knocker.

"Oh, it's you lot again," said the big woman who came to the door. She was wearing sandals and frayed blue jeans and a billowing pink garment that could only have come from a maternity wear shop. Her hair had been pinned up but was falling back down across a chubby neck, and she smelled of cigarette smoke. Tailby put her age in the late thirties, forty at most.

"Just a few questions, Mrs. Sherratt," he said.

"He's not back."

"I know. Has he been in touch?"

"No."

"There are some things I need to ask you."

Molly Sherratt looked down the road at the children gawping and nudging each other.

"For God's sake, come in then," she said.

Tailby ducked to go through the door and picked his way through a hallway cluttered with bicycles and shoes and piles of clothes. Mrs. Sherratt led him into a tiny kitchen with fitted teak-effect units and a brand-new automatic washer. The remains of somebody's breakfast still stood on the counter—an open packet of cornflakes, half a carton of milk, a knife sticky with butter, and a toaster sitting amid a sea of blackened bread crumbs.

"I was just washing up," said Mrs. Sherratt defensively, watching the detective's instinctive survey of the room.

"Carry on. Don't let me interrupt."

"I don't see that you could be doing anything else."

"I'll try not to be long," said Tailby politely.

She turned on a tap and began to squirt washing-up liquid into a blue plastic bowl until the suds concealed anything that might have been in there. Tailby saw that the door of the washing machine stood slightly open, and the interior was packed tight with dirty clothes. Presumably Mrs. Sherratt had been just about to do the weekly wash as well.

"I've told your lot all I've got to say already," she said.

"We need to know as much as we can about Lee so that we can find him. That's the reason for all the questions, I'm afraid. It *is* important that we find him."

"To eliminate him from inquiries. That's what the other ones said."

"That's right, Mrs. Sherratt."

She clutched the washing-up liquid bottle to her bosom without closing the cap, so that a small squirt of sticky green liquid spurted onto her pink smock. She seemed not to notice.

"Lee hasn't done anything," she said.

"He worked at the Mount," said Tailby, "so he knew Laura Vernon. And since his whereabouts are unknown . . ."

"I know, I know, that's what the others kept saying. But it means nothing. He often goes off for a day or two. He's a devil for wandering off for a bit, is Lee. But that doesn't mean he's done anything wrong, does it?"

"If you could help us find him, Mrs. Sherratt, we'll soon be able to establish that, won't we?"

"Anyway, he didn't work there anymore. At that place. They gave him the push last Friday. Them Vernons. Unfair, it was."

"Did he resent the fact he had been sacked?"

"Course he did. He was unfairly dismissed. He'd done nothing wrong."

In Tailby's experience, nobody's son or daughter had ever done anything wrong. They were all angels, pure as the driven snow, every one of them. It was a wonder there was any crime at all.

"Mr. Vernon claims that Lee was pestering his daughter."

"Rubbish. Lee has a steady girlfriend. They might be getting married."

"Might they?"

"That's why he was set on getting a bit of a job, earning some money. There's nothing 'round here for the young ones, you know. God knows, them Vernons didn't pay him much, but at least he was trying."

"I'm sure you're right. But it doesn't prevent him from having taken a fancy to Laura Vernon, does it?"

Mrs. Sherratt sniffed. "Well, if you want the truth, she wasn't his type. I don't want to speak ill of the dead and all that, but he could never bear them stuck-up types, all posh accents and jodhpurs. It was more likely the other way 'round. I reckon *she* took a fancy to *him*. He's a good-looking lad, my Lee. I bet that's what it was, and Mr. Hoity-Toity Vernon wouldn't like that, his girl fancying the hired labor."

"And, if that was the case, you don't think Lee might have responded?"

"No. Like I say, she wasn't his type."

"Did he mention Laura Vernon much?"

"Hardly at all. He hardly mentioned any of them much. Course, he didn't see much of *him,* or the girl either, except in the school holidays. It was mostly *her* he saw, when he went up there."

"You mean Mrs. Vernon?"

"That's right. Not that she would do anything but give him his orders, I suppose. None of them Vernons has ever mixed with anybody in the village, you know. They think they're better than the rest of us, just because they've got a bit of money to spend on big houses and flashy cars. Well, it isn't so. Having money doesn't make you a good person, does it? It doesn't give you any better morals than the rest of us. Some of us know what's right and what isn't. If you ask me, them Vernons have forgotten all about that, with their money."

Tailby's attention was wandering. His gaze drifted out of the kitchen window, across a small garden with a few vegetables struggling to force themselves through the weeds. There was a rickety garden shed and a small flock of house sparrows fluttering their wings in a depression in the dust in front of its door. A low wooden fence separated the garden from the field at the back of the property. It would present no barrier for anyone to climb over if he wanted to approach from the field instead of from the road.

"So, as far as you are aware, there was no relationship between Lee and Laura Vernon, apart from the fact that she was the daughter of his employer?"

"I told you, he didn't like her."

"He actually said so?"

"Yes. Yes, I'm sure he did. Stuck-up little madam, he called her, something like that."

"Why did he call her that? Did he give any particular reason?"

Mrs. Sherratt screwed up her face, which Tailby took to be a sign that she was thinking. "It was not long after he had started working up there that he said it the first time. He'd had a bit of a run-in with her one day, I think."

"You *are* referring to Laura now, aren't you?"

"I said so, didn't I? She was at home from school one day. It must have been their holidays or something. I don't know. But he said she was out in the garden, weighing him up, asking him questions. Lee said he made a joke, and she took exception. Told him to keep his remarks to himself, sort of thing. He was a bit put out when he told me about it, and he never liked her after that."

"Was that anything to do with why he was sacked, do you think?"

"I couldn't say. Because she took against him, you mean, and told her dad? I don't know. But he hadn't done anything wrong, I know that."

"You don't think Lee might have arranged to meet Laura after he had been sacked by Mr. Vernon?"

"No, I don't. He'd be glad to get away from her, if anything. He wouldn't have touched her, not in any way."

"Mrs. Sherratt, where does Lee usually go when he's off wandering for a day or two?"

"I don't know," she said. "He doesn't tell me."

"Not to his girlfriend?"

"I doubt it. But you can ask her, can't you? I gave the other lot her name and address, to be helpful."

"Yes, I know," Tailby sighed. They had already interviewed the girl-friend in question, along with several others whose names had been suggested by Lee Sherratt's drinking pals. If he really was intending to get married, it hadn't stopped him spreading himself around half the female population of the valley. But none of them admitted to knowing where Lee headed for when he went wandering. Here at Wye Close, officers had also already searched the house, turned over Lee's room, and checked out that garden shed.

"Besides," said Mrs. Sherratt, as if suddenly remembering something. "That girl at the Mount. She was only fifteen, wasn't she?"

"Yes, Mrs. Sherratt, she was."

"Well then."

Leaving the house, Tailby crossed the street to the Vauxhall again.

"Give it a few minutes, then check that garden shed 'round the back again," he said, "but don't make a fuss about it. You never know, the saintly Lee might just have appeared by some miracle."

Helen Milner found her grandfather sitting on a boulder on the path leading up toward Raven's Side. A small cloud of pipe smoke marked his position. His knees were spread, and his back was as straight as if he had been sitting on one of the old upright chairs at the cottage. At his feet was Jess, chewing at a stick. The dog had stripped the bark to shreds and was splintering the soft inner flesh of the wood with her teeth, dropping the fragments on the ground like a scattering of confetti. Jess looked up cautiously as Helen approached, gave her a soulful look, and went back to her stick. Her teeth gleamed white and sharp as they ripped into the wood.

This was not Harry's usual route for his morning walk. But below the ridge the reason for the change in routine was obvious. A white caravan sat in the corner of a field, where it had been dragged by a Land Rover. It was the furthest spot the caravan could reach before the woods began and the ground grew steep and rocky as it plunged toward the valley bottom. Three more four-wheel-drive vehicles were parked behind it. Farther down the slope, figures in white boilersuits and hoods were moving slowly around in the undergrowth, which had been cut down and removed in a wide circle. Other men and women could be glimpsed in the trees on either side. Some were on all fours, as if they were praying to some strange god for guidance in their bizarre task. Blue plastic tape had been wound around the trees, and it danced and flickered in the sun, signaling the spot where Laura Vernon's body had lain.

"If the ground wasn't so dry, they'd never have got that caravan to that spot," said Harry as his granddaughter crouched down beside him.

"What do they use it for?"

"Making a brew and having their snap in, as far as I can tell."

Helen could see a constable in shirtsleeves standing by the field gate between the caravan and the woods. His face was turned up to the hill, and now and then he put a hand up to shade his eyes as he squinted into the sun. He was watching Harry.

"They know you're here," said Helen.

"And they don't like it either, but there's bugger all they can do about it. It's a public footpath, and I'm not anywhere near their precious tape."

"Have they said anything?"

"Oh aye, they sent some bugger up to talk to me half an hour ago. He wanted to know who I was and what I was doing here. Then he took my name and wrote it down in a little book. He knew who I was then, all right. I thought he was going to ask for my autograph. I've never been so famous. You'd think I was somebody off telly."

"Did the policeman ask you to move?"

"He did."

"And what did you say?"

A gleam of amusement came to Harry's eyes. Helen sighed.

"Oh, Granddad. You shouldn't. It doesn't do to upset them."

"Bugger that. Somebody has to keep them on their toes."

Looking at her grandfather, Helen wondered whether she had been right to come. She had been into school for a preterm staff meeting, but had been given permission by her head to leave early. She had made use of the time to make a mad rush across the countryside to check on her grandparents. She had found Gwen subdued but calm, and Harry missing. Now she had tracked him down, he did not seem like the Harry she knew. Even more than on the previous day, he gave the impression that in some way he was enjoying himself. But she knew her grandfather was not a cruel or callous man. He would not revel in the death of a young girl. But somehow he saw the event as a challenge of his own he had to face. Perhaps it would have been better if she hadn't come at all. She did not want to end up in an argument with him.

"Have you seen the newspapers?" asked Harry.

"Some of them."

"A lot of rubbish they print," he complained. "Two of them have spelled my name wrong."

"I suppose there'll be more in the local papers."

"They're not out until later in the week. It might be over by then."

"Do you think so, Granddad?"

Harry had his pipe in his mouth, his jaw clamped into a habitual grimace. Helen couldn't read his expression at all. She wondered what had happened to the rapport she had always had with him, the sense of knowing what he was thinking without his having to say it out loud. Her understanding of him seemed to have died. It was dead since yesterday.

"Maybe it will," he said. He puffed at his pipe as if giving the question some thought. "If the coppers pull their fingers out. Or even if they don't. Maybe it will be over all the same."

"It says in the paper they're trying to trace the Sherratt boy."

He snorted. "Much good that youth will do them."

"He's disappeared. I suppose it looks suspicious."

"He was never going to last long at the Mount," said Harry. "Not him. I can't think what made them take him on."

"According to Dad, Graham Vernon said he wanted to give him a chance."

"Oh aye, him," said Harry. "He'd give anything a chance. He'd give the devil a chance to sing in the chapel choir."

"It looks as though he might have been wrong this time."

Harry took his pipe from his mouth and tapped it against the boulder.

"I tell you what, lass. He was wrong, all right. He's been wrong all his life."

"I know you don't like him . . ."

"Like him! If it were left to me—"

"I know, I know. Don't let's go over it all again, please."

"Well. You're right. It doesn't need saying over again."

The silence stretched into minutes. Helen had never felt uncomfortable with silence between them before. Now, though, it was different. She had no idea what Harry was thinking. She moved her shoulders, easing her bra straps where her skin was tender from spending too long in the sun the day before.

"I think I'll walk Jess on a bit farther," said Harry. "It'll give that lad's eyes a rest."

"Granddad. Don't get into trouble, will you?"

He pulled himself upright, regarding her with dignity. "Me? Don't you know me, lass? I'm a match for any of that lot."

She watched him tug at Jess's lead, flexing his stiff legs and straightening his jacket. The toe caps of his boots gleamed so brightly they were dazzling. For a moment, Helen caught a glimpse of herself, distorted and blackened, turned upside down on the toes of her grandfather's boots. She had never known anyone else with such innate dignity and self-control. If occasionally he said things that shocked people, it was only because he believed it was right that you should say what you thought and because he didn't really care what people thought of him. His pride in himself made her feel proud of him, too, and she felt her eyes fill as he moved slowly away.

"I'll see you later, then," she said.

"No doubt."

After a last glance at the police activity down the hill, Helen walked back to Dial Cottage to see her grandmother. She was surprised to find her father standing in the hall, hovering between the doorways to the front and back rooms as if he had forgotten where he wanted to be. He was dressed for the office, in a dark suit with a gray pinstripe, a white shirt, and a tie in red-and-gray diagonal stripes.

"Dad?"

"Hello, love. I was in the area and just called in to see how Gwen and

Harry were managing after yesterday. We've got to look after them when they've had such a shock, haven't we?"

"That's right. It *was* a shock," said Gwen. She was in her chair in the back room, toying with a piece of knitting. It was shaping up into a long-sleeved cardigan made from bright pink wool, and Helen had a horrible feeling she knew whom it was intended for. But at the moment, her grandmother's fingers were moving the needles without making any impression on the wool, as if she had to be doing something with her hands.

"Granddad's out there with Jess, watching the police."

"He's better off out there," Gwen said. "At least he's not under my feet."

"What are the police doing? Have they been here again? Have they been . . . digging or anything?"

"Digging?" Helen looked at her father in astonishment, wondering why he didn't come farther into the room. There was a sheen of sweat on his forehead, and she smiled at his old-fashioned reluctance to go without his suit jacket even in such heat. "Why should they be digging, Dad?"

"I don't know. That's the sort of thing they do, isn't it? Digging people's gardens up and all that."

"Looking for what?"

"I've no idea."

Gwen's mouth had fallen open. "They'd better not try to dig my garden up. It's taken years to get it like it is."

"Don't worry, Grandma, they won't do that."

"Of course not," said Andrew. "I don't know why I said that. I just wondered what they were doing out there, that's all."

Helen realized he was hovering in the doorway so that he could keep an eye on the view of the street through the front window, as if there was something going on out there that he didn't want to miss. He was fidgety and nervous, and she remembered that Laura Vernon's death would be having an impact at the office, too.

"I don't suppose Graham Vernon has been into work today, Dad?"

"No, no. He phoned to say he would be at home for a few days to look after Charlotte. And to help the police, of course. He said we could contact him there if we need him. But in the meantime I'm to carry on as normal. I've got to take over all his appointments and meetings."

Andrew looked at his watch as he said this, shooting back a white cuff containing one of a pair of gold cuff links that Helen had bought him. "I can't stop long," he said. "I've got to be back in Sheffield by twelve for a lunch."

"I'll have to be going soon, too, Grandma."

Gwen dropped her knitting and reached out for Helen's arm. "I daren't go out, Helen. Will you fetch me some bread and tea from the shop before you go?"

"Why daren't you go out, Grandma?"

"Why? Can't you imagine what people are saying about us? They're looking at me if I even go near the windows. That's why I closed the curtains."

"Take no notice, Grandma. People will soon forget."

Helen had noticed the extra activity in Moorhay. There were more walkers than usually passed through, even in summer. Many of them were not dressed for walking, but stopped and peered into the windows of the cottages they passed. The car park at the Drover was full, and there were cars parked along the roadside, their roofs shimmering with heat. There were even two cars in the lay-by where the Hulley's bus stopped twice a day. The bus driver would be annoyed when he came.

Andrew began to mop his brow with a white handkerchief as he cast another glance toward the front window. "So the police haven't been back then, eh, Gwen? That's good, isn't it?"

The old woman didn't look convinced as she fumbled for some money in an old purse. "I suppose so. And an extra pint of milk, Helen."

"I'll get off then, if you're all right, Gwen. Take care of yourselves, you and Harry, won't you? Bye, Helen."

Helen said good-bye and watched her father let himself out of the front door. She wondered, for a moment, where he had been passing from if he was on his way back to Sheffield.

Helen paused in the street after leaving Dial Cottage. She had recognized a figure farther up the road, emerging from one of the houses near the village hall. Ben Cooper was with the woman police officer who had come to the house with the more senior detectives to talk to Harry. She was carrying a clipboard and she looked serious and businesslike.

Helen hesitated, unsure whether she should speak to them, not knowing whether Ben would want to acknowledge her in front of his colleague.

"I cannot believe," Fry was saying, "the way some of the people in this village speak to you, Ben. What do they think you are? Jesus Christ?"

Cooper shrugged. He thought of his first taste of Moorhay hospitality the day before, when the man mowing the graveyard had glowered at him with suspicion, and the woman watering her flower beds had refused to speak to him. They hadn't known who he was then, hadn't even known he was a police officer. He had just been some casual stranger in sweaty clothes, running madly through the heat, his behavior unconventional, his intentions dubious. But that was not the picture of the place he would want to present to a genuine stranger, a real outsider, like Diane Fry. It was not how villages like Moorhay really were, at heart.

"They just know me, some of them. Or they've heard of me, at least. It makes a difference. There are some folk who don't like talking to outsiders much."

"I suppose you think if I was going 'round on my own they wouldn't even give me the time of day."

"Oh, they'd probably do that," said Cooper, "but it'd be the time in Papua New Guinea."

"Ha, ha."

"I'm only joking."

"Yes, I know. I could practically see you reading the script. But what gets me is that they all trot out your father's name, like some mantra. Sergeant Cooper this and Sergeant Cooper that. If you're Jesus Christ, who must he be?"

"Just an old-fashioned copper."

"You'd think he was a member of the family. They all look at you like a long-lost relative."

Fry saw Helen Milner first. Their eyes met, and Helen turned away, as if she had decided not to speak to them after all.

"And here's another one," said Fry quietly.

Cooper noticed Helen then. Fry glowered at him as he smiled toward her.

"Did you want to speak to us, Helen?"

"No, no, it's all right. Well, only . . . to say hello. How are you getting on? Are you any nearer catching the man you want?"

"We're just the troops on the ground, you know. We don't get to know the bigger picture in an inquiry until the big chiefs decide to tell us about it."

"Oh." Helen looked a bit disappointed.

"Of course, at this rate, it will be the other way 'round," said Fry. "We'll all be waiting like a lot of Dr. Watsons for Ben here to condescend to tell us the answers."

Helen frowned, puzzled by the tone of the comment. "Perhaps I'd better let you get on. I can see you're busy."

"No, wait," said Cooper. "How's Mr. Dickinson?"

She thought Ben looked different today—less formal, a bit more relaxed, now that they had renewed their acquaintance. Yesterday he had seemed to see her as a stranger, to be treated like any other member of the public. But perhaps *relaxed* wasn't the right word. He looked less tightly focused, more readily distracted. His hair was tousled in a way that reminded Helen powerfully of the younger Ben she had known so well. And Gwen was right—his eyes were deep brown. She had almost forgotten.

"Granddad's fine. A bit, well . . ."

"Yes? Is he upset? It's understandable."

"A bit quiet, that's all I was going to say."

"And your grandmother?"

"It's all a bit much for her to take in."

"She's taken it worse than your grandfather, I suppose. People of that generation—"

"Don't let Granddad hear you say that."

"Miss Milner, did you know Laura Vernon?" interrupted Fry.

"Oh, well, I did meet her once."

"When was that?"

"A couple of months ago. It was at a party that the Vernons gave. A Midsummer Party, they called it. Yes, it was in June."

"What do you know about Laura?"

"Oh, absolutely nothing. I don't really know her parents either."

"But you were invited to their party. How was that?"

"My father works for Graham Vernon. I suppose they invited me out of politeness."

"Oh, of course. But you met Laura at this party."

"Yes."

"What did you make of her?"

"Laura? She was a very pretty girl. Big, dark eyes. Very mature for her age."

Fry waited. "And?"

"I don't know what else to say really."

"Her looks don't tell us much about her personality, Miss Milner."

"As I say, I didn't really know her."

"But I'm sure you're a good observer. What do you do for a living?"

"I'm a teacher."

"Of course. So you're used to assessing children. What did you think of Laura Vernon?"

Helen lowered her eyes to avoid the policewoman's direct stare. "I suppose I thought she was rather too precocious. She was a bit brash, a bit pushy. Arrogant, even."

"Arrogant?"

"Well, she struck me as the sort of girl who had been told so often how clever and attractive she was that she had come to believe it and expected everyone to behave accordingly. We see the type in school sometimes. They can be very disruptive."

"Thank you. That's very helpful."

Cooper had his head cocked to one side, watching Helen as she answered Fry's questions. Helen thought he must see how disconcerted she was by the abrupt approach.

"Finished?" he asked Fry.

"Ready when you are."

"I might call in and see how your grandparents are for myself sometime," he told Helen.

"Grandma would be pleased," she said. "I think she took a liking to you. It would cheer her up. She remembers you, you know."

Fry was becoming impatient. "We've got some properties to call on yet, Ben. We'd better go."

"Sure."

"And your family, Ben," said Helen, as he turned away. "How are they?"

But it seemed to Helen that Ben Cooper must not have heard her question as he walked away toward his car. He didn't reply, didn't even look around, but gave a small gesture, a half-apologetic wave. It was Diane Fry, following him, who took the trouble to turn and look back.

Juliana Van Doon gazed down at the naked body and shook her head at the question.

"No rape. No genital abrasions, no semen traces, or any other bodily fluids. Sorry, Chief Inspector."

"No sexual intercourse, forced or otherwise?" said Tailby. He knew it sounded as though he was disappointed, but he didn't worry about what the pathologist might think of him. She was experienced enough to know it was only because such traces would have made his job a lot easier.

After the clothes had been removed, the body had been photographed and all external signs had been recorded. The clothes themselves had been set aside for forensic examination. Now Mrs. Van Doon was ready for the autopsy itself, the careful dismantling of the victim's body in search of minute scraps of information.

Stewart Tailby had attended too many postmortems over the years. The first ten or twelve had been a cause of humiliation, as his stomach had revolted at the smell of exposed intestines and the wet, sucking sound as organs were removed. His tendency to turn faint and leave the room to vomit had been a source of hilarity in his first CID posting. Though he had learned, like everyone else, to mask his feelings and control his stomach, he had never learned to accept in his heart the absolute necessity of the final horrors and indignities that were inflicted on a victim of violent crime. The fact that these gruesome acts were perpetrated in the name of forensic science—and ultimately, he supposed, in the name of justice—made no difference at all.

In the autopsy room, some police officers chose the pretense of graveside humor. That was not Tailby's style. He retreated instead behind a facade of silence and detachment, coated in a thin veneer of formal jargon and easily repeatable, meaningless phrases. In a way, he could be physically present, yet keep his feelings aloof from the things that had to be done. Tailby knew that he was already considered a cold and austere man by his colleagues and junior officers; some even said he was pompous and self-important. But it was a small price to pay to maintain your distance from realities that struck too close to home.

"That's not to say the victim was unfamiliar with sexual intercourse," said Mrs. Van Doon. "Not at all, not at all."

"No?"

"I would say the young lady was far from being a virgin, Chief Inspector. Fifteen years old? Very promiscuous, some of these young people now."

"You'd think that the risk of AIDS would make them think twice, wouldn't you?"

"This one won't be worrying about AIDS, in any case."

The pathologist was dressed in a green T-shirt and baggy green trousers, with her mask hanging around her neck ready for work. With her hair tied back and her face devoid of makeup and harshly lit by the mortuary lights, the pathologist still looked striking. It was all down to the bone structure, thought Tailby. That, and the thoughtful gray eyes. He had once, as a young detective, harbored secret dreams about Juliana Van Doon. But time had passed and the feelings had faded. He had married and been divorced since then. And his feelings had died completely.

Tailby would have liked to have been able to leave the postmortem room before the pathologist reached the stage of opening the body and removing the organs. Before she used the stainless steel saw to cut through the sternum, and before the electric trepanner sliced off the top of the girl's damaged skull. He told himself that there would be little to learn from the gory process in this case, except that Laura Vernon had died in perfect health.

"The bruise on her leg?" he said.

"Ah. Interesting, yes. Not unknown, I understand, in sexually motivated killings. You would be asking yourself why there is only this one sign of a possible sexual assault. Was the attacker interrupted? Yes, interesting."

"Not a bruise made by a blow, then. A hand gripping the leg? But I would expect two separate marks, at least."

"No, no, no," said Mrs. Van Doon. "You misunderstand. If you look more closely, you will see small punctures where the flesh is swollen. This is not an injury caused by the bruising of fingers. I suspect these are teeth marks, Chief Inspector."

Tailby perked up with sudden interest. "Someone bit her," he said. "Someone smashed her skull, then bit her on the thigh."

"Possibly," said the pathologist. "Interesting?"

The detective peered more closely at the mark. It looked no more than a bruise to him.

"Can you be sure?"

"Well, no. I need to obtain the opinion of a forensic odontologist, of course. I have already contacted the University Dental School in Sheffield. We can get photographs and impressions, and excise the area around the bite to preserve it. And then we can compare the impression with a suspect's dentition. It's up to you to produce the suspect, of course."

"It's an odd place for a bite."

"Yes. They are usually on the breasts in these cases, rather than on the thigh. In fact, I saw a report recently about a research project conducted by a forensic odontologist. It was entirely concerned with how bite marks differ according to the shape of the victim's breast, the cup size, the age of the victim, and even the amount of droop in the breast."

Tailby was intrigued. "How on earth did he manage all that?"

"Designed a mechanical set of teeth and recruited twenty female volunteers—goodness knows where from."

"Students, I suppose," said Tailby, reluctantly impressed.

"But I'm sure bites on the thigh are not unknown in sexual assaults either. In the absence of any samples for DNA analysis, Chief Inspector, this is probably the best you could have hoped for."

Tailby stared at the pathologist. "So, let's see. The attacker strikes her over the head two or three times. When she is on the ground he pulls down her jeans and her pants, then bites her once on the thigh." It didn't quite ring true somehow, though he knew there had been far more bizarre and ghoulish cases, far more perverted killers who committed much worse acts on the bodies of their victims.

"Ah, you would like to indulge in a little mutual speculation, Chief Inspector?" said the pathologist. "On that basis then, why not consider another scenario? A voluntary sexual act. The bite on the thigh is someone's idea of erotic foreplay."

"Possible. Then something goes wrong."

"The girl objects to the bite, perhaps."

"Yes, she pulls away, changes her mind. They argue; he gets angry."

"Sexually fuelled frustration. A powerful force."

"I can buy that," said Tailby. "There's no way of telling which of those it was from the nature of the bite, I suppose?"

"Mmm. A good odontologist may be able to reproduce the angle of the bite and the depth. He might suggest the position of the attacker's head at the moment the bite was inflicted."

Tailby looked again at the naked limbs of the fifteen-year-old girl. Her body was shockingly white except for the areas on her flank and the left side of her chest, where lividity had set in, the blood settling to the lowest point of gravity during the time she had lain dead in the bracken on the Baulk.

The bite mark was situated high on the inside of her right thigh, where the living flesh had been at its softest and most vulnerable. The picture suggested by Juliana Van Doon of the position of the attacker's head made Tailby feel more uneasy than anything else he had heard so far.

But the pathologist was fiddling with a table full of gleaming, sharp instruments, eager to get on with the next stage of the process of reducing Laura Vernon to her component parts. Tailby and his team had to do the same thing, in a way. That was the essence of victimology, the process of getting to know the intimate details of the victim as a means of establishing the connection to her killer.

"If your scenario is correct," he said, "Laura's attacker will be much easier for us to find—he must have been known to her."

"Presumably, Chief Inspector. Yes, it's preferable to a random attack by someone from outside the area, isn't it?"

"From our point of view, certainly."

"I hope that I am able to help you, then."

In the clinical atmosphere of the mortuary, Tailby felt able to voice the fear that he would never talk about much, even to his own staff. "That's what I'm always afraid of, you know—a case that drags on for months, unsolved, because we can't even get a lead on a suspect. It's a detective's nightmare."

"You have in mind, of course, a recent case."

"The girl in Buxton, yes. There are similarities, aren't there? B Division's inquiry has been unsuccessful so far, after more than a month. The view is that the victim was chosen at random by her attacker. In those circumstances, it was only ever a matter of time before we had a second victim."

"It would be a tragic thing," said Mrs. Van Doon, flourishing a scalpel over the chest of the corpse, "if the poor girl here were simply to be known as Victim Number Two."

"It would be even more tragic," said Tailby, "if we ended up with a Victim Number Three."

-10-

"OK, what have we got—anything?"

"Cars, lots of cars. Most of them unknown. You have to expect it in an area like this."

"Tourists," said DI Hitchens. "They always complicate the issue."

They were in the tiny beer garden at the back of the Drover, squashed around a table under a parasol that kept the sun off their plates of ham and cheese sandwiches and their slimline tonics. The only other customers outdoors were two workmen eating scampi and chips and drinking beer at a far table. Everyone else had chosen to sit inside the pub, in the cool rooms, or at the front, where there was a view of the road.

Cooper and Fry had met up with four sweating PCs who had been working their way down the village, and they were all now clinking ice cubes desperately as they exchanged the pitifully thin information from their clipboards. DI Hitchens had arrived late, brazenly downing a whiskey and stealing their sandwiches. He looked like the squire visiting his workers, trying to appear interested in what they had to say but ready to move on to more important calls on his time at any moment. He pulled up a chair next to Fry, cool as only a man could be who had just got out of an air-conditioned Ford.

"I've got plenty of hikers," said Ben Cooper, "mostly ones and twos. But there was a bigger group through 'round about the right time. They were seen on the Eden Valley Trail early Saturday evening."

"God, how will we trace them?" asked Hitchens.

"They were young people. They may have been heading for the sleeping barn at Hathersage or one of the youth hostels."

"OK, we'll check them out. There's going to be an appeal in the papers and on the telly in the morning. We'll try and get the hikers mentioned specifically. And the—what was it—Eden Valley Trail?"

"It's a popular footpath. It runs just under the slope where Laura Vernon was found. You can see the path quite clearly from there."

"OK, thanks, Ben. At least we're in with a chance of finding a witness or two. Anything else?"

"Only a lot of talk," said Cooper.

"You're lucky," said one of the PCs, an aggressive-looking bald-headed man whose name was Parkin. "Most of them just wanted me off the doorstep."

"Well, I can understand that," said PC Wragg. "They've probably heard your jokes."

Wragg was the officer who had accompanied Cooper to Dial Cottage when Helen Milner had first rung in to report her grandfather's find. He didn't look any fitter now than he had the day before, and he was drinking orange juice as if he had a lot of fluid to replace. Like the other uniformed officers, he had loosened his clothing as much as he could, but he was handicapped by the entire ironmonger's shop of equipment he wore around his belt—Kwik-cuffs, side-handle baton, CS spray, and God knew what else was considered necessary for the job of calling on members of the public in a quiet Peak District village.

"I've got a new one," said Parkin. "There's this prostitute—"

There were general groans. They had all heard Parkin's awful jokes before.

"Not now, Parkin," said Hitchens.

Fry was leafing through her notebook. "I got one woman. Mrs. Davis, Chestnut Lodge. She says she's met Laura Vernon several times. Apparently Mrs. Davis's daughter goes to the same stables as Laura did, and they got quite friendly. She describes Laura as a very nice girl."

"What does that mean exactly? *Nice.*"

"The way she spoke about some of the other children she came across, I think it means that she approved of Laura's background, sir."

"Mmm. Did you get her to expand on that?"

"As far as I could. She said Laura was polite and knew how to behave. She said she was very good with the younger children, helping to show them what to do when they were learning to ride. Mrs. Davis told me a story about Laura looking after a boy who had fallen off his horse. Apparently, she was the only one he would let comfort him when he had hurt himself. Mrs. Davis said Laura's mother was a nice woman, too."

Somebody snorted. DI Hitchens didn't look impressed. "It doesn't mean much."

"But they all seem to know of the Vernons, these people," said Fry, "every one of them."

"Yes, and not too charmed by them either, on the whole," said Wragg.

"It's that sort of village, though."

"What do you mean, Diane?" asked Hitchens.

"They're close, this lot. They don't like newcomers, people who don't fit in. I mean, they're not exactly welcoming, are they?"

"I don't agree," said Cooper.

"Well, you wouldn't."

"It depends on how you approach them, that's all. If you come to a village like this, willing to fit in, they'll accept you. But if you stay aloof, make it look as though you think you're better than they are, then they're bound to react against you."

"And the Vernons are like that, aloof, you reckon, Ben?"

"Sure of it, sir."

"Hey, what about some sort of conspiracy against the Vernons? Local vigilantes, like, who get together and knock off Laura Vernon as a warning? Clear off out of our village—we don't want you. That sort of thing."

"Don't talk rubbish, Parkin."

"That sounds like something out of the Dark Ages," said Fry.

"Or *The X-Files,*" suggested Wragg.

"All right, all right."

"Any positive reactions to the trainer?" asked Hitchens.

"Nothing."

"Some of the old biddies don't even know what a trainer is."

"That other trainer has to be somewhere."

"Sir, if it's chummy from Buxton, the one B Division are after, then he'll probably have taken it home with him as a memento, like they reckon he did with the tights off the other one."

"Yes, that's possible, Wragg. But Mr. Tailby doesn't believe we can assume the two cases are linked at this stage."

"But that means we have to do everything from scratch, when they might turn out to be the same bloke after all."

"Have we turned up anything on the known offenders, sir?" asked Cooper.

"Not yet. It's early days. DI Armstrong is on to it."

"Well, she's wasting her time anyway."

"Thanks for the benefit of your views, Parkin."

Cooper saw that PC Parkin was watching Diane Fry carefully for her reactions. Fry only needed to make one ill-considered comment, let slip one unguarded reaction, and a report on her behavior would be circulating around the division very quickly. A reputation among your colleagues could be made or broken on first impressions.

Sometimes, he knew, the worst thing of all was to inadvertently earn yourself some childish nickname, which you could then never live down, no matter how hard you tried.

"We were lucky that the body was found so quickly really," said Hitchens. "It's given us a head start. Sometimes we're not so lucky. The old bloke with the dog did us a big favor."

"Have you been involved in any other inquiries like this, sir?" asked Fry.

Hitchens told them about a murder inquiry in the late 1980s, when a teenage boy had gone missing from his foster home in Eyam. They had set up an incident room right in the center of the village, linked to Divisional HQ. Over a period of months they had gradually spread the search over an area within a five-mile radius of Eyam. They had used the Mountain Rescue Team, Search Dog Teams, Cave Rescue Teams, the Peak Park Ranger Service, Derbyshire Countryside Rangers, even members of ramblers clubs and scores of other volunteers. They had put up search and rescue helicopters over the hills. But they had never found the boy.

"A man walking his dog in just the right place would have been a godsend then," he said.

"And there was that one in 1966, do you remember?" said Parkin, turning to Diane Fry.

"I wasn't even around in 1966," said Fry, "thanks very much."

"Eh? Well, it's only, what . . ."

"Thirty-three years ago."

"So it was. Well, it's in the history books anyway."

"Not into sport, Diane?" said Cooper.

"Yes, but playing it, not the armchair kind. Nineteen sixty-six? Let me guess—you're talking about football. The World Cup? That'd be the only thing you know about, I suppose."

"Yeah," said Parkin. "They had the trophy nicked, did you know that? The World Cup itself, the Jules Rimet Trophy. Before the finals."

"Did somebody leave it in their car or what?"

"And you won't believe this—but it was found by a dog. Chucked in a hedge bottom, it was. Wrapped in fish-and-chip paper."

"The dog?"

"The trophy. It was wrapped in fish-and-chip paper."

"Pickles," said Cooper.

"No, it was definitely fish and chips."

"The dog was called Pickles. It got introduced to all the players before the final."

"Surely *you* don't remember it?" said Fry.

"No, but like Parkin says . . ."

"It's in the history books, right. Well, I must be reading the wrong history books. All that stuff passed me by. I suppose I must have overlooked it somewhere between the assassination of President Kennedy and the end of the Vietnam War."

"Well, probably," said Parkin, and sneered.

Cooper winced. "I think I'll just pop to the gents before we leave."

It was a relief to get inside the Drover and out of the heat. The landlord, Kenny Lee, nodded to Cooper from the bar as he slipped into the toilets. The sudden solitude and the smell of urine did nothing to help Cooper keep his mind off the previous night. It had been a very long night, as the farmhouse had filled with members of the family—his brother first, then his sister and her husband arriving from Buxton, and then his uncle and his cousins, all pitching in to help clear up the mess, to support Kate and look after the children, Amy and Josie. Meanwhile, the doctor had called to sedate his mother, and later the ambulance had arrived to take her to Edendale General, where it would not be her first visit to the psychiatric unit. And then the endless discussion had begun—a discussion that had gone on until the early hours of the morning, by which time they were all exhausted and no nearer to an answer to an insoluble problem.

There was a pay phone in the passage near the bar, and Cooper fished in his pocket for a few coins. He was put through to the psychiatric unit at the hospital, where the staff were professionally cautious. All his call established was what he already knew—that his mother was still under sedation and not fit to have visitors. Try again tomorrow, they said.

In the meantime, tonight there might finally be a family decision. And he knew that there was a chance his mother would have to be taken away permanently from the home she had known all her life. It would be the final humiliation in her descent into schizophrenia.

When he came out of the pub and walked back out into the beer garden, something made Cooper stop and stand still in the shade of the side wall. He was standing several yards behind Diane Fry, and he saw what he might not have seen from his seat across the table. He saw DI Hitchens's arm on the back of Fry's chair as he leaned close toward her to speak directly into her ear. He saw the DI's hand move upward from the chair to rest for a moment on her shoulder. Behaving like a courting couple, as his mother would have said.

And then he saw Fry nod briefly before Hitchens took his hand away. And Parkin told another poor joke that nobody laughed at.

The phone was ringing again. It had hardly stopped ringing for days. Though the answering machine had been left on and she had been told to take no notice of it, the continual noise was driving Sheila Kelk mad.

Sheila came to the Mount three days a week to clean, and Tuesday was one of her days. The fuss about the girl being found murdered had not put her off coming—far from it, in fact. Mr. and Mrs. Vernon would need her, she had told her husband. A house still needed cleaning. She might be able to provide some other service to poor Mrs. Vernon, to be of some comfort to her. Mrs. Vernon might, just might, want to confide in her, to tell her all about what had been going on.

But here she was, going over the sitting room carpet for the second time, wishing the sound of the Dyson would drown out the constant ringing. She had been here longer than her four hours already, and no one had so much as spoken to her.

In a temporary silence from the phone, Sheila switched off the vacuum cleaner, flicking a cloth over a piece of pine furniture that she had never quite been able to put a name to. She thought of it as a cross between a sideboard and a writing desk.

While she polished, she listened for the noises from upstairs. From Mrs. Vernon's bedroom, of course, there was still no sound. But the heavy footsteps were still moving directly overhead, where Sheila knew Laura's room lay. Mr. Vernon was still up there with the policemen. He had not been in a good mood; he had been angry, in fact. Understandable, of course. But being rude and refusing even to speak to her was going too far, Sheila thought.

The phone began to ring again. Four rings before the answering machine cut in. She couldn't understand why the Vernons were getting so many phone calls. Back home at Wye Close, the phone often didn't ring from one week to the next, and then it would only be some girl she didn't know, who would try to sell her double glazing.

Sheila Kelk was so absorbed in listening to the movements above, that she didn't notice someone had come into the room behind her until she heard the voice.

"Working overtime, Mrs. Kelk?"

She jumped, her hand going to her mouth as she turned, then she relaxed as quickly.

"Oh—it's you."

"Yes, it's me," said the young man. His jeans were grubby, and when he walked across the carpet toward the far door, his shoes left imprints on the pile. Sheila wanted to complain but knew it would make no impression on Daniel Vernon. He was dark and fleshy, like his father, but sullen and quick-tempered where Graham Vernon was polite and sometimes charming, on the outside at least. Daniel was wearing a white T-shirt with the name of some rock group on it that Sheila Kelk had never heard of. The armpits and a patch on his back were soaked with sweat. She guessed that Daniel had probably walked from the main road after hitching his way from Devon.

"Where's my mother?" he asked.

"Taken to her bed and won't get up," said Sheila.

"And I suppose these apes tramping about the house are policemen."

"They're looking at Laura's room."

"What for, for God's sake? What do they think they'll find there?"

"They don't tell *me*, I'm sure," said Sheila.

When the phone went again, Daniel automatically walked over and picked it up on the second ring.

"No, this is Daniel Vernon. Who am I speaking to?" He listened impatiently for a moment. "Your name means nothing to me, but I take it you're some sort of associate of my father's? Yes? Then, in that case, you can fuck off."

Daniel slammed the phone back down and glared at Sheila.

"Oh, I don't think your father would like you to do that," she said, shocked.

He walked toward her angrily, and she backed away from him, dragging the vacuum cleaner with her so that it remained in between them, like a lion tamer's chair.

"My father, Mrs. Kelk," said Daniel, his face contorted into a snarl, "my father can fuck off as well."

Tailby was watching Graham Vernon carefully, not asking too many questions, content to let the silence prompt the other man to talk.

"We're a very close family," said Vernon. "We've stayed very close to our children. In other families, they start to drift away when they reach their teens, don't they?"

Tailby nodded, as one father to another, understanding the way it was with teenagers. In his own case, though, they had done more than drift—they had positively stampeded.

"Charlotte and I, we have . . . we had a good relationship with Laura. We took an interest in what she was doing at school, in who her friends were, in how she was progressing with her music and her riding. And she took an interest in what we were doing. Not many families can say they have that sort of relationship, can they? Laura used to ask me how business was. She would ask me about some of the people she had met. Business contacts, you know. She was so intelligent. She knew who was important without me telling her. Amazing."

"She met your business contacts here?" asked Tailby. "They visit you at home?"

"Oh yes. I think entertaining is important. We both do, Charlotte and I. You have to treat your clients right. It's a question of mixing business with pleasure, if you like. A nice house, a good meal, a decent bottle of wine or two. A normal, happy family around. It makes a good impression on clients, I can tell you. It's the key to long-term success."

"Of course." Tailby wondered where a happy family came in the list of requirements. Somewhere between the Bordeaux and the beef Wellington?

"And your son, Mr. Vernon?"

"Daniel? What about him?"

"Is he part of this . . . I mean, does he meet your clients when they visit?"

"Well, he has done, on occasion." Vernon got up from the chair and poured himself another whiskey. He didn't offer the policeman one, having already been refused once.

Tailby had noted that there was a drinks cabinet in Vernon's study as well as in the sitting room, and no doubt another in the dining room. Not that Vernon himself called this room his study. It was an office, and it looked like one—with a personal computer and laser printer, a fax machine, a phone, and a bookcase full of presentation folders in tasteful dark blue with gold block lettering. From the high sash windows there was an excellent view of the garden, right down to the avenue of conifers and the rocky summit of Win Low in the distance.

"He's at university, Chief Inspector. Exeter. Studying politics. Not my idea of a subject, but there we are. He's a bright boy, and he'll make a success of something one day, I suppose."

"He was close to Laura?"

"Oh, very close. They doted on each other."

"He'll be extremely upset, then, by what's happened."

"He was dreadfully cut up when we told him. He'll take it very hard indeed."

Tailby considered this. He wondered if the son would put on a better show of being cut up than the father was doing. Shock and grief took people so many different ways, of course. And Graham Vernon had already had two days in which to go through the range of emotions expected of a man whose fifteen-year-old daughter had gone missing and had then been found, battered to death. There had been emotions, certainly. Anger most of all— but directed almost obsessively in one direction, toward the boy called Lee Sherratt, who had, it was claimed, lusted after young Laura. The intelligent, innocent, extremely attractive Laura. But if there had been genuine grief in Graham Vernon's heart, then Tailby had missed it.

"It's a little early to be back at university, isn't it?" he said. "Surely August is still the summer holidays for these students?"

"Of course." Suddenly, Vernon looked as though he might be losing patience. "But there are always things to do before the term starts proper. Summer schools, revision, settling into new digs."

Tailby nodded. "Tell me again about Lee Sherratt."

"Again? Surely you know enough about him already? I don't think there's any more I can tell you that will help you to find him, if you haven't managed it already."

"We're looking as hard as we can, sir. I'm hopeful we'll locate the boy soon. But I'd just like to get the alleged circumstances clear in my mind."

"The *alleged* circumstances?" Vernon looked a little red in the face.

"His relationship with Laura."

Vernon sighed. "He's a young man, isn't he? Twenty years old. You know what young men are like. Laura was a very attractive girl. Very attractive.

You could see by the way he looked at her what he was thinking. I had to get rid of him in the end. It never occurred to me when I took him on—I blame myself for that."

"So he looked at Laura," said Tailby. "Anything else?"

"Well . . . he took any excuse to strip off his shirt when he worked in the garden. Whenever he knew she was watching him. I thought of telling him not to, but it would only have drawn attention to the fact."

"It's not what I'd call a relationship," said Tailby.

"It was obvious that he wanted to go further. I don't need telling about young men like Sherratt, Chief Inspector. I had to nip it in the bud. I couldn't have him pestering my daughter."

"Did she say he was pestering her? Did she complain?"

"Well, in a way."

"Mmm. Yet from what you say, it sounds as though Laura was equally interested in the young man."

"For God's sake, she was only fifteen. That age is . . . difficult. They're easily influenced, in the full flush of adolescent hormones. Surely you understand that."

It was obvious to them both that Vernon was floundering.

"So you sacked him."

"Yes. Last week. I told him we didn't need him anymore. He wasn't very pleased, I can tell you."

"You tend to deal with these things yourself, do you, sir? Rather than your wife."

"What do you mean?"

"Well, you're away all day on business. Sometimes you work long hours, no doubt. You arrive home late in the evenings. But your wife is at home most of the time, I gather. She would have had more contact with a gardener. Yet you would do something like that yourself, rather than letting your wife do it."

"Yes."

"I just thought, it might have been difficult to find the opportunity to speak to Sherratt, if you weren't at home during the day."

"I made a point of it on this occasion, Chief Inspector."

"I would also have thought it might be difficult for you to get the chance to observe the boy."

"Observe him? You're losing me."

"I'm going on your description just now. You described him looking at your daughter and showing off to her while she watched. That suggests to me, sir, that you must have spent some time observing him. Perhaps I should say, observing them both."

Vernon was pacing toward the windows with his whiskey. His hand was moving again now, touching his lips as if he feared his mouth might react of its own accord. "I don't know what you're getting at. It's quite natural. Are those men of yours finished up there yet?"

"Shall we see, sir?" suggested Tailby.

Sheila Kelk's gaze passed over Daniel's shoulder to the doorway from the main hall. The tall policeman stood there, smiling politely, raising a slightly quizzical eyebrow. She wasn't sure how long he had been standing there.

Daniel turned and stared at him. "And who exactly are you?"

"Detective Chief Inspector Tailby, Edendale CID. Here with Mr. Vernon's permission, of course."

"Oh, sure."

There were more footsteps in the hall behind Tailby.

"Daniel?" Graham Vernon looked tired rather than impatient now, the conflicting pressures starting to wear him down. He looked from Tailby to his son. "We didn't expect you quite so soon."

"Mr. Daniel Vernon, is it? I'd like to have a chat with you sometime, sir, when it's convenient."

Sheila looked at Daniel and received a glare so venomous that her mouth shut suddenly, and she began to drag the Dyson toward the dining room, away from the scene of confrontation.

"Of course, Chief Inspector." The young man walked toward the policeman, staring up at him with an expression of undisguised fury. "I'm absolutely dying to tell you a few things you may not know about my parents."

-11-

"Where to next, then?" said Cooper.

"What's up with you? Eaten too much cheese at lunch?"

"I'm fine. Where to next?"

"Thorpe Farm," said Fry, consulting the map.

"That's one of the smallholdings. There's another one at the end of the same lane. Bents Farm. We'd better make sure we don't miss it out."

Cooper had to wait while two women on horseback passed them, the horses walking slowly and elegantly, their muscled hindquarters shining with good health. The riders nodded a greeting and looked down into the car to study them, as if motorists were unusual in Moorhay. Someone appeared at the door of the bar at the Drover, wedged it open, and propped a blackboard outside. From the tiny shop and post office came the sound of laughter.

Across the road, a workman was playing a transistor radio as he repointed the wall of a cottage. An old lady emerged from the open doorway to speak to him on his ladder, probably asking him if he wanted a cup of tea. She saw the Toyota and said something else to the workman, who turned around to look. Cooper had already visited the old lady, who had seemed to know more about everyone in the village than was good for her. But she had known nothing about Laura Vernon. Nothing at all.

It seemed to Cooper that there was more life about the village of Moorhay today than ever before when he had been there previously. It was as if the murder of Laura Vernon had given it a new vitality, had brought its inhabitants together in the face of adversity. Or maybe it had just given them something to talk about.

He turned the Toyota confidently into a rutted lane overshadowed by trees, with a tall strip of grass growing up the middle that brushed along the underside of the car. The trees were mostly beech, with some huge horse chestnuts creating a dense canopy overhead. In the autumn, the children of the village would be drawn to this track with their sticks and stones to knock down the conkers.

"Who lives out here, then?" said Fry. "I suppose it's your auntie Alice or something, is it? It's bound to be someone who greets you like the prodigal son. Some second cousin or other. Have your mother and father got big families? Inbreeding affects the brain, you know."

"I don't know these places," said Cooper.

Within a few yards of leaving the road the track took a turn, and they were reduced to a crawl to protect the suspension. Already they might as well have been miles from the village. The trees completely cut off their view of houses that were only a couple of hundred yards away. It was a very old patch of woodland they were driving through, and Cooper could see it was not managed, as a woodland should be, to remain healthy. Many dead branches and boughs brought down by winter gales lay rotting among the remaining beeches. They were covered in lichen and clumps of white fungi, and the bracken and ferns were chest high. Parts of the stone wall in front of the wood had collapsed, and a makeshift post and wire fence used to block the gaps had long since given up the battle. A handsome cock pheasant walking along the edge of the wood paused with one foot in the air, its claws frozen in surprise. The greens, reds, and golds of its plumage were vibrant and iridescent, and for a moment Cooper wanted to stop the car and reach out for the bird. But it suddenly burst into a run and dodged and weaved its way back into the dense undergrowth, its tail extended straight out behind it.

The pheasant had started a train of thought for Cooper about poachers, and he turned toward Fry to mention it. But he realized that she hadn't even noticed the bird.

"There are no signs," she complained, frowning out of the window, as if the AA had failed her.

"There don't need to be," said Cooper. "Everyone in Moorhay will know that Thorpe and Bents Farms are this way." And though the thought inspired by the bird stayed with him, he decided to keep it to himself for a while.

Soon the trees gave way to a view up the slope of the hill. The land here was largely rough grass. It was divided by stone walls, then divided again by strands of electrified fencing. A hundred yards up the slope was a jumble of makeshift buildings—wooden hen huts and sheds, a row of breeze-block pigsties. Two old railway carriages stood rotting in the corner of one paddock, and an ex-Army Nissen hut with an arched corrugated iron roof stretched the full width of one field.

A rich smell drifted through the open windows of the car—mud and soiled straw and the odors of animals of all kinds. Somewhere there was certainly a fully operating dung heap. There seemed to be poultry everywhere—in the fields, on the track, perched on the roofs of the buildings. There were red hens and speckled gray hens, a variety of ducks, and a dozen large white geese that immediately waddled toward the car, honking an aggressive warning at the intruders. Their noise started dogs barking somewhere in the midst of the shantytown, and a goat could be heard bleating from one of the sheds as Cooper drove up to a gate across the track.

He waited for Fry to get out and open the gate. This was, after all, the usual practice for the passenger on a gated road. But he saw she needed coaching.

"Would you open the gate for me?" he said.

"Are those things safe?"

"What, the geese? You just have to show them you're not frightened of them."

"Thanks a lot."

Fry struggled with the wooden gate that was tied to its post with a length of baling twine and at the other end hung on only by its top hinge. But at last the car was through.

"Are you sure anybody actually lives up here?" said Fry. "Where's the farmhouse?"

"Well, though they're called farms, these places, they're really just bits left over from the days of the old cottagers, when everyone had their own plot of land, with a cow and a pig. They're the bits that the bigger farms haven't swallowed up yet and the developers haven't got 'round to buying up for housing. There'll be a cottage somewhere. They'll know we're here, with all this noise."

Cooper pulled up against the back wall of the Nissen hut. There was a rickety garage next to it, where a white Japanese pickup truck was parked with a metal grille across the back. Enormous clumps of brambles grew over a wall which ran up to a range of low stone buildings that seemed to be growing out of the hillside.

"Do you want to take this one?" he said. "I'll drive on up to Bents Farm and pick you up again on the way back down."

"Fine."

Fry got out and hesitated, looking at the threatening geese.

"Take no notice. Remember, you're not frightened of them," said Cooper as the Toyota bumped away.

Fry took a deep breath and began to walk up the slope toward the cluster of buildings. The geese immediately fell into formation behind her, hissing and honking and darting at her ankles with their long beaks. One of them pulled itself up to its full height and beat its wings angrily.

Fry fixed her gaze on the buildings ahead. They looked neglected and badly in need of repair. There were slates missing from the roofs, and a gable wall of one of the outbuildings had bulged and slipped into an unnatural shape like something out of a Salvador Dalí painting.

After a few steps, she realized she was walking on an uneven flagged path, the stone flags almost invisible under creeping dandelions and thistles. A trickle of water ran onto the path from a broken drainage pipe protruding from a stone wall. Where the water gathered on the dusty ground, it was stained red, as if it had run through rusted iron.

Fry cursed out loud as she tripped over the edge of a sunken flag. Behind her trooped the geese, still honking in outrage at being ignored. They made a strange procession as they approached the buildings.

"Not exactly on undercover operations, then?" said a voice.

An old man was leaning on a fork on the other side of the wall. He was standing in a paddock that had been converted into a large vegetable patch. His red-checked work shirt was open at his chest to reveal wiry gray hairs, and his sleeves were rolled up over plump arms. Ancient trousers that had once been brown were barely held together at the waist and sagged alarmingly over his crotch. They were pushed awkwardly into black Wellingtons. His face was red, and there were irregular bald patches on his scalp that were turning dangerously pink.

In the corner of the paddock was a small lean-to building like an old outside privy, with an adjoining fuel store converted to a toolshed. On a wooden chair in front of the door sat a second old man. He had a stick propped in front of him, wedged between his knees, with its end dug into a patch of earth. His cuffs were rolled back over his long, thin wrists, and he had a sharp knife in one hand, with which he was trimming cabbages.

"Do you gentlemen live here?" asked Fry.

"Gentlemen, is it?" said the man with the fork. "Are you a gentleman, Sam?"

The thin one laughed, flicking the knife so that it caught the sun, its blade sticky with liquid from the stems of the cabbages.

"Are you the owner, sir?" Fry asked the first old man, raising her voice above the continuing noise of the geese.

"Hang on a minute," he said. "Let me turn the siren off."

He thrust his fork deep into the ground with a heave of his shoulder and walked to the wall. Then he picked up two clumps of weeds with balls of dry earth sticking to their roots. He hurled them one after the other at the geese, shouting at the top of his voice.

Fry thought the sounds he was making could easily be some local dialect descended directly from the ancient Scandinavian of the Viking invaders. But probably they were just noises. The geese, at least, understood him, and turned and waddled away back down the track to wait for the next intruder. Without the geese, it was quieter but not silent. There was a continual background clucking and muttering of poultry, a dog barking, the grunting of a pig. And, not far away, the yelling of the goat.

"I'm Wilford Cutts. This is my place. Over there's my pal Sam."

Sam waved the knife again and slashed at another stem. It severed in one clean blow, and the trimmed cabbage was dropped into a bucket.

"Sam Beeley," he called.

"Are you police? I suppose you're asking about that lass," said Wilford. "The Mount girl."

"Laura Vernon, yes."

"I saw the lass about sometimes, I suppose. Is that what you want to know?"

"Were you in the vicinity of the Baulk on Saturday night or Sunday morning?"

"Ah. Sam'll have to tell you what I did Saturday night. I can't rightly remember."

"I'm sorry?"

"I'm quite fond of a drink, you see. At my age, it only takes a couple of pints and the old brain goes a bit. Do you know what I mean? Ah, probably not."

"Where do you go drinking?"

"Where? There's only one place 'round here, lass. The Drover. As for

Sunday morning, well, I'm always here. All this lot to see to, you know. It takes a while."

"Feeding the animals."

"That's it."

"Do you live here alone, Mr. Cutts?"

"Alone? Well, you'd hardly call it that, would you?" he said, turning to look across the jumble of buildings, where any sort of animal could have been lurking for all Fry knew.

She turned at the sound of an engine, and saw a battered blue Transit van struggling up the track. As it reached the gateway, a bent little man in a tweed jacket and a cloth cap got out of the driver's seat to wrestle with the gate. He, too, took no notice of the geese.

"I'll have to leave you to it for a bit," said Wilford. "I've got a customer."

He walked off, waving to the driver of the van until they had maneuvered the vehicle against the end of one of the wooden hen huts. Both men went into the hut with bundles of sacks from the van.

"Stop and have a chat, lass," said Sam. "It'll make a change. Wilford can get to be a bit of a boring old bugger after a while."

"Have you known Mr. Cutts for long?" she asked.

"As long as I can remember. Mind you, my memory's not what it was, so he could be a complete stranger."

Sam began to laugh, his chest wheezing painfully and his false teeth clicking. Fry winced as he raised a thin hand to straighten his cap and the blade of the knife came dangerously close to his eyes.

"My family came down from Yorkshire when I was very small," he said, when a fit of coughing had passed. "We went to live at Eyam. My old dad went to work in the lead mines, and I followed him down there, as lads did in those days. Wilford was the son of one of my dad's mates. We worked on the picking table together with a few other lads, then moved on to be jig operators. That's the way it went in those days, you know. You moved in small circles, just a few families and people that you knew. None of this wandering about that everyone seems to do now."

Fry's attention strayed around the smallholding, her eyes wide in amazement at the ramshackle constructions and makeshift fencing. She was wondering whether the way the animals were kept was strictly legal. She made a mental note to look up the appropriate regulations when she got back to the station.

"You've been friends an awfully long time, then," she said vaguely.

"Sixty years, or a bit more. It was before the war when we met."

"That'd be the Second World War, I suppose."

Sam peered at her to see if she was making fun of him, but seemed to realize that she had not even been born until nearly thirty years after the war was over.

"Aye, I suppose there have been a few other wars since then," he conceded. "We joined up together as well, for a bit. Royal Engineers, of course. They were right glad to get miners. They welcomed us with open arms. We went over to France on D day and stayed there till the end." He chuckled. "It brings back a few memories still, does that."

"Really?"

"French tarts," said Sam.

"What?"

The old man chortled. "That's what I remember mostly now. All the rest of it has pretty well gone, all the bad bits. But I remember the tarts in France. We were a long way behind the front, of course. Rebuilding bridges, that sort of thing. Those French towns and villages were full of girls. And they were right glad to see a few Tommies, I can tell you. We had a high old time. Me and Harry, that was. Wilford didn't approve, of course."

"Harry?"

"Harry Dickinson," said Sam. "You might have heard of him. Here's your mate."

Fry turned and saw Cooper's red Toyota coming back down the track, turning in by the Nissen hut. He parked behind the Transit and leaned out of the window.

"There was no one at home up the lane," he said.

"You're Sergeant Cooper's lad, aren't you?" said Sam.

"Jesus," said Fry.

"I'm sorry, I don't think I know you, sir."

"Sam Beeley."

The goat's bellow was suddenly deafeningly near.

"She's out again," said Sam. "I'll have to tell Wilford."

"What's the matter with it?" asked Fry. "Is it ill?"

"In season," said Sam, as if they were talking about a vegetable that was sometimes unavailable.

"Will she be going to the billy, then?" asked Cooper.

"She's off tonight. A bloke up Bamford way is taking her. He has a billy of his own."

There was a clattering of hooves, and a brown and white head topped by a pair of horns appeared briefly over the roof of the outhouse before the goat dropped nimbly into the paddock and skittered off into the deep grass at the far end.

"Bugger," said Sam. "She'll eat all the cabbages before we can cut them."

"Do you want a hand to catch her?" suggested Cooper, getting out of the Toyota.

"No, no. We'd never get near her. Wilford will fetch her back—she comes to him. She's only a goatling, and she's a bit wild. He calls her Jenny."

"Mr. Beeley was telling me about when he first met Mr. Cutts," said Fry, anxious that the interview was drifting far away from her. "Their fathers knew each and they worked together, is that right?"

"Of course, we all had jobs to go into then," said Sam. "Local jobs. There were always jobs in the mines then, or the quarries. It's different for the young ones 'round here now, I suppose. The lad here will tell you that."

Fry noticed that Sam didn't doubt for a moment that she was from out of the area and knew nothing about it, while Ben Cooper would understand. Since she had been in Moorhay, she felt as though her lack of local origins had been pushed into her face, quite unconsciously and without malice, but very effectively. She had been treated politely by people at every property they had visited, but none of them had looked at her with the unspoken recognition and sense of mutual understanding with which they had looked at Ben Cooper when they realized who he was.

"It's been different 'round here for a long time now, Mr. Beeley," said Cooper.

"I suppose it has, lad. I suppose it has. But, like I told you, my memory's not that good. I remember the war, but not much since, if you know what I mean."

From the hut where Wilford and his visitor had disappeared, a great cacophony of cackling and screeching erupted, accompanied by the flapping of scores of wings.

"What are they doing in there?" asked Fry.

"That bloke with the van is buying some of Wilford's birds, see," said Sam, as if it were perfectly obvious. "Wilford left them inside today, those young Marans. But they're a bit active. It's better if you can move them at night—they don't give you as much trouble then."

"It sounds horrendous."

"They're good layers, them Marans," said Sam.

"Mr. Beeley, did you know Laura Vernon?"

"I know the family. Comers-in, aren't they? Half the village seem to be comers-in these days. They've only been there a year or two, at the Mount. They walked in the pub one night, you know, when they first arrived. Eh, you should have seen their faces. They never thought they'd be mixing with the hoi polloi like us. But they couldn't walk straight out again, so they had to sit there and drink their gin and tonics like a right pair of southern pillocks."

"They're from Nottingham, I believe."

"Aye."

Sam shifted his feet on the dry earth. One of them seemed to stick and move suddenly sideways, as if he had lost control of it through cramp. His shoe clanged against the side of an enamel bowl half full of water, left there for the geese presumably.

"Mr. Beeley, we're asking everybody what they might have seen in the area of the Baulk at about the time Laura Vernon was killed," said Fry.

"Oh, you want my alibi, eh?"

"No, that wasn't what I asked for, sir."

Sam chuckled. "Only I don't go in much for running after young girls these days. It's my legs, you see. Got them both bust once, in the mine. They mended, but they were never right after that. Now that I'm getting older, they don't work too well at all."

"Were you in the area on Saturday night?" asked Fry. "Or Sunday morning?"

"What's that accent?" asked Sam, cocking his head and scratching his ear with the knife. "You Welsh or what?"

"I'm from the Black Country."

"Eh?"

"Birmingham," snapped Fry.

"Ah. I've never been there. Wouldn't want to, either."

"Saturday night, Mr. Beeley?"

"Saturday night? Well, I'd be in the Drover till about eleven o'clock, with Wilford. It was a bit busy that night. Tourists, you know, in the summer. B and B people. A lot of cars about, too." He shook his head sadly. "I don't live far from the pub. I can just about walk that far. And we do tend to have a few drinks on a Saturday. No driving to do, you know."

"There were tourists in the pub. Strangers to the village, then."

"Full of them," said Sam.

Wilford and the van driver emerged from the hut, tugging at several bulging sacks. A cloud of dark feathers drifted out of the hut behind them, settling on their shoulders and sticking in their hair. From the sacks came a steady complaint of trapped birds and an occasional rustle of feathers. The two men were sweating and disheveled and breathing hard. Wilford was very red in the face and giving a series of faint, gasping laughs. The little man from the van looked wild-eyed, even frightened by his experience in the hut.

"Sunday morning," said Sam. "Well, I don't get up too early these days. But I was dressed by about half past ten, when my son came to collect me. That's Davey. Him and his wife always take me for Sunday dinner at their place in Edendale."

"Do you come up here much to help Mr. Cutts?" asked Cooper.

"I'm not much use to him really. But I have to find something to fill my time."

"Does he have any other help?"

"A lad or two, that he pays a few bob for the heavy work. And Harry comes up here, too, to help."

"Harry Dickinson again?"

"Yes, that Harry. *You'll* know him," he said to Cooper.

The sacks thudded one after another into the back of the Transit, and the driver clambered in and began to coast back down the track. No money seemed to have changed hands between the two men.

"Give us a hand here, Sam," called Wilford. "We've got one that's badly. Broke its legs on the wire, I reckon."

"Goat's out again, Wilford."

"She'll wait."

Sam limped over toward the hut, and Wilford tossed him a hen that had been hanging upside down from his hand, its wings outspread, its beak gaping and panting. Fry had never seen a hen so close before, and was startled to see the thin red sliver of flesh that protruded from its beak, like the darting tongue of a snake. The bird had soiled itself, and the soft feathers around its anus were stained yellow. Fry swallowed, swearing never to eat an egg again.

"Sam's a dab hand at this," said Wilford cheerfully. "He doesn't look to have much strength in his wrists, does he? But it's all in the technique, see."

"It's just practice and a bit of a knack," said Sam, taking a firm grip on the bird. He tucked its body under his armpit, folding its wings closed and pressing it tight against his side. Then he closed the fingers of his right hand around the hen's scrawny neck and pushed his thumb hard into its throat. He twisted and pulled suddenly. There was a faint crack and the bird's eyes went dull. The wings beat desperately, their dying strength defeating Sam Beeley's efforts to hold it still as they flapped wildly, releasing a spray of pinion feathers that drifted onto his trousers and boots. The bird's legs kicked frantically, and its tail lifted to eject another spurt of yellow. Then its claws relaxed and hung downward, pointing limply at the ground with pitiful finality.

"You've killed it," said Fry, astonished.

The two old men laughed, and she was amazed to see Cooper smiling, too.

"It's called putting them out of their misery," said Sam. "If you do it right, and do it quick, they feel no pain."

"It's disgusting," said Fry. "It's revolting."

"I suppose," said Sam, holding out the limp bird toward her, "that you won't want to take it home for your tea then."

Fry took a step back as a dribble of saliva ran out of the bird's gaping beak and dripped into the dust. Its scaly legs looked cold and reptilian where they were gripped in Sam's bony fingers.

"No?"

"Never mind. I'll take it in for Connie," said Wilford.

Cooper and Fry got back into the car. Fry wound up her window to keep out the musty smell of dried poultry droppings drifting from the door of the shed. The two old men stood watching them turn around, and Sam gave them a small, cheerful wave.

When they reached the bottom of the track, another van was turning in.

-12-

"And now the good news," said DCI Tailby.

Tired heads perked up all around the incident room. Most of the officers were finishing the daytime shift, winding down from the hectic first full day of a murder inquiry. Others were taking over for the evening, beginning their stint by getting up-to-date at the evening briefing.

Ben Cooper and Diane Fry sat together, reluctant, despite themselves, to break the professional bond that had formed between them by being paired up as a team. Fry still looked alert, her eyes fixed on Tailby, her notebook open on her knee. Cooper was weary, almost dazed, as if things weren't connecting for him properly. But he felt the tension within him increasing as the day came to a close. He couldn't stop his mind drifting away from the job toward a clamoring swarm of formless anxieties about his mother—sudden, stabbing fears about the immediate future, mingled with piercingly clear little memories of how she had once been, before her illness, in the not so distant past. He knew he would have difficulty tonight in making the transition from work to home. Wasn't the one supposed to be an escape from the other?

As Tailby began to speak, Cooper looked down at Fry's pen, which was already starting to move across her notebook. He was surprised to see the page half covered in drawings of spiders with black, hairy bodies and long legs, their shapes etched deep into the paper with heavily scrawled ballpoint pen.

"Make sure you all read the reports," Tailby was saying, "but I'll sum up the main points. Late this afternoon a witness came forward. A gentleman by the name of Gary Edwards. Mr. Edwards is a bird-watcher. On Saturday evening, he was positioned on the top of Raven's Side on the north of the valley at Moorhay. He was, it seems, watching for pied flycatchers, which are a rare species known to breed in this area. Mr. Edwards had

142

traveled from Leicester purely on the chance of seeing a pied flycatcher, so that he could tick it off on a list of British species. I'm told this activity is called twitching."

Cooper saw some of the officers smiling, but he knew Tailby wasn't joking. It was very rare that he did. The DCI looked up at them over his reading glasses, then back down again at the report in his hands.

"Mr. Edwards thought the oak and birch woodland near the stream was a likely site. At one stage, though, he says he was watching a pair of merlins nesting on the cliff face below him. While he was doing this, his attention was taken by a bird flying toward the woodland, which he felt might be the said pied flycatcher. He followed the flight of this bird with his binoculars."

In Cooper's hands was a summary of interviews conducted with Graham and Charlotte Vernon, and with Molly Sherratt, as well as with the bird-watcher. Some of the details were marked as new information and would be followed up with actions the next day. There were also reports of the attempts made by DI Hitchens's team to trace Lee Sherratt, without success. From the tone of the summary, Cooper was left in no doubt that Sherratt was considered the obvious suspect. All they had to do, it was inferred, was to find Sherratt and let the forensic evidence establish his guilt. The rest was all for show.

"It should be stated at this point," said Tailby, "that Mr. Edwards was equipped with a pair of Zeiss roof-prism type binoculars with a magnification of times ten and a forty-five-millimeter–diameter object lens. A powerful bit of kit. He says he trained these binoculars on the area of woodland into which the bird had disappeared, and he waited to see if there was any further movement. There was. But it wasn't a bird."

Tailby paused, like an actor savoring the effect, trying to get his timing just right.

"Mr. Edwards further states that he followed a movement in the undergrowth of something black, only to find the head of a dog appearing in his view. Due to the small field of vision of binoculars of that power, he took them away from his face and with unaided vision saw a man with a dog. We believe from Mr. Edwards's statement that this was near the spot where Laura Vernon was found. The time: approximately seven-fifteen."

There was a little stir of excitement. The bird-watcher had been in position within an hour of the incident, on a good vantage point, with a powerful pair of binoculars. Who could ask for anything better? What more had the twitcher seen?

Cooper observed that Fry had been scribbling notes rapidly, turning over the page with the spiders and turning again. Now she was sitting bolt upright, alert and eager. He could see that she was getting ready to take the first opportunity to put in a question, to make sure she was noticed.

"Unfortunately for us," said Tailby, "Mr. Edwards then completely lost interest in the area of woodland. He reasoned that the human and canine presence would disturb the bird population. Particularly the pied flycatcher, which is of a somewhat secretive and sensitive nature, apparently. His attention returned to the merlins. Mr. Edwards then remained on Raven's Side until nine-thirty approximately, but he saw nothing further of interest to us."

Fry stirred. "Over two hours, sir? What was he doing all that time?"

"Yes. DC Fry, isn't it? That is a question that was put to him, Fry. He states that he was waiting for dusk on the chance of observing little owls hunting."

"Tell him to get a life," said someone from the back.

"I don't need to point out that this could be an absolutely vital witness," said Tailby, ignoring the interruption.

Ben Cooper raised a hand. "The man with the dog, sir. Are we thinking it was Harry Dickinson? According to Dickinson's statement, he walks in that area regularly."

"Unfortunately, Mr. Edwards wasn't able to give us a description. He was too far away and did not study the man through his binoculars."

There were general sighs of disappointment.

"More interested in pied flycatchers than people," said the same voice.

"However, Mr. Dickinson will be spoken to again today," said Tailby. "In the initial interview he was not asked about Saturday evening. It may be that he was on the Baulk at that time and he saw something useful. Mr. Dickinson will be among the actions for the morning."

"It would be a bit of a coincidence, wouldn't it, sir?"

"How so, Cooper?"

"I mean, Dickinson being in the area at the time Laura Vernon was killed and maybe seeing the murderer. And two days later being in the same area and finding the trainer which led us to her body. That's what we're saying here, isn't it? A bit of a coincidence, surely."

"What would be *your* interpretation, Cooper?"

"I think we ought to press Harry Dickinson harder."

Tailby frowned. "At the moment we are not considering him as a suspect, merely a potentially useful witness."

"But if—"

"Now," said Tailby, turning away, "we have to look at the immediate family. Obviously, we need to bear in mind the possibility of a family row of some kind. The parents have to be under suspicion." Tailby waited for somebody to ask him why. No one did. But he told them anyway. "Murders occur mostly within families. The statistics tell us this."

All the faces in the room continued to look at him expectantly.

"For that reason, we will be looking more closely at the Vernons. Particularly the relationship between Laura Vernon and her father. I have spoken to Graham Vernon myself, and I have to tell you I'm not happy in that respect."

"Haven't we got a TV appeal lined up with him, sir?"

"Yes, with both parents in fact. That's scheduled for the morning. We will, of course, be watching them closely during the appeal."

Cooper saw Fry nodding calmly, as if it were perfectly normal to suspect parents of murdering their own daughter. He wondered what cases she had worked on in the past to feel like that or whether it was as a result of experiences in her own family. The thought made him feel very sad. His own family had been a totally happy one, and he thought the destruction of a family was the worst thing that could happen to anyone.

"And then there's the brother," Tailby was saying. "Daniel Vernon. Nineteen years old and a student at Exeter University. We're led to believe that he was away in Exeter at the time that Laura went missing and has only now arrived back in Moorhay. But we checked, and his term doesn't start for another two weeks. So what has he been doing? I need his movements traced—when did he leave and how did he get back? From a brief look at him earlier this afternoon, I'd say he was a pretty angry young man. On the other hand, you don't need me to tell you that the victim's family must be treated with care. I don't want any complaints about officers being heavy-handed or insensitive."

The DCI paused to allow this to sink in, then turned to gesture at an impressive aerial photograph of Moorhay, taken by the helicopter crew and blown up to enable the probable route of Laura Vernon's last journey to be superimposed onto it.

"Meanwhile, I intend to begin a full search of the Vernons' garden," he said. "This is in view of the possibility that Laura may have met someone there shortly before she was killed. Remember the sighting of her talking to a young man earlier in the evening. We need to find evidence to establish the identity of that young man. It is, however, a very large garden."

The officers in the incident room could see that there were extensive lawns and flower beds in the Vernons' garden, along with two greenhouses and a small summerhouse, as well as plenty of odd corners near the back, where a gate led out onto the hillside path.

The area of pale scrub where Laura had last been seen was clearly visible between the back wall of the garden and the vast expanse of dark woodland. The long shadows of a line of conifers fell across the patchy gorse of the scrubland like the bars of a cage.

"We are also following up Laura's other contacts. DI Hitchens's team is gradually piecing together her background. We believe she had at least one regular boyfriend, according to what her classmates tell us. The parents deny this, but we all know parents, don't we? They're the last people to find out. The youth's name is Simeon. That's with an *e*. We don't have a surname yet, and apparently he doesn't attend the same school Laura Vernon did. DS Morgan is confident of tracing him, though. Yes, Luke?"

"Absolutely."

"As you know, DI Armstrong is working on the known offenders list and possible links to the Susan Edson case in B Division. There are some similarities on the surface. The age and sex of the victim, obviously. But note the fact that an item of clothing is missing in both instances—in Laura Vernon's case, a Reebok trainer. In the Edson case, a pair of tights. It is likely these are now in the possession of the attacker or attackers. Please be aware of this. But we follow up all possible lines of inquiry. We are not assuming a definite link at this stage. But I confess to a certain concern in that respect."

The murmurs of agreement sounded like the low rumble of a lorry outside or the muttering of a disappointed crowd in the stand across the road when Edendale FC had lost again. Ben Cooper felt something equally distant and unidentifiable grumbling deep in his mind—a dark, hovering anxiety that growled and whined and threatened to emerge from where it was lurking and rip the certainties out from under him. But it was something that was impossible to pin down among the other worries that swirled about in there, all the other things he hardly dared to think about.

"Also, no murder weapon has yet been identified," said Tailby. "The nature of the injuries suggests a hard, solid object. Scientific Support are still at the scene and will continue the search, and I remain hopeful. Two sets of prints have been taken from the trainer, but they match only with the victim's own prints and those of Mr. Dickinson, who was printed for comparisons. However, as you will see, we do have a very promising piece of forensic evidence. I refer to the suspected bite mark on the victim's thigh. The services of a forensic odontologist have been obtained, with the intention of obtaining a cast of the bite which can be matched to the teeth of a perpetrator."

Around the room, officers could be seen whispering to each other as they asked what an odontologist was.

"Obviously," said the DCI, "a priority remains Lee Sherratt. Sadly, we've drawn a blank on his whereabouts so far. His mother states she doesn't know where he is and hasn't seen him since Sunday afternoon. He is, she says, 'a bit prone to wandering off.' Whatever that means. We would very much like to interview Lee Sherratt in connection with the killing of Laura Vernon. All officers are being issued with his photograph. Keep your eyes open."

Ben Cooper jerked to attention. His mind had been drifting away again. It was almost as though DCI Tailby's last words had been addressed directly to him. Yes, he needed to keep his eyes open. If he didn't, the dark thing that lurked and whined might jump out at him before he could see it.

Charlotte Vernon lay on the sofa in the sitting room at the Mount. She was wearing nothing but a black satin print wrap, but her hair was washed and brushed and she had made up her face and painted her toenails. Though Graham would normally enjoy the sight of his wife's body, today he felt waves of growing irritation that she had not yet taken the trouble to get dressed. Somehow, her nakedness seemed emblematic of the stripping away of an important veneer from their lives, a lowering of standards that he feared could symbolize the gradual disintegration of the family.

"He can't do this," said Graham. "We can't let him."

"And how do you intend to stop him?" asked Charlotte. "He hasn't felt the need to listen to you for years."

"I thought . . . You could speak to him, couldn't you, Charlie?"

"He might listen to me," she agreed.

"Well then. Catch him before he goes out."

"I didn't say I would do it."

"Why on earth not?"

Charlotte considered, reaching for the glass that never seemed to be far away these days.

"It would help him to get it off his chest."

"It might help him, but it wouldn't do me any good!"

"Or the business?"

"Well, obviously. I can't afford things like this, this sort of damage to my reputation. You know, Charlie, it's critical."

"And what about me?"

"Sorry?"

"Would it be good for me? That's what I'm wondering. Would it change you, Graham? Would it change things between us? To get it all out into the open, I wonder?"

"Charlie—do you want things to change?"

"I don't know."

"For God's sake, what *do* you want? I turned a blind eye to what you were doing, didn't I?"

"A blind eye? Is that what you call it?"

"Well? Didn't I?"

"Yes, I suppose you did. And you thought that was what I wanted, did you? Really?"

Graham sighed with exasperation. "I never will understand you."

Charlotte was back on the cigarettes and Bacardi with a vengeance, having come out of the artificially calm state induced by the doctor's sedatives. Everywhere in the house there were ashtrays filled with butts, which were only emptied three times a week when Sheila Kelk came to clean. Graham hoped that Mrs. Kelk hadn't been frightened off by Daniel. But then, on second thoughts, she was far too nosey to stay away just now.

He looked at his wife's hair and glimpsed the darkness at the roots. She looked tired, despite the amount of sleeping she had done under sedation. When she looked at him now, it was with open hostility and distrust. The death of their daughter had come between them like a wedge.

"Has anybody been here while I was out of the way?" she asked.

"What do you mean?"

"Has anyone been to the house?"

"Policemen. You know they want to search the garden? A fingertip search, they call it. God knows what they expect to find there."

"Apart from those policemen. Apart from Daniel. Has anybody been that I didn't see?"

"Mrs. Kelk, of course."

"Not Frances Wingate."

"No, Charlie."

"Not Edward Randle."

"No. I told them all not to come. All our friends. It's what you said you wanted. I asked them to stay away until you felt like seeing people."

"So Frances hasn't been."

"I've told you."

"And no one else."

"No."

Charlotte lit another cigarette, pouting her lips to suck on it and narrowing her eyes.

"I don't know why I ever trusted you," she said.

"Why do we have to do this now, Charlie?"

"While I've been lying there," she said, "I've been thinking. You're not completely unconscious, you know, when you're sedated. Your mind keeps working. And without any distractions, you seem to see things more clearly. All the memories came back to me. All the memories of Laura."

She walked to the cabinet, and her groping fingers found the empty frame again among the photographs.

"When will they let us have the photo of her back?"

"I'll ask," said Graham.

"I need to get back whatever I can of her."

"I understand."

Charlotte turned toward him, tears glittering in her eyes, anger twisting her mouth into an ugly shape.

"I blame you, you know, Graham. Do you realize that? When I think about . . . everything. All this. I've lost my little girl, and now they're taking away my memories of her. How could you let it happen?"

Graham moved to put his arms around her when he saw the tears, but she pushed him away roughly.

"Keep away from me. How can you think about it at a time like this? You're an animal."

"I wasn't, Charlie. I wasn't."

"Laura told me everything," she insisted desperately. "She didn't keep secrets from me."

The phone was ringing. Graham moved to answer, then changed his mind and left it. The answering machine switched in. It would be another client, anxiously wondering what was happening. When would Graham be back in operation? When could they expect him to be at their beck and call again? He didn't resent them. Their businesses had to go on, even if Vernon's didn't. Graham thought for a moment of passing everything on to Andrew Milner, letting him take all the responsibility permanently. But he dismissed the thought as soon as it came. He would be back in harness soon enough—surely it wouldn't take the police too long to sort things out, to come up with someone they could charge. As long as he could stop Daniel from stirring up trouble.

"We have to hold together somehow, Charlie. Will you talk to Daniel?"

She raised her head, dabbing at her eyes. They both listened for the sounds of their son, heavy-footed on the stairs, getting ready to go out. But she answered with another question.

"There isn't anything that I don't know, is there, Graham?"

"What do you mean?"

"About Laura. I need to know exactly what happened, and why. Are there things that you're keeping from me?"

Graham saw that something important depended on his answer. Should he tell the truth, or was it a lie that his wife wanted to hear? He thought of the sort of information that Tailby and his team might already be collecting—details that could shatter even Charlotte's illusions about their daughter. The direction of Tailby's questions about Lee Sherratt, and even about Daniel, had made that possibility clear. And who would Charlotte blame for that? She said she no longer trusted him. But what she thought of him might mean the difference now between holding together and everything falling apart. The truth or a lie? A crucial decision, but to hesitate would be fatal.

"They haven't told me anything," he said.

Charlotte finished drying her eyes, pushed back her hair, and stubbed out her cigarette in the nearest ashtray among a pile of old stubs.

"I'll catch Danny now, shall I?"

"Good girl," said Graham.

Cooper tapped Fry on the shoulder as the meeting broke up. "Are you in a rush to get home?"

"Well . . . no."

"I wondered if you fancied a game of squash. I could do with a game to wind down, and you said you were into sport."

Fry considered for a moment. Ben Cooper was not her ideal choice of a companion, for squash or anything else. On the other hand, it would be vastly preferable to another early night in front of the wobbly old TV with her own thoughts. Besides, she was confident she could beat him. That thought made her mind up for her.

"Can we get a game at short notice?" she asked.

"I can," said Cooper, grinning. "Just let me make one phone call. We'll get a court at the rugby club on a Tuesday night, no problem."

"Fine then. Oh, I'll need to call at the flat to get my racquet and kit."

"I've got mine in the car, but I'll follow you home and we can go together. OK?"

"All right, yes. Thanks."

"It seems strange to be going off duty with the inquiry at this stage, though. No money for overtime. Can you believe it?"

"They think they've got it sewn up, once Lee Sherratt's in custody. "

"That's what I think, too. They're relying totally on forensic evidence. It seems to be some sort of holy grail these days."

"Forensics don't lie, Ben. Only people lie."

"And it costs too much to keep a manpower-intensive inquiry going for days and weeks on end. I know, I've heard all that."

"It's true. We have to live in the real world."

"It worries me that the only suggestion of any motivation for Lee Sherratt is what the girl's father says about him. That's not enough, surely."

"Enough for Mr. Tailby to build a case on, providing the forensics back him up."

Cooper shook his head. "It doesn't feel right."

"*Feel* right? That again."

"OK, point taken."

"Feelings don't come into it."

"At one time," said Cooper, "it was money that didn't come into it."

"That sounds to me like your famous father speaking." She saw Cooper flush, and knew she was right. "A proper Dixon of Dock Green, isn't he, your dad? Why don't you explain to him one day that it's not the 1950s anymore? Things have moved on in the last fifty years. If he walked down the street in his uniform in a lot places in this country today, he'd get his head kicked in before he could say 'Evening, all.'"

Cooper went completely rigid, and his face suffused with blood. He breathed deeply two or three times before he managed to get himself under control. His hands were shaking as he pushed the papers he was holding into a file.

"I'll see you down in the car park," he said, in a voice thick with emotion.

As he walked away, Fry immediately began to regret agreeing to play squash with him. It had only been some sudden burst of comradeship, all too easy to give in to in the police service. There was always a feeling that it was "us against them" in the closed environment of a police station. But then she shrugged, knowing that it would be for only one evening. She would have no problem keeping Ben Cooper at arm's length.

"All right, Diane?" asked DI Hitchens, approaching her from behind and standing close to her shoulder.

"I'm fine."

"What are you doing when you go off duty?"

"I'm playing squash with Ben Cooper. Apparently."

"Really? Good luck then."

"And I'm going to thrash him, too."

"Are you? So you're a squash expert as well, then?"

"Not really, just averagely good. But I'm fit, and I'll have him begging for mercy on that court. Old Ben looks like a real softy to me."

"Ben? I don't think so. He's a bit of a chip off the old block really. Soft on the surface but tough as old boots underneath, like his dad."

"So you're a fan of Sergeant Cooper's, too, are you, sir?"

"We all are in this station. How could we be anything else?"

"And what exactly has he done to earn this adulation?"

"If you want to know about Sergeant Joe Cooper," said Hitchens, "I suggest you stop off downstairs in reception for a few minutes. You'll find his memorial on the wall near the front counter. It's about two years since he was killed."

-13-

Cooper screwed up his face, bared his teeth, and let the power surge through his muscles. He glared at the ball, swung back his arm, and released a ferocious serve that flew off the front wall like a rocket and hit the back corner so fast that Fry hardly had time to move.

"Thirteen–three."

They changed sides of the court, passing each other near the "T." Cooper refused to meet Fry's eye. He was completely absorbed in his game, as he had been since the start. His concentration was total, and Fry felt she might as well have been a robot set up for him to aim at. As they passed, she smelled the sweat on his body like the sweet resin of a damaged pine tree.

"Your serve's incredible."

Cooper nodded briefly, lining up the ball with his left side turned to the front wall. He waited a few seconds for Fry to get in position, then, with a grunt, unleashed a cannonball that bounced straight at his opponent's face, making her instinctively want to get out of the way, rather than try to hit it back. Returning Cooper's serve was proving a futile exercise anyway.

"Fourteen–three. Game point."

Fry had given up trying to make conversation during the game. Her comments brought no response, other than another crushing serve. Those that she managed to return resulted in an exhausting rally, during which she ran herself ragged backward and forward across the court, while Ben Cooper kept control of the "T." He would thrash the ball time and again against the front wall, now just above the tin, now curving high into the air over her racquet. She could see that her arms and legs had turned lobster red with the exertion, and the perspiration was trickling past her sweat band to run down the sides of her face and soak into the elastic of her sports bra between her breasts.

Cooper served again, and she managed to get her racquet under the ball, lobbing it toward the near corner. He darted across court and collected the shot with ease, ready to bounce his return to the far side. Fry stretched to reach it, ducking low and hitting the ball straight and hard back along the side wall. Glad to have made a return, she spun around, almost off-balance, in an effort to get back to the "T," and collided with Cooper on his way to return the shot. Their racquets clashed and their hot limbs tangled sweatily for a moment before they could separate themselves. Fry breathed hard and rubbed her knee where she had knocked it against some part of Cooper's body that felt like rock.

"Obstruction," he said.

She nodded. "OK. Game, then."

"And match. Unless you want to play three out of five."

"Oh no. I think I'd be safer conceding."

"Whatever."

Cooper collected the ball. For the first time, a small smile touched his lips.

"I win then. Thanks for the game."

"I'd say it was a pleasure, Ben, except that you play like a machine."

"I take that as a compliment from you."

"I'm absolutely wrecked."

Cooper shrugged. "You tried hard."

At another time, Fry might have found his tone a bit patronizing and reacted quite differently. But just now she was in a placatory mood. She tucked her racquet under her arm and held out a hand.

"Shake, then."

Cooper looked at her, surprised, but shook automatically. His hand felt as hot as her own, and their perspiration mingled in their palms as their swollen fingers fumbled clumsily at each other. Fry held on to his hand when he tried to pull it away again.

"Ben—I'm sorry," she said.

"What for? Playing so badly?"

"For the things I said about your father today. I didn't know."

"I know you didn't," he said. She felt the muscles in his forearm tense. The beginnings of a smile had vanished again, and his face was set, revealing no emotion. She saw a trickle of sweat run through his eyebrows and into his eyes. He blinked away the moisture, breaking her stare, and she let his hand go.

"DI Hitchens told me tonight. He sent me to look at the plaque in reception at the station. Your father was killed arresting a mugger, wasn't he? He was a hero."

Cooper seemed to study the squash ball, turning it over in his hand to find the colored spot and squeezing against the warm air trapped inside.

"It wasn't the mugger who killed him. A gang of youths were standing around outside a pub, and they joined in to try to get the mugger free. It was them who killed him. There were too many of them. They got him on the ground and kicked him to death."

"And what happened to them?"

"Nothing much," he said. He pulled a handkerchief from the pocket of his shorts to wipe his eyes and his forehead. "Oh, they found out who they were, all right. There was a big enough outcry about it in Edendale. But there were seven or eight of them, all telling different stories when it came to court, with the usual set of defense solicitors looking for the get-outs. It could never be proved which ones actually kicked my father in the head. I mostly remember that it came down to a debate about the bloodstains on their boots. Their argument was that they just got splashed because they were standing too close." He paused, his eyes distant and full of remembered anger and pain. "Three of them got two years for manslaughter, the others were put on probation for affray. First-time offenders, you see. Of course, they were all drunk, too. But that's a mitigating circumstance, isn't it, as far as the courts are concerned? An excuse."

"I really didn't know, Ben."

"Do you think I would have asked you to play squash tonight if I thought you knew? I'm not that desperate for company." He ran the handkerchief around the back of his neck. "I'm not sure it was a good idea to play in this weather anyway."

"You should have said something about your father. Why didn't you tell me?"

Cooper looked down at his feet.

"If you really want to know, I get fed up of hearing about it. It's been constantly rammed down my throat for two years now. I have to look at that bloody plaque every time I walk through reception. Do you know there's even a little brass plate screwed on to one of the benches in Clappergate? That's so that the Edendale public don't forget either. I've got so that I avoid walking down that part of Clappergate. I go 'round by another street to avoid seeing it. And then all those people who remember him. Thousands of them. Even those who'd never heard of him before he died, they knew all about him by the time the papers had finished with the story."

"Like in Moorhay—"

"Yeah. Like in Moorhay. 'It's Sergeant Cooper's lad.' 'Aren't you Sergeant Cooper's son?' It hurts every time. Every time I hear somebody say it, it's like they're twisting a knife in an old wound to keep it fresh. My father's death devastated my life. And people are never going to let me forget it. Sometimes I think that if one more person calls me Sergeant Cooper's lad, it's going to be too much. I'm going to go berserk."

He squeezed the squash ball in his fist, bounced it off the floor, and smacked it almost casually against the back wall with his racquet, so that it flew high into the air and dropped back into his hand.

"Were you working in E Division when it happened?"

"I was already in CID. In fact, at that very moment I'd just arrested a burglar, a typical bit of Edendale lowlife. I heard the shout on the radio while I was sitting in the car with him. It's not a moment I'm likely to forget."

"And it didn't put you off the police service?"

He looked surprised. "Of course not. Quite the opposite. It made me more determined."

"Determined? You've got ambitions?"

"I have. In fact, there's a sergeant's job coming vacant soon," he said. "I'm up for it."

"Good luck, then," said Fry. "You must have a good chance."

"Oh, I don't know anymore," he said doubtfully. "I thought I had, but . . ."

"Of course you have." She glared at him, irritated by the sudden slump in his shoulders. He had talked about his father with anger and passion, but he had changed in a few seconds, and now he had the air of defeat.

"You reckon?"

"You seem to be very highly regarded. Everybody knows you 'round the division. Not to mention the general public."

"Oh yeah, the public," he said dismissively.

"If *they* had a vote on it, you'd be mayor by now."

"Yeah? Well, we all know how much we can trust *them*."

But Fry had done her apologies now and was getting fed up with his reluctance to shake off whatever was making him so moody and morose. She watched him bounce the ball again and swing his racquet at it, hitting a slow lob that curled back toward them.

"You know, it must be really nice to have so many friends," she said, "and such a close family, too."

He took his eye off the ball, puzzled by the change in her voice.

"I don't suppose you'll ever move away from here, will you, Ben? You'll marry somebody, maybe some old school friend, and you'll settle down here, buy a bungalow, have kids, get a dog, the whole bit."

"Sure," he said. "It sounds great."

"I can't think of anything worse," she said, and smashed the ball into the ceiling lights.

Charlotte Vernon had found Daniel in Laura's room. On the dresser was a pile of letters that had been tied neatly in a pink ribbon. Charlotte had seen the letters before but had not touched them. She had not touched anything of Laura's yet. It seemed too much of an acknowledgment that she had gone forever.

"I wrote to tell her that I would be home last weekend," said Daniel. "She wanted to talk to me, she said."

"What about?"

"I don't know. It sounded serious. I told her I would be home for the weekend. But I wasn't. I didn't come home."

"You always wrote to her far more than you wrote to us, Danny."

"To you? You never needed letters—you always had your own concerns. But Laura needed contact with the outside world. She felt she was a prisoner here."

"Nonsense."

"Is it?"

Daniel turned over another letter and ran his eyes briefly over his own scrawl. His mother walked to the window and fiddled with the curtains as she peered down into the garden, squinting against the sunlight reflecting from the summerhouse. She moved a porcelain teddy bear back into its proper place on the window ledge, from where it had been left by the police. It was a Royal Crown Derby paperweight with elaborate Imari designs on its waistcoat and paws, a gift to Laura from Graham after a business trip. Charlotte averted her eyes from the room and turned to stare at her son, studying his absorption until she became impatient.

"What exactly are you looking for, Danny? Evidence of your own guilt?"

Daniel went red. "I certainly don't need to look for yours. Yours or Dad's. It's been pushed in my face for long enough."

"Don't talk like that."

Charlotte had been upset herself by the fact that her son had failed to return to his home, even for a day or two, between the doubtful attractions of a holiday spent in Cornwall with his friends and the peculiar sense of obligation that drew him back to university so long before the start of term. She didn't know the reason he stayed away. Now she pulled a face at the streaks of dirt on Daniel's jeans, the scuffs on his shoes, and the powerful smell of stale sweat. He looked tired, his fleshy face shadowed with dark lines and a day's growth of stubble. He reminded her so strongly of his father as he had once been, nineteen years ago, before success and money had superimposed a veneer of courtesy and sophistication. Graham, too, had been a man whose passions were barely kept in check.

"There's one missing," said Daniel suddenly.

"What?"

"A letter. I wrote to Laura from Newquay last month. But it's not there; there's a gap. Where is it? She always kept them together."

"The police have been through them," said Charlotte uncertainly. "I suppose they might have taken one."

"What the hell for?"

"I don't know. It depends what was in it, doesn't it?"

"Are they allowed to do that?"

"I suppose your father will have given them permission. You'll have to ask him. I don't know what they were looking for."

Daniel put the letters down. He tied them together again with the ribbon, securing it carefully and neatly despite the trembling of his hands.

"It's bloody obvious what they were looking for."

As he headed for the door, Charlotte caught his arm. She could tell he hadn't washed today, perhaps for more than one day. The back of his neck was grubby and the collar of his T-shirt was stained. She longed to propel him physically to the bathroom and demand his filthy clothes for the wash, as she would once have done when he was a year or two younger.

But Charlotte knew her son had passed well beyond her control. What he did in Exeter was a mystery to her. He no longer told her about his course, about his friends, or where he lived. She could no longer understand the angry, disapproving young man he had become.

"Danny," she said, "don't condemn us so much. There's no need to stir up old arguments that aren't relevant to all this. Let the police find out what happened to Laura. The rest of us have to go on living together without her." She watched his sullen expression and saw his face was closed against her. She felt his muscles tense to pull away from her, to shake off the last physical link between them. "Your father—"

But it was the wrong thing to say. Daniel knocked her hand from his arm. "How can I not condemn you? You and my father are responsible for what happened to Laura. You're responsible for what she became."

He paused in the doorway of Laura's room, his face suffused with rage and contempt as he looked back at Charlotte. "And you, Mum, you couldn't even see what it was that she'd turned into."

The three old men were crammed into the front of Wilford's white pickup as it wound its way down from Eyam Moor toward the Hope Valley. They had avoided the main routes, leaving them to the tourists. But when they reached the A625 they would meet the evening traffic coming back from Castleton.

They huddled among empty feed sacks and neglected tools. The floor of the cab was littered with crumpled newspapers, an old bone, a plastic bucket, and a small sack containing a dead rabbit. Sam was squeezed uncomfortably between the other two, shifting his bony knees to find room for his stick under the dashboard and wincing at every bump they hit. Wilford was driving, his cap pulled low on his head to stop his hair blowing about in the breeze from the open window. He drove with sudden twists of the steering wheel and sharp stabs on the brake as they approached each bend. Harry, on the outside, looked as though he were sitting in a limousine. His hands were spread on his knees, and his head moved slowly from side to side as he studied the passing scenery.

In the back of the pickup, riding in the open on a bed of hessian sacks, was the brown and white goat. It was tethered securely to the backboard of the cab with a short length of chain so that it could not reach the sides. Every now and then it turned its head and bellowed at a startled cyclist.

The snaking twists of the road slowed a lumbering quarry lorry ahead of the pickup. All around them were the familiar tucks and folds of the hills and the strange, unpredictable rolls of the landscape that concealed the history of the ancient lead mining industry. There were overgrown hollows and mounds running across one field, indicating the line of a rake vein. Here and there stood an isolated shaft, walled off for safety. Many years ago, two bodies had been pulled out of one of these shafts in a notorious murder case.

"Even with all their scientific tests," said Harry, "the coppers still go 'round asking a lot of questions."

"Course they do," said Wilford.

"But it's like in the song," said Sam.

"What's that?"

Sam begin to sing quietly in a cracked, off-key voice. The tune was just recognizable as one familiar to them all—"Ol' Man River" from the musical *Showboat*. After a moment, the other two joined in with the song, tuneless and punctuating their singing with laughter.

"Don't say *nothing*," said Sam firmly, when they had finished.

Just outside Bamford, Wilford drove the pickup into an untidy farmyard and sounded his horn. Two half-bred Alsatians ran out of a kennel until they hit the end of their chains and barked and snarled at the wheels of the vehicle. A man of about forty with wild hair and a vast bushy beard came out of the house and wandered toward them.

Wilford greeted him as "Scrubby."

"You brought the young nanny, then?" he said.

The goat screamed hysterically from the back of the pickup. The noise was so loud in the yard that the dogs stopped barking, stunned into silence.

"Aye, happen that'll be her now," said Wilford.

"Bugger's been giving directions all the way here," said Harry. "It's worse than having the wife in the car."

"You've not brought any dogs, have you?" said Scrubby. "Only it upsets them two over there."

"Not in here," said Wilford.

The three old men climbed carefully out of the cab, creaking as they straightened their legs. Harry put his arm around Sam and helped him down the step until he could support himself with his stick.

"Bloody hell, what's that?" asked Sam, as a ripe, musky stench slithered across the yard and grabbed the back of his nostrils. "It smells like someone's been sick and set fire to it."

"Ah, that's the billy," said Scrubby. "He's in breeding condition a bit early this year. I reckon the young 'un can smell him all right."

A rapid smacking sound was coming from the back of the pickup. The goat was wagging her tail so fast it was beating a tune on the metal sides. She was straining at her tether until the collar bit into her neck deep enough to choke her. She yelled again when she saw Wilford.

"Are you going to mate her now? Can we watch?" asked Sam.

"Course you can. I don't even charge for tickets."

The goat tugged them over to a low stone building, not much bigger than a pigsty, with an enclosed yard on two sides. The building seemed to be the source of the smell. The three old men bent to peer through a small opening into the gloom of the shed. They could make out something large and hairy moving restlessly inside, pawing at the gate with its hooves and rubbing its head on the walls.

"Bloody hell," said Sam. "He's got a pair of bollocks on him as big as your prize turnips, Wilford."

The goat looked suddenly as though she might change her mind and go home.

"Come on, Jenny," said Wilford gently.

Together, they pushed the goat into the yard, and Scrubby drew back a bolt on the door. They let out a concerted breath as the billy emerged, steaming and snorting. He was twice the size of the young goat, with a powerful chest and a dense, matted coat. He had thick, twisted slabs of horn curling onto the back of his head like gnarled tree roots, and along his spine the hair was going thin, revealing gray patches of flaky skin, tough and wrinkled like the hide of an elephant. The two goats began to circle together, sniffing excitedly at each other's rear end. The billy's top lip curled back to expose his bare upper gum in a grotesque, leering grin as he savored the scent of sexual promise.

Scrubby was looking curiously at Harry, scratching at his beard and tugging at an old bit of baling twine lashed around the gate of the enclosure.

"I heard you're the bloke who found that lass that was murdered over your way."

"Aye, news travels well 'round here."

"It's a bit of a funny do that, isn't it?"

"Bloody hilarious," said Harry.

"I saw her picture in the paper. Bashing her head in is about the last thing most young blokes would want to do with her."

"Oh aye?"

"Don't you think so?"

"She was only fifteen," said Wilford, without looking around.

Scrubby seemed to recognize something in the tone of the reply.

"I suppose so," he said.

In the enclosure, the billy was trying repeatedly to maneuver himself into a position to mount Jenny from behind, but the goatling was getting frisky. She was lighter on her feet than the billy, and every time he approached her she skipped away, turning to face him, then trotting off again, her tail wagging provocatively. The billy was growling from the back of his throat with his mouth hanging open, producing a deep moan like a wild animal in pain. He kicked at Jenny with his front hooves, smearing dirty marks on her flanks. As he got more frustrated, he began to gobble excitedly. His tongue flopped out of his mouth and saliva flew. The feet of the two goats were churning up the surface of the enclosure, and dust coated the white hair on their legs. In avoiding the billy, Jenny tripped, stumbled to her knees, got up, and skipped away again.

"It doesn't look like she's cooperating," said Scrubby.

Sam nodded. "Playing hard to get."

"She's only a young 'un," said Wilford. "She doesn't know what's happening."

"She has to stand still, though."

Scrubby reluctantly climbed over the fence into the enclosure. The billy growled at him, then returned his attentions to the nanny.

Next time the young goat came within reach, Scrubby grabbed her by the neck and pulled her toward him. He twisted her collar until he had her in a stranglehold, with her face turned up toward him and her eyes rolling in alarm. She was panting by now, her nostrils pink and flaring and her sides heaving.

"You have to do this sometimes with the young uns," said Scrubby. "They get the hang of it after the first time. The old chap there knows what he's about, though."

The billy glared at him once, then took a few short steps and launched himself onto the young goat, digging his hooves hard into her sides and throwing the weight of his hairy body onto her back. Scrubby hung on grimly, tightening the nanny's collar so that she couldn't escape. She began to moan and whimper, and her breath came in short gasps. The billy balanced himself on her bony pelvis and thrust into her. The young goat's back legs buckled, and she began to collapse under his weight. Scrubby hauled her forcibly upward to keep her off the ground. The billy thrust three more times in rapid succession, then tossed back his head and gradually slid off. It was over.

Scrubby eased his grip on the goatling's collar, and she began to cough spasmodically. Her legs were trembling and a string of white semen dripped from the bare patch of skin on the underside of her tail.

There was silence for a moment, except for the painful coughing of the goat.

"She didn't enjoy that much," remarked Wilford in a strange voice.

"She's just immature, that's all."

"Is that it then?"

Jenny crouched and a stream of pale yellow urine hit the dirt. The billy stepped forward to sniff at the stream, then began to lap at it eagerly with his long tongue. The old men screwed up their faces and shuffled uneasily.

"I'll just hang on to her for a bit, while he gets his breath," said Scrubby. "Then he can have another go."

The three men were quiet in the pickup on the journey back to Moorhay. The visit to Bamford seemed to have subdued them.

"Reckon she'll be all right?" said Wilford as they climbed the hill out of the Hope Valley.

"He looked as though he knows his animals," said Sam.

"It seems hard on them, when they're so young. She was a bit innocent."

"Innocent?" said Harry. "She was screaming for it all the way there, wasn't she?"

The others nodded uncomfortably, and Sam gave a painful cough. He looked exhausted by the drive, and had lost his willingness to make a joke. Wilford stared grimly through the windscreen until Harry spoke again as they breasted the rise that looked down on to their own valley.

"I think," said Harry, "I might tell them a bit of what I know, after all."

Sam and Wilford nodded again. After that, nobody spoke all the way home. And nobody sang.

-14-

Ben Cooper and Diane Fry emerged from their showers damp and tingling, and drank a fruit juice in the rugby club bar before heading back to Edendale. Cooper had seen a glimpse of Fry's flat in Grosvenor Road, and he thought he knew why she had been so easy to persuade with an excuse not to go home. But she could not know his own reason, and so far she had shown no curiosity. She did, however, want to talk about work, to go over the day's results.

"God, that Moorhay place," she said. "Is everyone 'round here as stroppy and awkward as that? The Dickinson man was the worst. Unhelpful or what?"

"He's an old man," said Cooper, "an old man who'd had a shock. How do you expect him to be? Most people around here are friendly and helpful, anyway."

"That I remain to be convinced of."

Her view of Harry Dickinson struck Cooper as superficial. His own feelings had been quite different. He thought of the moment when he had found the body of Laura Vernon, of Harry standing like a black mark against the sun-drenched hillside. Stroppy and unhelpful? Maybe. Deeply disturbed and afraid, definitely.

"Anyway," said Fry, "hold on a minute. That wasn't what you said at the briefing this afternoon. You wanted Dickinson to be pressed harder."

"That's different."

"Yeah? An old man who'd had a shock. So what do you want to press him harder for? That sounds suspiciously like gratuitous harassment to me, pal. Where's the caring, sharing Ben Cooper here? Come off it, *you* think he was unhelpful, too, don't you?"

"I think he knows something he's not saying," admitted Cooper.

"And that's not the same thing?"

"Maybe Mr. Tailby and Mr. Hitchens didn't ask the right questions," he said thoughtfully. "Maybe it's not to do with Laura Vernon at all. I don't know."

"Well, you could always ask your girlfriend, I suppose," said Fry.

"Who?"

"You know—the granddaughter, Helen Milner. Got the hots for you, hasn't she? She was following you around Moorhay like a lost dog."

"Rubbish."

Fry shrugged. "I stand by the evidence, Your Honor."

Cooper refused to rise to the bait.

"What did you make of the other two, then—Harry Dickinson's friends?"

"My God, don't remind me. That place was like something medieval. When I left West Midlands, they kept telling me that the countryside was primitive. Now I know it's true. That dead hen . . . How Wilford Cutts's wife can put up with that, I don't know. No doubt she would have had to cook it in a stew tonight."

"And chop off its head and legs and pluck it and take out its innards," said Cooper. "That's women's work. So they say."

"Not this woman. I'd make him stuff his dead hen where it hurts most."

Cooper sniffed his orange juice suspiciously, worried by the distinctly metallic tang.

"You know," he said, "I don't think this inquiry will get any further until Lee Sherratt is traced."

"He's a fair bet."

Cooper shook his head. "I'm not sure. We're just accepting Graham Vernon's word as gospel and hoping the evidence will turn up somehow. It's lazy thinking."

"OK then, Sherlock. You obviously know better than Mr. Tailby and Mr. Hitchens put together. What's your theory, then?"

"You don't want to hear about my gut feelings, I suppose."

"You're right, I don't. I asked for a theory. Something that relies on a few facts."

"I suppose you play it by the book always. Do you never follow a hunch, use your instincts?"

"By the book," said Fry.

"So you get yourself into a difficult situation. The first thing you do is call in, then sit back and wait for the backup to arrive?"

"Well, usually," said Fry. "That is the sensible course."

"The safest for you, certainly. Would you never break the rule?"

She thought about it. "OK, there are times when you might have to take the initiative."

"Eureka."

"I'll let you know when that happens. All right?"

"Sure. Send me a fax."

A couple of rugby players walked past on their way out from the bar, smelling strongly of beer. They slapped Ben Cooper on the shoulder and ruffled his hair as they made jokes about making sure his balls were warmed up. They smirked across the table at Fry without speaking to her.

Fry was rapidly losing interest in Ben Cooper. Other police officers' private lives were a serious turnoff, she found. Just occasionally, there was someone she felt she needed to know more about. But there was no way Ben Cooper could be one of them.

"What do you know about DI Armstrong?" she asked him, when the rugby players had gone.

"Not much. I worked with her briefly when she was a DS, but B Division poached her from us. She seemed to get promoted pretty quickly. I can't say she's dazzled anybody with her results since she was moved up to DI."

"I suppose you're going to tell me she got the job because she's a woman."

"No, but . . . Well."

"And maybe she did. So what? Makes a change, doesn't it?"

"Not to me, it doesn't."

Fry drained her glass and slapped it on the table. "I think it's about time we left. There's just no atmosphere in here."

By the time they left the club, it was dark. Cooper pressed his key fob and the Toyota flashed its lights for him in the car park. The skeletal shapes of the white rugby posts were visible standing guard over the black, deserted pitches.

"Do you actually play rugby, then?" asked Fry as they got into the car.

"No, I could never see the attraction in it," he said.

"Oh? I thought team sports were a boys' thing."

"I don't know about that."

"Especially in the force. They like team bonding and all that, don't they?"

Cooper shrugged. "I've managed to keep out of it so far. I prefer the individual sports. But I am in the Derbyshire Police Male Voice Choir."

"You are kidding."

"No, it's good fun. We do a few concerts—for the old folks mostly, that kind of thing, especially around Christmastime. The old dears love it. It's good PR."

"Do you sing soprano?"

"Tenor."

A couple of miles down the road toward Edendale, Cooper turned the Toyota off onto a side road and headed back out of the valley.

"Where are you going?" asked Fry.

"I've had an idea," he said, "something that came to me when we were talking about DI Armstrong."

"What exactly do you mean?" said Fry, with a warning note in her voice.

"You remember I said she was 'poached' by B Division?"

"Are you still harping on that?"

"No, no, you don't understand. I was thinking about poaching."

"Come again?"

"Just up here there's a big estate, the Colishaw Estate. That's an 'estate' as in a large area of privately owned land. Not a housing estate."

"I think I've got that, thanks."

"The Colishaw Estate runs shoots. That means they breed a lot of pheasants. There are deer on the estate, too. Not to mention rabbits and hare and partridge."

"Is this a nature lesson? If so, could we possibly do it tomorrow?"

"Obviously, it's a big target for poachers," said Cooper patiently.

"Right."

"The professional gangs used to be a big problem, but they don't bother so much anymore. There's no money in it now. But the local men still get down there."

"Chasing the pheasants and rabbits."

"You don't exactly chase them."

Cooper pulled the Toyota onto the verge near a patch of woodland, where signs warned PRIVATE PROPERTY. There was little traffic on the road, and the night was totally black but for the stars in a clear sky. The Toyota's sidelights illuminated a wall and a length of barbed wire.

"There's an old hut down there," he said, pointing into the wood. "It's always been a favorite for poachers to lie up in. It's well away from where the keepers patrol, even when they bother. Jackie Sherratt was a notorious poacher. He used to use it all the time. He must often have taken his son Lee there. As part of his training."

"Sherratt? Hold on. You think—?"

"It's possible. I think Lee could have chosen the hut to lie up in. No one will have thought of checking this out. It's too distant from Moorhay. But a lad like Lee wouldn't think anything of moving this far."

"Don't tell me—you want to check it out?"

"Yes."

"Right here and now?"

"Why not?"

"Are you crazy? It's the middle of the night!"

"I'm going down anyway," said Cooper. "You can wait here if you like." He got out of the car, pulling a sturdy torch from the glove compartment.

"We can't do this."

"I can," said Cooper. "You'll obviously have to go by the book, won't you?"

He climbed over the wall and began to walk into the wood, finding the start of a narrow path that had been invisible from the road.

"Hold on, for God's sake," said Fry, slamming her door.

He smiled and keyed the electronic locks.

"Can't be too careful."

They set off close together, sharing the light of the torch. Cooper had always felt a part of the world he worked in, especially when he was out working in the open. But Diane Fry, he thought, would be forever a stranger to it. He was alert for any sounds in the wood, but she seemed completely absorbed in herself, as if the darkness meant not only that she couldn't see but also that she could neither hear nor smell what was around her, nor even feel the nature of the ground underfoot. Cooper was listening hard. Any countryman knew that the sounds that animals made could tell you whether there was a human presence in the area.

At that moment, he could hear the echo of a faint screech deep in the wood, a fleeting sound like the scratching of a nail on glass, or chalk across a blackboard, but with a plaintive falling note at the end.

"Little owl."

"Eh?" said Fry.

"Little owl."

"What *are* you talking about? Is it cowboys and Indians? You Big Chief Little Owl, me squaw?"

"I'm talking about the bird. Can't you hear it?"

"No."

They both listened for a moment.

"It's gone now," said Cooper.

Fry seemed genuinely reluctant to go into the woods in the dark. He was surprised by her behavior. Afraid of the dark? Surely not Diane Fry; not Macho Woman.

"Are you nervous?" he asked.

"Of course not."

"We could leave it until tomorrow, if you like. I could suggest it at the morning briefing, and see if anyone can be bothered to put out an action for it. We're not getting overtime for this, after all. It doesn't make good business sense, does it? If you want to look at it like that."

"Since we're here, let's just do it, then we can go home."

"On the other hand, if he *is* down there, he'll probably have moved on somewhere else by tomorrow."

"Can you just shut up and get on with it?"

Diane Fry found the darkness disturbing. The deeper they moved into the wood, the more she wished that she had brought a torch of her own, that she had refused to go along with the idea, that she had stayed in the car after all. Or better still, that she had never stupidly agreed to play squash with a jerk like Ben Cooper. She had known it had been a mistake from the start. She should never have let herself get involved, not even for one evening. And now it had ended up like this. With a stupid escapade that she could see no way of getting herself out of.

In front of her, Cooper was walking with an exaggerated carefulness, lifting his feet high in front of him before placing them cautiously back on the ground. He pointed the torch downward, shielding its light with his hand so that it would not be visible in the distance. At one point he stopped to rest against a tree. When he straightened up again, Fry felt him stagger as if he was drunk. She grabbed his arm to support him but felt no resistance in his muscles. Peering into his face by the dim light, she saw that his cheeks were drawn, and his eyelids were heavy.

"You're exhausted," she said. "You can't go on with this. We'll have to turn back."

"Not now," said Cooper. "I'll be all right."

He shook himself vigorously, and they set off again. Soon, a darker area of blackness began to form up ahead. Cooper switched off the torch and signaled her closer so that he could whisper into her ear. His breath felt warm on her cheek, which was starting to feel a faint chill in the night air.

"That's the hut. You stay here while I take a look through the window at the side there. Don't make a sound."

Fry began to protest, but he hushed her. Then he was gone, creeping through the trees toward the side of the hut. Soon his shape had vanished into the gloom, and she found herself on her own. Immediately, she felt the sweat break out on her forehead. She cursed silently, knowing what was about to come.

As soon as she was alone, the darkness began to close in around her. It moved suddenly on her from every side, dropping like a heavy blanket, pressing against her body and smothering her with its warm, sticky embrace. Its weight drove the breath from her lungs and pinioned her limbs, draining the strength from her muscles. Her eyes stretched wide, and her ears strained for noises in the woods as she felt her heart stumble and flutter, gripped with the old, familiar fear.

Around her, the night murmured and fluttered with unseen things, hundreds of tiny shiftings and stirrings that seemed to edge continually nearer, inch by inch, clear but unidentifiable. Next, her skin began to crawl with imagined sensations. It was as if she had stood in a seething nest of tiny ants that ran all over her body in their thousands, scurrying backward and forward, scuttling in and out of her intimate crevices, tickling her flesh with their tiny feet and antennae. Her flesh squirmed and writhed as an icy chill seeped into her bones.

She had always known the old memories were still powerful and raw, ready to rise up and grab at her hands and face from the darkness, throwing her thoughts into turmoil and her body into immobility. Desperately, she tried to count the number of dark forms that loomed around her, mere smudges of silhouettes that crept ever nearer, reaching out to nuzzle her neck with their teeth and squeeze the air from her throat.

And then she seemed to hear a voice in the darkness. A familiar voice, coarse and slurring in a Birmingham accent. "It's a copper," it said. Taunting laughter moving in the shadows. The same dark, stained pillars of menace all around, whichever way she turned. "A copper. She's a copper."

*   *   *

The light fell on her face, blinding her. She knew there was a person behind the light, but she couldn't make out his eyes. She tensed automatically, her hands closing into fists, the first two knuckles protruding, with her thumbs locked over her fingers, and her legs moving to take her balance. Concentrate. Pour the adrenaline into the muscles. Get ready to strike.

"Are you OK?"

A concerned voice, northern vowels. Whispering. Unthreatening. Fry let the muscles relax slowly, coming back to an awareness of the woods, to the fact she was in Derbyshire, many miles from Birmingham. The reality of the horror was months behind her, and only the wounds in her mind were still raw and terrible where they were exposed to the cold wind of memory. She took a breath, felt her lungs trembling and ragged.

Cooper leaned toward her face, so they were only a few inches apart. "Are you OK, Diane?"

Instinctively, she reached out a hand to touch him, like a child seeking affection, a protective embrace. She felt his solidity and his reassuring warmth, and closed her eyes to grasp at the elusive sensations of tenderness and affection. The feeling of another human body so close was unfamiliar. It was a long time since she had wanted someone to hold her and comfort her, a lifetime since there had been someone to wipe away the tears that she now felt gathering in the corners of her eyes.

"What's wrong?"

Fry pulled back her hand, blinked her eyes, drew herself upright. Control and concentration, that's what she needed. She breathed deeply, filling her lungs, forcing her heartbeat to slow down. Control and concentration.

"I'm fine, Ben. What did you see?"

"He's in there all right. He's got a candle lit, and I could see his face in a sort of half profile."

"You're sure?"

"It's definitely him."

"What do we do now?"

"Are you joking? We nick him."

Fry sighed. "All right. Let's nick him, then."

Cooper put his hand on her arm and gave it a squeeze. She bit her lip at the friendly gesture and firmly shook him off.

"There's just the one door, and there's no lock on it," he said. "We'll go in fast, one either side of him, take him by surprise. I'll do the words. OK?"

"Fine by me."

They approached the door, paused to look at each other. Cooper nodded, flicked the catch, and kicked the door inward on its hinges. He was in the hut fast, moving to his right, allowing Fry space to get alongside him.

A young man was bending over a wooden table against the far side of the hut. A candle threw a fitful light on his face and cast his shadow on the opposite wall. There was an old chair and a small cupboard in the room, and even a worn carpet on the floor. But the hut smelled of earth and moldy bread.

Cooper began to reach for his warrant card, which was deep inside the inner pocket of his jacket.

"Lee Sherratt? I'm a police officer."

Sherratt turned around, slowly and deliberately, and only then did Cooper see the gun. It came up in his hands as they lifted from the table, the barrel swinging outward and upward, with Sherratt's fingers turning white where they gripped the stock, one index finger creeping toward the trigger guard, a blackened fingernail touching the steel of the trigger, applying the first pressure. . . .

Cooper stood numbed with surprise, his right hand pushed into his pocket, immobile. His mind had come to a halt, no instincts sprang up to tell him what to do. The last thing he had been expecting was that he would die here, in the poacher's hut, on a threadbare carpet gritty with soil and fragments of stale food.

Then Diane Fry came into view. She was moving at twice the speed of Sherratt. Her left foot lashed out in a straight-legged sideways kick that impacted Sherratt's wrist and knocked the rifle out of his hands toward the wall of the hut. Even before the gun had landed, she regained her footing, shifted her balance, and was striking a closed-fist rising blow to his solar plexus. Sherratt folded backward into the table, then collapsed facedown on to the floor and vomited on the carpet. Fry stepped back to avoid the mess.

"You don't have to say anything unless you wish to do so, but what you say may be given in evidence," she said.

"Shit," said Cooper.

Fry dug into her pockets and pulled out her Kwik-cuffs and her mobile phone.

"I suppose I could have called in first and waited for the backup," she said, "but, like I said, there are times."

-15-

"But where are they, sir?"

"We don't know exactly. Somewhere on the Pennine Way, we think."

"But that's two hundred and fifty miles long."

"And there are twenty-two of them, apparently," said DCI Tailby. "And they've all got to be interviewed. Paul?"

DI Hitchens was sitting next to Tailby at the head of the briefing room. He seemed to be moving into a central position again in the Vernon inquiry.

"The hikers seen on the Eden Valley Trail are all students from Newcastle on a week's walking holiday. Apparently, they stayed overnight on Saturday at the camping barn at Hathersage, intending to reach the start of the Pennine Way via Barber Booth sometime on Sunday. But nearly three days have elapsed, and we estimate they will be somewhere in West or North Yorkshire by now. The local police are trying to locate them for us."

Tailby nodded. "DI Hitchens is in charge of this line of inquiry. When the students are located, he will travel to Yorkshire to interview them, accompanied by DC Fry."

There was a faint trickle of comment, quickly hushed. Ben Cooper saw the DI look around and grin at Fry.

"Mr. and Mrs. Vernon are coming in today to film their television appeal, which will be broadcast later," said Tailby. "We are, of course, hopeful of some results from the public." He smiled to himself as he said it—a small, self-mocking smile, as he thought of the phone calls that would certainly pour in from the cranks and the eccentrics; the overzealous and the neurotic; the well-intentioned but mistaken; and the sad, sad cases desperate for a bit of attention. From among the hundreds there might, though, be one or two calls that would provide vital help.

The DCI looked down at his checklist. "Have we anything on Daniel Vernon yet? Who's on that?"

A burly DC leaning against the side wall raised a hand in acknowledgment.

"Yes, Weenink?"

"I checked with his faculty at Exeter University. Vernon is about to start the second year of the political science course. It's social dialectics this term, apparently. I always thought that was a sort of sexual disease." Weenink waited for the expected laughs, smirking as he thrust his hands into his pockets and slouched more casually. "Term doesn't start for another two weeks; but the new intake, the first years, arrive before that to register and find their way about, get fixed up with digs, all that sort of thing."

"But Daniel Vernon is a second year student," said Tailby impatiently.

"He's a buddy," responded Weenink.

"What?"

"A few of the established students turn up early to give advice to the newcomers. Some of these kids turn up at university on their own and they've never been away from home before. The older ones befriend them. So they call them buddies."

"You found this out from the faculty?"

"From the Students Union. Vernon checked in there on Saturday morning and worked over the weekend meeting new students. The Union president remembers him being called away sometime Monday night."

"And he arrived home on Tuesday? How? Has he a car? Did he use the train?"

Weenink shrugged. "Don't know, sir."

"I'd like you to concentrate on pinning his movements down precisely," said Tailby. "I need to know whether we can eliminate Daniel Vernon from the inquiry. Laura Vernon was seen talking to a young man in the garden at the Mount just before she disappeared on Saturday night. That could just as easily have been Daniel as any boyfriend, unless he has a solid alibi for the period." He waited for Weenink to nod his understanding. "Meanwhile, as you all know, we have Lee Sherratt in custody, thanks to a bit of initiative last night by DCs Cooper and Fry."

The DCI said the word "initiative" as if he wasn't entirely sure it was something he approved of. It was, after all, contrary to current philosophies. Police work was now a team activity, a question of routine legwork and good communication, comparing and correlating, inputting vast amounts of data and seeing what came out of the computer or what matched up at the forensics lab. Unplanned nighttime arrests in remote spots by off-duty detectives did not fit the plan.

Cooper was still smarting from an early-morning dressing-down by Hitchens for his total disregard of proper procedures, for not letting anyone know what he was doing, and for his criminal foolishness in putting himself and a fellow officer at risk. Words like "rash," "irresponsible," and "foolhardy" had been used, and in his heart Ben Cooper could not deny that they were justified. But Lee Sherratt *was* in custody.

The DCI was still talking. "There was an initial interview with Sherratt last night, and the tapes are already transcribed. He will be interviewed again this morning by myself."

Cooper put his hand up. Tailby's eyes swiveled toward him.

"Let me guess, Cooper, you're going to ask about Harry Dickinson."

"Yes, sir."

Tailby shuffled some papers.

"He was unavailable last night, but there's an action allocated this morning to ask him about the bird-watcher's sighting on Saturday night."

"We ought to press him," said Cooper. "He hasn't been cooperating so far."

"We shouldn't be wasting too much time on him," protested Hitchens. "He's just an awkward old sod."

"With respect, sir, I think it was more than that. He was upset about something."

"Upset? Bloody rude, more like."

"No, there was something else." Cooper shook his head.

Tailby frowned. "Justify it, lad. Where's your evidence?"

"I can't really explain what it was, sir, but I could feel it. It's . . . well, it's just a feeling."

"Ah. For a moment there, Cooper, I thought you were going to say it was feminine intuition."

Several of the officers began to titter, and Cooper flushed.

"We could check Mr. Dickinson's movements out more carefully. Just in case."

Tailby nodded. "All right, that sounds thorough. Do you want to action this yourself, Cooper?"

"Of course."

As Tailby finished the briefing, Hitchens got up and came over to Fry.

"Off to sunny Yorkshire then, Diane. Call home and pack an overnight bag for when we get the call. These students can be elusive, so it might not be until tonight."

Cooper waited until Hitchens had moved away.

"You should be in on the interviews with Sherratt," he said. "It was your arrest."

"It doesn't matter," said Fry. But Cooper could see that it did. He wasn't comfortable, either, with the idea of her being away with DI Hitchens. But it was her own business, of course. Nothing to do with him. If she wanted to take the opportunity of sleeping her way to the top, let her get on with it.

"In the hut there, with Lee Sherratt . . ." he said.

"Yes, Ben?" She turned to him, ready to brush aside the thanks.

"That was a lucky blow. He walked right into it. But a side-handed strike would have been better."

"Oh, really? You know that, do you?"

"I'm a *shotokan* brown belt," he said.

Fry gave a chilly smile. "Well, hey, that's great. I've been looking for a dojo 'round here. I'm falling behind in my training. Can you suggest somewhere?"

"Come along with me. I can get you in at my club. Maybe we can have a friendly bout. It'll be a bit of practice for you."

"In case I have to pull you out of the shit again, do you mean?"

Cooper grinned. "It's always worth learning a bit more, getting your techniques right. Will you come along? When you get back from Yorkshire?"

She stared at him—an appraising stare, as if she were weighing up an opponent, measuring his capabilities, judging how much of a threat to her he could be.

"Do you know, I'd really love to do that, Ben. And I'll keep you to that bout, don't you worry."

Lee Sherratt sat sullenly in an interview room, staring at the two cassette recorders and twin video cameras. His skin was faintly swarthy, as if he had a fading suntan or hadn't washed for a long time. His hair was black, and the stubble on his cheeks made his complexion look even darker. His eyes wandered around the room, looking at anything rather than the detectives facing him. He was a well-built youth, but at the moment his muscular shoulders were held high, betraying his tension.

Tailby knew it wasn't Sherratt's first experience of being interviewed in a police station. There were minor offenses on his record—juvenile car crime but no violence, not even a drunk-and-disorderly. Yet Graham Vernon had called him a violent yob. Of course, there was the gun.

DI Hitchens started the tapes and checked that the cameras were running. "Interview commenced nine-fifteen A.M., Wednesday, twenty-fifth August. Present are Detective Inspector Hitchens . . ."

"Detective Chief Inspector Tailby . . ."

Hitchens nodded at the two men across the table.

"Lee Sherratt."

"And John Nunn."

Somehow the duty solicitor looked more uncomfortable than Sherratt did. Probably he was not used to being involved in a murder inquiry. But Lee Sherratt had no solicitor of his own, and right now he had the sense to know he needed one.

Hitchens was leading, after consultation with Tailby. He had a transcript in front of him of the interview conducted the previous night, without the benefit of a solicitor.

"Lee, a few hours ago you told us that you had no intimate relationship with Laura Vernon."

Sherratt nodded, staring at the table.

"For the tape, please."

"That's right."

"If you wouldn't describe your relationship with Laura as intimate, how *would* you describe it?"

Sherratt looked uncertainly at the solicitor and back at Hitchens. "We didn't have a relationship. Not what you mean."

"You knew her, didn't you, Lee?"

"Well, yeah. She lived there, at the Mount."

"So you must have had a relationship with her."

"Not really."

Hitchens sighed. "Would you say your relationship with Laura Vernon was one of friendship."

"No, she wasn't friendly."

"But you weren't complete strangers. You had met several times. You knew her name, she knew yours. You had spoken to each other."

"Course I'd met her."

"So how would you describe that relationship, if it wasn't friendly?"

The youth frowned, struggling for the right sort of word to offer. He looked at his solicitor again, but Mr. Nunn had nothing to suggest. Sherratt rubbed his cheek with a broad hand, scraping the stubble.

"She was a stuck-up little cow," he said at last. Mr. Nunn jerked as if he had been kicked awake and looked at the cassette recorder.

"Perhaps my client might like to reconsider that remark," he said.

"Certainly," said Hitchens generously. It wasn't an answer to his question anyway. "Let's try another question. Why did you hate her, Lee?"

Mr. Nunn shook his head. "No comment," said Sherratt proudly, relieved to have been given a clear signal at last.

"Did you *like* her?"

"Detective Inspector, this line of questioning—"

"I'm merely trying to establish the nature of the relationship between Mr. Sherratt and the victim," said Hitchens genially. "Shall we agree, Lee, that if you thought Laura was a 'stuck-up little cow,' then you didn't like her very much?"

"No, I didn't like her," said Sherratt. His eyes fell again, and his chair creaked as he shifted his bulk.

"Right. But did you fancy her?"

"No comment."

"Come on, Lee, she was an attractive girl. Mature for her age, they say. Sexy, even. You must have noticed. Didn't you fancy her? I'm sure other lads would have done."

"She wasn't my type," said Sherratt, with a smirk.

"Ah. I see."

Hitchens turned over a few sheets of paper. They were interview reports. He read a few paragraphs, taking his time as the tapes whirred.

"According to Mr. Graham Vernon," he said at last. "That's Laura's father, Lee, your former employer. According to Mr. Vernon, you had been pestering his daughter. Trying to chat her up, he says. Ogling her. Spying on her in the house. Following her around. And, he says, you tried every chance you had to touch her. And that your attentions were unwelcome."

"It's not true," said Sherratt before Mr. Nunn could decide whether to shake his head.

"Why would Mr. Vernon say things like that if they weren't true?" asked Hitchens.

"He's weird," said Sherratt dismissively, as if it needed no further explanation. His eyes began to roam around again. He studied the clock on the side wall as if wondering how long he had to last out.

"Weird, how?"

"Well . . ."

"Weird because he didn't like you pestering Laura?"

"No comment."

"Did it make you angry that he thought you weren't good enough for his daughter?"

"No comment."

"You were just the gardener after all, Lee. A servant. And not a very good gardener, by all accounts."

There was a flash of anger in Sherratt's face now as he glared at Hitchens. "I worked hard," he said sullenly. "I'm as good as them. Why shouldn't I be?"

"Did Laura look down on you, too?"

"You what?"

"Did she treat you like a servant, Lee?"

"She was a stuck-up little cow." Sherratt looked defiantly at his solicitor. He was starting to get more confident now. Tailby saw the change in his manner and tapped Hitchens's leg. It was time for him to come in, to change tack.

"Some of these stuck-up cows like a bit of rough, don't they, Lee? They're desperate to get it from a proper man, aren't they?"

Sherratt turned around to face Tailby, a knowing leer slipping onto his face before he could think of controlling it. Nunn coughed and shook his head several times.

"I bet you're the man to give it to them, aren't you, Lee?"

"Chief Inspector, I don't think that is a relevant question."

"Did you have sex with Laura Vernon?"

"I didn't," said Sherratt.

"Just a bit of heavy petting, then."

"No."

"So how would you describe your relationship?"

Sherratt leaned across the table. The veins stood out in his neck as his chin jutted forward. "I told *him* already. We didn't have one."

"But you met Laura when her parents didn't know about it, didn't you?"

"No."

"So her parents *did* know about it?"

"What? No, I never met her."

"But you've already said, Lee, that you met her during the course of your job at the Mount."

"Well . . . yes."

Even the solicitor was looking confused now. Tailby leaned forward.

"Now we've cleared that up, would you like to clarify your other statement?"

"What was that?"

"You've told us that you didn't have sex with Laura Vernon. Would you like to change that statement?"

"No. I didn't do it with her. I told you."

"Lee, when you were taken into custody last night you agreed to provide samples for forensic examination and DNA testing."

The dark eyes wavered nervously. "Yes."

"Do you understand what a DNA test is? Do you understand that this will enable us to match those samples we took with evidence found at the scene?"

"I wasn't at no scene."

"For example," said Tailby, "I mean the used condom we found in the greenhouse in the garden at the Mount."

Sherratt blinked and his face went a shade of yellow under the dark color. His solicitor shook his head.

Tailby merely smiled, his eyes colder than ever. "A used condom contains semen. A good source of a DNA sample. Will we find that it's yours, Lee?"

Cooper called first at Dial Cottage. Before he could knock, the front door was opened by Helen Milner. She was looking over her shoulder, calling to her grandmother.

"I'm off now!"

She was taken aback when she saw him standing on the step. She was back in her shorts and a sleeveless cotton top, and her limbs seemed to glow in the brightness pouring through the doorway from the street.

"Oh, hello, Ben."

"How are you?"

"Fine. Who have you come to see?"

"Your grandparents, actually."

Was that a flash of disappointment that passed across her face?

Intrigued, Cooper studied her expression. But it quickly became a friendly smile.

"Grandma is in. She'll be pleased to see you."

"Hold on. Do you have to rush off?"

"I've got a few things to do. But—well, they're not desperate."

Faced with Helen again, Cooper found himself searching for what it was he wanted to say to her.

"I'm sorry it had to be like this when we met again."

"It's your job, I suppose," she said.

The local postman was working his way down the road in his van, stopping every few yards to deliver his handfuls of mail. The radio in his van was tuned to Peak FM, and every time he opened the driver's door, the village was treated to a blast of relentlessly lively pop music. But the chances were that the messages he was delivering were not so bright or so cheerful as the music.

Helen had unlocked the door of her red Fiesta, which stood at the curb near the cottage. Cooper leaned on the roof of the car, trying not to flinch as the hot metal burned his arm through his shirt.

"It's a good job. But it can get in the way sometimes."

"How do you mean, Ben?"

"It comes between you and other people."

Helen nodded. "Everybody sees you as a policeman first and foremost, I suppose."

"All the time. But you didn't, did you?"

"What?"

"On Monday. When I came here, to Dial Cottage. You saw me first as Ben Cooper."

Helen laughed. "No. I saw you as the teenager I remembered at Eden-dale High. I would barely have recognized you if it hadn't been for the photograph in the paper the other week."

"But you said I hadn't changed much," he protested.

"It's what you say, isn't it?" Helen studied him. "Yes, I suppose at first it didn't occur to me you were the police, Ben. I just remembered you as you were."

Cooper smiled. "It brought memories back for me, too," he said.

The post van coasted past them and pulled into the curb in front of the Fiesta. The postman emerged in a burst of Abba and stared at them curiously as he passed. But he had no letters to deliver to Dial Cottage.

Helen wound down the windows of her car, trying to let out the stifling air. Cooper straightened, sensing he would be unable to keep her any longer.

"So aren't you a policeman all the time, then?" she said. "What are you like when you're just being Ben Cooper?"

"You'll have to find out one day, won't you?"

"Maybe I will."

Helen turned away and walked back to the door of Dial Cottage. Cooper watched her red hair swinging on her bare shoulders and admired the movement of her calves. He met her eyes hastily when she glanced over her shoulder as she pushed open the door.

"Grandma! You've got a visitor," she called.

Gwen appeared in the passage, her face lighting up at the sight of Ben Cooper standing next to Helen. She was wearing an apron, and her hands, which she was trying to wipe on a towel as she came to the door, were covered in flour. She patted Cooper's arm.

"Come in, and I'll put the kettle on again. Won't you stay for a bit, Helen?"

"Sorry, must go."

Gwen stood on the step waving and smiling conspiratorially at Helen as she walked to her car. Cooper waited hopefully while Helen started the engine and fastened her seat belt. He was rewarded with a quick glance and a flash of her smile. The warmth that spread over his skin was due to more than the sun and the hot pavements.

He was roused by Gwen Dickinson tugging his arm. "Are you coming in then, or are you going to stand out here gawping all day?"

Cooper was embarrassed by her knowing twinkle and tried to slip back into his professional role. "Is your husband not at home, Mrs. Dickinson?"

"No, he's not in," she said. "He'll be up at Wilford Cutts's place, if you want him. He's always there, or at the pub."

"Perhaps I could have a few words with you, since I'm here."

"As long as you sit down for a bit and have a cup of tea."

Cooper followed her into the kitchen, feeling again the coolness of the cottage, with its thick stone walls to keep out the heat. On Monday, he had thought the chill was partly due to the circumstances, the sensation he had had of the close presence of death. But even today the inside temperature was enough to make him shiver as he left the sun behind.

Gwen Dickinson boiled the electric kettle and heated a teapot. She opened a cupboard and emptied half a packet of digestive biscuits onto a plate.

"I'm sorry they're not chocolate ones," she said. "Young men like chocolate biscuits."

"That's all right."

"Is Harry in trouble?" she asked, turning to Cooper and looking him directly in the face.

Cooper shook his head. "He's an important witness," he said.

"Because he found the shoe."

"The trainer, yes. But we have reason to think he may also have been on the Baulk at the time that Laura Vernon was killed."

Gwen stared at him, clutching the plate of biscuits. The kettle boiled unnoticed behind her, releasing a cloud of steam around her head, until it switched itself off.

"What does that mean?"

"He might have seen something," explained Cooper. "Or someone."

"Oh, I see."

She gazed absently at the kettle and at the plate in her hand. She put the biscuits down, switched the kettle back on, poured the boiling water into the teapot, and picked the plate back up.

"Won't you sit down?" she said. "Take one of the armchairs."

"Let me carry the tray," said Cooper, noticing the unsteadiness of her hands.

"Has somebody said they saw him?" asked Gwen when they were seated opposite each other on either side of a small glass-topped coffee table. "Did they see Harry?"

"Yes. At least, we think it might have been Harry. On the Baulk."

"But he goes there every day," she said, looking more comfortable, "to walk Jess. Every day."

"Does he go at regular times? That's normal for a responsible dog owner, isn't it? A regular routine."

"Yes, regular. Nine o'clock in the morning, after his breakfast, and six o'clock at night."

"He doesn't vary?"

"Regular."

"And on Saturday night?"

"The same. Six o'clock. He sits down for his meal when he comes back. He says it gives him an appetite."

Cooper nodded, waiting while Gwen poured his tea. Her legs below the hem of her dress looked painfully swollen, and the lower sleeves of her blue cardigan were stuffed with bits of tissue, ready for the next onset of tears.

"Did your husband mention seeing anybody when he was out that night?"

"Do you mean the Mount girl?"

"Not necessarily. Anybody."

"No," said Gwen. "He never said anything like that." She paused for a moment, and offered Cooper a biscuit. "You don't know Harry very well, do you?"

"No, I've only met him briefly."

"Well, you see, he wouldn't say if he had, anyway. He's like that."

"He wouldn't tell you if he met somebody while he was walking the dog?"

"No, he wouldn't see any reason to."

"But since then? Since he's known that Laura Vernon was killed down there? If he remembered seeing somebody, might he not mention it?"

"Not to me," said Gwen simply.

"I see. Did your husband go out again later, Mrs. Dickinson? After his meal?"

"He usually goes down to the Drover," she said.

"And that night, did he go out as usual?"

"Yes, I'm sure."

"What time would that be?"

"I can't remember," said Gwen.

"After seven o'clock?"

"Oh yes, he wouldn't have finished his tea before that."

"After eight o'clock then?"

"I can't really say. It might have been."

Cooper heard the aggressive tone in his own voice and hesitated, seeing Gwen begin to tremble. He felt sorry for her and didn't want to increase her distress. She was only one of those innocent people who got caught up in something they didn't understand. He thought of his own mother, for whom things had got too much. He didn't want to be even partly responsible for pushing someone else toward the edge.

"Just a few more questions, Mrs. Dickinson, then I'll leave you in peace. I know it must be difficult for you."

"It's all right," she said. "Those other men frightened me, but I don't mind if it's you."

He smiled, touched by the old woman's faith but not sure whether he could live up to it.

"I wonder whether Mr. Dickinson would have taken his dog with him when he went out the second time? When he went to the pub?"

"Jess? Oh yes, he doesn't go anywhere without her." Gwen took a deep breath. "Are they saying he met the Mount girl down there?"

He was surprised at the question, and wondered why it had come into Gwen Dickinson's mind. He deliberately avoided an answer.

"You keep calling her the Mount girl, Mrs. Dickinson. But her name's Vernon."

"Yes, I know that. The Mount is where she lives, isn't it?"

She nodded her head toward the window. But all that could be seen was the garden, the edge of the trees, and the sunlit hillside beyond.

"Do you know Mr. and Mrs. Vernon, then?"

"They're comers-in."

"Is that yes or no?"

Gwen threw out her hands. Cooper knew the meaning of that gesture. It indicated that you could never really know comers-in, not in the proper sense. You might say hello to them in the street or in the shop, let them buy you a drink at the pub, or even share a pew with them at St. Edwin's these days. But you wouldn't ever know them—not like you knew the people who had always lived in the village, whose parents and grandparents and great-grandparents you knew, and whose grandparents had known *your* great-grandparents. Many of them might well have been first or second cousins to each other. Those were the people you knew.

"We were never introduced," said Gwen. "They weren't *known* 'round here. Not really." She peered anxiously at him to be sure he understood.

"Of course."

Yes, you only really knew people when you knew everything about them. You needed to know it all—from the exact moment they had been conceived in the long grass behind the village hall to the first word they had spoken, and the contents of their fifth-form school reports. You needed to know what size shoes they wore, how much money they owed the credit card company, when their bout of chicken pox had been, and which foot had the ingrowing toenail. You had to know who their first sexual encounter had been with, what brand of condom they had used, and whether the experience had been satisfactory. Now that was *knowing* somebody.

"But I have seen them," admitted Gwen, "the Mount lot."

"What about the girl? Laura?"

"She never went to school in the village—she was already too old when they came. She didn't even go to the big school in Edendale. Private, she was. That place out at Wardworth, what do they call it?"

"High Carrs."

"That's right. They always took her out by car every morning and back in the afternoon. At weekends they were always away out somewhere, shopping in Sheffield and the like. Riding lessons and I don't know what. She never had anything to do with any of the other girls in the village, nor any of the boys either, though plenty would have liked to know her better, I don't doubt. They kept her shut up in that place or well away from here. So she was never really part of the village then, was she? Not her, nor that brother of hers either. They couldn't be, not like that."

"And how well do you think your husband knew Laura?"

Gwen flared up suddenly, her lip lifting to reveal her false teeth in something that was almost a snarl. Cooper bit off too large a piece of biscuit and nearly choked.

"Are you sure you've been listening?"

"Of course I have."

"Didn't I say he never tells me anything? How would I know if he knew her? She's never been here, she's never been to the cottage. So how would I know?"

"I'm sorry," he said, and meant it. "I'll have to ask him myself, of course."

"You think he'll tell *you* anything?"

"It's in his own interests. It won't help to be uncooperative with us."

"Try telling *him* that. I wish you luck with it."

She relaxed into her chair, calming down again as quickly as she had flared. She looked up at him coyly, as if ashamed at her show of temper.

"I heard he had a bit of a disagreement with my bosses," said Cooper, probing gently at something that was intriguing him.

"And thought he was very clever doing it," Gwen said. She sighed and put down her cup half drunk. "He always was contrary. A stubborn man. Ever since I've known him, he's been like that. When I was a girl, it was one of the things I liked about him. I thought it was a man's pride then.

Now . . . well, like I say, he's stubborn. A right awkward old bugger, Harry Dickinson. Everybody knows that."

From the way the old woman spoke, it seemed to Cooper that it was the stubbornness that was still, really, the thing that she liked most about Harry. Now that the physical attraction had gone and the romance had long since settled into a numb familiarity, there was still a quality in her husband that could make her voice soften and her pale eyes shift out of focus, as if she were looking beyond the walls of the cottage to the shadows of a happier past. Their marriage might not be happy, but surely something else had taken the place of happiness—a sort of stability, a necessary balance. The old couple were like two of those ancient rocks propped against each other on Raven's Side—jagged and weathered, their hard surfaces gouging into each other, but worn to each other's shape by the years. But if one of those rocks should crumble, there was no future for the other.

"Of course, he thinks more of those pals of his than he does of me, these days," said Gwen. "Sam Beeley and Wilford Cutts."

"I'm sure that's not true," said Cooper.

"That's what Helen says as well. But I'm not sure. Not at all."

"He's known them a long time, hasn't he?"

"Forever. From when they were young lads together. Before he met me. When you get married, you think you'll be the most important thing in the other person's life. But Harry never let me come between him and his pals."

For a moment, Gwen's voice hardened again, her eyes focused on Cooper as if he had reminded her of the present. "They worked together, you know, in the mines," she said. "And they joined up together. They were young men then. Served in the same regiment and came back from the war closer than ever. Then they went back to the mines—but the war had killed the lead mining like it killed all those men. It was the other things that they mined by then, not the lead."

"Fluorspar and limestone."

Lead had been mined in the area since Roman times. Cooper knew that it was still produced in the last remaining local mines, but only as a by-product to the other minerals that were demanded by modern industries. Limestone aggregate dug out of the mines and quarries in the area found its way into everything from aspirin to tile adhesive, from washing powder to concrete. And there were other things too—barytes, zinc blende, and calcite; and the unique ornamental fluorspar they called Blue John. The supply of minerals beneath the Peak District seemed endless. But nobody wanted the lead anymore.

"They must have been retired a few years now."

"Oh yes. But it hasn't stopped them spending all their time together. Sam Beeley's wife only died a couple of years back, but Wilford Cutts now—his Doris has been gone a long time."

"Mrs. Cutts is dead?"

"Pneumonia it was, poor soul. Since Mrs. Beeley died as well, they've been worse than ever, the three of them. Up at the smallholding all day and in the Drover all night. It's obvious that I don't count at all."

"Men like a chance to be with other men, to talk about the things that don't interest women much."

Gwen looked sharply at him, and he felt as though she was seeing straight through him.

"Oh? And do you do much of that yourself, then, lad?"

"Er . . ."

She waved a hand, sparing him a reply. "Never mind. I can see what sort of lad you are."

"Mrs. Dickinson, I do think your husband may know something he's not telling us."

Gwen laughed suddenly. Her hands danced on the front of her green cardigan, blue veins shimmying beneath the skin like worms exposed to the light.

"If he didn't, it'd be the first time in his life!" she said. "I told you—he's the closest old bugger you ever met. And nobody knows better than me."

"Has he really never confided in you, Mrs. Dickinson?"

"Dafthead. That's what I'm telling you, isn't it? If you want to know who he tells things to, try them other two. They're the ones he spends all his time with. No use asking me what he knows, I'm the last one he'd tell."

Cooper emptied his cup and dusted the crumbs off his fingers.

"Thank you for the tea, Mrs. Dickinson."

"You won't mind the things I say, will you? I'm just a silly old woman sometimes."

"You've been very helpful."

"You're a nice lad. Will you come back again tomorrow? Come a bit earlier, when Helen's here. She's been talking about you, you know."

Cooper hesitated. The invitation was tempting. There was a part of him that felt there was a chance here to introduce something pleasant into his life for a change. And he knew that chances, if not taken, had a habit of never coming around again. Then he thought of all the responsibilities that weighed on him. He was in the middle of a murder inquiry, for heaven's sake. Not to mention the crisis at home, and, above all, his mother in need of all the love and support he could give.

"I'm sorry, I can't promise that. There's such a lot to do at the moment."

"I suppose so. But she'll be sorry not to see you."

"You think I might find your husband at Thorpe Farm?"

"Sure to. Him and Jess went out hours ago."

"I'll pop up and see if I can find him, then. And don't worry—it's only routine."

Gwen escorted him to the door of the cottage. Then she put her hand on his sleeve.

"You can't make me give evidence against him, can you?" she asked.

"Why would we want to do that, Mrs. Dickinson?"

She shook her head wearily. "Oh, I know. It's only routine. I know."

And Ben Cooper didn't know the answer to his question either.

-16-

The smell of the smoke was acrid and strong, like burning rubber. But it was nowhere near as strong as the other smell, which lay like an evil fog on the ramshackle buildings and overgrown paddocks of rough grass. It was the sweet, sickly stink of advanced decomposition, the odor of organic matter rotted to the point of putrefaction and the escape of fermenting gases.

Cooper had found the three old men by using his nose. They were building a vast compost heap, well out of sight of the track to the house at Thorpe Farm. From a seat on a bale of straw, Sam Beeley was supervising the operation, while Harry Dickinson and Wilford Cutts had their jackets off and their sleeves rolled up on their white arms as they wielded two forks. Two young men were mucking out a nearby breeze-block building, producing a constant trail of wheelbarrow loads of dark, wet, strawy manure. It arrived in the barrows steaming and black, like enormous Christmas puddings. A few yards away, a pile of dry bedding was smoldering viciously, creating a blanket of thick gray smoke that drifted away from the buildings and dispersed in the bracken on the hillside. Its smell couldn't mask the stench of the fresh manure piling up in heaps on the ground. The smell was overpowering.

Wilford saw Cooper approaching and pointed at him with his fork, stabbing the air.

"Look what's coming! Here's trouble, you lot."

"Nay, he's a hero, that lad," said Sam. "He's just come from arresting the number one suspect. Solved the case, he has."

"On his own?"

"With one hand behind his back, probably."

"Happen he's come to volunteer," said Harry, leaning on his fork. His shirt was open at the collar, and there was a distinct line where the tan of his neck met the bleached white skin of a throat and chest that hadn't seen the sun for years. He looked like parts of two totally different men stuck together. Cooper thought stupidly of Frankenstein's monster, the creature with a head sewn crudely onto someone else's body.

"Ah, grab a spare wheelbarrow, then," said Sam, "unless you know anything about making compost."

"All you do is pile it up and it rots down again," said Cooper, determined to stay on friendly terms. "Is that right?"

"Oh no, not at all."

"Not at all," echoed Wilford. "There's an art to compost. It needs nurturing, like a child."

One of the young men came past with another load of manure. Cooper stepped back as a lump of evil-smelling muck slipped off the barrow. He could see it consisted of wet, soiled straw and partly decomposed animal droppings in indistinguishable clumps. As soon as the manure had landed, small brown flies appeared from nowhere and settled on it, probing into the mess with their noses.

"This is good stuff," said Wilford. "Take a whiff of that lot."

"You use it on your vegetable patch, I suppose."

"Vegetables now, they need a particular sort of compost."

"Blood and bone. That's what you want for vegetables," said Harry.

Sam cackled. "Blood and bone. Blood and bone," he said. "Oh aye."

There were dogs barking from a shed in the background. But the smallholding was quieter than Cooper remembered it from his previous visit with Diane Fry. There was a strange stillness about the scene in front of him, as if the old men were posed around some bizarre work of art they had created for the National Gallery.

"There's plenty of nitrogen in blood," said Wilford. "Phosphorus in bone. Nowt like it for your brassicas."

Another barrowload of manure was tipped onto the heap. Wilford and Harry forked it over, and Harry walked up the slope and trod up and down the heap in his black wellies.

"I'd like to speak to you, Mr. Dickinson, please," said Cooper, staring up at him.

The compost heap had reached a height of about four feet. Harry loomed high above Cooper, a strange scarecrow figure marching up and down on the compost like a sentry on guard duty. Cooper had to shade his eyes against the sun to look up at the old man.

"In a minute," said Harry.

Wilford passed him up two thick wooden stakes about six feet long. Harry chose a spot carefully and drove the first stake deep into the compost. It plunged into the heap with a squelch and a burst of putrid odor. Then he heaved his weight onto the end of the stake until it stopped moving, with the last couple of feet still protruding.

"You've got to give it a bit of air," explained Wilford as Harry drove in the second stake.

The youth with the barrow came past again and gave Cooper a sideways look and a conspiratorial grin. He had very short fair hair and a ring in his right ear. He was about the same height as the detective and had well-developed muscles in his arms and shoulders. He was wearing torn jeans and was stripped to the waist. His torso was oily with sweat from the exertion and the steamy heat inside the building. A few yards away, the other youth was throwing some branches and armfuls of straw onto the fire to keep it going. The straw caught, and flames instantly leaped into the air.

Closer to, the vast compost heat was shimmering and steaming, with clouds of dung flies swirling through the haze seeking out the choicest, smelliest patches. Cooper covered his mouth and nose, feeling slightly sick. He was used to farmyard smells, but this was a special creation in itself.

"Mr. Dickinson, I really need to talk to you."

"It won't smell when it's ready, you know," said Sam.

"Now, please," snapped Cooper, starting to lose his temper.

The three old men made an elaborate show of being impressed by his authoritative tone. Harry stood to attention in his wellies and saluted slowly. Wilford hoisted his fork over his shoulder like a rifle. Sam got up from his bucket and peered at Cooper over the top of the compost, grinning slyly.

"You'll get on all right, lad," he said. "You could be chief constable one day. All you have to do is get rid of all the other people ahead of you first."

The old men laughed, and Cooper scowled. The heat was really starting to get to him. He felt drained of energy and irritable. He was relieved when Harry picked his way carefully down the side of the compost to join him.

"I'm about finished here now," said Harry. "If you hang on while I fetch Jess, you can give me a lift home and talk all you like."

"Fine," said Cooper, pleased at the chance to get away from the small-holding.

"Blood and bone," called Sam, as Cooper began to walk back across the field. But Wilford followed him and caught up with him by the gate.

"You'll be questioning Harry again," he said. "That's what they call it, isn't it? Questioning."

The aroma of the compost clung to Wilford's clothes and skin and hair, and small clumps of it dropped from his boots as he moved. He was breathing a bit too fast, with his chest heaving and his face strained.

"I'm on the Laura Vernon inquiry, as you know, sir."

"Those Vernons. They're not all they're cracked up to be, you know."

"What do you mean, sir?"

"They've got a lot of money and they reckon to be posh, but they're not. They've been bad for this village."

"People like that will always be resented."

"Oh aye, but everybody knows . . ."

"Knows what?"

Wilford shrugged and lifted his cap, running his hand through his hair. The uneven white patch that had refused to catch the sun stood out on his freckled scalp.

"It doesn't matter, I suppose. You'll be asking more questions about the girl."

"Of course we are. That's what we've been doing all week. If you know anything—"

"No, no. But it's true, though, isn't it?" He looked at Cooper to seek reassurance. "A sin will always catch you out. Like we used to say in the mines, it'll always come to day."

Cooper didn't know what to say to that. But Wilford wasn't expecting a reply in any case. They passed several of the makeshift buildings along the track and came to the stone-built shed where the nanny goat had been on Tuesday when it had escaped.

"The goat's gone quiet," remarked Cooper.

"Aye. Quiet enough."

He poked his head around the corner of the goat's shed, but it was empty. There was no sign of the animal in the paddock either. Harry had disappeared behind another shed in a wire enclosure, and emerged with the black Labrador on a leather lead in one hand and a plastic carrier bag in the other.

When they reached the Toyota, Harry sat on a wall and took off his dung-covered Wellingtons and a pair of thick socks, exposing thin white feet. He took a pair of clean shoes and socks from the carrier bag and put them on.

"I'm not overfond of the job, you understand," he said, "but it's only natural stuff, manure. The missus'll moan, though, when I get in."

When Harry got into the passenger seat of the hot car, Cooper realized exactly why Gwen Dickinson was likely to complain.

Andrew Milner drove up the gravel drive of the Mount and parked in front of the mock pillars, close to Graham Vernon's Jaguar. He looked enviously at the sleek blue car, conscious of its importance as a symbol of the difference in status between himself and his employer. Andrew merited only a three-year-old Ford Mondeo, like any ordinary salesman.

He picked up a document case from the passenger seat, took a deep breath, and walked toward the front door. There was a closed-circuit TV camera high on the front wall, pointing down toward where he stood. Andrew kept his face turned away from its lens as he approached the steps. The sun reflecting from the white walls of the house created a protective barrier of heat and glare that he had to fight his way through.

"Excuse me. Mr. Milner?"

Andrew looked around, startled. He found a dark, intense young man staring at him from the other side of the Jaguar. He looked dirty and unkempt, and for a moment Andrew thought he must have been trying to steal Graham Vernon's car, until he recognized him.

"Oh. It's Daniel, isn't it?"

"We met once, didn't we?"

"Yes. Look, I'm sorry about, you know—"

"It's not your fault. You work for my father, but you're not like him, are you?" Daniel walked around the Jaguar. He was carrying a bunch of keys with a remote control device for the door locks and alarm. "I was going to borrow Dad's car, but I've changed my mind. I think I'd rather walk."

Andrew watched in astonishment as Daniel tossed the keys into a stone urn standing by the front steps. They vanished into the roots of a small shrub.

"I thought somebody around here ought to say sorry to you," said Daniel.

"To me?"

The young man came closer. "Sorry that you got involved. You and your family. I don't suppose my parents would ever mention it. They don't care, you see. They don't see the effect on anyone except themselves."

Andrew didn't know what to say. He clutched his document case closer, searching his reserve of social small talk for a reply. "You're studying at university, aren't you?"

Daniel laughed, then looked away as if suddenly losing interest. "I'm at Exeter, doing political science. A different world."

"Such a dreadful thing to happen," said Andrew, exhausting his stock of phrases.

When the young man spoke again, it was as if he were addressing the blue Jaguar, as if he had forgotten that Andrew Milner was there.

"They had already rung me at Exeter as soon as Laura disappeared, you know. But I just thought she'd gone off with this bloke, the boyfriend, Simeon Holmes. It was bound to happen sooner or later, I thought. I intended to come back home, but only after Mum and Dad had got over the shock of finding out their daughter was a secret nympho."

"I see."

"I should have come back straightaway. Shouldn't I? Don't you think so?"

"It's not for me to judge. Really—"

"No, not for anybody to judge but me," said Daniel bitterly. "Sorry to have bothered you."

He set off to walk down the drive, his hands thrust into the pockets of his jeans and his shoulders hunched angrily. Andrew watched him until the young man stopped a few yards away and turned back to shout in derision.

"Don't just stand there, go on in! I'm sure you'll find my mother available!"

Andrew shook his head, bewildered, but went on up the steps to ring the bell. Charlotte Vernon answered the door, looking smart in a silk blouse and cream slacks. She stared at Andrew for a moment, then broke into astonished laughter that carried a hint of hysteria.

"You! What on earth are you doing here?"

Andrew flushed, pulling nervously at his tie. His forehead was creased in permanent anxiety. "I'm sorry, Charlotte. I've got some papers that I need Graham to sign."

"Oh, really? *Important* papers?"

He waved a hand helplessly, hardly daring to look at her, conscious of the sweat running down inside his collar. He suddenly remembered the car keys in the urn outside, and wondered how he could mention them.

"Lost for words?" said Charlotte. "You'd better come in, I suppose. But it'll have to be quick."

"I'm sorry. Are you going out?"

"We've got our big moment of fame."

"I beg your pardon?"

She stood close to him, touching his arm, widening her eyes instinctively as she enjoyed his embarrassment.

"Graham and I are doing a television appeal. The police seem to think it will do some good."

"Oh, I see."

Andrew clutched his document case closer to him, so that it covered his groin like a protective talisman. His eyes roved around the hallway, looking toward the doors as if hoping for rescue. He tried to sidle gradually toward where he knew Graham's office lay.

"I'm sure Graham will be wonderful on TV, aren't you?"

"Oh yes. He's very articulate."

"Articulate. That's good. Yes, he talks very well, doesn't he? Very convincing. But what do *you* think, Andrew?"

He found himself almost squashed against the wall, close to an antique inlaid cabinet he had always admired. His hand slid across its lid as he groped for support, leaving a sweaty palm print on its polished surface.

"About what happened to Laura, you mean?"

"Yes—that, Andrew."

"They've taken Lee Sherratt in for questioning, haven't they?"

Charlotte laughed. It was a deep, throaty laugh, roughened with cigarette smoke and tinged with hysteria. Then she stopped laughing suddenly and tightened her grip on the sleeve of his jacket.

"Is that the best you can do? Is that what you're relying on? It won't be enough, believe me."

Andrew Milner felt her eyes leave his face and move away, staring over his shoulder. He turned his head and saw Graham Vernon watching from the door of his study, a sardonic smile on his face. Andrew became horribly aware of Charlotte's body pressed close against him, her breast squeezing into his arm, her pelvis thrust against his hip.

"Did you want to see me, Andrew?" asked Graham. "Or is Charlotte looking after you?"

*   *   *

Once in his own home, cleaned up and seated in his chair in the front room with his pipe, Harry looked much more approachable than he had among his friends. He had a copy of that morning's *Buxton Advertiser* on the table by his chair. On the front page was a color picture of the well dressing ceremony at Great Hucklow. This year the villagers had created a picture from flowers on the theme the Millennium—Two Thousand Years Since the Birth of Christ. According to the story, the team had worked through the night to finish the display for the opening ceremony.

"It says here the police are assessing the result of forensic tests," said Harry, tapping a story at the bottom of the page. "And they expect to make an arrest soon. Is that right?"

"I suppose it must be."

"Detective Chief Inspector Stewart Tailby, who is leading the inquiry, said: 'I remain hopeful.' Is that just a lot of rubbish, or what?"

"I want to ask you about Saturday night," said Cooper.

"Oh aye? Any particular Saturday?"

"Last Saturday night. The night we believe Laura Vernon was killed."

"That Saturday. Well, let's see. It was warm."

Cooper had read the transcript of the initial interview with Harry Dickinson, and he was determined not to let Harry divert him from his questions.

"Tell me what you did that evening, Mr. Dickinson."

"From when?"

"Let's say, six o'clock."

"Took the dog for a walk," said Harry straightaway. "Six o'clock regular. Jess likes her routine. We go down the path onto the Baulk. Under the cliff on Raven's Side, that's her favorite spot."

"Do you always go there?"

Harry sucked on his pipe. "Sometimes I vary it a bit. If I'm feeling a bit rebellious, like."

"But that night you walked toward Raven's Side?"

"That's right."

"Go on then. What did you do while you were out?"

"Do? Not much. The usual. Smoked a pipe. Let Jess off the lead for a run and to do her business. Sat for a bit. Walked back."

"Who did you see while you were walking your dog?"

"Oh, just the usual bunch of murderers," said Harry.

By the old man's chair was a little mahogany cabinet, well polished and worn with age. On the upper level was a shelf with a pipe rack, a leather tobacco pouch, and the other paraphernalia of a pipe smoker. Below it was the door of a small cupboard. A tin of black shoe polish, a cloth, and a shoe brush stood on the floor in front of it. Cooper glanced at Harry's gleaming shoes and looked back up to meet his eyes again.

"It was a serious question, Mr. Dickinson."

"Ah, but you made an assumption. You assumed that I saw someone. Are you trying to trick me or what? Because it won't work, I'll tell you that."

"No tricks, Mr. Dickinson."

Try silence, thought Cooper. The use of silence is a powerful tool. It puts the interviewee under pressure to speak. So he waited, expecting Harry to claim that he had seen no one. But Harry puffed at his pipe, staring into the distance, shifting to a more comfortable position in his chair. The only sound in the room was the ticking of the carriage clock. Outside, a van went by. The babble of the television came from the next room, where Gwen was watching a quiz show. Cooper started getting restless. Harry looked as content and self-contained as if he were still sitting on the Baulk with his dog at his feet, gazing at the outline of the Witches, thinking perfectly calm thoughts of his own.

"Did you see anyone?" said Cooper at last.

"Some hikers," said Harry, "now that you ask."

"Did they see you?"

"I doubt it. They were down by the stream. Young folk, they were, larking about. The young ones don't notice much, do they?"

"How long were you out?"

"Half an hour, until I came back here. Gwen had my tea ready, and I fed Jess."

"And later in the evening?"

"I went out again, to the Drover. About half past seven. I met Sam and Wilford, and we had a few pints. Lots of folk there know me. Ask Kenny Lee. That's what they call an alibi, isn't it?"

"Did you go straight there?"

"Why shouldn't I?"

"You didn't take a long way 'round—via the Baulk, for instance?"

"Why should I do that? I'd already been once."

"Did you take the dog?"

"Jess was with me. But Kenny makes you put the dogs out the back when you're in the pub. He says they upset the tourists."

Cooper wondered whether Harry would get around to asking him the purpose of the questions. He decided he wouldn't.

"We have a witness who saw someone answering your description at about seven-fifteen, in the area where Laura Vernon's body was found." The description had been vague enough, so he wasn't actually being misleading.

"Have you now?" said Harry. "That's handy then. That'll help you no end."

"But you've just told me that you were back here in the house at about six-thirty, Mr. Dickinson. Is that right?"

"Aye, that's right. My tea was ready."

"And you said you didn't go out again until seven-thirty. So, according to you, you were here in the house at seven-fifteen. Is *that* right?"

"Yes."

"You can't have been in both places at once."

Harry shrugged. "That's your problem, I reckon."

"What about Sunday?" asked Cooper, desperate for a change in the conversation.

"What about it?"

"Did you go out on the Baulk with your dog that day?"

"Nine o'clock in the morning and six o'clock at night. Regular."

"On the same path? To Raven's Side?"

"Yes."

"And on Monday morning the same?"

"Nine o'clock."

"It's a bit odd then, isn't it, that you didn't find that trainer before Monday night? When you had already made four visits to the area. One about the time Laura Vernon was killed, and three afterward. Without seeing a thing?"

Harry tapped his pipe into the fireplace, stared at the empty grate, and looked up at Cooper. He narrowed his eyes and set his jaw. Cooper thought he was in for another uncomfortable spell of silence.

"I was going to talk to Vernon," said Harry suddenly.

"What?" Cooper was taken by surprise, both at the information and the fact that Harry had actually volunteered it without having to have it dragged out of him with red-hot pincers.

"On Saturday night. I thought I saw Graham Vernon while I was out with Jess. I was going to talk to him."

"Why was that, sir?"

"I had something I wanted to discuss with him. Personal."

"What about?"

"Personal."

"How well do you know Mr. Vernon?"

"I don't. I've never met him."

"So why did you want to speak to him?"

"I've said it twice. I'm not intending to say it again."

"I could insist, Mr. Dickinson. I could ask you down to the station to help with inquiries, and we'll conduct a formal interview and ask you to make another statement."

"I'm making a statement," said Harry. "It was personal. That's a statement."

"But you do see that if it was anything to do with Mr. Vernon's daughter—"

"I can tell you that. It wasn't."

"To do with your own family perhaps?"

Harry smiled benevolently, as if at a clever student. "Happen so, lad."

"Where did you meet Mr. Vernon?"

"Assumptions again."

"Sorry?"

"I said I *wanted* to talk to him. But I couldn't find him. He'd disappeared again."

Cooper's mind was setting off on a different track now. He saw Harry Dickinson out wandering on the Baulk at the same time as both Laura Vernon and her father, not to mention whoever had killed Laura. And he pictured the bird-watcher Gary Edwards, who had been in a wonderful vantage point, but had only seen one of them. And then he realized that, if Harry *had* met Graham Vernon while he was out, then their conversation would surely have meant that Harry would have been later back at the cottage than usual. But would it have kept him out until after seven-fifteen? Gwen would have to be lying, too. But then she would, wouldn't she, to protect Harry?

"Next question then," said Harry.

Cooper decided he was getting into deep water. "No more questions for now, Mr. Dickinson."

"No?" Harry looked suddenly disappointed. He pursed his lips and cocked his head on one side. "That's a poor do. I was hoping for a proper grilling. An interrogation. You know, like *Cracker.*"

"Sorry?"

"That fat bloke that used to be on the telly."

"Robbie Coltrane, you mean. He played a criminal psychologist."

"Aye. He always used to give 'em a proper grilling. Shouting and swearing at 'em and all. Threatening to thump 'em if they didn't tell the truth." Harry squinted at Cooper critically. "Aye well. You're not him, though. Are you, lad?"

"No, Mr. Dickinson, I'm not Cracker. I'm not Inspector Morse either."

Cooper got up to go, shoving his notebook in his pocket. "Somebody will want to talk to you again, probably, Mr. Dickinson."

"Fair enough. You'll no doubt find me without any trouble."

"Thanks for your time, then."

Cooper reached the door and looked out at the village, struck by the contrast between the bright sunlight hitting the street and the cool, shady corners and heavy furniture of the room behind him. Passing through the door of Dial Cottage was like stepping out of the entrance to a deep cave. In ancestral memory, caves must have represented security. But there was always danger, too. There was always the possibility that a dangerous wild beast might be lurking in that cave. Cooper turned to say good-bye to the old man and found the sharp blue eyes fixed mockingly on his face.

"No. And you're not even Miss Marple," said Harry.

-17-

DCI Tailby's office was one of the few rooms in the Edendale Divisional HQ with air-conditioning. In the past couple of weeks, there had been a lot of excuses for meetings that had to take place in the DCI's office and nowhere else. Ben Cooper, though, was sure his visit that afternoon was justified by something besides the unbearable temperature.

"Very interesting," said Tailby when he had finished summarizing his interviews at Dial Cottage. "But do you feel you pressed him hard enough, Cooper?"

Cooper remembered what he had said during the morning meeting and wondered if the DCI was making fun of him. He was glad he had decided not to mention any of what had taken place at Thorpe Farm before he had managed to get Harry into the car.

"He's a bit of an awkward character, sir."

"I know. Perhaps we'll have to bring him in and interview him under caution. That would upset his apple cart, eh?"

"Possibly."

"So what do you make of it, Cooper? Do you believe him?"

"Well, yes, sir, funnily enough."

"Mmm?"

"Well, I believe what he said, because of the things that he didn't say, if you follow me."

"I don't think I do, Cooper."

"Well, it seems to me that he neatly avoided telling a lie. Where there were things he didn't want to tell me, he just avoided it. Because of that, I think everything he said was true. I think it's probably against his principles to lie."

"Are there still people around like that? I may be a cynical old detective chief inspector, but I thought that idea went out with George Washington."

"It's old-fashioned, I know, but there are still people 'round here who were brought up like that. My feeling is that Harry Dickinson is one of them. That's a good reason why he says no more than necessary. The less you say, the less temptation there is to lie."

"Tell the truth or say nowt."

"That's it, sir. Exactly."

"That's what my old shift sergeant told me many years ago when I was a new recruit," said Tailby, "but it *was* a long time ago. Things change, Cooper."

"Not everything changes, sir. With respect."

Tailby ran a hand vigorously through his hair, as if trying to mix the gray at the front with the darker hair at the back to create something that looked less like a session with the Grecian 2000 that had gone badly wrong. His face was even gaunter than usual, and he looked tired.

"All right. So has the bird-watcher got his times wrong? Was it earlier than he thought when he saw Dickinson and his dog?"

"It's possible. You can lose track of time when you're up on the hills. It can be very deceptive."

"We'll have to check with him." Tailby shuffled a file of reports. "Damn it, there's no mention of whether he had a watch on, or whether it was usually accurate. A bit of a sketchy interview altogether, in fact. Who did that?" He grimaced. "Oh yes, DS Rennie."

Unconsciously copying the DCI's gesture, Cooper raised a hand to push a lock of hair back from his forehead and found some of the strands stuck to his skin by sweat.

"I can't reconcile the idea of all those people we're interested in being on the Baulk at the same time," he said. "Laura, Harry Dickinson, Graham Vernon. And a fourth person—the killer? It seems like too much of a coincidence."

"We can't let Dickinson get away with refusing to say why he wanted to talk to Graham Vernon," said Tailby.

"Can we show that his reasons are relevant to the inquiry?"

Tailby considered it. "The whole question of Dickinson and Vernon being out on the Baulk at that time is very relevant."

"The bigger question is—what was Vernon doing?" said Cooper.

"The Vernon family have got some more questions to answer, I'm afraid. There's clearly something not right about their account of events just before Laura vanished. Yet they were very convincing during the appeal this morning. Graham Vernon will come over very well on TV."

Ben Cooper felt distinctly unimpressed by the thought of Vernon's television persona. In his own experience, anything that was said for the sake of the TV cameras was even less likely to approach the truth than the normal tangle of fabrications and evasions he had to deal with every working day. Lies told under a bright gloss of lights and cameras were lies just the same.

He watched Tailby fiddle with the knot of his tie like a man worried about his appearance, and he knew the DCI felt the same way.

"What about Daniel Vernon?" asked Cooper.

"Oh, there are several reliable witnesses to place him in Exeter at the critical times. Seems he's a member of some left-wing group with social consciences. I can't imagine where he got ideas like those from. A shame that, too—I had a feeling about young Daniel. In the end, I let DC Weenink call 'round at the Mount to ask him about his transport arrangements. It emerges that his father had offered to pay for his rail fare or even to drive down to Devon and collect him when Laura turned up dead on Monday. But Daniel preferred to hitchhike, and it took him all night and half the next morning. We traced the driver of a cattle transporter who dropped him at Junction 28 on the M1 in the early hours."

"Interesting."

"People aren't so willing to pick up scruffy youths by the side of the road as they were in my day."

"I didn't mean—"

"I know what you meant, Cooper. And I agree. But it can wait for a while."

Cooper wondered whether this was the signal for him to leave. But the DCI seemed to be in an amenable mood, so he decided to press on.

"How is Lee Sherratt shaping up, sir?"

"He's denying everything. Says he had no relationship with Laura Vernon at all, that he hardly knew her, in fact. But the used condom shook him, all right. The DNA will pin him down on that. All we have to do is wait for the results."

"Suggesting he had been indulging in some outdoors sex? But it won't prove the sex was with Laura Vernon."

"It'll be enough to put him under pressure. But we have another alternative anyway. DS Morgan has traced the boyfriend."

"Ah."

"A lad by the name of Simeon Holmes. Aged seventeen. He lives on the Devonshire Estate in Edendale. Do you know it?"

Cooper knew it well. He had patrolled the beat there as a young bobby, watching out for stolen cars being raced around the streets, or gathering information on local drug dealers who operated from the sprawl of prefabricated concrete houses mistakenly slung up in the 1960s.

The Devonshire Estate occupied low-lying land in the valley bottom which had once been wetlands and water meadows until they had been hastily drained for the housing scheme. For thirty-five years the damp had gradually been creeping back into the foundations of the houses, staining the walls with mold and rotting the doors and windows. Many of the houses had become virtually uninhabitable, with fungus growing through the floorboards and water pouring through the roofs. But there was almost nowhere else for the poor of Edendale to go. It was the closest thing the valley had to an inner city area.

"How does he come to be Laura Vernon's boyfriend? He sounds like entirely the wrong type."

"He's not someone her parents would approve of, I don't suppose," said Tailby. "Rides a motorbike for a start. He says he met Laura here in town one lunchtime when they should both have been at school. In fact, he says she initiated the relationship, and had been skipping school ever since to meet him in various convenient spots."

"Bunking off."

"Is that what they call it these days? I thought it was bonking, not bunking."

"Missing school, sir, not the other thing."

"Oh. Well, by all accounts they were doing the other thing as well. Holmes says she told him she was sixteen."

"They always say that."

"It's bloody difficult, though, isn't it? I certainly couldn't tell you whether one of these girls out there was fifteen or sixteen. Sometimes they look every bit of eighteen and turn out to be twelve. The CPS wouldn't entertain a prosecution for statutory rape anyway. Not at seventeen."

"There are certainly plenty of leads, then, sir."

Tailby sighed. "Too many. A positive overabundance of suspects. I'd much prefer to narrow it down to one at an early stage. But at least it avoids the talk of a link with the Edson case."

"Were there any reports of motorbikes in Moorhay from the house to house?" asked Cooper.

"Several. They're being sifted out from the computer. Holmes is coming in shortly to be interviewed. Perhaps we ought to have a look at him ourselves, you and I. We could leave Harry Dickinson and the Vernons until later. This lad seems to be more than happy to talk. What do you say, Cooper?"

"I'd like to do that, sir. Thank you."

Then the phone rang, and Tailby took a call from downstairs. He nodded with the beginnings of a small smile.

"Change of plan," he said. "DI Hitchens can tackle Holmes instead. If you pop downstairs, you'll find Mr. Daniel Vernon waiting. Apparently he has a few things he wants to tell us."

One of the twin tape decks had developed a faint, irritating squeak. Diane Fry thought it could almost have been designed to do that deliberately, to unnerve an interviewee. But today it was likely to unnerve the interviewers first.

"We go to the arcades at lunchtime from school, see. Sometimes we stay all afternoon. Nobody bothers about us."

Simeon Holmes was still dressed in the bottom half of his black biking leathers, but he had taken off the jacket as a gesture toward the stifling atmosphere of the interview room. He was wearing a black Manic Street Preachers T-shirt that revealed smooth, well-developed arms and shoulders, and there were small blue tattoos at the base of his neck on either side. His hair was cropped close on top, but had been left to grow long at the back. He had a gold earring in one ear and a small birthmark near one eyebrow. Diane Fry remembered that DS Morgan had described Holmes as the sort of muscular lout that some girls liked. And he had a five hundred cc motorbike as well.

"But you're a pupil at Edendale Community School," said Hitchens with barely concealed amazement.

"That's right, mate."

"How can you take all afternoon off from school?"

"We get study periods, see? It means we can do what we like, with no lessons to go to."

"Do what you like? Do anything but study, I suppose."

Holmes shrugged. "Everybody does it."

"I see."

Hitchens exchanged glances with Fry, who raised her eyebrows. It was no surprise to her what lads like Simeon Holmes got up to.

"You told Detective Sergeant Morgan that you met Laura Vernon at one of the amusement arcades in Dale Street."

"Tommy's Amusements, yeah. I was playing one of those computer fight games, you know? Tommy's has the best games, and I was knocking up a high score. There were a few of us in there, maybe six or seven of us."

"Fellow sixth formers?"

"Some of them."

"And?"

"Well, one of my mates, who was near the front window, shouted to me that there was this tart messing with my bike outside. So I went out, and there she was, sitting on the saddle and waggling the handlebars. A bloody cheek, it was, to be honest. If it'd been a bloke doing that, I'd have decked him. I don't like people messing with my bike. But it was this tart Laura."

Fry's nose twitched. There was a curious smell in the interview room that had been getting stronger during the past few minutes. It was warm and stuffy in the small room, but the smell was something more than just the sour odor of stale male sweat.

"You didn't know Laura before that?" she asked.

"Never set eyes on her before."

"You're sure?"

"I would've remembered, luv, believe me. I don't forget a good-looking tart."

Holmes grinned at Diane Fry, who remained impassive, much as she would have liked to have "decked" him. She had never much liked being called "luv" by youths like Simeon Holmes.

"She was an attractive girl, wasn't she?" said Hitchens.

"Yeah. She was."

Was there a slight flinching? Fry had seen before the people who seemed almost unperturbed by the death of someone they knew well, until they were referred to in that awful past tense. The fact of their death seemed to come home in one tiny word.

"So why was she on your motorbike?" asked Hitchens.

"She was just looking, she said. A lot of birds like bikes, you know. They find 'em dead sexy. They can't wait to get their legs astride one."

"Is that why you ride one?"

Holmes grinned again. "Not really. But it helps, you know?"

"So are you saying she was interested in the bike, not in you?" asked Fry.

Holmes looked at her, ignoring her frown as the grin stayed on his face. "Give over. Well, you might have thought so at first—she was pretending to play it a bit cool, like. But all I had to do was give a bit of chat, you know, and we got talking straight off. She came in the arcade to watch me play. Yeah, and later on one of the other lads in there, who knew her—he told me she'd been asking about me a couple of days before. She wanted to know who I was, what my name was, you know. So she'd obviously fancied me. The bike thing was just a bit of a ploy." He turned toward Hitchens again. "Birds do that sort of stuff, you know?"

"Yes, I know," said Hitchens. For a moment, Fry thought the DI was going to give Holmes a matey wink. If he did, she was going to have to walk out.

"Birds like her especially," said Holmes.

"Like what?"

"Well, she was from the posh school, you know. High Carrs. The kids there aren't supposed to be down in town during school hours, not even the sixth formers. But she'd sneaked out. She was like that, Laura. Didn't give a toss about school really."

"She was a bright girl, though, from what we hear."

"Sure. Dead bright. She could have sailed through her GCSEs, I reckon, but she couldn't be bothered with all the studying. She was more into music. I reckon her parents put her right off school. It happens, you know. Some parents push their kids too hard and they go totally the other way. It's a shame really."

"Teenage rebellion, eh?"

"Yeah, right. Did it yourself, eh, mate? Well, maybe Laura would have come out of it, if she'd got the chance."

"Yes, Simeon. But you didn't exactly encourage her to go back to school, did you?"

"Well, no. We hit it off pretty well, you see, from the beginning. She started coming down to the arcades regular. I was a bit surprised, to be honest—she was a bit too upmarket for me, if you know what I mean. Not my usual type. But she was dead keen. Yeah, dead keen. And I didn't say no. Well, you don't, do you?"

The curious smell was definitely coming from Holmes. Fry discounted the sweet smell of alcohol, the rank bite of cigarette smoke. No drugs she had ever come across smelled quite like that. Perhaps it was something to do with the motorbike leathers. Some kind of oil used to soften up the leather maybe, which was now being evaporated by the heat in the interview room. But to produce that sort of stink it would have to have been something like rancid pig fat.

"Didn't Laura get into trouble at school for breaking the rules?" she asked.

"Dunno. She never said. She wouldn't have given a toss anyway."

"But her parents might have."

Holmes shrugged. "She didn't talk about them much."

"Basically, you would say that Laura instigated the relationship?" asked Hitchens.

"What? Oh, yeah. She started it, all right. Dead keen, like I said."

"Had she had other boyfriends?"

"Sure. She was no little miss innocent. Don't go getting that idea."

Fry leaned forward to put her next question.

"When did you start having sex with her, Simeon?"

Holmes looked from Hitchens to Fry, the worry that had been behind the grin coming to the surface now.

"Look, this is about who killed her, right? That's what you lot are bothered about. I mean, you're not going to come on heavy about the age thing, are you?"

"What do you mean, Simeon?"

"Well, she told me she was sixteen, you know, but . . ."

"You knew she was younger, didn't you?"

Holmes looked at Hitchens appealingly. "You're not interested in that, are you? It isn't important now, is it? Now she's dead."

"That's what I think, too," said Hitchens.

"Right. Well, I didn't want you thinking I was making excuses, like. But, to be honest, she was gasping for it, big time. Couldn't wait to get my trousers off. Being frank, like."

"Oh really?"

"Well, it's right. She wanted to do it all the time. We used to go into the park, or we'd get on the bike and drive out somewhere into the country. Up on the hills. She liked that."

"So you had sex often?"

"All the time—well, every time we met, if we had long enough. And sometimes when we didn't have long enough, too, if you know what I mean. Yeah."

Fry thought if Holmes grinned again she would have to slap the cuffs on him and read him his rights on a charge of offensive behavior.

"Was she a virgin before she met you?" she asked.

"No way."

"Are you sure?"

"Well, look, for one thing you can tell when you do it the first time, you know. By how they react and other things." He hesitated, looking sideways at Fry. "Anyway, she knew what it was all about, all right. In any case, the lad that she'd asked about me, he'd already had her himself. He told me about her. Reckoned there had been others, too."

"Plenty of boyfriends, then."

"Yeah. She was dead keen on the blokes."

"Were there other boyfriends while you were seeing her, perhaps?"

"Dunno really. Could have been, I suppose. She never mentioned to me if she had."

"It wouldn't be unusual, for the sort of girl you seem to be describing. She might even do it deliberately, to make you jealous."

"I'm not the jealous type," said Holmes. Then his smile shrank and faded, and he looked at Fry again. "Oh yeah, I see what you're getting at. You've got an idea that I got jealous of some other bloke and bashed her, right? Well, you can forget that right off. She was OK, Laura, good fun. But things like that don't last, you know? We all move on. It's what I would have expected, for either her or me to find someone else and it'd be over. A good few weeks together, and that's it. It wasn't a problem. I didn't see her as much in the holidays anyway—she couldn't get away from the parents, you know."

"We have a witness who saw Laura talking to a young man on the path behind the Mount shortly before she was killed on Saturday night," said Hitchens.

"It wasn't me, mate. I've already told the other bloke where I was. I was at Matlock Bath with about fifty other bikers."

"Yes, so you said." Officers were already busy checking out the names and places Holmes had given to DS Morgan. Depending on what they came back with, the youth might have to be sent home for now.

Fry would be pleased to get out of the interview room soon to get some fresh air, because the smell was becoming overpowering. She noticed Hitchens pull out a handkerchief as if to wipe his nose, but keeping it there a long time.

"Besides," said Holmes, "I've never been near her place. Did someone say it was me they saw?"

"Not specifically," said Hitchens.

"There you are then."

Holmes was relaxing now. Fry hated to see him relaxing. He might start to grin again. "When you had sex with Laura," she said, "did you like to bite her?"

He stared at her with distaste. "Get lost," he said.

"You refuse to answer?"

"It's none of your business."

"Would you be willing to let us take a mold of your teeth?" asked Hitchens.

"What the hell for?"

"To help eliminate you from our inquiries, Simeon. If you didn't harm Laura Vernon, then you have absolutely nothing to worry about."

Simeon Holmes wasn't quite so stupid as he pretended. Fry could see him figuring it out. A question about his sexual techniques and a request for a mold from his teeth. They hadn't exactly been subtle with their questions. Because of his casual manner, Holmes might be easy to underestimate. But he had a choice now. He could work out that a mold might prove his guilt, if he was guilty. But if he was innocent, it might also clear him and get the police off his back. Fry and Hitchens both waited patiently to see which way he would jump.

"OK," he said. "No problem."

Hitchens's face fell in disappointment. But before he could say anything else, there was a knock on the door and DS Rennie stuck his head into the room. He did a quick double take at the fetid atmosphere and his face screwed up in disgust. Hitchens announced a break in the interview, switched off the tapes, and went out into the corridor to speak to Rennie.

Left alone with Simeon Holmes, Fry was able to study him afresh. The young man met her eyes directly. But a layer of affectation seemed to have dropped away from him in the last few minutes, the final shreds of some assumed role dissipating as DI Hitchens left the room. Fry couldn't quite figure out what it was. She didn't think he had been lying during the interview. And yet . . . How old was Holmes? Seventeen?

"You must be in the sixth form at the Community School now, Simeon," she said.

Holmes raised his eyebrows, saying nothing but looking meaningfully at the motionless tape machines.

"Just asking," she said.

He grinned slowly—that annoying, self-satisfied grin he had. But still nothing.

"Only I was thinking," said Fry, "that I bet you've got a bit more brain than most of your mates."

"Dead right."

"And I bet you do quite well at school when you turn your mind to it. What are your best subjects? Let me guess—mechanical engineering? Car maintenance perhaps?"

Holmes sneered. "Chemistry and biology actually. I take my A levels next year."

Intrigued, Fry found herself looking at a new Simeon Holmes, one who even sounded quite different.

"Not much use for stripping a bike, surely?" she said.

The guarded look began to fall back across the youth's face. Fry could almost see the transformation taking place in his features as he reverted to his role with a dismissive snort.

"Perhaps you were thinking of going on to university," she said. Then she held herself quite still, tingling with satisfaction, as she saw the beginnings of a blush seep into Simeon's neck and across his cheeks. She had found something that embarrassed him. Something that he wouldn't want to talk about with his biker mates.

"With good grades in chemistry and biology you could study—what? Medicine?"

His mouth opened, moving compulsively. Deep in his eyes there was a small spurt of pain and distress, as if Fry had struck close to the most vulnerable part of his anatomy. She hurried to press home her advantage.

"Is that it? Would you like to be a doctor one day, Simeon?"

But the spell was broken as DI Hitchens opened the door just in time to hear the last two sentences. His face contorted at the thought that he might go along to his local surgery and find this youth was his new GP. Then he nodded Diane Fry out of the room, leaving Simeon Holmes starting to grin again in the midst of his peculiar smell.

"We can hand this one back to Morgan," said Hitchens. "They've found those hikers. We're off to West Yorkshire, Diane."

Ben Cooper had not seen Daniel Vernon before. He wasn't impressed at first sight, but he had learned not to judge people younger than himself too quickly. It was a mistake to dismiss someone because they did not dress as you did or behave in quite the same way. Daniel Vernon was a student. That probably meant he went to all-night raves and took cannabis and Ecstasy. He probably took a different girl home every night and lay in bed all day. He probably thought nothing of stealing traffic signs from the roadside, beer glasses and ashtrays from pubs. But in a few years he would be a respectable, well-off member of the community demanding better protection from the police.

Daniel looked as though he had drunk too much cheap beer in the Students' Union. He was dressed in a grubby white T-shirt with the name of an American university written across the front. The T-shirt smelled of sweat.

Cooper took Daniel up to an interview room, where Tailby was waiting. They hardly needed to ask any questions before Daniel had begun to talk. He was eager to get something off his chest, and it quickly became clear what it was.

"I find it astonishing," said Tailby a few minutes later, "that you should be so eager to come in here and tell me such things about your parents."

"It's true," said Daniel. "I couldn't give a toss what they do among themselves or with their tacky friends. But they were blind to what it was doing to Laura. She thought it was OK, all that. She wanted to try things out for herself. She got a taste for sex when she was about thirteen. She told me all about it, though she would never listen to my advice. Mum, she never suspected, even now. Dad—" He shrugged. "Who knows?"

"You tried to talk some sense into her, didn't you, Daniel?"

"I tried. But it was a waste of time."

"We found your letters, you know."

"Yes, I know you did. You took the one I wrote to her after she'd told me about Simeon Holmes."

"Yes, Holmes," said Tailby. "Do you know him?"

"No. But it was the way Laura talked about him that made me write to her like that. It sounded more serious this time. She wasn't just playing anymore. My big worry was that she would let someone like him get her pregnant. I wanted to be sure she was still taking the pills she got from the doctor. She told me she was."

Daniel looked up at Tailby with a question.

"She wasn't pregnant," said the DCI, though he refrained from explaining how they knew. Or rather, how the pathologist knew. There was such a thing as too much information. "But why have you decided to tell us all this now, Daniel?"

"I don't doubt that my father has been telling you things about Lee Sherratt and Laura. I won't have you believing them. Laura wasn't interested in Sherratt, or him in her."

"But your mother . . ."

"My mother had the hots for him. She likes them young. And he was quite willing. My father knew, of course. He knew what was going on. He always knows."

"You're saying that your mother was actually having an affair with her gardener?"

"Sounds very D. H. Lawrence put like that, doesn't it?"

"Does it?"

"But Lee Sherratt is just a youth from the village who saw the chance of getting his end away with an older woman. He isn't exactly a Mellors."

Tailby wasn't sure what he was talking about. "Your father believes Sherratt may have killed your sister."

"If he did," said Daniel. "If he did kill her—it was my father's fault."

"Ah. How do you make that out?"

"He let it go on," he said, "until it had gone too far. He enjoyed it."

"What?"

"Oh yes."

Daniel pulled at his T-shirt, which was sticking to his sides where the sweat was beginning to dry. He fidgeted in his chair, his jeans squeaking on the leather. He looked from Tailby to Cooper, the expression in his eyes shifting and changing. When he spoke again, his voice had altered. It was quiet, less aggressive, with an adolescent edge to it that spoke of an inner pain he could no longer conceal.

"One day," he said, "I came across my father in his room. I wanted to speak to him about something I needed for university, just before I went away. I knocked on the door, but he must not have heard me. It turned out he was otherwise engaged."

Daniel gave him a small, ironic smile. Tailby didn't react. His face was expressionless but for one eyebrow slightly lifted—indicating a mild interest only. It spurred Daniel on more than a probing question would have done.

"He was standing at the windows. He was using binoculars, looking at something in the garden. At first I thought he was watching birds. I was surprised—I didn't know he had taken up a hobby. He was never a man for hobbies, except golf—and even that is a business tool."

"Go on."

"I was about to ask him what species he had seen. There have been woodpeckers in the garden sometimes. Then he heard me come in, and when he turned toward me I saw him. I mean . . . I saw his face. He was startled and angry at being interrupted. But most of all, he looked guilty. He asked me what I wanted. I wanted to know what he was looking at, but he wouldn't say. He started to bluster about trying out the binoculars before he loaned them to a friend. But as I stood there, looking out of the window, I saw my mother."

The young man was silent for several seconds, until Tailby thought he had finished. The DCI began to frown, frustrated at the seeming point-lessness of the story. But Daniel had more to tell.

"She was with Lee Sherratt. In the summerhouse down there. He was naked from the waist up, as he often was, and he was grinning. My mother had been wearing a red silk shirt, with the ends tied at the front in a sort of loose bow. When I saw her, she was just putting it back on. It was the first time I had seen my mother's breasts."

The silence grew in the interview room. Somewhere in the station someone started whistling. A telephone rang half a dozen times before it was answered. Tailby dared not move in his seat for fear of breaking the moment.

"But that wasn't the worst," said Daniel. "The most sickening thing of all was my father. When I came into the room and he turned away from the window, I noticed two things straightaway. The first was the binocu-lars round his neck. The second was his erection."

The young man was staring at the desk, as if interested in the ballpoint pens and a scatter of paper clips. Tailby remembered Graham Vernon's desk in his study. There had been a framed print propped against a table lamp, a photograph of a wedding couple, taken in the 1970s by the look of the bridegroom's hairstyle and the lapels of his suit. Graham Vernon was recognizable by his salesman's smile and the sincerity of his direct gaze at the camera. But allowing for the changes in fashion, in his youth Graham Vernon had looked very much like this young man in front of them now.

"It was sticking out at the front of his trousers like a monstrous growth," said Daniel. "It was unreal. At first I couldn't figure out what it was, you know. I thought he had something in his pocket. But he never carries anything in his pockets because it spoils the cut of his suit. Then I realized. The fact is, it turned him on to watch my mother having sex with the gardener. That's my father, Chief Inspector." His voice cracked. "That's the bastard I call my father."

Tailby nodded slowly. He had spent too long in the police service to be shocked by other people's sexual activities. They were merely facts to be noted now, data to be filed away as possible motives, to be assessed for their relevance to other details in the mass of information that was pouring into the incident room. The life and background of Laura Vernon were being pieced together, bit by bit, like a badly designed jigsaw. Everything that cast light on her circumstances was important. But how much could be trusted of what was said by an angry, bitter young man who hated his father and had just had his sister murdered?

-18-

The blue police tape still fluttered from the trees. A PC still stood guard farther up the path. But the Scenes of Crime officers and forensic scientists had gone. They had other things to do now—the scene of a suspected arson to attend in Matlock, a serious assault case at Glossop, a linked series of aggravated burglaries in Edendale.

"It's too hot. It affects my brain. I can't think straight out here."

Ben Cooper found himself back on the baking hillside again, standing with DCI Tailby at the murder scene.

"So what was the weapon?" asked Tailby. "A bough of a tree, a lump of wood? But there are no traces of bark in the head wounds, and Mrs. Van Doon says there would be. Besides, the injuries were made by something hard and smooth, not rough. So. A stone? Quite possibly. But no sign of it. You wouldn't take a thing like that away with you, would you, Cooper?"

Cooper was not too surprised to be asked his opinion by the DCI. He had worked under him before and had seen the contrast between the ease with which Tailby talked to individual officers, even a humble DC, and the awful stilted pomposity that seemed to overwhelm him when he had to deal with members of the public. The standard police jargon flowed unthinkingly from his lips when he had to address someone who was neither suspect nor fellow detective. There was no room in his vocabulary for normal conversation with ordinary, innocent citizens. It was as if they had to be held at arm's length, kept behind a barrier of meaningless formality.

Despite his experience in criminal investigations, Tailby's career was seriously handicapped by his lack of public relations ability. In time, he would probably be shunted to an administrative post, where he could compile reports and write memos in as pompous a style as he liked. Cooper thought it would be a loss. But everyone had their fatal flaws—sometimes they were just less obvious.

"If it *was* a rock, and you had your wits about you, sir, all you'd have to do would be to toss it into the stream."

They walked a few yards to look down into the gulley where the Eden Valley Trail footpath ran. The bed of the shallow stream was littered with handy-sized stones. There were hundreds of them. Thousands of them. And all of them constantly being washed clean in front of their eyes by the cool, rushing water.

"Let's see if the Vernons are in," said Tailby wearily.

Graham Vernon looked flushed, and his face was puffy, even before he started to get angry. Looking at the drinks cabinet, Cooper guessed that the man had been turning to the alcohol too much to help him cope with the situation.

"I can't imagine why you're giving any credibility to this lurid picture of my daughter, Chief Inspector. You can't seriously be taking notice of what the boy Lee Sherratt has been telling you?"

Predictably, Tailby was responding to Vernon's indignation by retreating into aloofness. They were like two well-groomed cats gradually throwing their veneer of civilization aside as they raised their fur to puff their bodies up to make themselves look bigger than they really were.

"Both Mr. Sherratt and Mr. Holmes have made statements, Mr. Vernon. And naturally we are taking the information which has emerged from those statements into account in our inquiries."

"Who the hell is Mr. Holmes?"

"Simeon Holmes was Laura's boyfriend."

Vernon began to splutter. "Her *what?*"

"Does it surprise you that Laura had a boyfriend?"

"Surprise me? You're talking rubbish, man. Laura had no time for boyfriends. She spent her time studying during the week. She worked hard. At weekends she had her music lessons. She practiced the piano for hours. On Sundays she would go riding—we kept her horse at the stables on Buxton Road. She was always either out hacking or we'd take her to a gymkhana somewhere. When she wasn't doing those, she was at the stables anyway. She was like a lot of fifteen-year-old girls, Chief Inspector— she was more interested in horses than boys. And thank God for that. Fifteen is too young to be having boyfriends."

"Nevertheless—"

"Who is this Holmes, anyway? Someone she knew at school, I suppose. I would have preferred to send her to a single-sex school, but it would have meant her boarding somewhere. My wife wanted to have Laura living at home. A mistake, it seems now."

Tailby ignored the turning down of Vernon's mouth, pressing on to prevent the man slipping into grief or self-pity.

"According to Mr. Holmes, Laura hated school. She used to play truant to meet him in Edendale. Or indeed to meet other young men, it would seem. Were you aware of that, sir?"

"No, I was not."

"Perhaps your wife would know more about that side of your daughter's life, sir."

"I'd rather you didn't ask my wife questions like that," said Vernon. "She is just starting to come to terms with all this, Chief Inspector. Don't knock her back, please."

"Mrs. Vernon seemed to cope very well in front of the television cameras this morning. I thought that went very well, sir."

"Clutching at straws."

Ben Cooper stood in the background, watching Vernon carefully. The man had a square, heavy jaw and a face like an unfit boxer's. It suited his aggressive manner, but went oddly with the atmosphere of the study. It was a large, high-ceilinged room with heavy pieces of furniture and a vast oak desk. A Turkish rug was thrown over a fitted oatmeal Berber carpet in front of an arched brick fireplace and a cast-iron log basket on the hearth.

"I know nothing of any boyfriends. Where does this Holmes live? Is he a friend of Lee Sherratt's? Have you thought of that?"

"I don't think that's very likely, Mr. Vernon."

"Well, you'd better be sure, hadn't you, Chief Inspector?"

"Lee Sherratt, of course," said Tailby calmly, "is telling a similar story to that of Mr. Holmes. Except that he insists that he had no relationship with Laura."

"Lies and more lies. Something for you to sort out, eh? You'd be better employed proving which of them killed Laura instead of asking me these ludicrous questions. I've told you what sort of girl Laura was. She was my daughter. Don't you think I would know?"

"You might know," said Tailby, as if to himself, "but would you tell me, I wonder?"

"What do you mean?"

"I mean that I have to doubt what you say to me in view of the things that your own son tells me. Things that suggest you have been lying to us, Mr. Vernon."

There was a silence in the study. Somewhere far away in the house, a vacuum cleaner started up. A telephone rang three times, then stopped. Tailby waited until Graham Vernon slumped and looked pained, as if an ulcer had suddenly flared in his stomach.

"Daniel. What has he been telling you?"

Tailby smiled grimly and asked Ben Cooper to read his notes of the interview with Daniel. Cooper read them in as steady a voice as he could manage, trying to put no particular inflection on the sections where the young man had become angry or upset. Vernon listened in silence until Ben had finished. By the end, Vernon's head was bowed and he couldn't meet their eyes. When Tailby spoke, he sounded almost sorry for the man.

"Now, Mr. Vernon. Shall we start from the beginning? What would you like to tell me about Lee Sherratt?"

The mood in the briefing room was subdued. Though they had followed up all the available leads, many officers felt that they still didn't seem to be getting anywhere. It was the start of a feeling that the inquiry might be running out of steam. Cooper recognized it and knew that Tailby would, too. It was the DCI's job, as senior investigating officer, to keep the troops motivated.

"OK," said Tailby. "We have traced and interviewed both Lee Sherratt and the boyfriend, Simeon Holmes. But to eliminate one or both from the inquiry, we still need evidence, and that's what I'm not getting. Forensics have given us very little so far. I remain hopeful of the bite mark, but we're still waiting on the odontologist in Sheffield. We're told tomorrow for a preliminary report on the bite—but comparisons with the molds that Sherratt and Holmes have provided will take longer."

Ben Cooper looked around the incident room, but saw no sign of Diane Fry or of DI Hitchens. He concluded that the party of hikers had been located and that the two of them were already somewhere to the north, following a lead that he himself had reported from Moorhay.

"Holmes's story of Laura Vernon being sexually experienced is backed up by the postmortem findings," said Tailby, "also by her own brother's statement. So if Holmes is right about the victim's sexual inclinations, can Lee Sherratt be believed when he says he had nothing to do with her? As Holmes stated in his interview, 'You don't say no, do you?'"

Tailby shuffled his papers. There was a diminishing number of officers in the incident room tonight. It looked as though the inquiry was already starting to be scaled down. Most of the TIE actions had been completed. Many of the individuals peripherally involved had been discounted: traced, interviewed, and eliminated.

Now, though, the leads that were being followed up were more focused. A shortlist of individual subjects were being targeted. Mr. Tailby had sifted his priorities and chosen his lines of inquiry. He had to feel fairly confident of the avenues that were worth pursuing. There was an underlying belief that the forensic scientists would produce the evidence that would seal the case.

"We also have the rest of Daniel Vernon's story," said Tailby, "which may be totally irrelevant. But if he is telling the truth, then it indicates that Sherratt is lying. And we might ask ourselves—if Sherratt was willing to conduct an affair with the mother, why not with the daughter? We remain to be convinced on that. Until Holmes's alibi is satisfactorily checked out, we have to consider that either of these youths could have been the one seen talking to Laura earlier that evening. On the other hand, it could have been someone else entirely. So we're struggling without the physical evidence. There's a weapon out there somewhere, but there's also a second trainer belonging to Laura Vernon. Both are crucial, but the trainer is going to be easier to identify."

The DCI paused and tried to look at each officer individually. Some of them met his eye, but others were busy reading notes or staring at the photographs and maps on the wall.

"So here's what we do," he said. "We go 'round the houses in Moorhay again. With all the publicity and activity in the village, no one's going to want to hang on to evidence like that—and I'm reckoning it will have been disposed of in the area. So we check out streams, ponds, ditches. And we look for signs of recent digging or burning. That would be the most obvious way to dispose of something like a trainer. Burying or burning. Someone must have been doing that in the last few days."

Tailby pinned another blown-up photo on the wall behind him. "This is Holmes. We're asking questions about both him and Sherratt now. But don't overlook other possibilities, of course."

Ben Cooper sat up with a sudden lurch of excitement when he saw the photo of Simeon Holmes. He had seen him already, and in Moorhay, too. Not only that, but at the time the youth had been digging. And a friend with him had been burning something. Cooper hesitated for a moment. It seemed bizarre—but he knew he had to speak now, not later.

"I've seen him, sir," he said, "earlier today. In fact, he must have come straight from the smallholding to be interviewed here."

All eyes turned on Cooper. Hesitantly, he told them about the vast compost heap that had been taking shape at Thorpe Farm that morning. He told them about seeing Simeon Holmes himself tipping barrowload after barrowload of fresh manure onto the heap, and about the old men carefully covering it over and treading it down. He told them about the unidentified youth with his small bonfire, and about what could have been a deliberately distracting conversation as he himself had stood in front of the heap.

As he spoke, he could sense the officers in the room pulling faces and drawing away from him as though they could actually smell the manure on his clothes.

When he had finished his story, he waited for a reaction. He was thinking of the words repeated by Sam Beeley and Wilford Cutts—"blood and bone," they had said. And again: "blood and bone."

Tailby stared at him, and groaned.

"Oh Jesus," he said. "We're going to have to dig it up."

A hastily assembled team arrived at Thorpe Farm an hour later in a variety of vehicles, which parked on the track between the jumble of outbuildings. A Task Force sergeant in a boilersuit and Wellington boots walked up to the house, where he found Wilford Cutts and Sam Beeley waiting outside, astonished at their sudden arrival. He served the search warrant on Wilford.

"You want to search my house?" said Wilford. "What for?"

"Not the house," said the sergeant. "The outside property."

"Outside?"

"Starting with the field over there."

Officers were gathering on the track, fastening their boilersuits and pulling on Wellingtons and gloves as spades and forks were issued from a van.

"You're never going to dig my field up," said Wilford.

Sam waved his stick and started laughing as he saw where the policemen were heading.

"Look at their faces," he said. "They're not digging the field up, they're going to dig up the muck heap."

The sergeant's expression told them he was right.

"What do you think you'll find?" called Wilford, but the sergeant walked away without answering.

A Scenes of Crime officer was raking through the remains of the fire and bagging the ashes as Tailby and Cooper came up from their car to the field. The two old men were standing by the top gate to watch the operation, and Cooper could feel their eyes on him as they approached.

"It was built by craftsmen, that heap," said Wilford accusingly. "Your bloody coppers are going to ruin it."

"Some of them buggers look as though they've never used a fork in their lives," said Sam, gazing in wonder at the boilersuited diggers.

"Mr. Cutts, I believe you had a young man by the name of Simeon Holmes working here earlier today," said Tailby.

"Oh aye," said Wilford. "Young Simeon and his mate. Good lads, they are. Hard workers. They mucked out the pig shed for us."

"And helped you build the compost heap there."

"Well, they did the heavy work, the barrowing and that."

"What's in the compost heap, Mr. Cutts?"

"Here now," said Sam. "We told your lad there exactly what was put in it. Didn't we, Wilford?"

"We explained it very carefully, as I recall."

Sam's attention drifted back down the field. He couldn't believe what he saw. "Some of them's shifting it, and some of them's just standing looking at it. What do they think it's going to do? Dance the hokey cokey?"

"And there was some burning, I believe? What were you burning, Mr. Cutts?"

"Some old straw. Some dead branches. General rubbish."

"Did you allow Simeon Holmes to put any extra items onto the fire or into the compost heap?"

"You what?"

"The other lad looked after the fire, in between barrowing," said Sam.

"And who was he?"

"Name of Doc, that's all. A mate of young Simeon's."

"A nickname?"

"I suppose so. Never seen him before."

"How did they happen to be working for you, Mr. Cutts?"

"Harry sent 'em up. I needed a bit of labor, and he said this great-nephew of his was a willing lad."

"His great-nephew! This is to do with Harry Dickinson again?"

"They're good lads, those two. You leave 'em alone."

"I do believe," said Sam, staring at the activities around the compost heap, "that those blokes of yours are actually counting the turds."

Cooper trailed after the disgruntled DCI as he strode off back toward the bottom of the field. The compost had begun fermenting as soon as the heap had been constructed, and steam could be seen rising in several places. The surface of the heap was alive with thousands of the reddish-brown dung flies. They rose in shimmering clouds when they were disturbed, only to settle again on the exposed patches of manure as work began on shifting the entire heap to one side.

The digging was hot and sweaty work, and the policemen could feel the pervasive smell of the manure infiltrating their boilersuits and being absorbed into the perspiration on their bodies. It was worst for the men working on top of the heap, where the heat rising from the compost itself made them feel as though they were slaving in the heart of a blast furnace or stoking the boiler of a vast steam engine. They stopped for frequent rests, their places being taken by other officers who had been moving the manure aside, turning and separating it as they did so to make sure no evidence went unobserved.

As the digging went on, the smell got steadily worse, and Cooper became more unpopular. Many venomous glances came his way as the top of the compost heap shrank and nothing more incriminating appeared than a tangle of blue baling twine or a rotted apple core.

Then a fork hit a solid object. Immediately, an officer dropped to his knees and used his gloved hands to dig into the stinking debris. Someone spread a plastic sheet on the ground, and the next few inches of manure were carefully transferred to the sheet, in case the material had to be packed up and sent to the forensic laboratory. The SOCO, who had finished with the fire, knelt alongside the officer, oblivious to the muck staining his knees and the swarms of flies that hovered around their sweating foreheads.

Finally, as a large clump of manure was scraped away, something white appeared among the dark fibers. It had been pierced by a tine of the policeman's fork, and now a burst of exposed muscle and tendon appeared like a bullet hole in the middle of the bare, white flesh.

-19-

Fry switched channels on the TV in her room until she landed on a news program. She watched an item about a sex scandal involving a government minister, heard about a breakdown in talks in Northern Ireland, and listened to news of a long-running war in some African country where thousands of people had already died in an inexplicable tribal conflict. It was all very predictable.

She lay sprawled on her hard bed, nibbling one of the complimentary biscuits from a cellophane-wrapped packet on the bedside table. She had kicked off her shoes and taken off her sweaty clothes, and was wearing her black kimono over her underwear. She was wishing she had been able to find the time to call in at a shop in Skipton for some chocolate.

Then a shot of the woods at Moorhay came on the screen. It looked as though the camera had been positioned on Raven's Side, where the bird-watcher Gary Edwards had stood. It focused in on the site where Laura Vernon had been found, but all that could be seen was the police tape. Then a reporter with a microphone appeared with a brief summary of the inquiry, and the scene switched to a shot of Edendale Police HQ, followed by a crowded room full of lights and microphones. At a table sat DCI Tailby, a police press officer, and Graham and Charlotte Vernon. The familiar photo of Laura appeared in a corner of the screen. They were about to broadcast the appeal recorded that morning.

Several minutes were given over to coverage of the Vernon inquiry. To be of real interest to the media, Fry knew that these days murders had to involve children or teenage girls, or possibly young mothers. But it also seemed to make a difference what part of the country they happened in. Somehow it seemed to strike at the heart of English middle-class conceptions for a murder to take place on their own rural doorstep. If Laura Vernon had died on wasteland in a run-down area of London or Birmingham, it would not have been seized on so eagerly. But this was a murder in scenic, sleepy Moorhay, and the tabloid newspapers had been full of it all week. Where Diane Fry had come from, there were murders for the papers to report every day. Some weren't given a high profile, even locally. And there were other crimes that hardly seemed worth mentioning. Like rape, for example.

After a few words of introduction from Tailby, it was Graham Vernon who was doing the talking. Fry knew that the film clip would be recorded and played back over and over again at Edendale, where they would be looking for little giveaways in the Vernons' performances, for discrepancies between the account they gave on screen and the statements they had given police.

It was accepted practice to encourage the relatives in such cases to tell their story under the glare of the lights and cameras, knowing their words were being heard by millions of viewers. It put a pressure on them in a way that could no longer be legally done in the privacy of an interview room.

But Vernon looked well in control. He appealed in a steady voice for anyone who had seen Laura on the night in question, or who knew anything about her death, to come forward and assist police. He encouraged people to consider whether they had noticed anything strange about the behavior of their husbands, sons, or boyfriends. Any bit of information, however trivial it might seem, could prove useful to the police. He sounded as though he had been coached in the phrases by Tailby himself.

Then Vernon changed to a slower, more intimate tone as he talked about Laura. He called her "our little girl" and described her as a bright, clever teenager who had had her whole life to look forward to but had been brutally struck down. He talked of how well she had been doing at school, and described her love of music and her passion for horses. He told the watching millions that Laura had been due to take part in a horse show today. But her horse, Paddy, was still in his stable, wondering where she was. As an actor, he was only second-rate. But that was how some people coped with these things.

Finally, the microphone was presented to Charlotte Vernon. Her eyes were dry and staring, and Fry wondered if she was still on some form of medication. She didn't say much, but at least she sounded sincere.

"We're pleading with everybody: just help the police to catch whoever did this to Laura." And she stared directly into the cameras, gaunt and grief stricken, while her husband put an arm around her shoulders to support her. It was the image that would appear in all the newspapers tomorrow.

The news program drifted off into a weather forecast—more sun tomorrow and no cloud until the evening. Fry reflected on the past few hours, the frustrating, time-consuming interviews with the student hikers. One after another they had been dragged reluctantly from their tents to the little office at the campsite near Malham. None of them had seen a thing—a fact Fry thought could have been established quite easily by a couple of North Yorkshire bobbies.

She wondered whose idea it had been for the two of them to travel all this way from Derbyshire, with the necessity of staying overnight in the little hotel in Skipton. Someone had felt sure the hikers would have seen something useful—or they had said they did. And why a detective inspector, who should have been heading one of the inquiry teams? A sergeant would have been quite adequate, or even two DCs.

Of course, it must have been Paul Hitchens's idea. She had left him in the bar, fueling up on beer and whiskey, enjoying the freedom of being away from the office. He had looked sour when she had taken only one glass of white wine and had refused further drinks, pleading tiredness. Late-night boozing in a Yorkshire pub was not her style.

Meanwhile, no doubt, the main part of the inquiry was getting along fine without her back at Edendale. She wondered what Ben Cooper was doing right now. Bubbling with brilliant insights and unerring flashes of instinct, probably. Like last night. It had been the most stupid thing she had ever seen, to go trailing through the woods in the dark and bursting in on a suspect without proper backup, or even calling in to tell control where they were. If that's where instinct and intuition led you, then you could keep it as far as she was concerned. She could not forget the moment that she had seen the gun in Lee Sherratt's hands. Then *her* instinct had taken over. But that was a different kind of instinct—a physical reaction, an essential defense mechanism honed by months of training.

In this case, though, she knew she had reacted not in self-defense but out of a gut-wrenching fear of seeing Ben Cooper injured. She knew it was terror that had made her strike the second, unnecessary, blow. Once she had disarmed Sherratt, he could have been arrested easily. But she had struck again out of fear and anger. Her old instructor would have been furious with her. It showed lack of discipline.

Fry wondered whether she had apologized to Cooper properly for the comments she had made about his father. He had seemed withdrawn and moody afterward. The escapade in the wood could well have been his way of proving something—in which case, had it been partly her fault that it had happened? Sighing in exasperation, she put it out of her mind. People were too complicated when they started having feelings. Why couldn't they all just get on with the job in hand?

Another old film was starting. Some romantic comedy from the 1950s with James Stewart. She switched off the TV and lay back on the bed. For a while she lay listening to the footsteps and other small sounds in the hotel corridor. She was wondering whether Paul Hitchens would come to her room.

"Sound asleep."

Ben Cooper had just come from saying good night to his nieces. Matt and Kate were watching television, curled up on the sofa together, a picture of domestic contentment. Life had to go on, after all.

But the sight gave Cooper no comfort; it only made him feel worse. Since Monday he had been finding it difficult just to walk up and down the stairs at the farmhouse, remembering the things he had seen.

He and Matt had spent an hour at the hospital, though their mother was still asleep. They had been warned she would be under heavy sedation for at least two days. She would not be awake and able to communicate with them until tomorrow. Yet the two brothers had still wanted to sit by her bed, looking at her face, watching her movements, and discussing in quiet voices their hopes and fears for the future. Matt said that the house and the phone had been busy for two days with members of the family calling to ask how Isabel was and offer their help. The Coopers were a large, close family, and nothing brought them together more effectively than a crisis. The same had happened two years ago, when the brothers and their sister, Claire, had never been alone after their father had been killed.

The death of their father had been a sudden, shattering blow. The illness of their mother had been a slow, lingering torture. Cooper's mind drifted away again, seeking memories of the times when they had all been together. It had only been two years ago, but it seemed like a century. It was called changing circumstances.

This time, though, he could not understand why he was finding little solace from the constant presence of his family. Their closeness seemed to create a weight of expectation he no longer felt capable of fulfilling. They all thought he was a clever, popular policeman and never doubted for a moment that he was destined for great things. It was a burden that he could no longer live up to.

Suddenly it seemed to him as though everything in his life was going wrong, one thing after another. The solid planks he depended on were being kicked away; his hopes were being trampled on remorselessly, one by one. Why had the crisis with his mother coincided with the arrival at Edendale of Diane Fry? He couldn't get out of his mind the idea that the two things were connected. They were a joint assault on his private and professional life, and he didn't know how to cope with the effects they were having on his feelings, his moods, and his judgment.

He had to admit that he had made a mistake in ignoring procedures to go after Lee Sherratt, and it had nearly ended in disaster—though he told himself that if Fry had not been with him, he would have done things differently. And then, out of the blue, he had found himself thinking about Helen Milner; he had been thinking about her ever since they had met for the first time in years during his visit to Dial Cottage on Monday.

In quiet moments since then he had speculated about the possibility that he had found someone he had enough in common with to think they could share a life together, someone outside the family. He had pictured himself introducing Helen to his mother, and knowing that she would approve. It was one of the two things that she wanted most—for Ben to find someone to marry; the other was her confident belief that he would make sergeant, like his father. Only that morning, he had been presented with an opportunity to renew the relationship they had once developed. But he had let the opportunity pass, and he had done it because of the job.

On top of that had come the humiliating fiasco with the compost heap at Thorpe Farm. He could imagine what was being said about him at the station. Within a few hours it would be the subject of gossip for every police officer in E Division, probably the whole county. The mountain he had to climb to be worthy of his father's memory was getting higher and higher. At this moment, it looked like Mount Everest.

"You've just missed the appeal by the Vernons," said Matt.

"Yeah? What was it like?"

"Stagey," said Kate.

Cooper nodded. He slumped into an armchair and stared at the TV screen without seeing it. His mind was a whirl of anxieties. He wondered how he was going to face going back into work tomorrow. And how he was going to face the visit to the hospital in the afternoon, which he had arranged to take time off for—the visit when his mother would be out of sedation. He didn't realize that Kate was speaking to him for several seconds.

"Sorry, what did you say?"

"Are you all right, Ben?"

"Yes, I'm fine."

"I was asking if you were in for the night now. I'll make some supper for later, if you are."

He couldn't admit that he found the idea of staying at home in the farmhouse for any length of time unbearable. There was a constant urge to go up the stairs and open the door of his mother's room, knowing she wouldn't be there. An urge to relive the worst moments of her illness as if it was some penance he had to go through.

"Er, no. I thought I might go out for a drink. Do you fancy coming, Matt?"

He didn't fail to see the quick squeeze that Kate gave to his brother's arm, which communicated her feelings sufficiently.

"No, thanks, Ben. I'll stay in tonight. I'm getting up early in the morning to shoot some of those rabbits in the south field. Maybe tomorrow, eh?"

"Fine."

Cooper got in the car and drove automatically toward Edendale. There were a handful of pubs in town that he went to regularly. But on the outskirts of town, when he saw the familiar landscape of stone gables and slate roofs spread out before him in the dusk, he changed his mind. He turned the Toyota into a side road and went over the hill into Moorhay.

The village looked peaceful once more. There were no tourists to be seen on the street, and no noticeable police activity, only a line of green wheelie bins along the roadside. The residents had retreated again behind their doors, some of them clutching their individual secrets, he was sure.

He drew up a few yards short of Dial Cottage and sat in the car for a while watching the doorway. It might have been the confusing light of the growing dusk or the stress of his experiences during the day or just his secret hopes acting on his senses. But he felt as though he could see Helen Milner emerging from the door of the cottage, just as she had done that morning—a warm, living glow against the inner darkness. He remembered that fleeting expression of disappointment when she realized she was not the one he had come to see. He remembered Gwen Dickinson's words: "She's been talking about you, you know." Could that be true? Had Helen been thinking of him, as he had thought about her?

Cooper repeated to himself the last few sentences that had been spoken between them. "So aren't you a policeman all the time?" she had asked. "What are you like when you're just being Ben Cooper?" "You'll have to find out one day, won't you?" And then finally she had said: "Maybe I will."

He turned the words over in his mind, assessing the tone of voice she had used, trying to recall the exact expression on her face, the precise movement of her head as she turned away, seeking the subtle meanings. There *would* be a day, he promised himself. Definitely there would be a day, one when he wasn't being a policeman. But not just now.

He started the Toyota and drove a hundred yards farther along the road to pull up on the cobbles outside the Drover. Inside, the pub was busy for a Wednesday night. But in their usual corner were the three old men— Harry Dickinson, Wilford Cutts, and Sam Beeley. Their heads turned as he came in and their eyes followed him to the bar. As he was ordering, he heard a comment from one of them produce a cackle of laughter. He felt his jaw clench and the blood start to flow into his cheeks, but he controlled himself with an effort. He was not going to let the old men wind him up.

The landlord, Kenny Lee, tried to make conversation, but sniffed and turned away when he was ignored. Having paid for his pint of Robinson's, Cooper walked over toward the table in the corner. The three old men watched him come, their eyes expectant, but their mouths tight shut. Harry stood up from his chair.

"Looking for me?"

"Not particularly. I just called in for a drink."

Harry looked disappointed and sat down again. Cooper looked around for a seat and found a worn wooden stool. He could feel them following his movements as he pulled the stool up to the table, sat down, and took a long draft of his beer.

"That's good stuff," he said. "I thought it would be. But I couldn't try it while I was on duty."

The old men nodded cautiously. Sam coughed and offered him a cigarette, which Cooper refused politely.

"Not many tourists in tonight, then?"

"It's Wednesday," said Sam.

He sensed the unspoken messages passing between the three men in the flicking of their eyes and the tapping of their bony fingers on the table. They were like a group of poker players about to take the shirt off the back of a stranger in town. But Cooper wasn't interested in what they weren't telling him. Not just now.

He let a silence develop, waiting for the old men to break it. Normally they would probably sit together for hours without saying a word, if there was nothing much to say. But he was a guest at their table, and they were the hosts. He was banking on their courtesy.

"How's it going, then?" asked Wilford at last.

"What's that?"

"You know what, lad. The murder case."

"It's not," said Cooper, and lifted his glass to his face again.

"Eh?"

"You've got suspects," said Sam. "You'll be questioning them. There'll be bright lights, the good copper and the bad copper. Wearing 'em down."

Cooper shook his head. "We can't do much of that these days. It's all the new regulations. They've got rights."

"Rights?"

"Unless we've got enough evidence to charge them, we have to let them go."

"And haven't you? Got evidence?" asked Wilford.

"Not enough. Not by a long way."

"That's a shame."

"It's very discouraging. Sometimes you feel like giving up."

Harry had said nothing so far. His eyes were fixed on Cooper as he spoke, watching his lips, studying his face as if trying to see behind his words.

"It wasn't our fault about the pigs, lad."

"No, I know it wasn't."

"Did you get in trouble?" asked Wilford.

Cooper shrugged. "I'll be very unpopular for a bit."

"It wasn't our fault," echoed Sam.

"We told you about the blood and bone."

"The heap rots 'em down, as long as they're not too big. Otherwise the knackerman charges you for taking 'em away."

"And you don't want to be paying the knackerman when you can dispose of 'em natural, like," said Sam.

"They weren't big enough for porkers yet, I suppose," said Cooper.

"No, no. Nowhere near. You couldn't have sold 'em."

"Funny thing about pigs, though," said Wilford. "Their skin is a lot like ours."

"It certainly gave those police mates of yours a fair turn," said Sam, starting to smile again.

"They thought they'd found a dead body or two," said Cooper. "For a while."

"Bloody hell, that doctor woman wasn't very pleased when she got there."

"The pathologist. That was a mistake."

"I've never heard language like it," said Wilford.

"Not from a doctor."

"And a woman, too."

"Do you know they get sunburnt, just like us?" asked Wilford. "Pigs, I mean. You can't leave 'em out in hot sun. Those two had been inside, you see, out of the sun. That's why their skin was so clean."

"And white."

"Aye. Middle whites, they were. Some folk like the old breeds, but the whites grow better."

Cooper closed his eyes, feeling the conversation running away from him already. Bizarrely, a memory popped into his mind of the slippery fish he used to try to catch by hand as a boy in the streams around Edendale. He knew they were there, lurking in the shady corners, and he could almost get his hands on them in the water. But it needed only a couple of wriggles and they were out of his grasp, every time. He suddenly felt utterly depressed and wondered what on earth he had hoped to achieve by coming here tonight. He was totally in the wrong place. But he had no idea what the right place for him was just now.

He drained his glass and stood up wearily.

"Off already?" asked Sam. "Company not suit you?"

"I'm wasting my time," said Cooper, as he walked away toward the door.

Outside, the sky was still light and the evening was warm. He stood for a moment, breathing in the motionless air and looking up at the shape of Raven's Side, looming above the village. He remembered then that there was one place where he always felt he belonged.

The door to the pub had been propped open to let out the heat, and he didn't hear anybody come up behind him. But he recognized the slow voice that spoke in his ear.

"If you ask the right questions, you'll find out what you want to know."

"Oh yes? I'm not sure about that, Mr. Dickinson. At the moment, it all seems pretty futile."

Harry looked at him with sudden understanding. "Fed up?"

"You might say that."

"Ah. I reckon you've got the black dog, lad."

"What?"

"That's what we used to say to the young uns when they were sulking or had a fit of temper. 'The black dog's on your back,' we'd say. That's what's up with you, I reckon."

Sulking? It was a long time since he had been accused of sulking. As if he were some temperamental adolescent.

"Yes, I've heard of it, thanks."

"Don't mention it, lad."

Now the old man had explained the expression, Cooper remembered that he *had* heard it before. He could hear a faint echo of his own mother's voice chiding him for having the black dog. It was one of those mysterious expressions from childhood that you only half understood at the time. The black dog. Words with a frisson of meaning that had always worked on his imagination. Looking back, he had a feeling that the young Ben Cooper had pictured some huge, terrifying beast coming down from the moors with red eyes and slavering jaws. The memory was confused now with the stories his Grandma Cooper had told, of the legendary Black Shuck and the Barguest—giant hounds with glowing eyes that waylaid unfortunate travelers on certain roads at night and took them straight to hell.

"The black dog's on your back," they said. It wasn't a very nice image. Once the picture had been planted in his mind, it had been difficult to get rid of. It had cropped up in his nightmares, waking him with snapping jaws and ferocious eyes. As a child, he would have done anything to get rid of that black dog from his back. Usually, his mother could help him do it. She could always cheer him up and chivvy him out of a depressed mood.

Now, though, when the tables were turned, he was helpless to remove an immense black dog from his mother's back.

Harry looked at him sharply, suspicious at the silence. Cooper shook himself and stared back at the old man.

"Well, I've got to go now, Mr. Dickinson. Maybe I'll see you again."

"I don't doubt, lad."

A few minutes later, Cooper was sitting on Raven's Side, looking across the dusk-filled valley toward Win Low.

He liked the names of the hills in this part of the Peak, with their resonances of the Danish invaders who had occupied Derbyshire for several decades. He had been taught at school that the raven had been the symbol of Odin, the chief of the Viking gods. And the Danes had not been alone in investing the hills with supernatural powers.

On the far side of the valley, the last rays of the setting sun lit the western flanks of the Witches in blood-red streaks, highlighting them in melodramatic three-dimensional relief. At any moment, they might launch themselves into the air on their broomsticks. No wonder the ancient inhabitants of the valley had been in awe of them. The rocky gritstone outcrops were a brooding and malevolent presence at the best of times, their shapes black and ominous on the sunniest day. It would be easy for superstitious villagers to blame them for all sorts of evils and misfortunes.

Cooper was sitting close to where Gary Edwards must have stood with his binoculars on the night that Laura Vernon had been killed. The view extended from the back gardens of the cottages in Moorhay in one direction to the roof of the Old Mill at Quith Holes in the other, and down over the sweeping woodland to the meandering road far below in the valley bottom. The stream was invisible from here, and the trees were thick in the area where Laura's body had been found.

The last shreds of the evening light were playing tricks in the deeper patches of woodland, distorting the shadows and deadening the colors until the greens and browns merged into each other in a mesh of dark patches tinged with violet. The light was slanting almost vertically down from the hill, flattening out the perspective and reducing the woods to a two-dimensional landscape where color meant nothing.

Cooper looked again at the summit of Win Low and the Witches. There was an ancient packhorse road crossing the tor, below the shadow of the twisted rocks. But it would be a brave traveler who went that way at night. It was all too easy to imagine the black hounds of the legends prowling up there on the dark ridge, waiting to pounce.

And once the black dogs of hell were on your back, you could never shake them off.

-20-

"Oh God," said Superintendent Jepson. "We'll never hear the end of it. This is the sort of thing the division will never live down. It'll be in the local press, the national tabloids—we'll make the joke item on the TV news. And for certain it'll be in the *Police Review*. We'll be the laughing-stock of every force in the country. I can hear the jokes about us now. It'll go on for years. Years!"

The superintendent had DCI Tailby and DI Hitchens in his office before the morning briefing. They had faced the difficult task of explaining to the divisional commander why a dozen officers had been employed to dig up a giant compost heap, and why the pathologist had then been called to examine two dead pigs.

"We could probably find something we could charge Cutts with," said Hitchens, "to justify the exercise, so to speak."

"No, no, no. That would only make it worse. Let's just play it down and hope it passes over after a day or two. Has the press office been briefed?"

"I did it last night," said Tailby. "They've got bare details, but after that they have to refer inquiries to me. I'll stonewall them."

"All right, Stewart, but I can't understand how it happened."

"Ben Cooper had one of his inspirations," said Hitchens.

"Ah, young Cooper. We had that business with the Sherratt arrest, too."

"It could have been a disaster if DC Fry hadn't been there."

"If Cooper had got himself shot . . ." Jepson shuddered. "It would be a total public relations catastrophe. Nobody's forgotten what happened to his father."

"We can't afford that sort of incident, no matter how you look at it," agreed Tailby.

Jepson turned to Hitchens. "You keep your ear to the ground regarding the staff in your department, don't you, Paul?"

"I try to, sir."

"You know we'll have to be making the decision on DS Osborne's replacement very soon. He signs off for good at the beginning of next month. DC Cooper was one we had in mind for the job, wasn't he?"

"He was top of the shortlist," said Hitchens.

"What's your view on that now?"

"Frankly, he appears to be a touch emotionally unstable. He was very moody yesterday. All over something and nothing, as far as I can gather."

"This new DC, though. Fry . . ."

"She's got better qualifications than Cooper. And she seems very stable, despite her past history."

Jepson nodded seriously. "Ah, the business in the West Midlands. Of course."

"A very nasty business," said Tailby. "But she's fine now, isn't she? Paul?"

"A bit of a cold fish, but solid as a rock, sir. Totally in control, I'd say. Very professional. No ill effects, she says."

"You've actually discussed it with her?" asked Jepson.

"Yes, sir."

"Good man. That's excellent management. Good relations with the staff."

"According to her record, she had the standard counseling. There's a note that she packed the sessions in, though, after she split up with a boyfriend. Seems he couldn't handle it, but she could."

"I suppose that sort of experience can actually make someone a stronger person," suggested Tailby.

"Ah, that's right. Baptism by fire and all that. Add Diane Fry's name to the shortlist. Let's see how she shapes up in the interviews."

"Ben Cooper, though . . . He'd be a popular choice, sir."

"Mmm. Emotionally unstable, Paul says. I don't like the sound of that. Cooper's a bit too immature yet for a supervisory post, I think. It's a pity, though. A local lad, wonderful local knowledge. Dedicated, hardworking, bright."

"It's not enough," said Hitchens.

Jepson sighed. "You're probably right. Do I take it we're agreed DC Cooper is not an option to replace Osborne?" He waited while the others nodded. "In that case, it'd better be done quickly. I'll see him this morning during the briefing and break the news. I'll jolly him along a bit, try to soften the blow. Suggest a bit of lateral development."

The three men sat for a moment, calmly assessing a job well done. Jepson stirred and sat upright, signaling a change of subject.

"What's the progress on the Vernon inquiry, then? Stewart?"

"We don't need to expend extra resources at this stage, sir. I expect forensic results today. They could wrap the inquiry up, I think."

"You've got two possibles, haven't you?"

"I'm confident forensics will tie in either Lee Sherratt or the boyfriend, Simeon Holmes," said Tailby. "That will be the breakthrough we need. We could be making an arrest soon."

"That sounds like a good press release," said Jepson hopefully. "If we can get that out to the media today, they might forget about the pigs."

"I remain hopeful," said Tailby.

Harry Dickinson was wearing his black-framed bifocals, which made his eyes look distorted and out of proportion, like smooth stones lying in deep water.

"And I tell you what, lass. If you see that young copper again, you can tell him if his mates are going to try to blame the Sherratt boy, they're wasting their time."

Helen Milner had done some shopping for her grandmother the night before at Somerfield's in Edendale. Things were much cheaper there than in the little village shop. Normally Gwen would be willing to catch the Hulley's bus from the stop near the pub for the journey into town for the sake of the money she would save from her pension. But this week she had refused to do the journey, worrying about what the other women would say to her on the bus, believing that the shop assistants would talk about her behind her back, that the checkout girls would refuse to serve her. Nothing Helen could say would persuade her she was imagining things. At times, she could be just as stubborn as Harry.

"He was the gardener at the Mount, but Graham Vernon sacked him," she said.

"Lee Sherratt? He was never a gardener. He can hump a wheelbarrow, but he knows nothing."

"They say he had a fancy for Laura."

"That's as maybe. It means nowt."

Helen slotted tins of peas and new potatoes into the kitchen cupboards, glancing sideways out of the window, where she could see Gwen pottering in the garden, carefully deadheading roses with a pair of secateurs. She looked frail and unsteady on her feet, her skin translucent in the morning light angling from above Win Low.

"Have you talked to Grandma yet?"

Harry was deep in his morning paper. Unlike many of the men his age, who preferred the sports coverage and sensational headlines of the tabloids, Harry took *The Guardian*. He said he liked to know what was really going on in the world. "All this stuff about TV celebrities and royal hangers-on. That means nowt to me," he would say.

"What should I talk to her about, then?"

"She's upset."

"When isn't she? The woman's got neurotic in her old age."

"Granddad, she's very worried. She thinks you're in trouble with the police. You have to reassure her. She won't listen to anyone else."

"Ah, they're all talking about me, aren't they?" said Harry.

"They'll talk. But nobody believes you're involved."

"Why not then?" he demanded.

Helen waved her hand, stumped for an explanation when challenged. "Well—"

"Aye, I know. It's because I'm old. You're just like them coppers. They haven't questioned me, you know. Not properly, not like they ought to have done, seeing as I found the body. They think I can't have done it, you see. Because I'm old. Well, they're wrong, and you're wrong, too."

"Don't be silly, Granddad. We know you didn't do it. Obviously."

"Oh aye. Obviously."

"Grandma knows. And Mum and Dad and me, we know that you've done nothing wrong. We would know—we're your family."

"And that's it? Just the few of you and no more?"

Helen felt a chill at his dismissive tone. "Your family has always meant a lot to you. You know it has."

Harry sighed and folded his paper.

"Well, hasn't it?"

"Of course it has, lass. But there are other things as strong as family. Stronger even. Women can't see it, because they're made different—family, that's everything for them. But there are other things. Friendship. When you've had a bloke at your back that you trust with your life, and he trusts you the same, that's different. That's a bond you can't break, not for any-body. You get so as you would do anything not to betray that trust, lass. Anything."

Harry was looking Helen in the face, a look deep in his eye that was almost appealing, asking for her help. And she did want to help him, but she didn't know how to. She waited for Harry to explain what he meant.

But he stared at the front page of the newspaper, where a picture of Central African refugees with desperate eyes stared back at him.

"You'd kill to help that sort of friend," he said.

Ben Cooper sighted along the barrels, shifted his grip on the wooden stock, and breathed in the scent of the gun oil as his fingers felt gently for the trigger. The shotgun fitted snugly into his shoulder, and the weight of the double barrels swung smoothly as he turned his body to test their balance. With that effortless movement came an eagerness to see the target in his sights, a desire for the kick and cough of the cartridge. He was ready.

"Pull!"

The trap snapped and a clay flashed across his line of vision. As if of their own accord, the barrels swung up and to the right to follow its trajectory, and his finger squeezed. The clay shattered into fragments that curved toward the ground.

"Pull!"

The second clay flickered overhead. Cooper carefully increased the pressure on the trigger, timing the extra squeeze as the target's line steadied and the clay shattered like the first.

"What do you think of it, Ben?"

"Nice," he said, lowering the shotgun and breaking it open. He laid the gun across the bonnet of the Land Rover, and his brother walked across from the trap gun they used for practicing. Matt was six years older than Ben, with the barrel chest and well-muscled shoulders and torso of a working farmer. He had the same fine light-brown hair and chose to hide his receding hairline under a green tractor driver's cap with a long peak like a baseball cap and the words "John Deere" on the front.

"Those were two good shots, Ben. Who were you picturing when you hit the clays?"

"What?"

"From the expression on your face, you had someone you really hate in your sights. Did it help to let it out?"

"Yes, a bit."

Matt studied his younger brother. "It's really getting you down, isn't it? We don't often see you like this. We will get Mum sorted out, you know.

Wait till you see her this afternoon—I bet she'll be more like her old self, and you'll feel a whole lot better about it."

"Maybe, Matt. But it isn't only that."

"Oh. Woman trouble, by any chance? Not Helen Milner, is it?"

Cooper stared at his brother in amazement. "What makes you say that?"

"It's obvious you must have bumped into her on this Vernon case. I put two and two together when I read about it in the paper. Her dad works for Graham Vernon, doesn't he? And the old man, Harry Dickinson—that would be her grandfather, right? If you've been hanging around there, I guessed you must have renewed old acquaintances."

Matt grinned as his brother looked at him, lost for words. "What do you reckon, then? Should I have been a detective?"

"I don't know how you worked all that out."

"Mmm. Helen Milner, eh? I always thought she had a bit of a thing about you, little brother, a few years back."

"All water under the bridge. She's different now. You should see her."

"Oh, but I have seen her. She's a teacher at Amy and Josie's school now. We talked to her at a parents' evening not so long ago. I hate to give away my secrets, but that's how I know about her dad and all that. We talked for quite a long while, actually. Some of it was about old times, some about the Vernons, too."

"Well then. You know what she looks like. She's probably got half a dozen blokes she's sleeping with. Why should she bother with me?"

"Do I detect a hint of bitterness? Is it a case of a heifer in heat and too many bulls to choose from?"

"People aren't like cattle, Matt."

"It'd be better if they were sometimes. Come to think of it, it's a pity you can't put raddle on people like you do on rams, then you'd know straightaway who was tupping who."

Matt looked at his brother expectantly, raising his eyebrows, but saw he hadn't even raised a smile.

"But there's more still, isn't there? Problems at work, is it?"

"Yeah, you're right. I've made a couple of bad cock-ups in the last few days."

"They'll understand you're under a lot of stress, though, won't they?"

Cooper fished the keys of the Toyota out of his pocket and looked at his watch. It was past the time he should have been setting off for Edendale to start his shift. But the chance to try Matt's new shotgun had been too much of a temptation.

"You've told your bosses about Mum, haven't you?"

"No, I didn't think they needed to know."

"But you have got time off this afternoon to go to the hospital?"

"I just told them I had a doctor's appointment."

"Bloody hell. They probably think you're going to see a psychiatrist or something, the way you've been these last few days."

"I'd rather keep the police force out of Mum's life, that's all."

"I see. Things are a bit bad then."

Cooper sighed. "Let's put it this way—I'd much rather stay here shooting rabbits with you, Matt, than go into the office this morning."

Matt walked back with his brother to his car, parked in the crew yard. "I take it the Vernon case isn't sorted out yet, then?"

"It feels as though it's running into the ground, Matt. We always dash 'round like mad at the beginning, of course. We collect masses of information, do dozens of witness interviews, house-to-house surveys, and TIE inquiries, getting background detail. God, there's so much in the computer after the first few days. Usually you get some clear lines of inquiry opening up that you can follow. But sometimes every one seems to be a blind alley and you get nowhere. Once a murder inquiry stalls, you can be looking at months and months before you get a result. If ever."

"And this is one of those, is it, Ben?"

Cooper paused with his hand on the car door. "I don't know, Matt. Maybe it's just me. But don't you ever get the feeling that you've been banging your head against a brick wall and didn't realize it?"

"It's a tragedy about the young girl. There's a bloke somewhere who shouldn't be running 'round loose."

"That's what keeps us going, I suppose."

He got into the driver's seat and lowered the windows. The interior of the car was already warm, though the morning had hardly begun.

Matt rested a brawny forearm on the door. "Still, the Vernons are no example to anybody, are they?"

"They're not my idea of good company."

"More than that," said Matt. "They create trouble for themselves, with what they get up to. Those orgies and things up there. I'm all for a bit of fun, but that's just sick."

Cooper looked at his brother, frowning, wondering what on earth he was talking about.

"Oh, I see. Well, if you don't believe me," said Matt, "you just ask Helen Milner."

By the time Cooper reached the outskirts of Edendale, he knew he was going to be late for the second time in a week. Another black mark. But he found he didn't really care. There was a dull pain throbbing at the front of his head, just behind his eyes, like the warning of an approaching thunderstorm.

At eight o'clock in the morning it seemed as though every few yards along the road there was someone clutching a dog lead. Their pets were nose down in every clump of grass, stopping to examine every lamppost and tree. It would be a rash murderer who tried to hide a body in this neighborhood. The search parties were out permanently.

The first person he saw on the second floor of Divisional HQ was Diane Fry. She was heading for the briefing room with three other DCs. They were laughing at something, and Cooper began to flush immediately, not doubting that it was him they were laughing at. Fry, though, saw him coming and stopped to let him catch up.

"You're late again, Ben. You'll be up on a charge if you're not careful."

"Doesn't matter," he said. "Have a good trip to Yorkshire?"

"Not particularly. I'd rather have been here."

"Waste of time, then?"

"Yes, as a matter of fact. There was no need for anyone to go, let alone two of us."

Cooper sneered before he could stop himself. "What a surprise. Still, I suppose you had a good time together."

Fry's nostrils flared. "I don't know what you're getting at, but I'll ignore it just this once."

He inclined his head, his shoulders slumping. "Sorry, Diane. I shouldn't have said that."

"Are you all right, Ben? You've got some funny ideas, but you've managed to restrain yourself from the snide comments so far."

"Yeah. I'm fine. It's this endless heat—it's wearing me out."

"Only I've been hearing something about some pigs . . ."

"Yeah, yeah, don't tell me."

He saw Fry studying him. Her eyes traveled from his dull eyes to his

244 / STEPHEN BOOTH

hastily combed hair and down to his badly shaved cheeks, his crumpled shirt. He was suddenly aware of the smell of stale sweat from his body and the way his hand shook when he rubbed his temples where the pain was beginning to throb again.

"Ben—what I said about your father. I did apologize. If there's anything else I can say . . ."

"I told you then—if one more person calls me Sergeant Cooper's lad . . . Just let me forget it, can't you?"

Fry stood back, shocked by the venom in his voice. "Fine. Oh, and there's a message for you. The superintendent wanted to see you straightaway, as soon as you got in."

"What about the briefing?"

"Straightaway. That was the message. Trouble, is it?"

"Bound to be."

"Hey, you haven't forgotten our date tonight, have you?"

"What?"

"You're taking me to your dojo. I'm looking forward to that challenge bout. You're going to teach me a few things, remember?"

The walls of the superintendent's office were lined with photographs, some of them going back many years. The faces of stiff, upright men with high collars and large mustaches seem to glare at Ben Cooper, judging him. It was as if they were saying that he did not come up to their standards. That was certainly the message that Superintendent Jepson was trying to put across.

"So basically, I'm saying it's just not your turn this time, Cooper. Be patient, and your turn will come, I'm sure. Give it a bit more time, and we'll look at things in a fresh light. There's always hope in the future. Think about a bit of lateral development."

Jepson studied the DC for his reaction. Hitchens was right—Cooper did look a little stressed and nervy. The dark patches under his eyes made him look older than twenty-eight, and he didn't seem to have shaved properly this morning. His hands were shaking slightly, even before he had been told the news that he would not be on the shortlist for the DS's job. Jepson wondered whether Ben Cooper had a drink problem. He would have to ask DI Hitchens.

"Does it come as a shock to you, Cooper?"

"I suppose I had wondered about it, sir. I had a psychological assessment done, you see."

"And what did it say in your psychological assessment report, Cooper?"

"It said I'm not assertive enough, sir. Too inclined to interiorize and empathize in inappropriate circumstances."

"Mmm. And do you know what that means?"

"Not a clue, sir."

"It means you're too bloody nice, Cooper."

"I see."

"And we can't have nice cops, can we? Not anymore. Oh aye, we've every other kind of police now, Cooper. They've all got their place in the modern service. We've got black cops, women cops, gay cops, even psychic cops."

Cooper took the last to be a reference to a story that had appeared in the local paper about a section officer who was a prominent member of the Spiritualist Church and had recently confessed to clairvoyant tendencies.

"Nothing can surprise me now," said Jepson. "Next we'll have transvestite cops, you'll see. Some bugger in Vice Squad will turn up in a skirt one day, and then it'll be anything goes. We'll have midget cops, zombie cops, blue-skinned cops from the planet Zog. Who knows? Maybe we'll have genetically manipulated PCs with muscles like King Kong and brains like turnips. No, scrub that, we've got those already. But God forbid we should discriminate against any of them, Cooper. The one thing that *won't* be tolerated is a prejudiced cop."

"Yes, sir," said Cooper, and tried a tentative smile, assuming Jepson was trying to cheer him up.

The superintendent looked at him suspiciously. He liked his junior officers to laugh at his jokes, but only when he was actually joking. "I suppose you think there's no reason why we shouldn't have nice cops, don't you, Cooper? No reason at all."

"No, sir. Just not as a sergeant, perhaps?"

"Well, who wants to be a bloody sergeant? It's the dog's arse of a job, believe me."

They both listened for a moment, trying to catch the echoes of the insincerity from the plasterboard walls. Jepson tapped his hands on his desk to break the moment, glaring at Cooper until he was forced to speak.

"Anyway, sir, I'm not as bothered as all that. I don't really resent it or anything."

"Bollocks. If I were you, Cooper, I'd be totally pissed off. You're just trying to be nice about it. There's your trouble, you see," he said with an air of triumph.

"I don't suppose I'll ever learn, sir."

"My advice is, go and shoot a few of those pigeons or whatever it is you do, get it out of your system. Have a few drinks. You'll soon forget about it."

Cooper dipped his head in acknowledgment as Jepson pursed his lips seriously for his final comment. "But no emotional outbursts, eh?"

He stared past the superintendent's head. There was a large framed photograph on the wall, with dozens of solemn men sitting or standing in long rows. They were the entire uniformed strength of Edendale section, pictured during a visit to the station by some member of the royal family in the 1980s. Cooper remembered the occasion and the photograph well. In the second row, among the other sergeants, was his father.

"I understand, sir. It doesn't matter. It really doesn't matter at all."

The doctor had explained that Isabel Cooper was on a powerful antipsychotic drug. He had spelled out the name of the drug, and Cooper had written it down carefully. Chlorpromazine. It blocked the activity of dopamine and caused changes in the nervous system. These could mean side effects, said the doctor.

As Cooper sat by her bedside, it seemed to him that his mother couldn't stop moving her lips and tongue or the muscles of her face. She was permanently grimacing, rolling her tongue in her cheeks like someone frantically trying to remove stray bits of food from her gums. Underneath the bedclothes, her legs were in constant movement, flexing and convulsing endlessly like the limbs of a long-distance cyclist.

The doctor had been eager to point out to Ben and Matt that the drugs they were using were not curative. They could not cure schizophrenia; they could only relieve the most distressing symptoms. And those symptoms seemed unending in the mouth of the doctor—thought disturbance, paranoia, hallucinations, delusions, loss of self-care, social withdrawal, severe anxiety, agitation. The condition could only get worse. But occasionally, just occasionally, they could expect remissions, when

Mrs. Cooper would almost be her normal self. The doctor seemed to think they would find this reassuring.

"I'm being a terrible nuisance to everyone," said Isabel, gazing with old eyes from the bed.

"No, Mum. Of course you're not. Don't worry about it."

"Is that Ben?"

"Yes, Mum. I'm here."

He had been sitting there for nearly forty minutes already talking to his mother. Matt had been with him for the first half hour, but had gone outside for a while. He needed some fresh air, he said.

"You're a good boy. I'm not well, am I?"

"You'll be fine, Mum."

She turned her head, grinning and winking helplessly as she reached a hand toward him. There was a dribble of saliva on the neck of her night-dress. A small vase of white gypsophila stood on the bedside cabinet, the same color as the sheets; the same color as her skin. Cooper was sweating in the heat of the hospital room, but his mother's hand felt cold and clammy.

"You're just like your dad," she said. "Such a good-looking young man."

He smiled at her and pressed her hand, guessing what was coming, dreading the need for an answer, not knowing what he could possibly say.

"Are you married yet, Ben?"

"No, Mum. You know I'm not."

"You'll find a nice girl soon. I'd like to see you married and have children."

"Don't worry."

He knew the words were meaningless. But in all his vocabulary there didn't seem to be any words that would carry a meaning they could both understand and draw comfort from.

Isabel's shoulders twitched and her legs jerked and squirmed, rustling under the hospital sheet like restless animals. Her tongue protruded over her lips as she blinked around the room with a puzzled expression. Then she focused on her son. She sought his face eagerly, her eyes desperate and pleading. She was sending out a mute appeal, begging him for some small drop of consolation.

"Just like your dad," she said.

He waited. His muscles were frozen and his brain empty of thoughts. He was a mesmerized rabbit waiting for the fatal bite. His lungs hurt from holding his breath. He knew he would not be able to refuse the plea in her eyes.

"Have they made you a sergeant yet, Ben?"

"Yes, Mum," he said, though it broke his heart to lie.

-21-

It was the first time Diane Fry had visited the Mount. She was not impressed by the mock porticos and the triple garage and the wrought-iron gates. She found the whole thing tasteless, a white box that was out of place set against the scenery of the valley behind it and the rows of stone cottages a few yards down the road. It could have been plonked down here from a suburb of Birmingham—Edgbaston or Bourneville, perhaps. It gave no impression of being part of the landscape.

She had been allocated the task of talking to Charlotte Vernon, following DCI Tailby's interview with her husband and son. Charlotte had been saying little so far and attention had not been concentrated on her. But now there were other questions that needed to be asked, particularly questions about Lee Sherratt. The boy was still Mr. Tailby's favored option, though Fry could see he had always kept in mind a second line of inquiry centered on the family. It was possible Charlotte Vernon might hold the key, one way or the other.

Fry was shown in by Daniel. He seemed subdued and sullen, rather than the angry young man she had read about in the reports. But when she told him what she wanted, he took her through the house without a word or a backward glance, finding no necessity for politeness. It was a pity his alibi had checked out so thoroughly.

Charlotte Vernon had been described by the officers who had seen her as an attractive woman; some had said very attractive. Fry had expected to find a rich man's spoilt wife, with nothing to do all day but look after her appearance, keeping her body in perfect condition, her hair expensively styled, her cosmetics flawless. But she found a woman in her late thirties, tired and resigned. The cosmetics were certainly there, and might have fooled a man. But Fry recognized that they had been applied without conviction.

Charlotte was wearing cream slacks and a silk shirt. She looked elegant—but then any woman wearing so many hundreds of pounds' worth of clothes on her back ought to look stylish. Fry had come prepared to feel sympathy for the woman, who had just lost her daughter. She was willing to put the son's story to the back of her mind, to listen to Charlotte's version of events. But there was something in the tilt of the woman's head as she lit a cigarette and settled herself into an armchair; something in the curl of her lips as she looked her up and down critically. In the end, Fry did not get a chance to show sympathy, as Charlotte Vernon opened the interview aggressively.

"Don't bother to treat me with kid gloves. I'm all right now."

"There are a few questions, Mrs. Vernon."

"Yes, I've been expecting you. Dan's been to see you, of course. I couldn't stop him. The poor boy—he gets so mixed up about sex. Some men take a long time to mature, don't they? I think Dan has got a bad case of delayed puberty."

"Your son has made a statement about your relationship with Lee Sherratt, Mrs. Vernon."

"You mean he found out I was having it off with the gardener, don't you, dear?"

Fry stared at her without expression. They were in a room full of beautiful old furniture with clear, tidy surfaces. There were three or four large watercolors on the wall, and an expanse of woodblock floor led toward French windows and a flagged terrace with stone balustrades. Fry would have liked to explore the bathroom and the kitchen, to examine the whirlpool bath, the automatic oven, the fitted wardrobes, the self-defrosting fridge and the digital microwave.

"Is that the way it was, Mrs. Vernon?"

"Certainly. Oh, only a couple of times, but we both enjoyed it. He was unsubtle but enthusiastic. And an excellent body. It's so good for morale at my age when you can still make the young men come running."

"Did you initiate the relationship?"

"I suppose I seduced him, yes. It didn't take much doing."

"When did your husband find out what was going on?"

Charlotte shrugged. "I don't really know. Does it matter?"

"I would have thought so."

"Why is that?"

"Presumably he objected."

"You presume wrong, dear. He gets a turn-on from it, old Graham. That's convenient for both of us, really. It means I'm free to take what lovers I like without any complications. Graham, of course, is quite free to do the same as far as I'm concerned."

"But he did object, didn't he? He sacked Sherratt from his job."

"True." Charlotte blew a slow smoke ring which hovered in the air between them. "But didn't Graham tell you that was because of Laura?"

"And was it?"

"If that's what Graham says, it must have been, mustn't it?"

"Were you aware yourself of Lee Sherratt's attitude to your daughter? In view of your own relationship with him?"

"Do I call you Detective Constable?"

"If you like."

"Detective Constable, I don't know what you imagine I did with Sherratt in the summerhouse, but we certainly didn't indulge in conversation about my daughter."

"But do you think——?"

"He was more than occupied with me, dear. I can be demanding when I'm aroused."

"And why bother with the lamb when you can have the old ewe, eh?"

Charlotte bared her perfect teeth in a snarl, then changed her mind and turned the snarl into a mirthless laugh.

"Very good, dear. I wouldn't have thought you were so good with the farming metaphors."

Fry was disappointed that she could not crack the woman's facade. If only she could get through the provocative, brittle exterior, she might expose a soft, vulnerable core that would yield something to the probing.

"Did you know about Laura's boyfriend, Simeon Holmes?"

"No, I didn't." Charlotte sighed. "Until your people managed to track him down. I suppose there's no doubt they had a thing together?"

"None at all."

"She was obviously a bit of a chip off the old block, wasn't she? She kept her bit on the side quiet, though. Laura usually told me her secrets, but not that one."

"Perhaps she thought you would consider him unsuitable. He's from one of the council estates in Edendale, rides a motorbike."

"Unsuitable? Not me."

"Really?"

"Well, I *was* shagging the gardener, dear."

Fry gritted her teeth. Charlotte stubbed out her cigarette and began to stir restlessly. The ashtray was already full of butts, and the air was pungent with stale smoke that mingled with an expensive scent.

"I hope I'm not shocking you," said Charlotte. "I know some of you people can be very puritanical. But Graham and I have always had that sort of marriage. It is rather an accepted thing among our circle of friends."

"You mentioned other lovers, Mrs. Vernon. I need to ask you for some names."

"Really? How many years would you like me to go back?"

"Just the last few months, shall we say?"

"Are our police looking at jealousy as a motive, then? How original."

"Names?"

"All right. There have been one or two of my husband's business colleagues. Just the odd occasion, you know. Nothing heavy."

She gave Fry three names, only one of which meant anything.

"Andrew Milner?"

"He works for Graham."

"I know who he is."

Fry stared at the woman, wondering if she was really the distraught mother who had appeared in previous reports. Perhaps she was on some drug that the doctor had given her. But she could think of nothing that would completely change a woman's personality to this. Charlotte studied her expression and laughed her cold laugh again.

"Oh yes, I'm not too fussy when I'm in the mood."

"And have you been in the mood much since Laura was killed? Does the thought of your daughter being attacked and murdered make you feel randy?"

Charlotte's face seemed to blur and quiver, and her eyes swelled alarmingly. Her limbs trembled and her shoulders slumped into an unnatural position. It was as if the woman had disintegrated suddenly into a broken doll.

"I go to that place every night, you know," she said.

"What place?" asked Fry, startled at the unexpected change.

"I go at night, about eight o'clock, when no one's around. Graham hates it. I take flowers for her."

"You go where?"

"That place down there. The place where Laura died." She looked up pleadingly. "I take her roses and carnations from the garden. Are they the right things to take?"

Back at E Division, Ben Cooper made his way wearily up to the incident room, where just two computer operators were at their terminals, and the office manager, DI Baxter, was stacking away some files. Cooper checked through the action sheets, but could find nothing allocated to him.

"I'm back on duty now, sir."

"Nothing for you, Cooper," said Baxter. "Some of the teams are being reallocated. Your DI wants you back in the CID room. You've to report to DS Rennie."

"Oh, shit."

"Sorry, son."

Baxter seemed about to reprimand Cooper for his outburst, conscious of the computer operators' eyes on him. But he looked at Cooper's face and changed his mind, not being one to kick a man when he was obviously down.

"Mr. Tailby thinks forensics—"

"Yeah, I know. Thanks."

Cooper stamped back downstairs. A DC was on the phone in the CID room, and Rennie was holding a report in the air, staring at it with an expression of admiration. He noticed Cooper come in and waved a hand casually.

"Ben. Welcome back to the real world."

Cooper kicked the chair away from his desk and thumped the pile of paper that had been sitting there since Monday.

"What's all this stuff?"

"Hey, calm down. We don't want any prima donna tantrums just because you're not with the big boys on the murder inquiries anymore."

"Yeah, right. Car crime. They want something doing about car crime, yeah? So what's new?"

"This is," said Rennie, waving the report. "Here, take a look."

The report landed on Cooper's desk. It bore the heading of the National Crime Intelligence Service. "What's this?"

"New ideas on detecting car crime. It's good stuff. The super is very impressed. It was the new lass's idea."

"Not Diane Fry?"

"That's her. Not bad for a lass, I reckon."

"And where is she? Is she already out working on this?"

"Not her," said Rennie. "She's still on the Vernon inquiry."

Fry phoned Vernon Finance, but was put through to a particularly unhelpful and protective secretary who told her that Andrew Milner was out of the office all afternoon. She eventually persuaded the secretary to give her his mobile number, and ate a tuna sandwich while she dialed. When he answered, Milner was clearly on the road somewhere. There was heavy traffic noise in the background, and he was shouting, as people did when they were using the hands-free adaptor in a car.

"Who did you say you were? Hold on, I'm just turning onto the A57."

When she got it through to him who she was, he went very quiet for a moment. Perhaps it was just the signal being broken up by the high ridges of Stanage Edge and the Hallam Moors.

"Give me a second, and I'll pull into a lay-by," he said.

Fry talked to Andrew Milner for several minutes, trying to catch the tone of the man's replies against the thundering slipstream of passing lorries and the intermittent fading of his cell phone signal. She thought he sounded nervous and defensive, but he stuck to a firm line on the suggestion of any relationship with his employer's wife. It was ridiculous, it was nonsense. Charlotte Vernon obviously wasn't well.

Eventually, Fry let him go when he pleaded that he was late for an important meeting. She felt sure that he was hiding something but couldn't pin down what it was. She needed some more information before she could know the right questions to ask. Time to talk to Andrew Milner's wife.

The Milners lived in a brick prewar semi on one of the hills overlooking the center of Edendale. The front door was set into an arched porch, with a round opaque window made up of shaped pieces of colored glass.

All the cars parked in the street had pink stickers taped to their windscreens, and notices on the lampposts warned that parking was by resident's permit only. But Fry found room for her Peugeot on a small drive in front of a carport. By the corner of the house she noticed on old brick chimney pot that had been planted with red geraniums.

Margaret Milner took her into a lounge dominated by leaded bay windows draped in net and a wheel-shaped chandelier supporting electric candles. A display cabinet contained limited-edition figurines, miniature cottages, and commemorative plates.

"Andrew's at work, of course," said Margaret. "He's been very busy since what happened to Laura Vernon. But Graham says he'll be back at the office next Monday. Apparently Charlotte is feeling better now. But people don't really come to terms with these things properly until after the funeral, I find."

"Have you been in touch with the Vernons yourself?"

Margaret hesitated. "I've tried to ring Charlotte, but nobody ever answers the phone. You just get the answering machine."

"I've just come from the Mount myself," said Fry.

"Oh?" Margaret didn't seem to know what else to say. She was wearing a long skirt and strappy shoes with flat soles, and she had a light sweater tied around her shoulders. She looked hot and uncomfortable, but then so did everybody in this weather.

"I've been talking to Mrs. Vernon."

"Is she— How is she taking it all?"

"Not quite in the way you might expect."

"Oh?" said Margaret again.

Fry walked across to the bay windows and peered through the net at the front garden. Close up, she could see that the geraniums were wilting and turning brown, and their petals had formed a dark-red pool around the base of the chimney pot.

"What sort of relationship would you say your husband has with the Vernons?" she asked.

"He works for Graham. It's a good job and Andrew works hard." Margaret sat down, straightening her skirt, perching uneasily on the edge of an armchair. She looked at Fry anxiously, worried by the fact that she insisted on remaining standing by the window, despite the hint. "He was out of work for a while, you know. It made him appreciate having a secure job."

"Just a relationship between employer and employee, then? Or something more?"

"Well, I don't really know what you mean," said Margaret. "They work very closely together. You have to have a fairly close personal relationship, I suppose."

"A personal relationship? Friends, then? Do you socialize with the Vernons? Have you visited their house?"

"Yes, we have. Once or twice. Graham is very hospitable."

Fry watched her closely, noting the shift in the gaze, the involuntary movements of the hands that fidgeted constantly, as if seeking something to pat back into place, something that could be put right with a quick shake and a smoothing of the palms.

"And Charlotte Vernon?" said Fry. "Is she equally hospitable?"

"Would you like a cup of tea?" asked Margaret with a note of desperation.

"No, thank you."

"I'll make one, I think."

"If you like."

Fry followed her into the kitchen, making Margaret Milner even more nervous as she slouched against the oak-effect units and got in the way of the fridge door being opened. Margaret stared at her over the top of the door with a plastic bottle of skimmed milk in her hand.

"What exactly is it that you want?"

"A bit of help, that's all," said Fry. "I'm trying to fill in a few details."

Cold air from the open fridge was filling the space between them, chilling Fry's skin and causing the warm air in the room to condense on the steel surfaces. Margaret seemed reluctant to reach for the handle to close it, afraid to reach too near to Fry in case she touched her and was contaminated by something that could not be killed by Jeyes fluid and bleach.

"I don't know what details I can give you. I really don't."

Margaret actually walked away, leaving the fridge ajar, to switch on the kettle. When Fry slammed the door, Margaret jerked as if she had been shot, slopping water onto the work surface.

"Would you know where to find Mr. Milner just now, if you needed to?"

Margaret glanced automatically at the clock. "His office would be able to tell you where he is. He has to drive around a lot. Meetings with clients, you know. He's so busy. He may not be home until late again tonight."

Home late and she never knew where he was? Fry wondered whether Andrew Milner really was as busy as he told his wife. She wouldn't accept that anything was impossible.

"Maybe there are times when you don't know where your husband is, but Graham Vernon does know."

"Of course."

"And sometimes, perhaps, it's Charlotte Vernon who knows where he is?"

For a moment, Margaret did nothing but stare at the simmering kettle as if it had muttered a rude word. Then she opened her mouth and eyes wide and began to flap her fingers. "Oh no, what do you mean?"

"I think it's fairly straightforward. Mrs. Vernon was quite open about it."

"Was she implying something about Andrew? It's quite ridiculous, isn't it? She's obviously not well. She must have been affected very badly for her to make up things like that."

"You don't think it's true?"

"True? What nonsense! Andrew? Nonsense!"

"You realize that the wife is often the last to know?"

"Oh, but really . . . Andrew?" She laughed suddenly, foolishly. "It's just not possible."

"OK." The kettle began to boil but was ignored. A small cloud of steam drifted across the kitchen, but dissipated before it could warm Fry's chilled hands. "One last detail, Mrs. Milner. Are you related to a boy called Simeon Holmes?"

"Simeon is my cousin Alison's son. They live on the Devonshire Estate."

"Were you aware that he was Laura Vernon's boyfriend?"

Margaret wrung her hands and stared out of the bay window. "Not until Alison told me last night. She said he had to go to the police station."

"Something else you didn't know, then?"

"No, no," cried Margaret. "Not Andrew. It's impossible!"

Fry trod in the slithery skin of geranium petals as she left the house. Though still scarlet on the surface, they were black and rotting underneath. Impossible? The only thing that was impossible was the idea that she might have been willing to sit and take tea with Margaret Milner among her miniature cottages and net curtains.

While she turned the Peugeot around, Fry thought of one more place to try. This one would be a pleasure, she thought, as she remembered the way Helen Milner had looked at Ben Cooper in the street at Moorhay.

Helen took a phone call from her mother as soon as Diane Fry had left the house in Edendale, and she had to spend some minutes placating her. When she had finally hung up, Helen rang her grandparents' number. She knew they didn't use the telephone much and had only been persuaded to have it put in for emergencies, with Andrew paying the rental. When it rang, she could picture the two old people looking at the phone in alarm, reluctant to answer it. Eventually, Harry would get up slowly and take hold of the handset, answering the telephone being a man's job.

"Granddad, it's Helen."

"Helen, what's up, love?"

"It's the police, Granddad. They've been asking questions about Dad."

"Have they now? That pillock with the big words or the nasty piece of work that was with him?"

"Neither."

"Was it—?"

"No, it was the woman. Detective Constable Fry."

"Her? She's nothing but a bit of a lass."

"Even so . . ."

Harry paused, considering. "Aye, you're right. Best to know."

Diane Fry found Helen Milner's cottage to be one of four tiny homes created out of a barn conversion.

The barn had a wavy roof and there was a clutter of old farm buildings at the back that no one had yet found a way of using. Inside, the walls were of undressed stone, with casement windows and pitch-covered beams. Most of the furniture was secondhand stripped pine, with wicker chairs and a rush mat on the kitchen floor.

Helen greeted her without any indication of surprise, and Fry guessed that the phone lines had been busy during her journey across Edendale. She expected this third member of the Milner family to be as unforthcoming as the others, to tell the same story of shock and ignorance, to use the same, familiar words of outraged innocence.

But she was amazed how long the visit lasted. And she was fascinated and enlightened by the story that Helen Milner had to tell her over the instant coffee in the hand-thrown pottery mugs. By the second coffee, Fry had almost forgotten what she had come for.

-22-

The three old men had met at Moorhay post office, where they had collected their pensions. The post office had been busy, not just with the regular Thursday pension queue but with hikers emptying the cold drinks cabinet and the little freezer where the choc ices and the strawberry-flavored iced lollies were kept. There was barely room inside the shop to maneuver around the displays of postcards of Ladybower Reservoir and Chatsworth House. Bulging rucksacks were piled outside while their owners flicked through the guidebooks and the sets of National Park place mats.

Soon the hikers would be moving on through the village to the tearooms and craft center at the Old Mill or the picnic site at Quith Holes; then they would head for the Eden Valley Trail, aiming to reach the Limestone Way to the south or the Pennine Way to the north. Within half an hour, they would have forgotten Moorhay.

Harry Dickinson had picked a small frozen chicken out of the freezer for Gwen. It was solid and heavy in his hand, and the frost bit painfully into his palm, numbing his fingers. But queueing at the counter to pay for it, he found himself marooned in a sea of young people, who bumped against him and elbowed him carelessly in the ribs. They seemed regardless of his presence, as if he were just another obstacle that had come between their grasping hands and the next Diet Coke.

A small vein began to throb in Harry's temple as a girl pushed in front of him in the queue. She was wearing a crop top that left her midriff bare and striped leggings that made her hips and backside look enormous. Her dyed-blonde hair exploded from the top of her head like badly baled straw, and when she opened her mouth to call to her friends, he saw a silver stud thrust through her tongue.

Jostling for position, she trod hard on Harry's toes with her Doc

Martens, and when he looked down there were dirty scuff marks and indentations in the shiny leather of his boots. If she had apologized, he would never have said anything. But she turned away without even seeing him. She might as well have trodden on a piece of litter that she could wipe off later.

Harry tapped the girl on the shoulder, and she stared up at him incredulously. Her lip turned back in a sneer, revealing a gray wad of chewing gum squashed between her teeth. He noticed there was a stud through her bare navel that matched the one in her tongue.

"Haven't you been taught any manners?" he said.

She looked at him as if he were speaking a different language.

"What's up with you, granddad?"

Her accent was local, and Harry thought he might actually have seen her around the village before. It made no difference.

"If you shove in front of me and tread on my feet, you might at least apologize."

"I've as much right to be in here as you."

"As much. But not more. You'll have to learn, lass."

"Oh, get lost," she said. She pushed her chewing gum forward through her teeth so that it smeared across her lips. Then she wriggled out her tongue and dragged it all back into her mouth again, staring insolently at Harry. But she quickly lost interest in him and turned away as the queue moved forward.

Harry hefted the solid weight of the frozen chicken in his left hand, staring at the back of the girl's head. The tight breast of the chicken was smooth and hard, and coated in a thick layer of ice. He grasped the legs of the bird and let it begin to swing.

The girl screamed and cannoned forward into a youth in front of her in the queue. Everyone in the post office turned to look as she snarled and cursed at the old man. She was rubbing the place on her back where the biting cold of the chicken had touched her warm, naked flesh like a branding iron.

"Sorry," said Harry.

Outside the shop, by the swinging Wall's ice cream sign, Sam Beeley slipped on a discarded Coke can and hit the pavement with a painful thump, his ivory-headed stick clattering into the gutter. There was a flutter of consternation until two tall young men with Australian accents helped him to his feet and picked up his stick. Three girls, who had leaned their hired mountain bikes against the shop window, made a great fuss of asking the old man if he was all right and dusting him down, eyeing the Australians. They all circled around Sam in a kaleidoscope of colorful shirts and brown limbs, like butterflies momentarily attracted to a dry, leafless plant before passing on to seek new scents elsewhere.

Finally, they left him to Harry and Wilford, who assured them he only lived a few yards away. Though supported by his friends, Sam didn't get very far before he had to stop and rest on a wall, gasping from the pain in his legs. He lit a cigarette and squinted at the churchyard across the road, where the gravestones gleamed white in the sunlight.

"You'll be carrying me over yonder soon," he said, without self-pity.

"We're all heading that way," said Wilford.

"I'll not race you. It'll happen soon enough."

"You have to accept the fact," said Harry, "that when you get to our age, death is always just around the corner."

"Do you remember that time in the mine, when I nearly got killed," said Sam.

"That was a good few years ago."

Sam looked down at his legs. "Aye, but it left me a memento."

The three men were silent, staring at the houses opposite, not seeing the cars that went past or the young hikers who had to step off the pavement to get around them.

It had been over twenty years since the accident had happened at Glory Stone Mine. They had been in a six-foot-wide worked-out vein, nearly a hundred feet high. The face sloped upward in a bank of calcite-like scree, with a miner drilling at the top, fifty feet up, silhouetted against the speck of his light. The sloping face was dimly lit, and the air was smoky from the blasting, with the roof nothing but a dusky darkness way beyond the reach of the lights. It was a vast and misty cavern of grays and blacks, thick with the acrid stink of explosives and dust.

Sam had been the miner at the top of the face. He had been in his fifties then, an experienced man who had spent most of his working life in the mines. When his drill split the brittle rock and the face had opened under his feet, his body had been thrown instantly backward, his arms and legs tumbling among their own thrashing shadows until he hit the foot of the slope and had been buried by an avalanche of calcite. Wilford had found Harry in the darkness, and together they had dug Sam out with their bare hands and dragged him to safety. They hadn't realized his legs were broken until he started to scream.

"If the pain got too much," said Wilford, to nobody in particular, "would you think of doing away with yourself?"

Sam looked thoughtful. "Aye, I suppose so."

Harry nodded. "If there was nothing left for you. No hope. I reckon you'd have to."

"Depends on what you believe in, though," said Wilford. "Doesn't it?"

"How do you mean?"

"Some folk don't believe it's right to do away with yourself."

"Ah, religion." Sam smiled.

"Well, it's a sin, suicide," said Wilford. "Isn't it, Harry?"

Then Harry lit his pipe. The others waited, sensing an impending judgment or decision. They knew Harry did his best thinking when his pipe was lit.

"It seems to me," he said, "there's different sorts of sin. Sin isn't the same as evil. God would forgive you a sin."

They nodded. It sounded right and reasonable. None of them had got through almost eight decades without committing the odd sin.

"It'd take a bit of courage, though. There aren't any easy ways."

"There's sleeping pills."

Harry cleared his throat contemptuously. "That's a woman's way out, Sam."

"You could throw yourself off somewhere high. Raven's Side cliff," suggested Wilford.

"Messy. And you wouldn't necessarily kill yourself."

They shuddered. "You wouldn't want that."

"I can't stand heights anyway. They make me dizzy."

"That's a point."

"There's hanging," said Harry, "if you know how to tie a knot right."

"And you have to get the drop just right, else."

Wilford pursed his lips, ran his fingers through his white hair. "Else what?"

"You don't die quick—you strangle yourself. Slowly."

"I've read somewhere that blokes pretend to hang themselves," said Sam. "They almost hang themselves but not quite. For a bit of fun, like."

"Bloody hell, why would they do that?"

"Sex," said Sam solemnly. "They say it gives you a bloody great hard-on."

"Ah. Well, that'd be a novelty, all right."

"You never know. It might be worth it, for once."

"There was a bloke in the paper," said Sam. "Seventy-four years old, he was. He had fastened his nipples and his testicles up to electrical terminals. They called it an *'autoerotic experiment.'*"

"Aye? What happened?"

"He had the charge too strong. It killed him. Blew his balls off, for all I know."

"Old age doesn't stop you wanting it. It just stops you doing it properly," said Harry.

They nodded wisely, watching the three young girls from the post office cycle past, long legs whirling as their spinning spokes flickered in the sun.

"That lass in the shop," said Sam. "The one with the big bum and the bolt through her tongue. That was Sheila Kelk's girl, from Wye Close."

"Oh aye?" said Harry, uninterested.

"They live near the Sherratts."

The council dustbin wagon rumbled and hissed somewhere on Howe Lane. The wheelie bins still stood on the pavement waiting for it, painted with white numbers or the names of houses. Inside the bins was the accumulated debris that could tell the whole story of people's lives.

"You could do it with a car," said Wilford. "They do that all the time 'round here. Blokes from Sheffield and that. They drive out somewhere on the hills where no one'll find them and gas themselves with the exhaust."

"You're right, Wilford. They do. Bloody nuisance, they are, littering the place."

"I haven't had a car for years," said Sam. "So that's a waste of time."

He pushed himself to his feet, leaning painfully on his ivory-headed stick as Harry supported his elbow. They only had a few more yards to go to Sam's house, but it might as well have been miles away.

"But *I've* got a car," said Wilford.

Cooper waited until Rennie and the other DC were out of the office before he phoned Helen Milner. Despite the events of the day, his brother's comments had been preying on his mind, and they had reemerged as soon as he sat at his desk. He needed to know what Helen was holding back.

She sounded cautious when she answered, but surprised him by how readily she began to tell him about the parties at the Mount, as if she had already rehearsed what she would say.

"They go to the Vernons for the food, plenty of alcohol, and plenty of sex," she said. "A bit of soft drugs, too, probably. There was no pretense about it. Everyone seemed to know what to expect when they went to the Mount. All except me, that is."

"Are we talking a bit of old-fashioned wife swapping?"

"I guess so. Graham and Charlotte Vernon certainly seemed to swap with anyone who was available. It became their hobby, I think. Some people take up train spotting or line dancing," she said sourly.

Her description of the sexual activities the guests expected went a long way toward justifying Matt's reference to orgies, as far as Cooper was concerned. There had been no old people at the Mount parties, only those of the Vernons' age or younger. Graham, it seemed, chose most of the guests personally; some came by recommendation from friends. Listening to Helen's account, though, it struck Cooper that the parties weren't just a bit of fun for Graham Vernon. They also helped his business. All the guests were clients or potential clients, and attendance at the parties tied them together in what Vernon would no doubt have called a mutually beneficial relationship. It put a whole new slant on the idea of corporate entertainment.

"Oh yes, it was business as well as pleasure," said Helen when he suggested it. "He probably claims back the VAT on the booze."

"Was Laura Vernon at these parties?"

"Yes, but only at the beginning. They made sure they had her there on show when people arrived. But before the action started, they packed her off to the home of some pony-club friend in Edendale, where they let her stay the night. Out of sight, out of mind, as Grandma would say."

"We know she was sexually experienced. Do you think she might have got involved with any of her father's friends?"

"One of the perks for Daddy's best clients? Maybe. It sounds about right."

Helen sounded very bitter, but it was more than just distaste at the casual treatment of a teenage girl. You didn't have to be a police officer to know that far worse exploitation was an all too familiar story these days. Cooper thought about his nieces, Josie and Amy, and clenched his fists. He dreaded to think what he would do if anyone came near those two.

"She enjoyed every minute of the attention while she was there," said

Helen, "but my feeling was that it was mostly a performance for Daddy. She was Daddy's girl, all right. Though Charlotte Vernon would tell you differently, I think. Charlotte thought Laura was as good as gold, and really believed that she had no idea what went on at those parties. I'm sure that provided an extra spice for Laura. The excitement of living dangerously, enjoying a big secret."

Cooper wondered what she based this judgment on, but had too many other questions piling up in his mind to go down a sidetrack.

"Daddy's girl?"

"You can take that how you like. Imagine the worst, if you want. As far as I'm concerned, Graham Vernon is capable of anything."

"You really dislike him, don't you?"

"Dislike him? Hate him, you mean."

He frowned. He thought that the word "hate" didn't sit too comfortably in Helen's mouth.

"And you, Helen?" he asked cautiously. "How did you get involved in these parties?"

"I was invited because I had met Graham Vernon at my parents' house a few weeks before."

"I suppose he took a fancy to you."

She sighed. "I can't believe how naive I was. Dad really didn't want me to go, but he wouldn't say why. I thought it would be exciting, you see. A bit more glamorous than the staff room of a primary school, anyway. When I arrived it all seemed good fun at first. Everybody was very friendly. Attentive, even." There was a strange vibration of the phone, as if she were shuddering at the recollection. "I had a bit too much to drink, but everybody else was the same. I sobered up pretty quickly when Graham Vernon got me in one of the bedrooms."

Ben Cooper thought at first he must have misheard her. Helen's last words didn't seem to conjure up a rational picture in his mind. The picture he had was completely wrong. Completely.

"Hold on. Are you telling me—?"

But Helen wasn't listening. She was absorbed in her own memories. "He's a big man, you know. He was far too strong for me. Before I knew what was happening, he had pushed me down among the expensive coats on the bed, and his whole weight was on top of me so I could barely breathe. He was laughing all the time, as if it was some sort of joke that I was struggling. I can remember now the smell of the wine on his breath, the feel of his fingers digging into my arms, the sight of his face so close to mine that I had to shut my eyes. . . ."

Cooper waited in silence. He wanted to ask her to stop now, to tell her that he had enough information, that there were times when you could know too much. But her words continued to spill down the phone line, cold and fast, like a stream loosened from its winter ice.

"The worst thing was that somehow I couldn't force myself to shout for help. It was because I was in *his* house, Ben. I was too embarrassed to cry out or scream. Too embarrassed! It sounds ridiculous, doesn't it? Totally pathetic. I didn't want to make a fuss."

Finally, there was a crack in Helen's voice, a single, painful flaw that betrayed the truth behind the unemotional delivery. Cooper had never felt so helpless, never so lacking in the right things to say.

"I think about all those women who have ever been raped," said Helen, "and who have then had to explain in court why they didn't fight back or shout for help. I never understood it before that night, Ben. I understand it now."

Cooper remembered reading a report of a court case, the trial of a notorious American serial killer who had been convicted of the brutal rape and murder of several women. Sentencing the killer to the electric chair, the judge had made a famous comment: "The male sexual urge has a strength out of all proportion to any useful purpose that it serves." But for some people, it did serve a purpose. The purpose of domination.

"I was saved in the end, when somebody started knocking on the bedroom door. There seemed to be a group of them out there, and something was causing them great amusement. Of course, I was convinced that it was me they were all laughing at. Stupid, isn't it? And when Graham Vernon finally let me go, I had to walk past them downstairs as if nothing had happened. I couldn't bear the thought of all those people looking at me, seeing the state I was in, all messed up, with my best dress crumpled and my hair all over the place. That was all I could think about at the time. But they wouldn't have cared what I'd been doing, would they? Because they were all the same as him. Graham Vernon. Don't ask me why I hate him, Ben."

Cooper wished he could reach out and touch her, to reassure her that everything was OK. But maybe it wouldn't have been the right thing to do, even if he had actually been there with her, instead of on the end of an impersonal phone line.

"Thanks for telling me, Helen," he said, knowing it sounded totally inadequate.

"As a matter of fact, it helps to tell somebody. And you're not difficult to talk to, Ben."

"I'm glad."

She paused. "Ben—"

"Yes?"

"Do you go off duty sometime?"

"Of course. Tonight." He hesitated, a fateful hesitation. "But—well, I've got something that I have to do."

"I see."

He hadn't forgotten his promise to Diane Fry, and he hated to let people down. But there were times when, no matter what you did, no matter how you tried, there was always someone that you were letting down. And it was usually yourself.

-23-

The Way of the Eagle Martial Arts Center was tucked away in the basement of a former textile warehouse in Stone Bottom, at the end of Bargate. The ground floor of the warehouse was occupied by a computer software company, and above it, on three more floors, were craft workshops, creative designers, a small-scale publisher of countryside books, and an employment agency. The steps down to the dojo were always bathed in the smell of freshly baked bread from the ventilators in the back wall of the baker's in Hollowgate.

Diane Fry followed Ben Cooper's Toyota as it turned off Bargate and bounced down the carefully relaid stone setts between a corner pub and three-storey terraced houses whose front doors were reached by short flights of steps lined with iron railings. On the left, a steep alley ran back up toward the Market Square and Edendale's main shopping streets.

The daytime car park for the craftspeople and office workers was closed by a barrier, but a small patch of derelict land had been partially cleared next to the old warehouse. They parked their cars in the middle of an area of mud-filled potholes fringed by broken bricks and shoulder-high thistles. There were several other vehicles there already, and the sound of dull thumps and hoarse screams filtered through the steel grilles of windows set near ground level.

The buildings were clustered so close together in Stone Bottom that they seemed grotesquely out of proportion from the ground as they leaned toward each other, dark and shadowy against the sky, set with long, blank rows of tiny windows. The slamming of their car doors echoed loudly against the walls and reverberated down the stone setts to the narrow bridge over the river Eden.

Fry collected her sports bag from her boot and joined Cooper at the door. Though the baker's had stopped work for the evening, they could still smell the warm, yeasty scent of the bread lingering around the basement steps and in the dark corners between the buildings.

"That's making me feel hungry. I haven't had anything since lunchtime, and I only managed to grab a sandwich between interviews."

Cooper shrugged. He had been at the hospital at lunchtime and he hadn't eaten any lunch at all. In fact, he hadn't even thought about food. The hunger that was gnawing at his belly now wasn't caused by the smell of baking but by the need to prove that there was something he could do right. Something he could do better than Diane Fry.

"What have you been doing today, then, Diane?"

"I interviewed Charlotte Vernon this morning. You wouldn't believe that woman, Ben. She tried to put on an act for me. Wanted me to believe that she was some sort of hard-faced, sex-mad bitch who didn't care about anything, let alone her daughter. Anybody could have seen through it. The woman is broken up inside. But why would someone put on an act like that?"

He paused, regarding Fry curiously. "I could think of several reasons."

"Such as?"

"She may feel she has to play the part that's expected of her. People do that all the time. They try to live up to an image they've created for themselves or meet the expectations that other people have of them, as if they have no real personality of their own. Or she may have been diverting your attention from something else. On the other hand, it could have been a double bluff. She may have been hiding the truth by pushing it in your face so hard that you would refuse to accept it."

"Amazing, Ben. You make people sound really complicated. In my experience, their motivations are usually very simple and boring."

"Motivations like ambition and greed? The old favorites? They can certainly make people ruthless and selfish, can't they?"

Fry bridled at his tone of voice, though she didn't know what he was getting at. "And sex, of course," she said.

"Oh yes, let's not forget sex." Cooper collected two locker keys and signed Fry into the visitors' book, stabbing the page with the point of the pen. "But sex isn't so simple either, is it?"

"For some of us it's very simple, I can assure you. But not for the Vernons and Milners, apparently."

Cooper paused to greet another dojo member passing through toward the changing rooms. He was a tall young man, a fellow brown belt student. All the students and instructors here knew Ben Cooper—he often thought of them as a second family, united by a common attitude and purpose. The chief instructor, the *sensei,* was the closest thing he had to a father now.

"Why do you include the Milners?" he asked.

"Oh yes. Charlotte Vernon named Andrew Milner as one of her many lovers. He and his wife have denied it. But his daughter had some very interesting things to say. Did you know Simeon Holmes is her cousin?"

"You've talked to Helen Milner today?"

"That's right. What's the matter?"

Cooper had his mobile phone in his bag, since it wasn't safe to leave it in the car. And his memory was quite good enough to remember Helen's phone number.

"You go ahead, Diane," he said. "I've told Sensei Hughes you're coming. You go and get warmed up. I've got a phone call to make first. I may be a few minutes."

Fry looked surprised. "Well, OK. Whatever."

The atmosphere in the changing room was the familiar one of sweat and soap. At one side were three rows of metal lockers for members' valuables. A thick *makiwara* practice punching board had been left against the wall by the door.

Cooper started to get undressed while he listened to the phone ringing. With one hand he unbuttoned his shirt and began to unroll his *gi,* the loose white suit that was obligatory in the training hall. It was tied up in his brown cloth belt, the mark of a successful fourth-grade student, just one level below the various tiers of *dans,* the black-belt masters. The ringing went on for so long that he nearly pressed the button to stop the call.

"Hello?"

"Helen?"

"Ben? What a surprise—twice in one day. You only just caught me, I was about to go out."

"Oh. Anywhere interesting?"

She laughed. "Parent-Teacher Association darts night, would you believe? We take a team 'round local pubs and clubs to raise money for the school."

"I never knew you could play darts."

"I can't. I think I'm supposed to be the comic turn."

"I won't keep you. There's something else I wanted to ask you. About the Vernons."

"Yes?"

"These parties you described at the Mount. You said your father knew about them?"

"Oh yes, he'd been there himself. Vernon thought it was a huge joke, inviting him and Mum along. Dad was totally shocked. He really freaked out over it when he got home. He said it was the most embarrassing night of his life, the biggest insult he could imagine, all that sort of stuff. Yes, I thought you might ask about that. It was the cause of what happened afterward, really."

"What do you mean?"

"Well, I'm sure that was the reason Graham Vernon invited me later. It was aimed at Dad, of course. To annoy him even more. I think that was the worst thing of all. He was taunting Dad through me."

"But your father let you go?"

"He didn't dare say anything. Vernon invited me in front of him, don't forget. Poor Dad. He was always such a coward. It may have been the biggest insult he could imagine, but still he couldn't make a stand over it."

"Did you tell your father what happened when you went to the Mount?"

"Oh yes. I told them both. I was angry, you see. So it all came out."

"What did he do?"

"Do? He protested to Graham Vernon."

"Protested? Is that all?"

"A mild protest, no doubt. He's never been allowed to forget that. Not by my mother or by my grandparents. Certainly not by Granddad, who despises him for it. He thinks Dad's a complete wimp. So the poor man has been taunted with it ever since. I feel very sorry for him."

"Are you saying that he simply didn't want to jeopardize his job by falling out with Vernon—even over something like that?"

"Of course. You obviously don't realize, Ben, but it's terrible what the fear of losing a job can do to a man of that age. Dad thinks if Vernon sacks him, he'll never work again. And that's all he lives for, his job. None of us would want him to become another suicide statistic. It happens to so many men now. When they lose their jobs, they lose their self-respect, and there's nothing left."

"And your grandfather? What did he say?" asked Cooper. "He doesn't seem to me to be the sort of man who would be content with a mild protest."

"No, not Granddad. He was furious. He said that he would have killed Graham Vernon, if he'd been there."

Her voice faded then, and he could picture the sudden concern in her eyes as she remembered whom she was talking to and what he was. For a few minutes, she had forgotten he was a policeman and had thought of him only as Ben Cooper, as a friend. A warm flood of gratitude ran through him.

"I know, I know," he said. "It's just an expression. Just something that people say. It doesn't mean they really will kill anybody."

"Oh no," said Helen faintly. "I think he would have done it."

Cooper listened to Helen's breathing at the other end of the line. The sound reminded him of the afternoon at Moorhay, when he had stood so near her in the narrow hallway of Dial Cottage. He remembered being able to feel the heat from her body and being aware of the way her breasts lifted and moved beneath her halter top as she had turned to close the front door.

"Apparently Cousin Simeon had been seeing Laura Vernon," she said. "I didn't know that."

"It meant he was bound to come into the inquiry."

"Of course. We don't see a lot of his parents, you know." Helen paused, and her tone softened and became more hesitant. "It was kind of you to visit Grandma yesterday, Ben. I didn't really think you would do it. But I remember now that you were always very thoughtful. You were never quite like the other boys I knew."

Cooper felt himself blushing. "To be honest, I was there looking for your grandfather."

"Oh. You were on duty then. She didn't say that."

"Yes."

"Does that mean you've been questioning Grandma?"

"Not . . . exactly."

Helen sounded desperately disappointed in him. He cast around for something to say that would make things better. He needed to know exactly where he stood with Helen. What Matt had said had left him confused. Could there possibly be a bit of light at the end of the dark tunnel, a light that Helen could provide? He needed that gleam of hope, and he needed it now. But in his present state of mind, the subtleties of the situation were beyond his grasp. He had only two options—ring off now or take the bull by the horns.

Before he could make the decision, the door of the changing room banged open and the tall brown belt student came in from the hall, sweating and grinning.

"Hey, Ben, I thought that friend of yours was just a novice. You never said she was so good."

"What?"

"Sensei Hughes is very impressed."

"Ben—are you still there?"

"Yeah—sorry, Helen, I'm on a mobile. Just a second."

Cooper eased the door open and peered through the big windows into the training hall. There was some kind of distorting effect of the glass that magnified the scene in the hall, exaggerating the size of the figures moving around there. He could see Diane Fry in her *gi,* going through her kata sequences, the formal exercises used to limber the body up for action. She performed a downward block, the cat stance, straddle stance, and rising block. Every movement was poised and perfectly balanced, the result of well-trained muscles flowing with precision and power, like an animal's. Around her waist, she was wearing the black belt of the top-grade *karatekas.*

"A fourth *dan,* too," said the student over his shoulder. "She's terrific, Ben. Where did you find her?"

"Helen—"

"Was there something else, Ben? Only I'm on my way out, remember?"

"I was wondering," he said, "if you'd like to meet up sometime, perhaps go for a drink or a meal. What do you think?"

Helen seemed to consider the suggestion but answered with another question.

"You think Granddad was involved in Laura Vernon's death, don't you?"

Cooper felt a flush of embarrassment creeping up his neck and was glad that she couldn't see him.

"We have to follow up all the possibilities."

The katas were beautiful when performed correctly. A work of art in themselves. And Fry was performing them perfectly. Knife hand, hook punch, elbow strike, finger jab. Front kick, side kick, back kick, crescent kick. Getting faster and more fluid as the body loosened up. Every turn of the wrist was tightly controlled, every jab of a sharp heel executed with flawless technique and timing. Not an animal at all. A machine.

"But most of the other policemen would leave him alone, Ben," said Helen. "They don't think he's worth bothering with. The pressure to keep questioning him comes from you."

"What makes you say that?"

"The woman detective—she told me it was you."

Roundhouse, spearhand, hammer strike, and stamping kick. A twisting hand to the groin, a chop to the throat. Diane Fry executed practice strikes at all the vulnerable points of the body—face, neck, solar plexus, spinal column, and kidneys. Every blow was fast and hard and perfectly focused. And every one of them lethal.

"She had no right to say that." No right? That was a ludicrous understatement. It was against all codes of behavior. And she couldn't have ruined his chances with Helen more effectively if she had been trying. But then a hard knot of anger twisted in his stomach as it occurred to him that perhaps she *had* been trying.

"It's true, though, isn't it, Ben? I can tell it is from your voice."

"Helen, I just know that there's something wrong. Something that involves your grandfather."

"Is there? How can you know?"

But Cooper shook his head, unable to answer. He was watching Fry, and he was flushing an even deeper red, though now the embarrassment was giving way to an intense rage.

"Let me know when it is that you stop being a policeman, Ben," said Helen. "In the meantime, I think it would be better if I said no to your suggestion, don't you? In the circumstances."

"Circumstances." What a word, he thought. So often used in a pretentious and meaningless way. Yet all of life could be reduced to that one word. Difficult circumstances. The wrong circumstances. Killed by circumstances.

Around Diane Fry an admiring half circle of dojo members had gathered—Cooper's fellow students, his second family. Sensei Hughes stood watching her, applauding when she had finished her kata. She bowed at the waist, stretched on her toes, breathing deeply, invigorating her muscles, letting the power spread throughout her body. She was ready for the next thing, ready for her *kumite,* her sparring bout. Ready to humiliate Ben Cooper in front of his friends.

The tall student looked on in amazement as Ben Cooper tossed down the phone, spun on his heel, and lashed out with a clenched fist at the practice punching board, denting the soft wood. His scream was not the one taught at the Way of the Eagle dojo, but it came from the soul.

Helen had listened very carefully to Ben Cooper's voice as he ended the call. She could tell he was trying to sound calm, like a man who hadn't just been rejected and hurt. But he had never been able to conceal his feelings very well.

Sensing his suffering, she felt all the more sorry for having caused it. She felt sorry because of what he had said about Harry. And because she knew that Ben was right.

Fry had been chatting to Sensei Hughes for ten minutes before it occurred to her to wonder what had happened to Ben Cooper. The sensei sent one of the students to look in the changing room, but Cooper had already left.

Fry shrugged, baffled. "He was making a phone call, so perhaps he was called away."

"Something urgent. Life in the police force can be very unpredictable. We understand that," said Hughes.

She was getting on well with the instructors and the other students, who all wanted to know where she had been trained. The *sensei* offered to include her in the next grading night, when he felt she could rise to fifth *dan* grade. At the end of the session, she went with a group of students to the pub on the corner, the Millstone Inn, where they ate lasagna and chips and talked about competitive sport of all kinds.

Only when she had got outside in the street and paused to say good-bye on the corner of Bargate did the tall brown-belt student tap Fry on the shoulder and mention Ben Cooper's behavior. He was a serious-minded young man and felt that what he had seen in the changing room demonstrated a lack of the self-discipline and the positive attitude taught by the dojo. He had known Ben for two years, and he was worried.

Suddenly Fry grew frightened. Through her mind ran a series of scenes from the last few days. There were a series of flickering images of Ben Cooper, first as the capable, self-possessed detective whose reputed success and popularity had been rammed down her throat until the sound of his name infuriated her.

But gradually the picture had changed, and Cooper turned into the morose, nervous, unpredictable man who had walked out of the dojo in an angry and violent state of mind. She knew that she had played her part in his deterioration; indeed, she had to acknowledge that she had done it deliberately. She had seen him as a challenge.

"Do you know where he might go? A pub somewhere?"

The student shrugged. "There are a lot of pubs he knows around Edendale. But his training's too important to him, so he doesn't drink a lot."

After four or five pints, Cooper was beginning to feel that nothing mattered. After seven pints and a couple of whiskey chasers, the black dogs appeared from every corner of the pub, prowling and snarling, waiting for him to turn his back on them, for the chance to pounce.

He had eaten nothing all day, and the beer sloshing in his stomach made his head dip and swell. His hands and neck were flushed with the effects of the alcohol, his hands trembled, and his lips were turning numb. Now the whiskey was burning its way through his system, stimulating his muscles and making him feel as though he could pull down walls.

The pub wasn't one of his regular haunts. He couldn't remember having been in it for years. As a result, though, he had not been recognized as he sat on his own, steadily deadening his thoughts and stupefying his feelings. Most people who saw his scowl and his unsteady hands would have left him alone with his personal black dog.

But nearby were a group of youths who were becoming rowdy and belligerent as the evening went on and they, too, became fueled by alcohol. In one of those ways that Cooper had never understood, they had spotted him as a policeman. Their voices grew loud in derision when he failed to react to the mocking exchanges.

"Pork on the menu tonight?" they shouted to the bar staff. "Nice bit of bacon? Kill a pig for me, love."

"Oink, oink. I wondered what the smell was."

"Look at his snout in that beer."

"Oi, pig, got an old sow at home?"

"Oink, oink."

The youths thought they were hilarious. Ben Cooper had heard it all before, ever since he was a young bobby on the beat, walking around the Edendale housing estates or patrolling the town center on a Saturday night. Never before, though, had he felt such a powerful, swelling anger that threatened to burst out of him at one more provocation. Charged up by the whiskey, he felt that he would actually welcome an outburst of violence. It would be a blessed release.

The youths, getting no response to their pig jokes, had switched tactics.

"Is that a truncheon in your pocket, or do you fancy me?"

"Ooh, put the handcuffs on me. I've been a naughty boy."

"Nah, he's not interested. The pigs are all too busy finding out who did for that tart at Moorhay. I don't think."

"What, Laura Vernon? Her?"

One of the youths guffawed and made an obscene gesture.

"Laura Vernon? She'd fuck with anything, that one. Young blokes, old blokes, her own dad."

"She'd even fuck with animals."

They thought this was totally hilarious. "Yeah, even pigs. Get it? Pig?"

One youth pushed his face closer to Cooper, leaning provocatively across his glass-strewn table, leering in sweaty proximity. He had a ring through his left nostril and small, pitted scars around his mouth.

"Don't you get it, then? Pig?"

Then he made his mistake. His face creased and his eyes narrowed as he peered at Cooper again, recognition dawning slowly.

"Hey, just a minute, aren't you that Sergeant Cooper's—"

The empty glass was in Cooper's hand before he knew it, and he was on his feet, clutching at the youth's shirtfront with his other hand. A chair went over, and the swinging glass smashed on the edge of the table. The youth's friends threw themselves forward, grabbing at Cooper's arms, bringing up their knees, snarling and spitting with ferocity as they reacted like a pack to a sudden threat.

Ben Cooper faced them, boiling with rage, a lethal crown of broken glass grasped tightly in his fist.

Becky Kelk was fourteen. She lived on Wye Close almost next door to Lee Sherratt. She went to the same school as Simeon Holmes. She had heard all about the girls that had been attacked, the one at Buxton and the one right here in Moorhay, that girl at the Mount. It had never occurred to her until now that she could be the next victim.

The policeman still guarding the murder scene found her by her screams. She was in a hollow behind a screen of brambles, not far from the path that led to the Baulk. Her pants had been removed and her striped leggings were torn. Her crop top and bra were disturbed, and there were grass stains on her shoulders and the imprint of a tree root in the small of her back. "I've been raped," she said.

The PC pulled out his radio immediately, scanning the area for signs of the assailant.

"How long since?"

"Just now."

"Did you recognize him?"

"It was the old man," she said.

"What old man?"

Becky Kelk knew where the old man lived, though she didn't know his name. She pointed unerringly up the hill toward the village, where Dial Cottage stood in the middle of its terraced row, its roof picked out by the last of the evening light.

They found Harry Dickinson waiting patiently in his front room. He was dressed in his best Sunday suit, his thin hair slicked back, a blue tie knotted carefully at his throat. The toe caps of his shoes were gleaming, and the *Guardian* was folded neatly on the table. He sat solemn and stiff in his hard-backed chair, his expression that of a man in a hospital waiting room, expecting the inevitable bad news.

When Gwen let the police into the front room, he showed no surprise and no emotion. He merely knocked out his pipe and laid it on the rack on the mahogany cabinet. He picked up his cap, smoothed the knees of his trouser legs, and stood up slowly.

"You didn't take long. I'll give you that."

-24-

"Hey, hey, that's enough of that!"

The burly landlord was wading his way in between them, a shaggy-haired Alsatian snarling at his heels and snapping at any available leg. Cooper pushed the youth roughly away and put the glass back on the table. They stood around in a panting group, shaking and trembling as the adrenaline continued to pump through their veins.

"You lot—out!" said the landlord. "You're banned."

"Bloody hell. We were just messing. It wasn't anything serious," said the leading youth.

"I don't care what it was. I won't have it in here. This is a respectable pub."

"What about him, then? PC Plod here."

"I've told you—out. Now!"

The three of them trooped out sullenly, grumbling loudly and slamming the door behind them. The landlord and his dog watched them with similar glowers on their faces until they had gone. The normal noises of the bar gradually resumed, couples leaning toward each other in openmouthed excitement. The jukebox had been playing an old Rolling Stones hit for the past few minutes. "I Can't Get No Satisfaction." A barmaid came out with a pan and brush to sweep up the broken glass.

"Sorry," said Cooper.

"I don't know you, lad, but I take it you're with the police."

"Yeah."

"You ought to know better, then."

Cooper slumped back into his chair, feeling suddenly weak in the legs. The landlord looked down at him, assessing him with a professional eye, weighing up exactly how drunk he was.

"I'll get someone to fetch you a coffee. Then you'd better go home."

"No, thanks. One more whiskey, then I'll go."

"Have sense."

"I'll be all right."

"You're not driving, are you?"

"Of course not."

"I suppose that'll be all right then. But that's it. No more."

Diane Fry had tried to do things in the right order. She had no home phone number for Ben Cooper, so she had dialed his mobile, but got no reply. That meant a tour of two dozen pubs. It was one way of getting to know the town better.

It was lucky that Cooper's red Toyota was distinctive. She spotted it eventually in a pub car park behind the bus station, where the stink of diesel fumes from the green TransPeak buses mingled with the smell of new plastic and burnt oil from the factory units on the Edenside Industrial Estate.

The Unicorn was near the corner of two streets of terraced houses, some of which had their ground floors converted into shops—motor spares, insurance, a Chinese take-away. The corner property had been demolished at some time, and the site had become a car park for the pub. There was no lighting at the end of the street or on the brick walls of the pub, and the glare from the bus station two hundred yards away only made the darkness blacker. But Fry saw the Toyota gleam suddenly in her headlights as she turned into the street and pulled up outside the take-away.

It was one of those bars where everyone turned to look at you when you walked in. At least, they did if you were a woman on your own. Even the landlord gave Fry a hard stare as she scanned the room to find Cooper at his table in the corner. His face looked bloated and his eyes were half closed as he nursed the remains of a single whiskey. She could see straightaway that he was hopelessly drunk.

"Ben?"

He looked up blearily as she stood over him. "What the hell do you want?"

She ignored the aggressive tone in his voice. "What do you think you're doing, Ben?"

"Getting pissed. What has it got to do with you?"

"Are you mad? Are you intending to make a complete idiot of yourself?"

"Probably. So what?"

There were too many people close enough to overhear. She sat down, leaning across the table to deliver her message eye to eye. "You're a police officer. Don't you realize, if this gets back to Division, you'll get your arse kicked all the way back to the beat. Bang goes the promotion, Ben."

"Oh yeah? It's damn well gone bang already. So why should I bother? Anyway, it's what you want, isn't it?"

"What are you talking about?"

"Oh, I can't be bothered talking to you. Just get lost and leave me alone, will you?"

She tugged at his sleeve. "Come on, Ben, let's get out of this place. I'll drive you home."

But he reacted violently, jerking his arm away, almost knocking over his whiskey. "I'm not going anywhere with you, bitch."

Now she began to feel angry. "I'm not going to put up with this, Ben. Are you going to come, or have I got to drag you out?"

"Leave me alone!"

He was on his feet, stumbling against the table, oblivious of the stares of the other customers. The landlord was coming out from behind the bar again to speak to him.

"I don't want you anywhere near me, Fry," he said, with as much dignity as he could manage. "Just stay away. All right?"

Fry gritted her teeth and restrained herself from slapping his flushed face as he drained the last of his whiskey and staggered out of the pub into the night. She knew she ought to go after him and remove his car keys—forcibly, if necessary—to prevent him from trying to drive home in his present state. But another part of her wanted to let him go and get stuffed.

"Are you a friend of his?" It was the landlord, leaning over her shoulder.

"Sort of."

"Well, take my advice—he shouldn't be wandering about out there in that state."

"I'm not his nursemaid. It might seem like it, but I'm not."

"Listen, take him home, or let us call him a taxi or something. But he shouldn't be out there on his own, I'm telling you."

"OK, OK."

She walked out of the Unicorn and stood in the lighted doorway, staring out at the dark street, conscious of the eyes on her back. The streetlights ended just below the pub, and the other side of the car park was in complete darkness. An alley ran along the edge of the car park. It wound its way between two high brick walls toward the back entrance to the bus station.

"Ben!"

There was no answer. She crossed to the car park, where Cooper's Toyota stood empty and locked.

She glanced back down the street toward her own car, but there was no sign of a figure staggering between the streetlights, no one slumped outside the darkened window of the Chinese take-away or the insurance brokers.

"Where the hell—"

Then she heard the noise. Taunting laughter moving in the shadows. The sound of stumbling feet, animal grunts, and stifled cries. A confused thudding and thumping, echoing dully from a wall somewhere. A chill ran across her neck as she stared into the blackness of the alley. She ran to the corner of the car park, peering into the gloom. Shapes were moving in the darkness, coming together and moving apart again, convulsing and thrashing their arms and legs as if involved in a primitive dance. She could distinguish four figures. Three of them had blurred features—collars turned up over their faces, caps pulled low on their foreheads. They struck and kicked at the fourth figure, one after the other, mechanical and brutal, aiming to hurt. The fourth figure was Ben Cooper.

"Ben!"

Three faces turned toward her; the fourth slumped against the wall, oblivious of her presence, waiting for the blow that would bring him to the floor, ready for the boots to go in.

Fry began to move forward, then paused and froze, thinking furiously. She had two choices. What she ought to do was to announce herself as a police officer, call for assistance, attempt to make an arrest before Ben Cooper was too badly injured, if she could. But to do so would make Cooper's behavior a matter of public record. He deserved a chance. Maybe no more than one chance. But a chance.

She did have a second option. It was dangerous, but if she was going to do it, she had to do it now. She ran into the alleyway, feeling the energy already pouring into her limbs, drawing in the deep breaths that expanded her lungs and quickened her muscles. The three youths turned toward her, astonished at her charge.

"Who's that?"

"It's a woman."

"She must be another copper."

"A copper!"

She could smell them in the darkness, see their shapes moving toward her through the shadows. Her brain began to flood with memories. It was the same old film that had run and rerun through her mind constantly, no sooner reaching its climactic end than it would start all over again. She felt hot and dirty, and suddenly hurting. A great rage came over her, swamping her resistance, and she badly needed something to hit out at.

The youths were grinning, even as they breathed hard through their flared nostrils and gaping mouths. They weren't taking her seriously, even though she was now within reach. One of them turned away to give a final kick at Cooper's battered body. Fry reacted. She hit him in the kidneys with a jumping lunge punch, swept his legs from under him, and broke his nose with a vicious knifehand strike.

With a startled shout, a second youth came at her from the left. But he had hesitated too long, and she diverted his swinging fist with an upper forearm block. She swiveled, cracked his kneecap with a side snap kick, and knocked him out with an elbow strike to the jaw.

Then an arm closed around her throat as she was grabbed from behind. The third youth was strong and much taller and heavier than she was. The impact of his body forced her up against the wall, trapping her arms and banging her forehead on the bricks. When she was firmly pinned, her attacker shifted his grip and began to squeeze her throat. A miasma of beer fumes filled her nose, and his breath pressed hot on the back of her neck. The feel of his body pushed up against hers and the smell of his sweat-soaked hands in front of her face brought back all the remembered terrors, all the black nightmares that had haunted her for over a year, the demons that gibbered and shrieked at the back of her brain every time she closed her eyes or found herself in the dark.

Now panic drove her to excess. She took a deep breath through her nose before folding suddenly forward at the waist, kicking backward into his groin with her heel, and driving her elbow hard into his solar plexus. He grunted in pain, and his grip loosened. She spun around, using a full rising block to break his grip completely. As he stumbled backward, she aimed a spearhand strike at his exposed throat, releasing the *kiai* shout from her diaphragm as the technique focused on the soft target.

From the moment she launched the final blow, she knew that it would be fatal.

Harry hadn't expected them to take his clothes away. It was years since he had stripped naked in front of strangers. Standing in the tiny surgery in E Division headquarters, he watched in bafflement as each item he removed was carefully bagged, labeled, and sealed. First they took his cap, his suit jacket, and his trousers. Then his beautifully polished shoes and his socks. They took his shirt and even his tie. They examined each piece of clothing meticulously, feeling into the pockets and the seams with their latex-gloved hands.

The surgery smelled powerfully of disinfectant, with a faint underlying taint of old vomit. Despite the warmth, the old man shivered as his white, shrunken thighs and sinewy arms were exposed to the harsh glare of the strip lighting. The hair on his legs was gray and coarse, and there were bare white patches on his calves where the skin was as smooth as a baby's, waxy and pallid, as if it had never seen the sun.

With each layer that was stripped away, Harry retreated a little bit more into an inner remoteness. A detached calm descended over him like a series of veils that concealed his inner self, preserving and even heightening his dignity. He stared fixedly ahead, ignoring the Scenes of Crime officer and the detective who took and examined and folded his clothes. He remained completely silent, his thin lips clamped shut, uttering no protest. The detective logged every item, writing carefully on the labels as if pricing up a pile of secondhand clothes that Harry was donating for a charity shop.

Finally they made him take off his vest and his underpants. They seemed particularly interested in his Y-fronts, turning them inside out and closely inspecting the folds of the front flap for stains before sealing them away with the rest of his clothes.

When Harry was completely naked, they gave him a white waxed-paper overall that felt icy cold against his bare skin and rustled as he moved. The sleeves barely covered his wrists, and the collar left his white neck and throat exposed.

They explained to him again that he was a suspect in an allegation of rape. They asked him if he was sure that he agreed to provide samples for analysis, which would help to eliminate him from inquiries. He agreed, not following the meaning of their phrases, thinking they were talking about his clothes, which already sat in a stack of plastic bags ready for the forensic laboratory.

But worse was to come.

"Have you any ailments?" asked Dr. Inglefield, pulling on his disposable gloves.

Harry stared at him. "I've had my checkup. I go to my own doctor, thanks all the same."

"I need to know if you have any ailments. Any skin conditions— psoriasis, eczema, herpes? Do you suffer from diabetes or hemophilia? Any sexually transmitted diseases? Hepatitis? Are you HIV positive?"

"I'm fit," said Harry gruffly.

"Are you under medication at all? Who is your GP? And you're sure you have no ailments? Nothing at all? It would be unusual in a man of your age . . ."

Harry shook his head.

"Very well, then. Visual examination first."

"What's all this in aid of? I thought you'd just want to ask your questions."

"That comes later."

They made Harry sit down while the doctor examined his head. His thin hair was combed through to obtain loose hairs, which went into small plastic bags. Then a couple of hairs were plucked out, the doctor scrutinizing them against the light to make sure the roots were still attached before dropping them into another bag. The DC attached more exhibit labels for the doctor to sign.

Harry waited stoically, giving them no further response, his face grave and dignified as if he were sitting in church waiting for a tedious sermon to be over. After a while, his manner began to affect the detective and the doctor, and they became nervous and silent as they went about their business.

Dr. Inglefield produced a set of swabs like large cotton buds, which he scraped over Harry's open palms and between his fingers.

"Open the suit, please."

"What's this for?"

"I need more hair samples."

Harry didn't move.

"Pubic hair. Mr. Dickinson?"

Very slowly, Harry stood up and unfastened the front of the paper suit. The doctor bent to examine his shrunken genitals. Again he produced the comb. He had to pull it through Harry's pubic hair several times before he was satisfied. Then, with his gloved fingers, he plucked a gray hair. Harry flinched—the first involuntary movement he had made since he had entered the surgery.

Another swab appeared. The old man stared into the distance as the doctor took hold of his penis and swabbed round the glans.

"I'm going to take a sample of blood now."

A syringeful of blood was removed from Harry's arm and split into two small plastic jars—one for DNA testing and one for blood grouping comparison. The detective collected the packages together and stored them in a fridge until they were able to go to the forensic lab. Now there was just one more sample left to collect. The doctor presented a small bowl.

"Spit into this for me please, Mr. Dickinson."

But that was one sample that Harry had no trouble providing.

Afterward, Diane Fry couldn't stop trembling from a mixture of rage and fear. She looked down at her hands in horror, appalled at what they had done. Where was the control? Where was the discipline? Where was the high-minded motivation? She needed reassurance, but all she had was Ben Cooper, comatose in the passenger seat of her Peugeot.

The most difficult part of the job had been getting Ben to the car and away. He would just have to pick up his Toyota tomorrow, when he was sober and a bit more mobile.

She had no idea where he lived, and could see no alternative to taking him home with her. The very last thing she wanted was to have anyone in her bare, soulless flat, let alone Ben Cooper. But what else could she do?

Cooper sat with his head lolling, a trickle of blood running down the side of his head onto his neck. A large bruise was forming over one eye, and his lips were split and swollen. Fry had never seen anyone look such a mess. She prayed that he wouldn't throw up in her car. On the way up Castleton Road she damned him to hell and back for getting her into this situation.

The only consolation she had was that she'd managed to divert her final blow at the last moment. But the strike to the side of the third youth's neck had been sufficient to lay him out on the floor of the alley with the other two.

She became aware of the Suzanne Vega tape playing on the cassette player. It had come on automatically with the ignition, but it sounded too depressing.

Impatiently, she flicked out the tape and replaced it with Tanita Tikaram, turning the volume up loud so that it beat against the car windows. The album was *Ancient Heart,* and Fry listened to Tikaram start to sing a familiar track. It had a line that always continued to run through her mind long afterward: "Now your conscience is clear." She glanced at Cooper, saw his eyes flickering half open, as if the music was getting through to him. But his pupils were unfocused, and he stared straight ahead for a moment, seeing nothing, as the noise thumped around him. Then his head drooped again.

When they reached Grosvenor Road, Fry shook Cooper and managed to rouse him enough to negotiate the front door and the stairs partly under his own steam, though he needed her arm wound tight around his chest. She could feel his heart beating under her hand through a tear in his shirt, and the sweet smell of beer on his breath made a heady blend with his distinctive male odor. It was a scent she had not smelled so closely for a long time.

She took him straight to the bedroom and dumped him on the bed, disentangling his rubbery limbs from around her body. Then she began to pull off his clothes—his scuffed shoes, his jacket, and his torn shirt—pulling and tugging violently at his jeans until they turned inside out and came away from his feet. Then she brought a bowl of warm water and a cloth and bathed the blood from his forehead and cleaned the weeping grazes on his back and legs. She noticed that his body was taut with lean muscle, and she guessed the injuries starting to appear on his chest and sides would prove to be nothing worse than bruises in the morning. No bones broken. Then, as she worked on a cut on his thigh, Fry became aware of the growing bulge that stirred in the front of his briefs. Cooper was getting an erection.

She looked up at his face. He had stirred and was regarding her with a bitter, aggressive stare through half-closed eyes. His face was red and his hair fell wildly across his forehead. At first she didn't think he even recognized who she was. Then his eyes came momentarily into focus and fixed on her face.

"Fry? What have you got that I haven't got? Why don't you ever get so that you can't take all the shit anymore? Are your tits made of steel, or what?"

She jerked away to the edge of the bed as if he had slapped her. She turned her back on him, clenching her fists and gritting her teeth, attempting to control her anger at the taunt. The blood flushed through her face and neck and into her throat at the ingratitude. Her palms itched to reach out and hold on to something, to prove the unfairness of the gibe. He was totally wrong. She was *not* a passionless bitch, not some machine with no feelings. He was so, so wrong.

She was conscious of Cooper's bare, lean body only inches away, and tensely aware of the dark, curling hair spreading down his abdomen toward his tautly swelling erection.

"I'll show you steel tits," she said. She pulled her blouse roughly over head and reached around to unhook her bra, in the same moment turning back toward him and leaning over his naked chest. Then she stopped. Her breasts were swinging free, her nipples beginning to harden with excitement as they brushed gently against his hot skin. The expression on her face changed and darkened with anger. She grabbed him by the shoulders and shook him violently. His head lolled forward, his cheek bouncing into the soft flesh of her breasts. Ben Cooper was unconscious and snoring.

"Bastard!"

Finally she went back to the sitting room, her mind repeating what he had said, over and over. *Steel tits.* What had he meant? She undressed, did her exercises automatically and without enthusiasm, pulled a rug over her, and lay down on the sofa. Her body was weary, but her mind was whirling endlessly. She tried to read a book, but found the pages were a blur. She discarded the book, turned over restlessly, and eventually put out the light. She pressed her face into her pillow, hugged her steel tits to herself, and wept.

-25-

The old man sat upright on the plastic chair in the interview room, staring at DCI Tailby and DC Fry with frozen dignity, as if he were the only one present who knew how to behave properly.

"Interview commenced at 1430 Friday, twenty-seventh August. Those present are Detective Chief Inspector Tailby . . ."

"Detective Constable Fry . . ."

Tailby nodded at Harry. "Could you identify yourself for the tape, please, sir."

"My name's Harold Dickinson."

"You're entitled to have a solicitor present, Mr. Dickinson. Do you have your own, or would you like the duty solicitor?"

"I'll not need one of them."

"Are you quite sure?"

Harry ignored the question, waiting for the next one. Tape or not, he seemed to say, there were times when speaking was a waste of breath.

"Have you been given food and sufficient rest?" asked Tailby formally. "Have you been given the opportunity to make a phone call?"

"Where's my dog?"

"He's being looked after, Mr. Dickinson," said Fry.

"She's a she, not a he," he said, with open contempt.

Tailby glared back across the table. "We have to ask you some more questions, Mr. Dickinson."

Harry stared at him impassively. Somehow he made his waxed-paper suit look as if it had come from a rack at Marks and Spencer. The disposable plimsolls they had given him looked almost as if they had been polished overnight.

"Well. You can ask," he said.

They interviewed Harry at intervals throughout the day, making sure he was fed at the correct times, insuring he got the proper rests, asking him repeatedly if he wanted a solicitor.

The Police and Criminal Evidence Act obliged them to make sure he understood questions, was not distressed or fatigued or under the influence of any substance that affected his level of awareness, and that he was offered refreshment and allowed access to toilet facilities.

They alternated their teams of interviewers, aiming to break his story by changing direction and the type of question they asked. This also allowed the officers to spend time on the tedious job of listening to their recordings on earphones and transcribing them onto Record of Interview sheets. They analyzed their results in between sessions and considered the next strategy. Besides, the interviewers needed a rest, too, after an hour with Harry Dickinson.

"Look, Harry, we all know that old men sometimes feel randy, too. Your sexual urges don't disappear altogether, do they? Eh, Harry? Not like some people think. I suppose the young girls still get you excited, don't they?"

DI Hitchens was leaning across the table, staring into Harry's face. He was watching for a crack in the impassive facade, probing and pushing for a reaction.

"It's just not a nice thought, is it, that your old granddad might be lusting after the young women like he always used to when he was young? Best to pretend it doesn't happen, eh? Sweep it under the carpet and keep quiet. What you don't know about doesn't hurt. But we know better, don't we, Harry?"

Harry said nothing, secure in his superior experience, looking at Hitchens as if he were a simpleton.

"Because sometimes it goes too far, doesn't it? Sometimes you just can't control yourself. Can you, Harry?"

The old man raised an eyebrow dismissively, suggesting that he knew more than a thing or two about control.

All the interviewers had been trained to use the proper interviewing techniques. Open questions were the key to the GEMAC procedure—Greeting, Explanation, Mutual Activity, Closure. The aim was to create spiral questions—open questions such as who, what, why, when, where, and how, followed by probing of the answers. The theory was that if someone was inventing a story, it was almost impossible to maintain a lie under detailed probing.

As for closed questions, which invited only a single-word reply—they were too much of a temptation for someone like Harry.

> *"We have the statement of a Mr. Gary Edwards, a bird-watcher, who saw a person answering your description passing along the path near the place where Laura Vernon's body was found. A person accompanied by a dog. Was that you, Mr. Dickinson?"*
>
> *Diane Fry looked up expectantly as Harry opened his mouth to speak. He was starting to look relaxed and calm, yet still somehow aloof from what was going on around him in the claustrophobic interview room. Ironically, he seemed immune to the stresses the interviewers were suffering. They knew that they would shortly have to allow him another rest break without having made any progress at all.*
>
> *"Observant chap, was he, this bird-watcher? Did he describe the color of my eyes and all?"*
>
> *"It was an old man that Mr. Edwards saw."*
>
> *"Do we all look alike, then?" said Harry, with an infuriating smile.*

"Idle and foolish remarks will be disregarded," the rule book said. But the interviewers found themselves seizing eagerly on every remark that Harry Dickinson let drop, no matter how idle or foolish. At least it was a reaction, something more than that same stony, contemptuous stare.

Harry had the air of a man patiently enduring an outrageous impertinence. He allowed them no emotional feedback, only the unspoken promise of a sober and abiding enmity.

> *"Is that the policy you use toward your wife, Harry? What they don't know about doesn't hurt. Women will think the worst of you, no matter what you tell them. So you might as well tell them nothing. Isn't that right? They're happier with their own imaginings anyway. Isn't that right, Harry?"*
>
> *The one thing Harry wanted was his pipe, but he wouldn't give them the pleasure of being able to refuse him. He looked from Hitchens to Fry with a blank, slightly puzzled expression, as if wondering how they came to be in his room.*

"Or does Gwen know all about your activities, Harry? Perhaps she'll want to tell us all about it. Because we've got her here, Harry. She's in another interview room now. What do you think of that?"

"Who's going to feed my dog?" said Harry.

Ben Cooper was in the CID room, handling the routine crime reported overnight. His head was thumping as if someone were driving a pneumatic drill through his brain. His mouth was dry and tasted foul, and his body ached all over. He had told DS Rennie that the injury to his head was the result of an accident on the farm. For half an hour he had been forced to submit to a barrage of sheep-shagging jokes, while his stomach churned and he fought the bile that constantly threatened to rise up in his throat.

He had woken this morning with no idea where he was. A strange bed in a strange flat, and no recollection how he had got there, apart from the clue of a thundering hangover and a body stiffened solid with bruises, as he discovered when he tried to move.

But there had been a note scribbled on the back of an old envelope on the bedside table. "Have been called into the office. I suggest you call in sick. Whatever you do, I don't want to know about it." In his groggy state, it had taken several minutes before he had been able to work out who the "DF" was who had signed the note.

Then a few gray, fragmented memories had started to trickle into his brain. The visit to the dojo he remembered; then the phone call to Helen Milner and how Diane Fry had shafted him, how she had planned to humiliate him. It was so obvious now that she had deliberately ruined his chances with Helen and had planned to make him look small in front of his friends at the dojo. She had not mentioned that she was a fourth *dan* black belt when he had boasted of his skill and invited her to a bout. She had lied to him, and when he realized what she had planned, he had walked out in a blazing fury.

Vaguely he remembered the pub near the bus station. It was the third pub he had been in, but he knew something had happened there. From that point on, though, the memories disintegrated completely. Had there been something to do with pigs? Yes, he thought there probably had. Which didn't go anywhere near explaining how he had ended up in Diane Fry's bed and what had caused his injuries. Had she beaten him up? It didn't seem beyond the bounds of possibility. She had kicked him in the teeth in every other way she could find.

Even sitting in the office when he eventually dragged himself into work, Cooper found the memories he needed still eluded him. All that he could think of were his black dogs—the series of disasters that had knocked the legs from under him, coming one after another.

Then he thought of his mother lying in hospital, and he groaned. How could he have forgotten about her and done something so stupid? He thought of his meeting with Superintendent Jepson and swore vehemently. No doubt that was Diane Fry's work as well—she had got in thick with DI Hitchens and used a bit of influence on him. No doubt it had been while they were away in Yorkshire overnight together. Very cozy. That was something he certainly couldn't compete with.

Then Cooper remembered lying to his mother and winced with shame. He remembered Helen Milner rejecting him, and felt despair. He was worth nothing to anybody. And now he had made a fool of himself at the very least last night, got horribly drunk, and done God knew what else besides. He might as well go home now to the farm and throw himself in the slurry pit. There was nothing but those evil black dogs running through his mind, snapping and growling. Black dogs and pigs.

Among the morning's crimes was a report of three youths suffering minor injuries in a late-night brawl in Edendale. A falling-out among drunks was presumed. The youths themselves weren't talking and had been sent home. There were other more pressing matters—a list of burglaries and car thefts, a ram raid at a building society.

And, as he had discovered from DS Rennie, there had been an alleged rape at Moorhay, for which Harry Dickinson had been arrested. Cooper shook his head and poked around in the drawer of his desk for some painkillers, but found none. Nothing was right this morning. Just *nothing*.

Later in the morning, Diane Fry herself appeared in the CID room. Cooper kept his eyes down, not knowing what to say to her. What *did* you say to a woman whose bed you had woken up in without a clue about what happened between you during the previous few hours? The only possible approach was to let her speak first—if she wanted to.

But she made him wait in agony for several minutes, moving papers around on her own desk, making notes, taking a phone call. Eventually she drifted over toward where he sat. He was aware of her presence but didn't look up, willing her to speak first.

"You look like shit."

"Thanks. I feel it."

Fry walked on past his desk. Cooper sat in a daze for a while longer, until she came back, clutching a handful of reports.

"You want some paracetamol or something?"

"I'll be all right."

"Just don't throw up all over the desk, will you? I can't stand the smell of sick."

"I'm fine. Really."

"Right."

Even in his befuddled state, he sensed Fry hesitating, hovering behind him like a baleful matron. She gave off no aura of guilt, only a mood of simmering anger tinged with reluctant concern. Cooper began to reconsider the possible scenarios of the night before. There were still huge blanks in his memory and there was no way he could make the stuff about pigs fit anywhere. But suddenly he knew for certain that he had done something awful, something totally stupid. So what was it that he was expected to say? Maybe it was "sorry." But how could you apologize for what you couldn't remember doing?

"Thanks anyway," he said feebly. "Thanks, Diane, for—whatever."

She sighed heavily, put down her papers, and wedged herself onto his desk. Cooper winced at the movement and her sudden proximity.

"I don't know if you're in a fit state to talk about it. But you know we've got Harry Dickinson in?" she said.

"Yeah." Cooper glanced up at her. She was looking at him with a mixture of pity and scorn. It seemed like an improvement. "What has he said?"

She snorted. "Damn all. He's more worried about his blasted dog."

"So where's this girl who says he attacked her?"

"Rape suite. They're interviewing her now."

"And do Mr. Tailby and Mr. Hitchens think they're going to break Harry Dickinson and get him to confess?"

Fry looked thoughtful as she pulled up a chair next to his desk. She absently pushed some of his files aside to create a few inches of surface to lean on.

"It's a funny thing, that, actually. When the lads picked him up, they said he acted as though he was expecting them. 'You didn't take long,' that's all he said. But now I keep getting the feeling that he's puzzled by what we're asking him. It's like we've been putting totally the wrong questions to him all along, and he can't understand why."

"A feeling, Diane?"

"Yeah. So?"

"Nothing."

Cooper was busy scribbling on a piece of paper with his ballpoint pen. The fog in his head was clearing gradually, revealing ragged patches of light. This was better than paracetamol for making your brain work.

"What are you doing, Ben?"

"I think you could be right about the questions you were asking. Just take a look at that. There's got to be a link."

He had sketched a rough diagram. It showed lines running between members of the Vernon and Milner families. Old Harry Dickinson was there, connected to Laura Vernon by the finding of the body; his son-in-law Andrew was linked to Graham Vernon through business; Helen Milner connected to Graham through the incident at the party; there was Helen's cousin Simeon, who had been Laura's boyfriend and had been helping Harry and his friends at the smallholding; and then there was Harry again, a wavery line running from him to Graham Vernon, representing the proposed meeting, purpose unknown.

Fry pointed at Harry's name.

"Strictly speaking, he didn't . . ."

"Find the body, I know. He only found the trainer."

"And that wasn't really him, it was his dog."

"But the meeting he talked about with Vernon is bound to leave a question mark. What *was* he up to? Besides, the bird-watcher saw him."

"Maybe. Maybe not."

"Harry Dickinson is involved. No doubt about it."

"A feeling?"

"No. A certainty."

He looked cautiously at Fry. Magically, the tension between them seemed to have dispersed as soon as they had begun to talk about the Vernon case. She had needed someone to talk to, and she had been drawn toward him despite the contempt which still lingered in her eyes. Whatever had happened between them, perhaps it could eventually be forgiven, or at least set aside so that they could get on with the job. One day, he might even manage to remember what it was that had happened.

"All right. So let's assume Harry's involved. Consider the possibility, then, that he's covering up for somebody. Who might that be?"

"Not Graham Vernon, anyway."

"No love lost there, certainly."

"It has to be family," said Cooper.

"Families stick together, don't they? They close ranks against outsiders when there's trouble."

"It's what families are for."

"Simeon Holmes, then. His great-nephew."

"Harry would protect him for the sake of the family."

"Family loyalty. They say it's a powerful motivation."

"But he says he was with about thirty other bikers at Matlock Bath, nearly twenty miles away," said Cooper. "Has anybody managed to break that alibi?"

"Have *you* tried being a police officer asking for information from bikers about one of their own?"

His head was beginning to thump again. For a few minutes, he had almost forgotten the pain.

"There's another thing, though, Diane. I think you ought to talk to the bird-watcher again. Gary Edwards."

"Him? Why?"

"There's something not right about his statement."

"That's true. Dave Rennie took that statement. Mr. Tailby said himself it wasn't up to scratch. Rennie never pushed Edwards on the time."

"So has he been seen again already?"

Fry frowned. "No. I don't think so. It would have been put through as an action, but probably got allocated a low priority when Sherratt was pulled in."

"And then just got filed somewhere in the system."

"And after they started pulling people off the inquiry . . ."

"Yeah, like me, for instance. Talk to him yourself, Diane. Will you?"

"You think he can positively tie in Harry? His description is too vague, you know."

"You've got to press him on it. There's something. I just know there is. You've got to do it."

There was a moment's silence, broken only by Fry's intake of breath. "Who do you think you *are*, Ben?"

Cooper looked up, startled by the tone of her voice. For a while, he had forgotten all the things that he had to worry about, all the reasons he had to hate Diane Fry. Now she was glaring at him, making it clearer than ever that the feeling was mutual.

"I only came in here to tell you what was happening because I thought you'd be interested. But the fact is, you're off this case. You've got plenty of other things you should be concentrating on. And there are several other reasons why I don't think I should have to listen to you telling me what I've got to do. So who *do* you think you are?"

Cooper felt the full flush of his anger coming back to him. He had never found anybody so infuriating as he did Diane Fry. How was it she was able to provoke him into saying things that he would never dream of saying to anyone else?

"Just at this moment I don't know who the hell I am. Sometimes I feel as though I'm not anybody really. As though I'm just rehearsing for a role that my family want me to play. Learning to be just like my father."

"Oh yes? At least you've *got* a family," she said.

"What do you mean?"

"Never mind. It doesn't matter." She pulled abruptly away from his desk, glancing around with distaste at the mess.

"Are you going to let me down, then?" he asked.

She didn't answer but changed the subject. "I've got some other news for you. Lee Sherratt has been bailed."

"What?"

"He claims he had no intention of using the gun. He says you startled him, and he had it in his hands at the time. Cleaning it. And it was only an air rifle anyway. You don't even need a license for one of those. OK, he admits he was poaching—but what's that? A few quid in fines?"

Fry was beginning to move away, back toward the interview rooms and another spell with Harry Dickinson.

"What about Laura Vernon?" asked Cooper.

"What about her? We can't tie Sherratt in with Laura Vernon. Mr. Tailby's done his best."

"Is he not hopeful?"

"There's no evidence. Sure, the semen in the used condom was his— but we have Charlotte Vernon's statement that *she* had sex with him more than once. And it *might* have been Sherratt seen talking to Laura at six-fifteen that night. In fact, I'm damn sure it was. But unless he admits it, there's no evidence of that, either. And Sherratt knows it perfectly well."

"But there's the bite mark. Have they taken an impression of his teeth for comparison?"

"Yes, but it was a waste of time. The report came back from the forensic odontologist at Sheffield. Mr. Tailby is furious that it took so long for a result like that to come through."

"Like what?"

"Ben—that bite mark is the wrong shape. Not only were the teeth not Lee Sherratt's—they weren't even human."

"So what do you imagine will happen to your dog, Mr. Dickinson?"

"What do you mean?"

Diane Fry thrust her chin forward aggressively. "If your dog attacked and bit Laura Vernon, it could be considered an aggravated offense under section three of the Dangerous Dogs Act."

"I don't understand."

"A court could make an order to have your dog destroyed. Put down," she said.

"You'd better put me down first."

"It's a possibility, though," said Hitchens, interested in Harry's reaction. "If the dog was responsible for the attack which led to Laura's death, it would be more than likely. What's the wording, Diane?"

"The Act refers to 'a dog that injures any person while dangerously out of control in a public place.'"

"You can't tell they're a dog's teeth," said Harry.

"Oh, yes, we can. We have experts on those sort of things these days, Harry. Experts with very expensive bits of equipment. Such as scanning electron microscopes and electronic image enhancers. They can tell."

"Aye?"

"Do you want to hear a bit of what one of these experts says? I've got it here." Hitchens pulled out the report from the odontologist. He deliberately skipped the bit about the bite mark being of insufficient depth to assess by normal methods, which was why the expensive equipment had had to be used. "Here we are. The odontologist says: 'It should be noted that human bite marks have a unique oval form, and most of the times there is found a suck mark in the middle of the oval injury. Most human bites exhibit markings from several of the six upper front teeth or lower teeth, sometimes both. Canine bite marks, however, have an angular shape, like a diamond, compared to the human bite mark, which is more curved. Following electronic image enhancement, the pattern injuries caused by canine teeth are clearly distinguishable under the electron microscope.'"

Hitchens looked up. "In other words, they were canine teeth, Harry. Laura Vernon was bitten by a dog. We think it was your dog."

Harry stared into the distance. The detectives waited, instinctively recognizing the time to be silent.

"What if I told you that I killed the lass, and she was bitten after she was dead? Would that do?"

Fry felt a surge of excitement and astonishment. After all the stonewalling that the old man had done, could it really be so simple? But DI Hitchens was more cautious. He had heard too many statements that sounded like confessions in the heightened atmosphere of the interview room but which failed to hold up in the cold light of a court hearing. And Harry's remark hadn't even been a statement; it had been a question.

"You'd have to convince us first, Harry. Do you want to tell us what really happened now?"

But Fry interrupted. She had a different question, which she couldn't wait to ask.

"Would you really sacrifice yourself for a dog?"

Harry turned his steady gaze on her. It was clear from the pain in his eyes that his tough exterior had been cracked at last. An intense emotion was breaking through the restraint, a passion that could no longer be controlled by closemouthed pride.

"You wouldn't understand," he said. "It's obvious to a blind man, you've not got an ounce of love in you."

-26-

"It's only a dog," said Fry.

Ben Cooper turned away. "Well, maybe."

"What did he mean, Ben? What he said in the interview."

"He was just trying to wind you up, Diane. Take no notice of him."

He regarded her with concern, worried that she seemed unduly disturbed by Harry Dickinson's gibe. He had been in the middle of a call to a motorist whose car had been stolen the previous night when Fry had stormed back into the CID room, anxious to talk about the interview. Cooper had barely had time to finish the call before she had been repeating the conversation word for word.

"But it's only a *dog.*"

"Let's go down to the canteen," he said.

It was obvious there was something about the old man that was totally foreign to her. Cooper thought he could almost get on Harry's wavelength sometimes. Almost, but not quite. It was still not possible to predict what he might do next. But to Diane Fry, he seemed to be some kind of alien.

A few minutes later, they were sitting at a table on their own, clutching two mugs of coffee, ignoring the noise from a group of uniformed officers nearby.

"They've had to release him, of course," said Fry, recovering as the caffeine reached her bloodstream. "No charge."

"Go on, surprise me."

"By the time they got 'round to interviewing the alleged victim in the rape suite, she admitted she'd made the story up. She'd let her boyfriend go all the way without protection, and when it proved a bit disappointing she suddenly remembered things like pregnancy and AIDS. Not to mention irate parents."

"She panicked?"

"Yes, inspired by half-digested sex education lessons and a vivid imagination. And with all the stories that have been in the papers, the first thing that occurred to her was to shout rape."

"Not the first time that's happened."

Fry shrugged. "We all know there are more false rape allegations than there are actual rapes. The boyfriend's fifteen, by the way."

"But why did she claim it was Harry?"

"Apparently the two of them had some sort of encounter in the village shop earlier in the day. Harry must have come out of it best, because she hadn't forgotten it. And she'd heard all the talk in the village, so she reckoned she'd be believed. Anyway, she said he was a miserable old bugger and he deserved anything that happened to him. Funny how their minds work sometimes."

"And what was it she said exactly, when the PC found her?"

"As I recall, her words were: 'It was the old man.'"

Cooper nodded, not surprised. "It was the old man." He thought of the old lead miners' saying, their hushed stories about the spirit they called "t'owd mon," who lurked in the unlit shafts of the mines. "The old man" was blamed for everything that went wrong in the mine, from unexplained sounds in the dark to unproductive veins and fatal accidents. But he was also its guardian, a collective spirit of long-dead miners and of the mine itself. What the girl had said was an echo of the myth. "It was the old man, the old man." An ancient mantra of superstition.

"She'll be in the False or Persistent Rape Allegation file now. Silly little cow. They've sent her home, too, with a morning-after pill. A WPC went to talk to her parents. Let them sort her out, if they can."

"What about Harry?" asked Cooper.

"What about him?"

"Was he all right?"

"Him? He'll be all right. Tough as old boots, if you ask me. And too proud by half as well. What are you worrying about him for?"

"It's not a pleasant experience, being pulled in as a rape suspect."

Fry shrugged. "Tough."

"Did anybody explain it to Gwen?"

"He can explain it himself, can't he?"

"I don't think he will," said Cooper thoughtfully. "I don't think he'll be making any excuses."

"Like I said, too damn proud."

"It's not just that. I think he wants as much attention as he can get. What was it he said when they went to pick him up?"

"He said: 'You didn't take long.' Now why would he say that?"

Fry set down her coffee cup thoughtfully. "You're thinking about your link, aren't you, Ben? Have you still got that diagram?"

"Yes."

He put the diagram on the table, straightening out the creases to show the connecting lines.

"I drew it for Mr. Tailby after we sent Dickinson back to his cell," said Fry.

"Did you? And?"

"I told him what you said. That the old man would protect someone for the sake of the family. But who might that be? That's the question. And Mr. Tailby agreed with you on that."

Cooper waited tensely, watching her face.

"But he definitely doesn't think it's Simeon Holmes," she said.

He sighed, his shoulders slumped. "That's what I was afraid of," he said.

He finished his coffee and contemplated going back to detecting car crime.

"Diane, do me a favor, though?"

She nearly said "another one," but held her tongue. "What's that?"

"Talk to the bird-watcher again."

She sighed. "You've got an obsession about him."

Cooper found the words hard to say, but knew he had to say them. For some reason, it was important enough.

"Please, Diane."

The atmosphere at the Mount had passed through every mood and emotion that Graham Vernon could think of, with the exception of the good ones.

For several days, Charlotte had succeeded in working her way up toward a brittle pitch of nonchalance that had shattered dramatically after the visit by the woman detective the day before. Now there was barely a word or a response to be had from her. All day she had clutched to her chest the photograph of Laura which had finally been returned by the police.

As for Daniel, once the shouting was over, an uneasy peace seemed to have descended. This morning, Graham had even begun to feel that he and his son might actually understand each other a bit better after this business was done with. But when would it be done with?

"What the hell are they doing now?" said Daniel.

"God knows," said Graham. "They don't tell me what they're thinking."

They were missing the village gossip that Sheila Kelk would normally have been delighted to pass on to Charlotte. The only other person that might have known what had been happening was Andrew Milner—but there was no way Graham was going to ask his employee for information of that kind.

Father and son stood together by the French windows in begrudging unity. Graham was glad that Daniel had at least cleaned himself up. His hair had been washed, and somehow he had found fresh clothes in the house. Even the kitchen had been cleaned recently, and Graham was sure that Charlotte hadn't done it. He was surprised, really, that his son was still in the house. And he watched Daniel for clues to his reasoning, fearing another rebellious gesture he would fail to understand.

But Daniel was staring into the garden, his eyes following the methodical movements of the dark shapes in the conifers that grew by the bottom wall.

"What are they looking for, Dad?"

"I just don't know," said Graham.

They watched the police team assemble for a few minutes on the lawn, brushing the soil off their knees as they discussed their next move. Then the officers dispersed again. They pulled on their gloves and approached the densely planted bushes on the eastern border of the property, gradually getting nearer the gate that led onto the Baulk. And they started looking again.

That afternoon, Cooper left Edendale to visit a family from East Anglia who were holidaying in a cottage near Bakewell. Their Mitsubishi had been taken from the roadside near one of the show caves at Castleton, full of the usual items—a camera, binoculars, mobile phone, a wallet, and checkbook locked in the glove compartment. They were fortunate that their insurance allowed them to get a hire car to finish their holiday, but he had a feeling they wouldn't be coming back to Derbyshire again. However, one of the family thought they might have caught a glimpse of the thieves near their car as they had headed for the cave. It was a very small clue in a hopeless task.

From Bakewell, he drove up the A6 as far as Ashford-in-the-Water. There were clumps and wisps of yellow straw lying all along the roadside, swirling in the blasts of air from passing traffic and settling to the ground again like broken shreds of sunlight.

The schools were still on holiday for another week, and the main roads throughout the Peak District were choked with cars and caravans. If the hot weather held a bit longer, the tourist honey pots would be at a standstill again at the weekend, with thousands of people sweltering in narrow, gridlocked lanes surrounded by the stench of exhaust fumes and hot tarmac.

In Ashford, the streets were lined with cars, and the bridge over the weir was packed with people watching the ducks paddling in the shallow water or the families picnicking on the grassy banks. There was a small car park behind the church in the middle of the village, but it was over-looked by houses and relatively safe. Cooper drove on.

Through Ashford a road ran up to Monsal Head, where the spectacu-lar view of the old railway viaduct crossing the wooded valley of the Wye attracted many motorists to stop. The railway line here had long since been dismantled and was now used as footpath. Across the other side of Monsal Dale was the parish of Brushfield and a plateau scattered with more of the hundreds of disused mine shafts that littered the landscape. He was deep in White Peak country here, a land of glittering streams and green pastures, where narrow side valleys had elbowed their way through the prehistoric fossil seabed to form craggy gorges.

Northward from Monsal Head he passed opencast limestone work-ings and turned right toward Foolow and Eyam. After a call at a disused quarry that was used as an unofficial car park for walkers following the Limestone Way, Cooper found himself crossing Eyam Edge and arriving, as he knew he must, on the road into Moorhay.

He parked the Toyota at the Old Mill at Quith Holes, persuading himself that this meant he was still pursuing his routine inquiries into car crime at local tourist spots. There were plenty of other cars at the Old Mill, and several families were seated at the tables set out on the grass. A cluster of cottages were set behind the mill on a narrow road protected by PRIVATE NO ENTRY signs.

Cooper crossed a small stone bridge near the original ford and took the path that skirted Raven's Side, wincing at the bruises on his legs and back but glad of the opportunity to loosen up his limbs. He had to consult his Ordnance Survey map, because he hadn't approached the path from this direction before. But by following his instinct and steering slightly downhill, he soon reached the area where he had walked to with Harry Dickinson four days previously.

Once again, he left the path and crossed the tumble of boulders to the spot at the top of the slope above the stream. There was no sign of the crime scene now, except for a wide, bare patch where the undergrowth had been cut down to the ground and removed to the forensic laboratory.

He peered down on to the stream below. He knew there was nothing he could see that wouldn't already have been found and identified by the SOCOs. But sometimes he did get feelings that he couldn't account for. He didn't talk about these feelings much at E Division. He couldn't afford to be considered an eccentric. In the police service, you had to fit in; you had to be a team player and follow the rule book. Now, though, he was hoping that some feeling, some small insight, might just strike him at the place where the body of Laura Vernon had been found. Somewhere at the back of his thoughts, indistinct and deadened by the remains of his hangover, was an idea that had been suggested to him sometime last night. Something to do with dogs. Or was it pigs?

Cooper found his mind filled with a vivid image. He saw a sharp, black muzzle filled with white teeth that snapped and tore at pale, dead flesh. Behind the fangs were jaws dripping with saliva and a pink tongue that curled and twisted and rolled out a rumbling growl from deep in a fur-covered throat. Fierce red eyes stared madly as the teeth bit and pierced. The white skin darkened and punctured, but there was no blood. He saw the dog finally letting go of its victim and looking up at the dark, contorted shapes of the Witches as it began to howl, its dirt-encrusted claws scrabbling in the earth with frustration. The black dog had come for a soul, and had been thwarted.

But that wasn't it. Cooper shook his head to clear the image. He knew the black dog was his own. He had carried it around in his mind since childhood, and it was him that it had come to claim, not Laura Vernon.

After several minutes, he was forced to give up and move on, with no great inspirations. He walked back to the path and looked up the hill. He ought to go back to Quith Holes now—back to the car and his routine inquiries. He was off the Vernon case.

But instead he turned and began to walk up the path toward Moorhay, his muscles protesting and the bruises on his ribs throbbing. Out of the trees, the sun beat on his back and neck, and he began to feel a bit light-headed. This was no way to restore himself as a candidate for a sergeant's job. But something had happened out here on the Baulk. Who had Laura Vernon met here? Had she met him by design or accident? Had she been followed, or had she walked down this path with someone she had spoken to behind the garden at the Mount?

The final results of forensic tests might reveal some of that information. So far, they had at least established that the bite mark on the victim's thigh had been the work of canine teeth. A dog, possibly. But it could just as easily have been a fox, coming across the dead body as it lay in the undergrowth attracting maggots. But would forensics reveal the identity of the killer? Cooper didn't think so.

When he got to within a hundred yards of Dial Cottage, he almost bumped into Harry Dickinson, who was standing under a tree in the shade, with his dog at his feet. He stared wordlessly at Cooper, like a man interrupted in his own sitting room.

"Oh, you."

"Aye, me. Like a bad penny."

"Not your usual time for walking the dog, is it, Mr. Dickinson?"

"I needed to get the taste of your police station out of my mouth, lad."

"So where have you been?"

"Minding my own business."

Cooper was hot and sore, and felt himself starting to get angry. But Harry only tilted his head, revealing his unfathomable eyes.

"Are you going to arrest me again? There are no young lasses in these woods, you know—not at this time of day."

"I don't think it's a subject to joke about, Mr. Dickinson. Do you?"

"Aye, maybe you're right, lad. Maybe I've had enough enjoyment for one day."

The hint of bitterness in the old man's voice made Cooper's ears prick up. Evidence of emotion was rare enough from Harry. There was an air of finality in his words, too, a feeling of something coming toward an end. He'd had enough—but enough of what?

"They had Jess in a cage at that police station," said Harry. "Shut up in a cage with a lot of mongrels and strays. What has she ever done wrong to anybody? Tell me that."

Cooper felt a strange sensation coming over him, a powerful physical surge that sent a shiver of excitement up his spine. His eyes were drawn down to the ground, where Jess, the black Labrador, was lying on the grass at Harry's feet. Her lolling pink tongue was the only splash of color in a tangle of black fur.

"Right," he said, catching his breath. "Yes, that's right."

Harry looked at him sharply, suddenly suspicious at the silence. Cooper shook himself and stared back at the old man, beginning to smile for the first time in days.

Gwen Dickinson saw Ben Cooper coming up the path. She had been watching for Harry from the kitchen window. Her face was drawn, and her eyes were red from lack of sleep and too many tears.

Cooper remembered that she, too, had been questioned in an interview room at Edendale, to be informed that her husband was a suspected rapist. Suddenly, he felt sick at the thought of what was done to people like Gwen—innocent people who happened merely to find themselves on the sidelines of a major inquiry as unwilling witnesses, possessors of some snippet of information the police were determined to get hold of, while the foundations of their lives were being pulled apart in front of their eyes. For Gwen, he knew, life with Harry would never be the same.

"What did he say?" asked Gwen when he reached the back door of the cottage. She clutched at his sleeve as if expecting him to put everything right. "I saw you speak to Harry."

"He didn't say anything. I'm sorry."

Cooper didn't know what he was apologizing for. But he knew he had disappointed Gwen by the way her face fell; and she turned to go back inside, shuffling her feet in a pair of old slippers decorated with pink roses.

"Come in. Helen's here."

"Oh no, it's all right. I don't want to intrude."

He began to back away, out into the sunlight. But Helen herself appeared in the kitchen at the sound of his voice. She was wearing jeans and a T-shirt and had a polishing cloth in her hand. Her red hair was tied back in a ribbon.

"Come in, Ben. Don't stay out there, please."

"Helen's been doing a bit of cleaning for me," said Gwen. "I can't seem to be bothered with it anymore."

As the old woman shuffled through into the sitting room and settled herself with a sigh into an armchair, Helen turned troubled eyes on Cooper.

"None of this was because of me, you know," he said.

"I know. I'm sorry, Ben."

"I'm off the inquiry anyway. They don't need me now."

Helen laid a hand on his arm, sensing his pain. "I'm really worried about Granddad now. I think he's planning something. That's why he's kept out of the way ever since he came back from the police station. Because he's worried I might be able to tell what he's thinking; he knows that I can understand him. We're too close, you see. I think that's the reason he's been behaving so strangely. He's trying to keep me and Grandma at arm's length, so we can't guess what he's up to. But he's certainly up to something. Can you help us, Ben?"

"Hasn't he said anything to you at all?"

"There was just one thing he said, when he first came back. It worried me even more. He said, 'It was meant for Vernon.'"

The sound of the phone was loud and jarring in the little cottage. Gwen jumped with alarm, but stayed in her chair, gripping the arms, her eyes turning pleadingly toward Helen. Her granddaughter went to answer it, and Cooper watched Helen's face change as she listened, turning pale under her tan. It was obvious there was more bad news.

Helen turned slowly back to Gwen and Cooper as she replaced the phone. But she couldn't meet Cooper's eyes. "That was Mum," she said. "The police have been and taken Dad in for questioning."

DCI Tailby smiled wolfishly at Andrew Milner, noting the nervousness in his posture and his gestures and the sheen of sweat that had broken out on his forehead. A cup of tea stood going cold on the interview room table in front of him, untouched and beginning to form a scum on its muddy surface.

"Mr. Milner, your daughter, Helen, has told us about the parties at the Mount."

"Oh," said Andrew, his face crumpling immediately.

"She has described an incident with Graham Vernon. Your boss, Mr. Milner."

"Yes."

"You know all about that incident, don't you? I refer to the occasion when Mr. Vernon lured your daughter to one of the bedrooms. From the description, it might well be considered an attempted rape."

"Yes, Helen told me. She was very upset."

"And how did you react when you heard about it, Mr. Milner?"

"Naturally, I was shocked and angry. I've always had a good relationship with Graham. I knew he had those parties, of course. Him and Charlotte. They got something out of them that I could never hope to understand. Different lives, Chief Inspector. Different from mine, anyway."

"You knew what these parties were like? But you didn't stop Helen going when she was invited?"

"Stop her? How could I?" Andrew spread his hands, appealing for sense. "She's an adult. She takes no notice of me."

"You didn't even warn her?"

"Well, I hoped that everything would be all right. I didn't expect Graham would try . . . something like that . . . with Helen, with my daughter. I thought it would be all right, you see. In any case, she wanted to go. I couldn't have stopped her. I thought it would be all right."

"But it wasn't all right."

He slumped. "No."

"Did you speak to Mr. Vernon about it afterward?"

"Yes, I did."

"What did you say?"

"Well . . . that I was upset about what Helen had told me. That she had complained he had assaulted her. Sexually, you know."

"And his response?"

Andrew twisted his hands, appealing to Tailby with his eyes for sympathy. He was reliving the moment, just as Tailby wanted him to do. In the end, Andrew sighed deeply and sagged a little further into his chair.

"He just laughed at me," he said.

"He thought assaulting your daughter was a joke?"

Andrew nodded. "Apparently. He said those sort of games were expected at their parties. 'Games' he called it. And then he said something like: 'Never mind, she's a big girl now.' I didn't know what to say or what to do. I felt so stupid. He made me feel as though I was the one who didn't know how to behave properly. He can always make me feel like that."

"Some fathers would have known exactly what to do," commented Hitchens.

"I suppose I'm not that sort of father. Not that sort of a man. I have never seen violence as an answer."

"Violence. Ah yes. Was that what I meant?"

"Wasn't it?" asked Andrew, surprised. He looked confused now and somehow accusing, as if the detective had pulled a trick on him.

"And, of course, Mr. Vernon is probably three or four inches taller than you, a stone or two heavier, younger, and fitter. It was better to show discretion, in the circumstances. Very wise."

Andrew inclined his head, accepting the point without objection.

"You could have reported it to us. You could have resigned," said Tailby. "Yet to choose to go on working for this man . . ."

"Chief Inspector, I can't afford to throw away my job. There are too few for a man of my age and background. I've got a wife, a mortgage. Things have gone badly for me in the past. I can't have it happen to me again. I need that job at Vernon's. Resign? No."

Tailby eyed the man, suppressing a surge of pity, keeping his face impassive. "Let me ask you about Mrs. Charlotte Vernon, then."

"Charlotte?"

"Mrs. Vernon has named you as one of her lovers."

Andrew's mouth dropped open, and he shook his head vehemently. "Oh no."

"Are you saying she's lying?"

"I was never that."

"Never? Why would she lie about it, Mr. Milner?"

"I don't know."

"But you had been to one of the Vernons' parties yourself, hadn't you?"

"Well, yes. But I wouldn't take part in . . . anything like that."

Tailby was silent for a few moments. Andrew Milner hung his head, waiting for the next question with the air of a man expecting the inevitable.

"Where were you on Saturday night, Mr. Milner?"

Andrew looked puzzled. "I gave a statement days ago," he said defensively.

"Ah yes." Tailby consulted his notes. "You had been to a meeting with some clients in Leeds. A bit unusual on a Saturday?"

"Not at all. We've been very busy. If the clients work on a Saturday, then we do, too."

"And you state that you were tired and stopped for a rest on the way home."

"At Woolley Services on the M1. I'd had a long day. I dozed for the best part of an hour, I think. It's not safe to drive when you're tired."

"Of course. And you state that you were then held up in traffic on the M1."

"And getting through Sheffield from the motorway, yes. There had been an accident somewhere, I think. And the usual roadworks, you know."

Tailby slapped the file with his hand. "Of course there were road-works. There always are roadworks. The rest of it is quite impossible to substantiate."

"I can't help that."

"So," said the DCI, "let's go back to your relationship with Mr. Vernon, then. You can't afford to resign, and you can't afford to upset the boss too much. Is that it? So you just grin and bear it when the man assaults your daughter. You accept the humiliation."

"I'm afraid that's what I did."

Tailby stood up. He towered over Andrew Milner, and Andrew cringed as the detective's expression changed to anger.

"No, I don't think so, Mr. Milner. I don't think you did just accept it, did you?"

"What do you mean?"

"I think that the humiliation rankled. I think it ate away inside you—the anger and the humiliation, the self-disgust. The shame that you hadn't been man enough to respond in the way that so many fathers would. You already hated Graham Vernon for his condescension, for the way he treated you like a servant. But now your hatred festered and you wanted to strike back. I think you saw a way of doing that in what must have seemed the most appropriate manner—through his own daughter. Revenge—wasn't that it, Mr. Milner? Vengeance for your humiliation, for Helen's ordeal and your own impotence. Tit for tat. Laura Vernon was an obvious target of your anger."

"I don't know what you're talking about."

"I think you do. Where did you *really* go on Saturday night, Mr. Milner?"

The silence grew, with Tailby leaning down toward Andrew, glaring at him as he waited for an answer. The tapes whirred uninterrupted, waiting for the next person to speak. Andrew Milner did nothing for a long time. Then his face seemed to convulse and collapse. His hands clutched at each other, and tears began to ooze down his cheeks.

-27-

Ben Cooper lifted the binoculars and swung them across the hillside, resting his elbows on the warm rock. The light was starting to fade, and the straggle of buildings looked gray and flat. For the first time in days, a bank of cloud had built up in the west and had blotted out the setting sun. But he could easily make out the white vehicle that had bumped up the track, and he could identify the three figures that were now moving slowly in front of the dilapidated farmhouse.

"All three of them are there now."

"Let's see."

He passed the binoculars across carefully, shifting his body to make his position more comfortable. He lay prone, keeping his profile below the skyline, knowing his dark clothes would make him almost invisible against the rocky outcrop.

"Harry has the dog with him."

"As always."

"They just seem to be standing around at the moment."

"They would normally go to the pub at this time. They're late already. Besides, why would Harry and Sam Beeley come up to the smallholding? Surely it's much easier for them just to meet Wilford down at the pub? They both live close to it, and Wilford's the one with the transport."

Diane Fry kept the binoculars to her face. Cooper watched her, anxious to see her expression. She had agreed to come with him to Raven's Side when she came off duty, but he knew he had a long way to go to convince her that he wasn't making a fool of himself again. Two days ago, when he had sat on Raven's Side and recalled the legend of the black hounds that haunted the hilltops, he had noticed the vantage point on the east side of the tors from which there was a perfect view of Thorpe Farm.

"Maybe they've just come to help Wilford feed the animals," she said. Cooper smiled. "What animals?"

Fry wondered what she was looking for as she swung the binoculars backward and forward again, surveying the buildings. There could be anything within those ramshackle sheds and huts. They would be a nightmare to search, if it ever came to it.

To the right of the buildings, she could just make out the famous compost heap. It lay like a vast heap of droppings freshly left by some monstrous creature passing across the hillside toward Moorhay. Even from this distance, she could see the tendrils of steam rising from its surface. She shuddered, imagining that she could even detect the smell on the evening air.

"It's certainly quiet in the fields," she said. "The animals must all be in bed."

Cooper snorted derisively, until she pulled the binoculars away and glared at him. Like him, she was dressed in denims and a dark jacket. She was uncomfortable lying on the hard ground, and uneasy about what they were doing. Memories of the incident on Tuesday night were still clear in her mind, when she had followed Ben Cooper into trouble at the poacher's hut. She could not understand why she had done it again—let him persuade her into doing something she knew wasn't right.

"Sorry," he said. "What are they doing now?"

"Nothing. Probably Wilford's wife has got something cooking and they're all going to be having their dinner in a minute."

He frowned at her. "What did you say? Who's got what—?"

"I said having dinner. Just like we should be doing, Ben."

"OK, OK. I'll buy you a Chinese meal later on. How about that? We'll go to Fred Kwok's. It's the best Chinese in Edendale. Fancy some deep-fried wonton later? "

"Make it right now, and I'd even accept meat pie and mushy peas at the Drover."

He was silent. But she knew that he would simply be looking at her with that pleading expression that baffled her and made her angry at the feelings it stirred up inside her. They were feelings she had long since tried to suppress. Feelings that she had already allowed to surface once recently, with humiliating consequences. She wasn't about to let it happen again.

"I'm sure I'm right, Diane," he said.

Looking at Cooper's face now, she knew that this was what it was really all about for her. This was why she had let him persuade her into this mad expedition, this spell of unauthorized surveillance. It was the sheer strength of his conviction, the intensity of his belief in himself. All he had done was put a few facts together with a whole load of half-baked ideas, instincts, and feelings that were entirely his own; and as a result he was filled with a pure, heartfelt certainty that he was right. She could see that Ben Cooper was a man who believed strongly in things; he had faith, he had genuine passion. It was ridiculously attractive.

"Ben—you've made this mistake once already. You're not even on the case anymore. You should back off now, or you'll regret it."

"And what exactly have I got left to lose?" he snapped.

"Shh. You'll let everybody down there know we're here."

"I promise you I'm right."

"OK, OK."

Immediately below their position was a patch of woodland clinging to the side of the hill. It was full of the quiet noises of creatures settling down for the night or stirring ready for their evening's hunting. The woods petered out fifty yards away, where the millstone grit erupted from the hillside and the ground became bare and rocky. At their backs were the tors themselves—gritstone outcrops sculpted by geological forces and the weather into strange, twisted shapes. Their names owed a lot to the dark imagination of the rural Peak dwellers—the Horse Stone, the Poached Egg Stone, the Mad Woman.

But I'm the madwoman, thought Fry. I'm mad for even being here.

Cooper knew he had to handle her carefully. She was like a coiled spring—one wrong word and she would walk off and leave him. But it was difficult to avoid the wrong word with Diane Fry. Besides, there were so many things he wanted to ask her, away from the office. Number one on his list was what had happened between her and DI Hitchens on their trip to Yorkshire. But it might be wise to save that one for later.

"Is Mr. Tailby still hopeful of Andrew Milner?" he asked, steering the way into a safer subject.

"Your diagram encouraged him. That and the lack of evidence against Simeon Holmes. If Harry Dickinson was protecting somebody, it has to be Milner."

"Yeah. Harry doesn't think much of Milner, but he'd protect him for the sake of his daughter. For the sake of the family."

"Family loyalty. As you say, a powerful motivation."

"Yes, it fits," said Cooper sadly.

"Milner had been pushed to the limit by Graham Vernon. Maybe he finally cracked and took revenge."

"Not only was he pushed to the limit by Vernon, but he was also reminded of his failure by his own family. Harry in particular taunted him with his weakness. If Harry found out what had happened, he would have felt guilty—partly responsible, in fact. He would try to make amends. I can see that."

Cooper cast his mind back to his first visit to Dial Cottage. He remembered the bloodstained trainer standing on the kitchen table on a copy of the *Buxton Advertiser*, the atmosphere of tension lying on the cramped rooms like a thick blanket. He remembered the old lady, distressed by something beyond the innocent discovery of a missing girl's trainer.

"I wonder if that was what the row was about," he said, "and, if so, who was on which side?"

Fry frowned, but let it pass. "Anyway, Milner's account of his whereabouts was crap from the start."

"Really?"

"There was no possibility of tracing anyone who could remember him. He could have been anywhere at that time."

"But he can't be placed at the scene either."

"The DCI thinks he's worth pursuing. And that one is no Harry Dickinson, either. Mr. Tailby will have been running rings 'round him back at Division."

Cooper was silent for a moment, lying quite still to ease the pain in his chest.

"Andrew Milner isn't in the frame," he said.

"But you just said it fits!"

"Of course it does. It fits the facts, anyway. But he can't have killed Laura Vernon."

"Why not?"

He shrugged. "He just can't, that's all."

"You're nuts, do you know that? You're a sandwich short of a picnic."

They didn't speak to each other for a few minutes. They lay listening to the noises in the woods. A small flock of jackdaws appeared and circled the face of a neighboring crag. Their harsh, metallic cries drowned out all other noises coming up from the valley until the birds gradually settled onto their roost.

The minutes passed without incident. The three old men were still gathered around the white pickup in front of the house. In another half hour the light would have gone completely. Fry passed the binoculars back to Cooper. Then she eased over onto her side and dug a hand into the pocket of her jacket. She pulled out a bag of colored sweets.

"I read somewhere you should have something with you when you're on the hills. For the energy."

Cooper took a sweet and sucked it thoughtfully. He looked at her with a faintly puzzled expression. She seemed to feel his eyes on her and turned away, pretending to study something in the woods. Beyond the valley, a jet airliner was leaving a faint trace across the sky toward Manchester.

"Diane—" he said tentatively.

"Yeah?"

"What happened to your family?"

Fry remained staring straight ahead. A tendon twitched in her neck as her jaw tightened. She showed no other sign that she had heard him.

He studied her profile, trying to tune in to what she was thinking, to get a glimpse of how she was feeling. But her face was stony and expressionless, her eyes fixed on something that might have been deep in the wood, or even beyond it.

A blackbird scratching in the old leaves beneath the trees whistled and chattered to itself. A partridge wound up its rusty spring somewhere down the hillside. They followed the sound of a car traveling up out of Moorhay toward Edendale.

"You don't have to tell me if you don't want to," he said gently.

She turned her head then. Her lips had narrowed to a hard line, but her eyes had returned from their invisible horizon to seek out his own.

"I just can't believe you sometimes, Ben."

"I'm that amazing, eh?"

"What sort of time is this to decide you want to discuss my private life?"

"I thought you might like to talk while we wait."

"Would it surprise you to learn that all I'd like to do at this particular moment is punch you on the nose?"

"Oh, I shouldn't do that. My screaming would give our position away."

"Right."

They stayed unmoving for five minutes more. The blackbird chattered among the old leaves on the woodland floor. A squirrel rustled the branches as it leaped from one tree to the next. A large, pale moth appeared, fluttering in front of Fry's nose until she waved it away. A tawny owl hooted from the slopes of the Baulk. Finally, she gave a deep sigh.

"I was taken into care by Social Services when I was nine. They said my parents had been abusing my sister, who was eleven. They said it was both my parents. We were fostered after that, but we kept moving on to different places. So many different places that I can't remember them. It was years before I realized that we didn't stay anywhere long because of my sister. She was big trouble wherever we went. Nobody could keep her under control. But I worshipped her, and I refused to be split up from her."

"What about you?"

"What about me? Do you mean was I abused, too? I can't remember."

"Was it—?"

"I can't remember."

The blackbird flapped away through the undergrowth, cackling its alarm call. The squirrel froze on an oak branch, its body upright, its head alert for danger. Cooper and Fry automatically ducked their heads and hugged the ground more closely. Gradually, the normal sounds of the hillside returned. The squirrel relaxed and moved on.

"So what happened to your parents?"

"For God's sake. I've no idea. And I don't want to know. All right?"

"And your sister?"

Fry hesitated. When she spoke, her voice had lost its hard edge. Her eyes had drifted away, back to the images floating somewhere in a darkness that only she could see. "I haven't seen her since she was sixteen. She disappeared from our foster home and never came back."

Her voice died, and Cooper thought she had told him all she was ever going to say. But then came a whisper, full of anger and unresolved pain.

"Of course, she was already using heroin by then."

A skein of geese passed slowly overhead in a straggly V shape. They honked hoarsely to each other, communicating their presence, binding themselves together as a living unit that moved as a single creature. A combine harvester was working late lower down the valley. Its headlights were on, and the clatter of its blades was clear and sharp on the air as it flattened a field of barley. A cloud of dust marked the combine's position, golden specks glittering in the fading light.

Fry tried to persuade her memories to fly away with the geese, to fall into shreds beneath the combine's blade, to disappear in a cloud of dust. But in the dark valley of her mind, the nightmares roosted permanently; the harvest never came.

"Diane—"

"What now?"

"I guess you must have taken me home last night."

"Who else?"

"Well . . . thanks."

"Think nothing of it. But don't expect the same favor too often. It wasn't exactly the most fun I've ever had in one night."

"Right."

He sucked the last of his sweet and polished the lenses of the binoculars on his sleeve.

"There's just one other thing, Diane. Most of last night is a complete blur. But there is something I can sort of remember. Something I wanted to ask you about. I can't get it out of my mind."

Fry went completely rigid, her arm and leg muscles locked tight as if she had multiple cramps. Her stomach tied itself into a painful knot, and she turned her face away, praying that he couldn't see her blush. How could she have hoped that he wouldn't remember that excruciatingly embarrassing moment? She had no idea what she was going to say to him. Her mind was a total blank.

"Diane—?"

She barely managed a grunt of acknowledgment, but it was enough to encourage him to continue.

"I remember some music you were playing in the car on the way back to your flat. I guess it sort of stuck in my mind while I was drunk, and I can't get rid of it again. I just wondered what it was, that's all."

Fry laughed out loud with relief. "That's ridiculous!"

"Some woman singer. I'm more into the Waterboys and the Levellers. But that tape sounded all right."

"It was Tanita Tikaram. It's called *Ancient Heart.*"

"Thanks."

"I'll lend you the cassette, if you like. You can make a copy of it."

"That's great—"

A bleeping sound came from Fry's jacket pocket. "Oh shit."

"What have you brought that thing for?"

Fry pulled out her pager and switched off the sound as she read the phone number. "It's somebody I've been trying to get hold of all day," she said. "He's just tried to ring me back at last."

"Important?"

"The bird-watcher—Gary Edwards."

"Ah. You remembered."

"Do you still think it's important? Should I go back to the car and phone him, then?"

Cooper hesitated for a moment. "Yes, you should."

She straightened herself up and scrambled over the rocks toward the car park that lay a few hundred yards below them at the Old Mill. "See you in a few minutes, then."

"Yeah."

Damn, thought Cooper. And just as he was getting around to asking her about Hitchens.

He swung up the binoculars again. He had to peer hard now to make out the figures by the white pickup. They seemed to have been gathered over a piece of paper, consulting together, nodding their heads, as if they were doing a crossword or something.

A few minutes after Diane Fry had left, he saw two of the dim shapes begin to move away from the house. He realized they were heading back down the track leading from the smallholding. The third stayed behind, leaning against the pickup.

Cooper followed the two figures as they passed through the first gate on foot and continued along the track toward the road. When they turned and crossed the road toward the squeeze stile that led to the path onto the Baulk, he knew he would have to follow them.

He looked at his watch. Nearly eight o'clock. Who else had mentioned eight o'clock? He flicked through his mental notes, and remembered Fry's account of her interview with Charlotte Vernon. It was this time, every night, that Charlotte visited the spot on the Baulk where her daughter's body was found.

*   *   *

"So let's just go back over it again, Mr. Edwards, shall we?" said Fry. "You were standing near the cairn on Raven's Side when you saw an old man with a black dog walk past the end of the footpath below."

"No."

"What do you mean no? That's what you said in your statement."

"No, I didn't. Where've you got that from?"

Fry stared through the windscreen at the car park and the lighted windows on the front of the Old Mill. She was still unsure what it was she hoped to establish by speaking to the bird-watcher. Gary Edwards had already insisted that he would stick by his estimate of the time he had seen the old man. His watch was accurate, and he was sure of the time. He always recorded the exact time of a sighting, he said.

Now, though, she did seem to have touched on something. She consulted her notes, taken from his earlier statement.

"I've got it right here, Mr. Edwards—the statement that you signed. Let me read part of it to you. Your statement reads: 'I saw the head of a dog through my binoculars. It appeared through some undergrowth. It was close to the ground, sniffing at a fallen branch. It was black.'"

"Right."

"You go on: 'Then I saw there was a man with the dog. He was an old man, wearing a cap. He passed out of my vision to the left, walking, not running. I took the binoculars away from my eyes and I saw the man and the dog move away into the trees. This was near the stream that runs by the footpath called the Eden Valley Trail.'"

"Well—"

"So the dog was a black dog."

"No, that's not what I said."

"It's here. You've signed it. 'It was black,' you said."

"You're not listening. Like the other bloke—he didn't listen either."

"Detective Sergeant Rennie?"

"Yes, him. He just wrote what he wanted to, didn't he? But listen. I only saw the dog's head through the binoculars. The *head* was black."

"So?"

"So maybe the rest of the dog wasn't. Get it? I couldn't tell when I took the binoculars away, see? I could only make out the rest of the thing then, when it came out into the open. But the light was funny by that time. It was late on, and the sun was so low. You lose the definition of the colors."

"OK, I know what you mean. But as far as you could tell, the dog was black, yes?

"No. Well . . . I reckon it was probably black and white."

"Why? You've just said—"

"Well, they usually are, that type of dog. When you see them on the telly—they're mostly black, with some white. They reckon it's good camouflage, so the sheep can't see them on the hillside."

"What are you talking about?"

"*One Man and His Dog.* It was a sheepdog type of thing, with a shaggy coat. A Border collie, they call it."

"A Labrador, surely. A black Labrador you saw."

"I'm telling you, I'm telling you. Will you write it down properly, for God's sake? I know a Labrador from a collie, see? And this was a Border collie. A black-and-white collie. Definite."

Fry sighed. "We'd better see you and take another statement in the morning, hadn't we, Mr. Edwards?"

"Whatever you like. But we'll have to make it quick. There's been a pair of snipe sighted on Stanton Moor."

As she finished the call to Edwards, a memory came back to Diane Fry, and she almost dropped the phone. The memory was of a photograph of Laura Vernon. It was the original photograph, the one from which her face had been enlarged for use in the murder inquiry. Fry had seen it only once. She had sneaked a look in the file when the girl was still officially just a missing person. It had been a photo of Laura taken in the garden at the Mount, at a time when she was laughing and happy in the sunshine. And at her feet in the picture had been a dog. A black-and-white Border collie.

Stewart Tailby called DI Hitchens into his office. It was late, but they were both too senior to qualify for overtime payments.

The two men were tired and tense. They were awaiting the results of fingerprint examination on a find made earlier in the evening. They hardly dared to say it to each other, but they knew the results could be crucial. Tailby had openly pinned his hopes on forensics so often during this inquiry that it seemed like tempting fate even to voice the hope that a set of prints other than Laura Vernon's would be found on the second trainer. That second trainer they had spent so many expensive man-hours looking for. The trainer which had now been found by searchers, where it lay in the roots of a hedge inside the back wall of the garden at the Mount.

Meanwhile, a tearful Andrew Milner had been sent home for the night, with the warning that they might want to talk to him again tomorrow—and the friendly advice that he should talk to his wife.

"So Margaret Milner was right that he hadn't been Charlotte Vernon's lover," said Tailby.

"But she didn't know about the secretary."

"Mmm. Has it occurred to you, though, that Graham Vernon might well have known about the affair?"

Hitchens snapped his fingers. "Of course. The hold he had over Milner wasn't just to do with his fear of losing his job. He knew Milner's dirty secret."

"And he certainly made the most of it. The result was that Andrew Milner felt unable to act even when Vernon made a move on his own daughter."

"Are we discounting Milner, then?"

"No. There's enough hate there. Hate for Graham Vernon, but self-disgust, too. It has to be directed somewhere."

Tailby leaned wearily on his desk, his shoulders stooped. The air-conditioning was still running, and his office was turning cold as the evening temperature dropped. "No, I'd like to eliminate Milner, but we can't. Not without confirmation of his movements that night. Poor sod. He couldn't even switch his story and claim he was with the mistress."

Tailby glowered at Hitchens's raised eyebrow, realizing the DI was amused either at his use of the old-fashioned term or his sympathy for the suspect. Perhaps both. Maybe he was getting too old for the job if his junior officers were laughing at him, thought Tailby. Maybe he ought to take that job in the Corporate Development department at County Headquarters in Ripley. They needed a chief inspector to take charge of Process Development. Whatever that was.

"We have no case against Andrew Milner," said Hitchens.

"I know that, damn it."

"Of the other names on the list, Simeon Holmes is in the clear. He was nearly twenty miles away at the time, and his story is well supported."

"Bikers," said Tailby.

"This lot weren't exactly Hell's Angels, sir. You'd be surprised at the types who gather at Matlock Bath in their best leathers on a weekend. Some of them that we talked to were married couples with kids. Some were in their fifties."

Tailby decided he disliked Paul Hitchens. It was his youth and his condescending smile. He would probably go far. In fact, he would probably be DCI very soon. What *did* Process Development mean exactly? He recalled that the three other CIs in Corporate had sections called Strategic Planning, Policy Development, and Quality Assurance. Not much help.

Hitchens was counting on his fingers, like a primary school teacher. "We know Lee Sherratt could have been there. He *could* have been the youth seen talking to Laura, but he's sensibly keeping mum. Without forensics, we'll not pin that one down. Nobody saw him who can identify him."

"OK. Take the father, Graham Vernon."

"Yes, sir." Hitchens held up another finger. It looked dangerously like an insulting gesture to a senior officer. "Graham Vernon *was* seen and identified. By Harry Dickinson. But, of course, Mr. Vernon went out to look for Laura when she didn't come back to the house for dinner. Perfectly natural. An innocent explanation. He looked around for a while, perhaps called her name a few times, then got worried when he couldn't find her, went back to the house, and phoned us. Just what we would expect from a concerned father."

Tailby's expression must have betrayed his feelings about Graham Vernon. "I know you didn't like him, sir. But we can't act on feelings, can we? We need evidence."

Hitchens was really warming up now. "Teaching your grandmother to suck eggs" was an expression that sprang to the DCI's mind. He wanted to stop Hitchens, to take back control of the conversation, but he felt powerless to halt the flow. His words had an air of inevitability.

"Harry Dickinson."

"Yes, Harry Dickinson. He was definitely there." Hitchens looked at his fingers. He seemed to have lost count. He was already holding up five fingers and was trying to find a sixth. "But was he there at the right time? Nobody can tell us so for definite. There's no firm identification of him, not even from the bird-watcher."

"He did find the body, Paul."

"Well, strictly speaking—"

"Yes, I know!"

Tailby knew he was losing his grip on the situation. He shouldn't lose his temper. But how could he stand this waiting? What were the finger-print people doing down there? Of course, he knew the difficulties of lift-ing latent prints from a leather surface, and it could take hours. They were praying that the suspect had handled the leather upper of the trainer, and that his hands had been sweaty. They were praying that he hadn't handled the trainer by its laces or by the cloth interior. They were praying he was someone they knew.

If they lifted a suspect print, the inquiry was back on track and they could start making comparisons for identification. If they lifted no prints, they had hit another brick wall.

"We may have to start pulling in every youth in the Eden Valley for elimination," said Hitchens with an air of too much satisfaction.

"We might as well pull in all the foxes in those woods and identify the one that took a bite out of Laura Vernon's leg. That's about as useful as forensics have been to us so far."

"It could have been a fox," said Hitchens. "Or it could have been a dog."

"Oh yes," said Tailby. "That's about the best we can do. It could have been a bloody dog."

But did the Vernons *have* a dog? Jesus, had nobody found that out? As Diane Fry punched the buttons of her phone again, she wondered how something so obvious could have been missed. Had *everybody* been fix-ated on Harry Dickinson? She banged the dashboard of the car irritably. No answer from the Vernons.

What was she going to do now? She could, of course, try to get hold of Mr. Tailby or DI Hitchens and ask them what to do. But what would Ben have suggested? The answer came to her as if he had been there next to her: Sheila Kelk, the Vernons' cleaner. Her address was on file back at the office. It only took a call to the duty operator in the incident room to get the phone number of the house at Wye Close.

Mrs. Kelk sounded terrified when Fry told her who she was, as if the council house she was speaking from might be full of guilty secrets.

"I just want to ask you something, Mrs. Kelk. Do the Vernons have a dog?"

"Oh, no. Mrs. Vernon doesn't like them."

"But there's a photograph in the sitting room at the Mount showing Laura with a black-and-white collie. So they must have had one when that picture was taken?"

"No, I think that was the gardener's. Laura always loved animals. Dogs and horses and that. I think she did mention that dog to me once, when I was dusting 'round the knickknacks on the cabinet. She told me its name, too, but I can't remember what it was."

"It belonged to the gardener? So that's Lee Sherratt's dog in the photograph?"

"No, no, not him. What, Lee Sherratt? He was never really what you'd call a gardener anyway. Or one for keeping animals either, I should think. He'd rather shoot 'em than look after 'em. No, it was the one before him. That photo must have been taken a year ago, I'd say."

"Who was that, Mrs. Kelk? Who did the dog belong to?"

"The old gardener. I'm sorry, it was before my time at the Mount, you see. I don't know his name. But Laura said it was an old man that used to come. A strange old man from the village."

-28-

Diane Fry drove up to the smallholding, this time having no trouble with the gates or the geese, which seemed to be notable by their absence. The stream of rusty water from the broken pipe had dried up, and an air of unnatural silence hung about the buildings.

Her headlights caught the white pickup, which had been parked near a small wooden shed. She parked in front of it and got out. Its doors were unlocked and the keys were in the ignition. Then she saw Sam Beeley. He was alone, leaning against a wall by the vehicle, almost invisible in the gloom. His expression was vague and sad and full of suffering, and his eyes were fixed somewhere in the distance. He seemed so preoccupied that he hardly noticed Fry's arrival until she was standing right in front of him.

"On your own, Mr. Beeley? Where are your friends?"

He looked at her vaguely. "Harry and Wilford? They've left me to it."

Sam looked shockingly pale, despite the strong sun that had been baking the area for weeks. The veins showed through in his neck and along the line of his jaw among sparse gray stubble. His skin hung in loose folds from his cheeks, and there were dark blue shadows under his eyes.

"Are you all right, Mr. Beeley?"

"Right as I'll ever be."

Fry turned and looked up toward the crags of Raven's Side, where she had lain with Ben Cooper half an hour before, looking down on Thorpe Farm. There had been no sign of him there when she had returned from the car park up the steep path. No indication of where he had gone, no attempt to leave a message. It was typically infuriating behavior—just what she had come to expect from him.

"Have you seen Detective Constable Cooper tonight? You remember Ben Cooper?"

"Eh? Sergeant Cooper's lad? I remember him." A ghost of a smile touched Sam's pale lips at the memory of the compost heap fiasco.

"Have you seen him? Has he been here?"

Sam looked at her blankly, shaking his head in incomprehension.

"And where have Mr. Dickinson and Mr. Cutts gone?"

He looked as though answering her would be too much effort. She wanted to get hold of his jacket and shake him until he responded, but thought he looked so frail that he would fall apart in her hands.

"Mr. Beeley, I need to know. Where have they gone?"

Sam rallied momentarily, as if the tone of her voice had pierced his lethargy. He moved a hand feebly, not quite completing the gesture. "Out on the Baulk."

The old man sagged again. He was clutching his ivory-headed stick as if his life depended on it, and his bony hands were tense and white at the knuckles where they gripped the Alsatian's head.

Fry thought of her first visit to the smallholding. *"He doesn't look like he's got strong wrists, but it's all in the technique,"* Wilford Cutts had said. She had seen those same hands break the neck of a large bird with one twist. She thought of the three old men, and she thought of Harry Dickinson covering up for someone involved in the death of Laura Vernon. Did it *have* to be family? She looked again at Sam, seeing him afresh. He looked like a defeated man, a man who had been in pain for years and was in agony right now, suffering in front of her eyes. But was his pain entirely physical?

"Can I have a look at your stick, Mr. Beeley?"

"My stick? I've had it a long time."

"May I?"

She held out her hand, and Sam hesitantly gave her the stick. It felt heavy and solid and was well made, so that it balanced properly and swung easily in the hand. The handle was worn smooth and shiny by Sam Beeley's hands. The back of the dog's head formed a hard, rounded ball of ivory, easily capable of crushing a skull if wielded with enough force. Or, of course, with the right technique.

She examined the handle closely. There were no traces she could see. But then it could have been cleaned. And in six days of use, any visible traces of blood or tissue could easily have been rubbed off onto the parchment-thin palms of its owner's hands. The forensics lab, though, would soon settle it one way or another.

"I have to ask you to come with me to the station to answer some questions," said Fry.

Sam nodded wearily. "I'll need to use my stick."

"I'm afraid you'll have to manage without it for a while."

"I can't walk without my stick," he insisted.

Sam was trembling even more than usual. He looked as though he needed an ambulance rather than a trip to the station. Fry hesitated, conscious of the mistakes that had dogged the inquiry so far. The last thing she needed was a sick old man suffering a collapse in police custody.

As her brain ticked over, she found herself looking past Sam into the doorway of the shed. The interior was pitch-black, but her eye was attracted by a quiet movement in the darkness. There was something in there that was blacker than the surrounding shadows, something with eyes that turned to watch her as she brought her mobile phone from the Peugeot. She needed advice on this one. Someone else could make the decision on whether to pull an apparently helpless old man in for questioning.

She got through to the duty officer in the incident room again, giving details of her location and asking for the whereabouts of Tailby and Hitchens. But the officer had news. And what he had to tell her made her forget about Sam Beeley for now.

Fry asked a few questions and requested whatever backup was available at this time of night. Then she ended the call and dialed again, this time trying Ben Cooper's number. She needed to tell him this bit of news. It was something he had to know before he encountered Harry Dickinson again.

According to the duty officer, a second search had been ordered that afternoon in the area of scrubland at the back of the Vernons' garden, this time seeking evidence of Andrew Milner's presence in the vicinity. The search had spread, almost by accident, into the garden itself. And there, at the bottom of a well-trimmed privet hedge, Laura Vernon's second trainer had been found late in the afternoon.

The man in the incident room was eager to talk. It was a lonely job in the evening, and nobody ever took the trouble to discuss the inquiry with him.

"It caused a bit of excitement 'round here, I can tell you," he said with relish. "It went straight to the lab, and they found two clear sets of prints on the trainer. I thought Mr. Tailby was going to hit the roof. Especially as the garden had been searched once already. But that's the way it always goes, isn't it?"

Fry held her breath, staring blindly at Sam Beeley and the shed behind him.

She heard that a fingerprint officer had worked late in the evening to lift the prints off the second trainer and compare them to those on the matching half of the pair. On the first trainer, they had found only Laura's own prints—identified by taking fingerprints from the body—and those of Harry Dickinson, who had carried the trainer back to Dial Cottage. Now the new fingerprint report had come through, and it showed that the two sets of prints were identical. It meant that Harry Dickinson had handled both trainers. But only one of them had been found with the body. Who else could possibly have touched the other one, except Laura Vernon's killer?

Ben Cooper's phone rang and rang unanswered. Fry knew, of course, that he had left his phone in his car. But still she let it ring. Echoing in her mind was that one sentence he had used that had trapped her into being here tonight, in this crazy situation. *"Are you going to let me down?"* he had said.

While she waited, biting her lip, she found her eyes growing accustomed to the darkness in the doorway behind Sam. And now she could see, all too clearly, what was in the shed.

For a while, Ben Cooper was able to keep the two figures in sight from a safe vantage point among the rocks on Raven's Side. Gradually, he worked his way down the steep hillside, using the cover of the rocky outcrops and the first of the trees on the lower slopes. The two old men weren't moving quickly. They looked as though they were out for a Sunday stroll, ambling along the path close together, almost shoulder to shoulder, apparently deep in conversation.

Cooper was glad of their absorption in each other as he scrambled down a stretch of open ground, stumbling on invisible rabbit holes and stubbing his toe on half-buried stones. Before he had reached ground level, Harry and Wilford had vanished around a bend in the path. He remembered a second path that ran at a diagonal across the face of the cliff and emerged onto the main path heading toward the Baulk. He found it quickly and broke into a run, lifting his feet high off the ground and letting them fall as softly as he could, afraid of unseen hazards that might trip him but desperate to gain distance on the two old men. The surrounding trees grew tall and dense; and a thick, muffled silence gradually descended around him, cutting him off from the world that had existed higher up on the tors.

As he ran, Cooper thought of Diane Fry's interview with Charlotte Vernon. If she really did visit the Baulk every night to contemplate the place of her daughter's death, then Harry Dickinson would surely know it. There seemed to be very little that went on in this area that Harry wasn't aware of. No doubt he had seen Charlotte picking her way along the path with her bunches of flowers, just as he had spotted her husband out on the Baulk. Cooper wondered what Harry's real intention had been when he set off to try to meet Graham Vernon the night that Laura had died. And he wondered whether Harry now meant to follow up that intention with Vernon's wife instead. There was no doubt in Cooper's mind that danger lurked in the woods tonight.

For once, Harry was without his dog, Jess. But he was accompanied by Wilford Cutts instead. Probably there was little to choose between them for loyalty.

Cooper reached the main path, breathing hard, and turned westwards toward the Baulk. Down below him now, on his right, was the stream and the Eden Valley Trail that ran alongside it. Faintly, through the covering of trees, he could hear the whispering of the water. A barn owl called—an eerie, long-drawn-out hunting cry that echoed across the valley and was enough to make him shiver, even though he knew what it was.

He wondered what luck Diane Fry might have had with the bird-watcher, and wished that he had her alongside him now. A fox barked somewhere ahead. Perhaps even the same fox that had sunk its teeth into the cooling flesh of Laura Vernon's thigh.

A couple of minutes passed as Cooper walked as fast as he dared, squinting ahead into the gloom, hoping he hadn't lost the two men. But eventually, as he rounded a bend by the disintegrated remains of a stone building, he came to a sudden halt at a glimpse of movement up ahead. He stood at the side of the path, under an overhanging elder bough, and watched the old men. They were standing at a point where the path diverged. Again they were very close together, merging into one dark, indistinct figure, as if they were holding each other, embracing like lovers. Then they turned, striding down the right-hand path without looking back. The path dipped in a gentle slope into a patch of denser trees and then toward ground that grew rocky and steep and was broken into deep ravines.

Cooper had to go more slowly as he found himself walking over the rocks. By the time he reached the first ravine, the old men had vanished into the night as if they had been erased out of existence.

He stood back off the path in the trees and waited. There was nothing else he could do. He wondered what Diane Fry would have done when she found him gone. Surely she would have the sense this time to call in and get some support. She wouldn't make the same mistake again. No way. She wouldn't make the mistake of following him into trouble.

As soon as she entered the woods, Fry knew that it would happen again. Though she had brought a torch this time, the narrow pool of light it cast at her feet seemed only to emphasize the blackness outside its reach, to make her isolation total and threatening. From among the trees, the eager darkness had begun to sidle in toward her, oozing around her body in swift, oily movements, and pressing in close with its nauseous and suffocating familiarity.

The night was full of tiny, whispering movements. They were like the soft seething on the surface of a bowl of maggots. They made her want to scratch her skin, where the small hairs were tense and moving. Then the invisible ants began to swarm across her body, nipping and biting as they went, their thousands of tiny insect feet scuttling over her arms and legs, itching her skin and burrowing under her breasts and into the moist warmth between her thighs, until she wanted to scream with revulsion.

She needed desperately to reach out and touch something solid for reassurance, yet could not move her hand for fear of what her fingers might encounter. Somehow she managed to keep putting one foot in front of the other, automatically, like a robot programmed for a single action. Every step she took made her afraid. Every movement was like a leap into a void, a step into the midst of unseen horrors.

She knew that she wouldn't be able to stop the shadows bringing back the memories that she had pushed deep into the recesses of her mind. They were memories that were too powerful and greedy to be buried completely, too vivid to be erased, too deeply etched into her soul to be forgotten. They merely wallowed and writhed in the depths, waiting for the chance to reemerge.

As she walked, she turned her head from side to side, watching the dimly seen trees for movement. They were like rows of solid bodies standing threateningly, surrounding her and closing in. She was alone among a dozen of them, two dozen, maybe more. Other bodies could be sensed, farther back in the darkness, watching, laughing, waiting eagerly for what they knew would happen next. Voices murmured and coughed. "It's a copper," the voices said. "She's a copper."

The memories churned and bubbled. There were movements that crept and rustled closer; there were brief, fragmented glimpses of figures carved into severed segments by the streetlights; the sickly reek of booze and violence. And then she seemed to hear that one particular voice— that rough, slurring Brummie voice that slithered out of the darkness. "How do you like *this,* copper?" The same taunting laughter moving in the shadows. The same dark, menacing shapes all around, whichever way she turned. A hand in the small of her back and a leg outstretched to trip. Then she was falling, flailing forward into the darkness. Hands grabbing her, pinching and pulling and slapping. Her arms trapped by unseen fingers that gripped her tightly, painful and shocking in their violence. Her own voice, unnaturally high-pitched and stained with terror, was trying to cry out but failing.

Nothing could stop the flood of remembered sensations now. The smell of a sweat-soaked palm over her mouth, her head banging on the ground as she thrashed helplessly from side to side. Her clothes pulled and torn, the shock of feeling parts of her body exposed to the cruel air. "How do you like *this,* copper?" And then came the groping and the prodding and the squeezing, and the hot, intruding fingers. And, perfectly clear on the night air, the sound of a zip. Another laugh, a mumble, an excited gasp. And finally the penetration. The ripping agony, and the scream that was smothered by the hand over her face, and the desperate fighting to force breath into her lungs. "How do you like *this,* copper? How do you like *this,* copper?" Animal noises and more laughter, and a warm wetness spurting and trickling inside her before the final withdrawal. The relief of the lifting of a weight from her body, as one dark shape moved away and she thought it was over.

But then it happened again.

And again.

Blindly, she continued walking, insensible to her surroundings, all her efforts directed toward controlling the reactions of her body. She tried to focus her thoughts on Ben Cooper, somewhere ahead in the woods, unaware of the danger he was in. *"Are you going to let me down?"* he'd said.

Finally, she found herself stepping out into a clearing, immediately feeling the difference in the ground underfoot. She became aware of a sound—a real sound, belonging to here and now, a sound that needed explanation.

Her memory was still forcing unwanted pictures in front of her eyes as she turned to identify the noise, seeking its source among the menacing shadows. She found that a large tree stood near her shoulder, tall and thickly shrouded in foliage, its crown dimly visible against the pale sky. Its leaves whispered and rustled like a vast colony of small creatures roosting directly above her head. She thought of thousands of tiny bats, scraping their thin, papery wings against their bodies as they prepared to drop in fluttering swarms onto her shoulders. There was nothing worse than something you could only hear but not see.

There was a sudden loud creaking as the wind caught the weight of a branch and a louder crackling among the leaves. She caught the unmistakable smell of urine and feces, drifting closer. And then there was a heavier movement among the branches as something swung toward her, lumbering out of the dark.

Three hundred yards away, Ben Cooper had picked up the trail again as one of the old men reappeared on the path. He heard the man coming before he saw him, could sense his breathing and hear a barely audible muttering.

After switching to the left-hand fork, the figure walked on for several hundred yards before suddenly striking off the path into the depths of the trees. Cooper found it difficult even to locate the exact spot where he had disappeared. Once in among the trees, he was lost. There was no hope of seeing anyone who might be lurking among the straggling clumps of brambles and the trunks of the old oaks and beeches that grew thickly here. Faintly, on the air, he caught a familiar tang of pipe smoke. But he finally had to admit that he had lost the old man he had been following.

Then Cooper lifted his head in despair as a high-pitched scream shattered the silence of the woods.

-29-

Dial Cottage was almost in darkness. The only light behind the curtains of the sitting room was a flickering pattern of shifting colors, a light that died against the window before it reached the garden or the blackness beyond.

Two torches shone onto the flagged path, throwing the shadows of shrub roses across the flower beds like skeletal fingers reaching toward the house. In the background was the sound of another siren approaching Moorhay from the Edendale road. The flashing blue lights of an ambulance were reflected off the night sky.

Ben Cooper and Diane Fry knew the ambulance would not be needed. Fry still had a clear picture in her mind of the old man hanging from a branch ten feet above the ground, the toes of his black work boots pointing to the earth, his head lolling to one side in a last mocking gesture. When she had moved reluctantly closer to the swinging body, she had seen that his right hand was clenched tight around an old leather dog lead.

She was aware that she had screamed when the wind had swung the dark, rustling shape toward her head and the dangling feet had bumped in her face. Then Ben Cooper had been there, cannoning into her at full tilt in answer to her cry. And somehow she had recognized him instantly, an instinctive response to his scent or the sound of his breath, so that she reacted not by attacking him, as she would a stranger rushing at her from the darkness, but by clinging to him desperately, finding at last the reassuring solidity that her body craved.

Then finally, together, they had cut the body down. Cooper had climbed up to the branch and sawed through the nylon rope with his penknife. The old man had clearly been dead before they got him to the ground. It had been a neat, clean job, with the knot of the noose tied properly and positioned below the angle of the jaw, with plenty of height to the drop. His neck had been snapped cleanly.

*　　　*　　　*

Ben Cooper hesitated as they reached the old wooden gate at the bottom of the garden, wondering if the same thought was in both their minds. But he didn't want to be the first to say it.

"So Sam Beeley had the dog," he said instead.

"The Border collie, yes. Kept well out of sight in a shed at Thorpe Farm."

They had waited only while the machinery of an official response to a sudden death had swung into action. The first area patrol car had already arrived with two uniformed officers following Fry's call to the incident room. An ambulance had been summoned, closely followed by the police surgeon to officially certify death. They had all been obliged to step carefully around the small heap of roses and carnations tied up with ribbons, slowly fading and shriveling on the ground, marking the spot where Laura Vernon had died.

Then Cooper and Fry had walked together up the path toward Moorhay. Cooper was following the route for the third time that week. But this time he was conscious of Diane Fry close at his side, her hand unsteady now as she pointed her torch toward the row of cottages.

Cooper knew that she had taken control at some point. It had been immediately after they had discovered the body, immediately after that spontaneous embrace, when her fear had seemed to empty itself into his arms like a dam bursting, relieving some unimaginable pressure. She had naturally taken command of the scene then, issuing instructions clearly and professionally, like someone born to the role.

And then he had discovered that she had already been to Thorpe Farm and spoken to Sam Beeley and had already found the dog. She had already phoned in to the incident room, and she had organized the backup. Everything done just right. The credit would be all hers.

But it was almost too perfect. Almost as if the reason she had agreed to come with him tonight was not to support him but just to seek that moment when she typed her own name on the report that cleared up the Vernon inquiry.

"Who's going to do it?" she asked.

Cooper nodded, relieved that she had said it first.

"I will, if you like."

They walked up the path. From inside the cottage came the dull, distorted sounds of artificial laughter. Cooper knocked. It was late, and the noise sounded too loud. When Gwen Dickinson answered the door, the sound from inside the cottage increased and it became clear that she had been watching television.

"Mrs. Dickinson, when did you last see Harry?" asked Cooper.

"You'd better come in," she said.

She took them through the sitting room, where a talk show was on the TV, into the front room of the cottage. Here, in the semidarkness, the same smell of pipe smoke lingered that Cooper had noticed in the woods.

"I knew there was something going on," said Gwen.

"We've found a body," said Cooper, "hanging from a tree on the Baulk."

"Oh my goodness." Gwen clutched at her bosom as if her heart would stop with the shock. She fumbled her way to an armchair behind her and sat down heavily. She stared across the room at the opposite chair.

"You know who it is, of course," said Cooper. But he wasn't speaking to Gwen.

"Of course I do," said Harry. His pipe was in his mouth and his head was resting upright on the antimacassar of his chair. But in the half-light of a single lamp in the corner, his stare was derisive. "He always knew to do the right thing, did Wilford."

Jess lay at Harry's feet, her black coat gleaming, one eye turned apprehensively toward the visitors, sensing the atmosphere.

"Are you saying he committed suicide?"

"Obviously," said Harry.

"And why would he do that, Mr. Dickinson?"

"Because he killed that girl. The Mount lass. It was the only way out. He couldn't have faced prison, you see. Not being kept in a cell, out of the daylight. He couldn't have stood that."

"He killed Laura Vernon. And you, Mr. Dickinson—you helped him all along?"

"It's what you do, for a friend."

Cooper perched on the edge of a hard chair. The Labrador stirred and lifted her head to study Fry as she moved restlessly across the room. A low growl began in the dog's throat, but Harry silenced her with a sound that was barely a hiss of breath.

"Do you want to tell us about it?" asked Cooper.

Harry was silent for a moment, looking from one to the other. He seemed not to be considering his words but weighing up what effect they would have.

"I saw Wilford on the Baulk that night, that Saturday," he said. "He was upset, and he told me what had happened. I said I would help him, of course."

"So you delayed things."

"Aye, I left it for a bit before I found the body. And I hid the other shoe thing."

Harry looked down to the side of his chair, where the small mahogany cabinet stood. The shoe polish, cloth, and brush were no longer on the floor in front of it but had been tidied away, presumably in the little cupboard. Cooper remembered that he had thought them incongruous and untidy in that well-ordered room when he had seen them there on Wednesday. He realized they had not been put away then because there was no room in the cupboard. The space had been taken up by a size-five Reebok trainer.

"I chucked it in the garden of the Mount on Wednesday night. It was supposed to make you think it might have been Vernon who did it himself." Harry sighed. "It doesn't always work like it does on the telly, though. It took you a long time to find it. And that other lass had stuck her oar in by then." He laughed sardonically. "That was a right turnup for the books."

"You mean Becky Kelk. The girl who claimed you'd attacked her."

"Nasty bit of work, she is. Never been taught how to behave, if you ask me. Still—I suppose I ought to look on it as a compliment."

"Mr. Dickinson," said Cooper, "the officers who came to your house said you seemed to be expecting them."

"I was," said Harry, "but not about that, you understand. It had come to my mind about fingerprints. The ones on that shoe would be mine. I knew you'd be coming for me again as soon as you found it. But I didn't expect all that other business. I thought you'd be asking about the shoe."

"Instead, Becky Kelk made a false allegation against you, and you were treated as a rape suspect."

"It was a bit of an education, all right."

"And you went through all that for Wilford Cutts?" asked Fry. "Even though you knew he'd killed Laura Vernon?"

Harry nodded. "Aye, because he was a mate." Then he turned to stare directly at Fry. "Besides, the girl was evil."

Cooper heard Harry's voice stumble into anger when he mentioned Laura Vernon. It happened every time, in every case he had ever seen. Every time that the life of a victim was turned over, they were revealed as a person of many facets in the eyes of those who had known them. Like Charlotte Vernon, some saw glittering diamond surfaces, precious and unflawed. Others, like Harry Dickinson, saw only base lead.

Cooper became aware of Gwen in the background, a faded shape against the dark wall. Her eyes were fixed and unblinking, and her expression made him flinch with its intensity.

"How did it happen?" he asked Harry.

"Wilford used to work at the Mount, you know. He created that garden up there. It was his skill. Not like young Lee Sherratt. He was never a gardener. He can hump a wheelbarrow, but he knows nothing about gardening. But Wilford found out what was going on up there, you see. Those orgies and things. He said it was wickedness, and he gave 'em a piece of his mind. So Vernon sacked him."

"Was this before your granddaughter went to a party there?"

"Yes, it was," said Harry. He looked at Cooper closely. "If you know about that, lad, you'll understand why I didn't disagree with him about those Vernons. Did Helen tell you about that?"

"Yes."

"She likes you. Will you be seeing each other? When this lot is over? You'd suit each other, I reckon."

Fry shifted impatiently and gave Cooper a signal with her eyes. Keep quiet, it said. Don't encourage him to wander off the subject. Obey instructions.

"Stick to the subject of Laura Vernon, Mr. Dickinson," she said.

"Aye well, Wilford kept his worst words for the lass. He called her all sorts. But she was as hard-faced as they come. It only provoked her to worse. You wouldn't believe a young lass could be as foulmouthed as that. She mocked Wilford. She saw him as a challenge, that's what it was. She told him he was the only man who had been to the Mount that she hadn't had sex with. Can you believe that? A lass of fifteen?" His eyes hardened to black buttons. "But that was the way she was brought up."

They waited while he sucked violently on his pipe, watching the cloud of smoke rise and drift toward the yellowed ceiling.

"Then she met Wilford on the Baulk that day. And she mocked him again, worse than ever. She offered herself to him there and then, pulling down her clothes, taunting him like the little whore she was. And then she reached out and touched him . . ." Harry seemed to have trouble swallowing, shifting the stem of his pipe in his mouth with a faint crunch.

"Wilford had these bursts of temper, you see. It was because of a thing that happened to him in the war. Did you know he was shot in the head? It did something to part of his brain, and now and then he got these rages. It was the right thing, you see. Wilford always did the right thing."

"The right thing?" Gwen had been keeping quiet, but now she turned on her husband.

"That's what I said."

"But he killed that little girl, didn't he? Murdered her. Beat her to death down there in the woods. How can you talk about the right thing?"

Harry was silent for several moments, staring out of the window into the darkness, as if he were seeing the hills, as if he were listening for the skylark and the distant rumble of blasting in the quarry. Perhaps he was tasting in his imagination the air and the earth, rolling on his tongue the lingering memories of an underground world, stifling and dark, where the only things you could ever trust were your own two hands and the man standing at your back.

"It's no good. You won't ever understand," he said.

Gwen's face crumpled into tears, and the detectives stood in the middle of the room, embarrassed.

"What happened during the war?" asked Cooper.

"Was it something to do with the French tarts?" suggested Fry, and Cooper raised his eyebrows.

"Aye, those French girls," said Harry. "Did Sam tell you? It's not something I've ever told Gwen. I never told her much about the war. Women only worry—they get everything out of proportion."

He nodded wisely at them. "We were lucky, me and Sam. But Wilford wasn't so lucky. He was always a bit too upright. Didn't approve, you know. But there was this lad he thought the world of—he was looking after him, like. And one day they came across this French lass standing in an alley. She wasn't very old, and she gave them the come-on, hot and hard. Wilford didn't want to know, of course, but the lad was excited. He went into this dark little house, and Wilford had to tag along, trying to talk him out of it all the way. The lad almost changed his mind, but the lass grabbed him and stuck his hand down her drawers. Well—"

Harry sucked his pipe, remembering.

"There were two Jerry soldiers hiding in that house, waiting for the girl to tempt a Tommy in. They bayoneted the lad. When Wilford walked through the door, the lad's guts were already spilled on the floor.

Wilford had his Bren gun ready, and he shot the Jerries. Then he shot the girl. But he got a Jerry bullet lodged in his skull, and they sent him home. He was never quite right after that, the old lad. His brain never healed somehow. You could never quite tell when he'd have these rages. He had one at the Mount, by all accounts. No wonder Vernon sacked him. And sometimes he'd get them with the animals, though it broke his heart to hurt them."

Fry drew her breath in sharply. Cooper looked at her, sharing the memory. He saw a cloud of dark feathers drifting out of a hut, settling on Wilford Cutts's shoulders and sticking in his hair. He remembered the van driver looking wild-eyed and frightened by whatever had happened inside the hut. And he remembered the hen dangling from Wilford's hand, its wings broken, its eyes glazed with pain, waiting to be put out of its suffering.

Harry continued, unaware of their exchange of glances. "When the Vernon child tormented him, he couldn't put up with it. It reminded him of France and the lad who left his guts on the floor of that house. She was like that French tart all over again. Evil. So he picked up a stone . . ." Harry's eyes focused on Fry, as if seeing her for the first time and wondering why she was there. "It was just a moment's mistake, you see. You can't forget sixty years of friendship for that."

"Friendship?"

"Aye. Friendship."

Harry studied Diane Fry. On her first visit to the cottage, he had ignored her as completely as he had during the interviews at the police station. Now, though, he was looking at her in a different way, as if he sensed a change in her. He looked from Fry to Ben Cooper, assessing them both curiously.

"*You* knew, didn't you, lad?"

Cooper nodded. "It was the pigs, of course."

Fry looked at him in amazement. "The ones in the compost heap? Come on. The pigs were a joke."

"No. It was after I had that bit of bother in the pub, you remember? Anyway, one of those youths in the pub said something about pigs. And it stuck in my brain. Like that music you were playing in the car. Tanita Tikaram? They're about the only two things I *can* remember."

The old man was nodding at Cooper like a proud father, encouraging him to do his stuff.

"What the hell have the pigs got to do with it?" asked Fry.

"Well, it suddenly dawned on me what was going on at the smallholding. They were helping Wilford get rid of all the animals. He didn't want to leave them behind. He couldn't just abandon them, because he cared about them too much. They were his family, if you like. Apart from the pigs, every last one of them went during the course of a week."

"Honestly?"

"You remember the hens, when we went to Thorpe Farm that first time? He sold all of them. When I went up a couple of days later, the goat had gone, too. And there were no geese. I should have figured it out then, but I didn't. It was the pigs that really clinched it. You can't just sell swill-fed pigs, you see. You've got to get movement permits from the Ministry of Agriculture before they can leave the premises."

"Because of swine versicular disease," put in Harry.

"But there wasn't time to do that, was there? He had to get rid of them quickly, and there was only one way he could think of. That was to have them humanely killed and bury them in the compost heap."

"So everything went? All that menagerie."

"Everything. The place is deserted now. All that's left of Wilford's family is the dog."

Harry nodded. "We kept her out of the way after we heard about the bird-watching bloke. You nearly saw her once, in the pub, but she was out the back with Jess. You see, Wilford needed time, that's all. That's what I was doing for him—buying him time. We couldn't let him get arrested. He knew what he had to do, but he needed more time. We helped him do it, me and Sam. Like you say, there's just the dog now."

"So he took all his family with him. As a matter of interest, Diane," said Cooper, "what gave you the idea that Wilford Cutts was married?"

"I don't know." She frowned. "Wasn't he?"

"His wife died years ago."

"Oh well, I don't suppose it's important. I just remember wondering how on earth Connie managed to put up with him and his friends. He spoke about her once, when I was there. Perhaps he'd just forgotten she was dead."

"His wife was called Doris," said Cooper.

Harry nodded. "Maybe you're almost Inspector Morse, after all."

"You also did your best to throw suspicion on Graham Vernon. Did you really see him on the Baulk that night? Or was that a lie?"

"No, lad, no lie. He was there, all right. He was out looking for the girl, I reckon. No doubt he had an idea in his mind of what she would be up to. The mother hadn't a clue, of course. She always thought the lass was some sort of angel."

The old man curled his lip contemptuously. "Aye, Vernon was there, all right. I *would* have had a few words to say to him, too, if I'd got near him. You know what about, lad, if Helen's told you. You don't need to ask me what I would have said to the man. But he saw me coming, and he cleared off sharpish. I wasn't complaining. It kept him out of the way. And it did no harm for you lot to be asking him your questions, did it?"

"And then you even tried to attract suspicion to yourself."

Harry shrugged. "It didn't matter if you thought I had killed the girl anyway."

"Didn't matter?"

"Well, I was innocent, wasn't I? I knew Wilford would prove it, in the end. He did the right thing, you see. He always said he would."

"But what you put yourself through," said Cooper. "It must have been appalling."

Harry shrugged. "It's what you do. For a friend."

But Fry wasn't satisfied. She was still angry. She stepped forward, and the old man looked up at her from his chair as they faced each other across a short stretch of carpet. "You've caused a lot of trouble for us, Mr. Dickinson," she said. "Do you realize you've just admitted to committing several offenses?"

"If you say so."

"Mr. Dickinson, you've deliberately misled the police. You've concealed evidence of a very serious crime. And that's only for starters. At the moment, there's no proof that Wilford Cutts's death was suicide. There may be more serious allegations to follow, depending on the results of forensic examination."

"Sam has the suicide note," said Harry, "if that's what you need. It was all done properly."

"I see."

Concern clouded Harry's impassive face. "Somebody ought to go and see Sam. He's not well."

"Detective Constable Cooper is just about to do that," said Fry.

Cooper looked at her, and their eyes met for a long minute. There was everything in their stare, all the pent-up resentment and jealousy, all the disdain for each other's views and methods, their lifestyles and back-grounds, all the memories of the things that had passed between them, all the pain of intimacy and betrayal. Cooper could sense that she was also asking him to trust her.

"Ben, please."

She said it as if it were a request. But now the words had a note of authority, naturally assumed, as of a right. She expected him to obey. This was *her* case, she seemed to say. And she was right, of course. Diane Fry had done everything properly; she had called in, she had sent for backup, she had secured the scene. As for Ben Cooper, he was officially off the inquiry. He shouldn't even be here. So how could he possibly expect to take any of the credit?

He nodded and went toward the front door, looking for a passing patrol car to flag down for a lift to Thorpe Farm. As he left the room, he heard Fry begin the litany.

"Harold Dickinson, I am arresting you on a charge of attempting to pervert the course of justice. You do not have to say anything, but it may harm your defense . . ."

Sam Beeley looked relieved when the police car came up the track to the smallholding. He was holding an envelope, sealed and addressed "To Whom It May Concern." Cooper realized that he and Fry had actually watched the three old men composing the letter on the bonnet of the pickup, but had thought they were doing a crossword puzzle.

He looked closely at Sam. "We'll take you to a doctor, Mr. Beeley. It's all over."

Sam waved his stick weakly. "Someone has to look after the dog."

"Oh yes."

Cooper went to the shed and opened the lower door. A black-and-white Border collie emerged from the darkness, coming eagerly to sniff his legs and lick his hand, gazing up hopefully into his eyes. He guessed that she knew her master had gone. Dogs always did seem to know these things. The bonds of trust and affection they forged with people were so powerful that they could only be broken by death.

He reached down to stroke the animal's head, an inadequate gesture of consolation.

"We'll look after you, Connie," he said.

-30-

A few evenings later, Diane Fry left her flat and drove her black Peugeot out of Edendale. She headed southward toward the limestone plateau, skirting Durham Edge and Camphill, where the flying club was. She gazed up at the gliders launching themselves into the air, soaring on the thermals rising from the valleys, and slipping sideways in the warm breezes stroking the tops of the hills. She felt as though she could take off like one of those gliders and fly over the countryside that was now becoming her own. No matter what view she got from up there, she wouldn't have been able to see her future any more clearly than she did now. Everything was working out fine.

She found Bridge End Farm and crawled down the track to park in the farmyard. She could see Ben Cooper standing by a field gate in the shadow of a barn. He was talking to an older, more heavily built man who had the same colored hair and the same open, boyish look to his face. This must be Matt, the brother who was the farmer. The two men were comparing the guns they held over their arms, and there was a dog on the ground at their feet.

Fry took the cassette from her glove compartment and slipped it into her pocket. Tanita Tikaram's *Ancient Heart*. He had asked about it and said he liked it. Maybe, just maybe, it would help to bring back some more memories.

Cooper turned as she got out of the car. His face was a picture of amazement.

"Diane—is something wrong?"

"No, Ben. It's a social call."

"I see." He seemed suddenly flustered and looked at his brother. "This is Matt, by the way. Matt—Diane Fry. A colleague."

"Nice to meet you," said Matt with a smile and a strange sideways look at his brother. "Sorry I can't stop to chat, though. There's a lot of work to do. I'll see you later, Ben."

"Our mother's home," said Cooper, as if it explained everything. But it meant nothing. Fry had never known his mother was away.

They stood and looked at each other in front of the barn. She had worked out what she was going to say, but now the words didn't seem to spring so easily to her lips. She was suddenly full of doubt. There was something about the way he had introduced her to his brother as "a colleague" that didn't sound right. In the end, it was Cooper who broke the uneasy silence.

"How was your meeting with the superintendent?" he asked. "A pat on the back, was it?"

She took a breath, clutching the cassette case in her pocket for luck. "Actually, he's asked me if I'll put in for the sergeant's job when they interview again next month," she said. "I thought I ought to tell you myself."

Before she could read his expression, Cooper had turned away to put his shotgun in the Land Rover, where he locked it into a steel box. Though she couldn't see his face, she could tell that his shoulders were rigid and arched with tension.

A tractor engine coughed into life in the field beyond the barn. A sudden clattering of machinery sent a flock of rooks spiraling into the air, where they wheeled against the distant silhouettes of the Camphill gliders. The hoarse, mocking calls of the birds drew echoes from the barns and the cattle sheds, and the noise multiplied and swelled until it seemed to fill the entire farmyard.

"I'm very pleased for you," said Cooper, with his back still turned. "I'm sure you'll make a very good detective sergeant, Diane. Always in control. Always doing the right thing. You'll get on fast. You'll shoot up that promotion ladder." He slammed the Land Rover door too hard. "Like you've got a rocket up your arse."

Fry winced. She had rarely heard him swear. Only once before had he spoken to her in that tone. It had been in the bar of the Unicorn, when he had been consumed with drunken rage. He had called her a bitch then, but somehow she had persuaded herself it was only the beer speaking.

Now she felt the conversation was drifting away from her badly. This was not the way it was supposed to have been. Desperately, she cast around for something to say and finally nodded toward the dog.

"Is she taking to it well?"

"Connie? Yes, she's a natural. Very loyal."

"A good companion, I suppose."

Cooper patted the head of the Border collie, who looked up at him adoringly. "Connie's more than a companion," he said pointedly. "A friend."

Fry turned at a sound behind her. Another car had pulled into the yard, one that she vaguely recognized. The door opened and a woman got out of the driver's seat, but hesitated and remained standing by the car, waiting for Ben. It was Helen Milner. Fry felt a chill run under her skin and seep into her arms, even as a flush started in her neck, and she knew she had made a fool of herself.

"Well. It looks as though your other friend's come for you, Ben. Better not keep her waiting."

Cooper turned angrily at the sneer in her voice, but controlled himself with a visible effort, remembering the superintendent's warning about emotional outbursts. He strode a few paces across the yard toward Helen's car before he stopped and faced Fry again. By now he was calm, and his words were chosen with care.

"You may not understand this. But we all need friends sometimes, Diane."

Then he turned and left her standing in the shadow of the barn. Fry found she had been squeezing the cassette in her pocket so tightly that its sharp edges were digging into the palm of her hand, and the pain was making her eyes water. She spoke then, but in a voice so quiet that Cooper could not possibly have heard.

"So they tell me, Ben," she said. And she watched him walk away.

A kestrel hung in a hot up-current of air, searching for moving prey among the limestone crags high in the daleside. In this valley, most of the lower fields had been turned to rye-grass leys and silage pasture. But halfway up the hill toward Great Hucklow there was still a single meadow full of wildflowers, oxeye daisies and marjoram, their colors contrasting with the uniform green of the pastures.

They had almost reached the meadow when Ben Cooper asked Helen to pull into a gateway. She looked at him curiously, wondering what could have gone wrong. But she turned off the engine and wound down the window, and for a few moments they watched a glider that was slipping silently across the valley, tilting its wings against the sun before disappearing over Durham Edge.

They were on their way to have lunch together at the Light House, because it had seemed like the natural thing to do. But for Cooper, it was more than that. He felt as though he was on the point of emerging from the darkness into another world, a moment to be tasted and savored. As Helen leaned out of the car window to track the movement of the glider, her hair caught the sunlight and turned it into an elusive, coppery haze that he could have watched forever.

But finally, his eyes were drawn back down the valley, where Bridge End Farm lay half in the shadow of the hill against a curtain of wych-elm woods. He could see the windows of the cool, dark rooms, where his mother lay asleep, dreaming drug-assisted dreams, escaping from a strangely altered reality. He could see, at the back of the house, his brother's tractor trailing a cloud of dust as it dragged a disk harrow across the top field. And he could just make out Diane Fry's black Peugeot as it began to crawl up the track to the road, hesitating at every pothole as if nervous of falling in. The face of the driver was invisible behind the reflection from the windscreen.

Then the echo of a bark drifted up the hillside. In the farmyard, waiting patiently by the gate, lay the Border collie that had once belonged to Wilford Cutts. The dog turned its head into the shade to follow the tires of the Peugeot, and the wiry texture of its fur softened and faded for a moment, darkening its outline against the dusty ground. But then the collie stirred again and looked up the hill, as if sensing Cooper's presence. Now the white patches on its face and flanks sparkled and shimmered as they picked up the glare of the sun from the limestone walls.

For Ben Cooper, it was all perfectly clear. From here, in this light, at this moment in his life, there was no way that he could make a mistake. He could see no black dog.

Stephen Booth's Web site:
www.stephen-booth.com

ABOUT THE AUTHOR

Stephen Booth was born in a Lancashire cotton town, in the north of England, and has remained rooted in the Pennine hill country during his career as a newspaper journalist. He is well known as a breeder of Toggenburg dairy goats and includes among his other interests wildlife, the Internet, and walking the hills of the Peak District, in which his crime novels are set. Stephen lives with his wife, Lesley, in a Georgian dower house in Nottinghamshire. They have three cats and five goats.